W9-BTR-884

THE FRAME-UP

THE FRAME-UP

The Golden Arrow Mysteries, Book 1

MEGHAN SCOTT MOLIN

47NORTH

This is a work of fiction. Names, characters, organizations, places, events, and incidents are either products of the author's imagination or are used fictitiously. Any resemblance to actual persons, living or dead, or actual events is purely coincidental.

Text copyright © 2018 by Meghan Scott Molin
All rights reserved.

No part of this book may be reproduced, or stored in a retrieval system, or transmitted in any form or by any means, electronic, mechanical, photocopying, recording, or otherwise, without express written permission of the publisher.

Published by 47North, Seattle

www.apub.com

Amazon, the Amazon logo, and 47North are trademarks of Amazon.com, Inc., or its affiliates.

ISBN-13: 9781503904187 (hardcover)
ISBN-10: 1503904180 (hardcover)
ISBN-13: 9781503904194 (paperback)
ISBN-10: 1503904199 (paperback)

Cover design and illustration by Danny Schlitz

Printed in the United States of America

First edition

*To the incredible Dr. Liechty, and
to Noah Wayne . . . the two* real
superheroes in my life.

CHAPTER 1

Instead of finalizing his coffee order, the schmo ahead of me in line is reading on his iPad, the headline MYSTERY DRUG BUST AT DOCKS splashed across the screen. While I can't fault him for being sucked in, if we don't hurry, we'll all get stuck on the 110, having to contemplate peeing into our cups. As irked as I am, I can't help but look over his shoulder. I read about the drug bust this morning in my Twitter feed, but I didn't see a picture of the crime scene. It's a doozy. Who doesn't love when two street dealers are trussed together, back-to-back on the Long Beach docks, left with a note for the police? *Actually* trussed together. Like in a comic book. I squint my eyes, lurking over the guy's shoulder probably a little too long, but . . . Is that an outline around the criminals? It can't be. But . . . if I tilt my head just a little, it *does* look a little like a rabbit. And if so, this tableau bears a striking resemblance to something I've seen before. It is probably a glare in the shop or a trick of the light, but my poor little writer brain has no defense against this sort of nerdy imagining. All I can see is a panel from my favorite comic come to life.

"All that's missing is a golden arrow," I mutter, giving the picture one last look as the line shuffles forward. I dutifully shuffle . . . straight into iPad Guy's heels.

He snaps the iPad closed. "What did you say?"

Oh crap. iPad Guy looks straight at me with the typical "I disapprove of your purple hair" frown on his face and completely ignores the counter girl yelling, "Next!" There's a lull in the shush and hiss of the coffee-making orchestra that suggests they're ready to make the next order.

"Nothing. Just that news story reminds me of a graphic novel. Are you ready to order?" I paste a smile on my face. I know better than to upset the Muggles. Even when they are *seriously* inconveniencing the rest of us in line.

Tap, tap, tap—Order-Taking Girl isn't pleased. Someone's getting spit in their foam, and it's not going to be me.

"No . . . I'm still decid—"

I step around the man and belly right up to the bar. "Tall cinnamon dolce latte, coconut milk, dash of chocolate on top." I already have my card out before Order-Taking Girl asks, and she knows by now not to give me a receipt. I don't need more paper filling up my messenger bag. Thank God for online banking.

I'm startled when iPad Guy sidles up next to me while waiting for the barista to finish his drink. I look him up and down, taking in the slightly rumpled dark bedhead, five-o'clock shadow, jeans, and rolled-up sleeves of his nice-ish work shirt, and peg him as an Americano guy. Okay, so he didn't really *sidle*. He's more businesslike than that. But he's definitely not hanging back in the typical stranger zone. I use my Genius Comic messenger bag as a blocker, putting it firmly between us. At least make it hard for the creepers to cop a feel.

"Hey," he says, looking at me again. Only his gaze doesn't linger on my short purple hair. It takes in my whole self, moving from my Converse sneakers to my black skinny jeans, messenger bag, Wonder Woman tee, bright-red blazer, and actually ending at my eyes, in a "I did not just look at your boobs, and here I am looking at your eyes because I value women as people" look.

I narrow my gaze in return. So it's like *that*, is it? I detest false altruism. Just stare at my boobs and get it over with, like every guy at every convention I've ever attended. I can never just live my life; I have to be boobs first, comic book writer second—if a guy even gets that far. I get weary of being a novelty in my world.

"What were you saying before, about a book, Miss . . ."

I ignore the blatant fishing for my name and huff a breath, glancing at the time on my iPhone. I'm running late for the office, and I need time to let the coffee soak up some of my morning grump. "A *graphic* novel. A comic book. The scene reminded me of a panel from my favorite one." Cue the disbelieving stare when man realizes woman has read comic books . . . and there it is. Game, set, match. If he's surprised I read them, it'd turn his hair platinum to find out that I *write* them for a living.

"MG! Cinnamon dolce latte!" Saved by the barista. I reach out, snag the cup sans to-go collar—*ouch*—and keep right on motoring out of the coffee shop. I hear "Herbal tea" called out behind me, and I snort. Not an Americano guy after all. *Herbal tea?* Hipster much? Or maybe it's for his sick girlfriend. He seems the type.

Through the glass storefront, I hear a symphony of honking peppered with angry yelling. The traffic outside is already picking up for morning rush hour, and downtown LA is a bitch in May. It's why I ride my bike whenever possible.

Heading for the door, I weave my way through a dude pitching a screenplay and a stay-at-home mom bitching about no "me time," even though she's clearly here without her children. Or they're off terrorizing the other patrons—a distinct possibility, seeing as LA fuels itself on broken dreams and hypocrisy. The dirty glass door screeches, letting a blast of gritty, gasoline-scented wind in as I push it open with my hip. It never closes behind me. I'm surprised when an arm reaches out to hold it open. I don't even need to look to know that it's Herbal Tea Guy. Usually the Muggles aren't this tenacious. Time to level up my game.

"Hey, I know you seem busy, but—"

The guy doesn't take a hint.

I turn to face him, my sassiest hip thrown to the side. *Rip off the Band-Aid, MG. Sometimes there's no other way.* With one look, I can tell this guy's interest is severely misplaced. I usually date the type of guy who can dialogue about Batman's backstory, and I'm definitely not J.Crew enough for Herbal Tea. I have a meeting to get to, coffee to consume, and regret for breaking my usual silence in the waiting line.

"Look." I stop him in his tracks with a glacial glance, right over the top of my fire-engine-red wire-rimmed glasses, a look I've perfected at comic convention open-bar nights. "I'm sure you're a nice person, and you're cute and all"—*if you're into the rumpled, sensitive, tea-drinking type*—"and I am sure you have a lucrative hipster job that allows you to drink cof—er, *tea*, at all hours of the morning, but I'm not interested."

He steps back, shock and a lot of embarrassment registering in his eyes. He's not used to being brushed off. Score one for the home team. "Well, that's prickly," he says, going blotchy red at the collar of his shirt.

"It's not prickly. I just don't put up with bullshit. And there's a lot of bullshit in this world." I spin around to continue my trek and don't look back. I have bigger fish to fry this morning. "Winter is coming," in the words of Jon Snow.

———◆

Stuck, stuck, *stuck*. À la Gregory House, MD, I throw the ball even harder against the wall of my office. To be more specific, the half-height modular wall that separates my working pod from Simon's. It's supposed to foster creative collaboration, but it just allows us to annoy the living daylights out of each other. Kyle and Andy have been talking the story from this morning to *death*—the one with the tied-up drug dealers. Neither one of them has noticed the rabbit outline or overall resemblance to *The Hooded Falcon*, and instead of coming up with something brilliant for my project, I'm wondering if I should jump into the conversation with my tinfoil-hat theory. It surprises me that Simon is silent on the topic; usually if someone is wearing tinfoil alongside me, it's him. But my problem is solved momentarily when Andy gets a call and leaves the room. I sigh.

Thwack, thwack, thwack.

"I think if you throw it harder, you'll figure it out. Maybe you'll hit yourself." Simon doesn't even raise his head, and I'm surprised he can hear me over the music screaming through his headphones. I stick my tongue out at him. Of course, like a good kid, Simon polishes his pages while I am sitting here with *nothing*. Well, not nothing. I have my basic outlines, but I'm stuck on the last frame of the page. It refuses to fill itself in, no matter how hard I try to bleed something brilliant onto the page. There's an idea that's been cooking in the back of my brain since my run-in with Herbal Tea Guy yesterday, but for the life of me I can't pull it out. I can only hope it's genius when it emerges, because I'll be just under the wire for this week's green-light meeting. And unlike the last three times, I have *got* to nail this presentation. My brilliance seems to go unappreciated in meetings. Just last month, my boss, Edward Casey Junior, was unable to overlook the *tiny* fact that I'd insulted the current story line—a beast of Kyle's making, not mine—before offering my own ideas. So I *may have* called the villain—my boss's favorite to date apparently—a direct copy of our competition's and *may have* used the words "trite" and "tired." What I saw as honest feedback he took personally. Fine. I need to work on my delivery, that's all. I'll keep working on my presentation for this month's green-light meeting, wow them with graphics, and prove I have the best ideas. Because I do . . . when I can figure them out.

I resume my throwing, and even Kyle shoots me the stink eye from across the room. He's just in a bad mood because he got all banged up playing *Pokémon GO* on Sunday night. He insists he was trying out parkour—from the new "nerd fitness group" he and Simon had joined—to nab a Jigglypuff, but my guess is he was staring at his phone and walked into a tree.

"Are you finished annoying the rest of us? You're not the only one with a deadline this week, you know." He's absentmindedly rubbing what looks like rope burn on his arm. I narrow my eyes. Kyle is about the nerdiest, most nonathletic guy I know, next to Simon. Papercuts would constitute an emergency in his book. *Rope burn? Has he taken up slacklining too?* That doesn't seem likely. Maybe he was injured in some *bedroom* parkour instead of at the park. Certainly something I'd lie about to coworkers too. I raise my eyebrows at him and throw the ball against the wall, maintaining eye contact. I can't say I'm always proud of my antics, but being the only woman in this office, I sometimes stoop to their level of boyish tactics.

Thwack, thwack, th—

The ball bounces off the wall funny and flies over my shoulder into the aisle near the printer. I'm halfway under the printer when I hear my name called. Busted for workplace "distraction" again, I bet.

"Oh, eff off, Andy. My draft idea for the green-light agenda isn't due until three p.m., and I have at least—" I pause mid-kneel, holding my red ball, and stare up at Herbal Tea Guy. What. The. Hell. I climb to my feet awkwardly, complete with hitting my hip on the table holding the printer.

"You have a visitor," Andy says. He's trying to smooth his flyaway curly blond hair. It would be surfer hair on a cooler person. "I had to go get him from reception."

"I can see that," I shoot back. Simon surfaces from his ad markers, staring at me. I don't think he's ever seen me with a guest in the office, *ever*. That's because I don't bring them. On purpose.

Herbal Tea Guy looks different than he did yesterday. He's wearing slacks and a neat work shirt, though I note that it's still rolled up at the sleeves. Even his skinny tie is fashionable. His five-o'clock shadow is gone, and I catch myself pondering whether I liked him better with scruff before I yank my mind back to the important question at hand: *Why is he here at all?*

"I brought you a coffee. Cinnamon dolce latte." He offers it to me like an olive branch.

My eyebrows shoot up, and my traitorous hand sneaks out to take the cup. Caffeine is my body's drug of choice, and it seems he's found my weakness. *And* remembered my order.

Andy is still staring at us, and I don't blame him. I still haven't said anything. He shifts from foot to foot and straightens his woefully rumpled button-down in a self-conscious way. "I, uh . . . I'll be over there if you need me." He motions to his desk, the central one in the pod as befits his team art director status. Andy's never been big on dialogue. That's my specialty. Usually. Except right now, when I'm gaping like a fish out of water. We watch him go in a growingly awkward silence.

"Must be nice to have a hipster job where you can drink coffee at any hour," the man says with a wink, looking pointedly at Kyle—watching us shamelessly in return, feet propped on his desk, large travel coffee mug in hand. Touché, Herbal Tea Guy.

And just like that I'm back, shields powering up. "Takes one to know one, I guess." *Or* go with childish insults. Whichever.

He smiles, and damn it if I'm not back to thinking about whether the scruff made him more attractive. Smiling definitely does. You know, if you're into hipster stalkers, *which I'm not.* The last part is a dictate to my subconscious to quit being ridiculous.

I'm finally about to boot this bozo out when he ups his ante again. "Is there a conference room or something that we can go talk in?" The question is quiet instead of suggestive, and his face is serious. Intriguing, and not at all how I picture hipster seduction taking place. He holds out a business card. This one seems to be a . . . gentleman stalker? I take it automatically and glance down. *LAPD. Detective Matteo Kildaire.*

Oh *crap.*

CHAPTER 2

"So, uh, how did you find me?" I sip my latte and try to suppress my moan of satisfaction. It's the perfect temperature and exactly what I want right now, stressed as I am about my deadline.

"It wasn't hard." He sets his coffee cup across from mine, spins one of the chairs, and sits down opposite me. We're jammed in the small conference room dedicated to our team just off the main workspace. The bad news is that everyone in my office seems to be taking every opportunity to walk past the glass door and glance in. The good news is that I love this room for the view. LA stretches out in front of the large window that makes up the back wall—the textile and fabric shops off Wall Street, my favorite part of the city.

"I thought you were an *herbal tea* guy." "Americano" is scrawled across his white cup, along with something that looks suspiciously like a scrawled phone number. Order-Taking Girl, you go-getter, you.

"I've been trying to quit drinking coffee, but work has . . . amped up since yesterday, and I'm off the wagon," he admits, taking a sip and meeting my curious stare. Studying me. I'm a little undone by his intense hazel gaze and long lashes. "It was easy to find you. Detective, remember? I noticed the Genius Comics name on your bag, called to see if anyone with purple hair worked here . . ."

"Et voilà," I finish for him. Seeing as I'm the only woman in the office most days, and well . . . the purple hair. Not exactly rocket science. Something tells me that despite the pretty gorgeous set of peepers this Muggle has, he's here on business. "All right, Sherlock, let's cut onions. What can I do for you?"

"I need to talk to you about what you said in the shop."

"You mean my completely ridiculous remark about the crime scene missing a golden arrow?"

"Yes. That."

Our silence spans two sips. *There's no way.* "You *found* a golden arrow?"

"Yes."

Internally, I'm scrambling. They *found a golden arrow.* And my tinfoil suspicion suddenly doesn't seem so coated in, well, tinfoil. But, then, why would the *police* be at my work? "So I'm, what, under arrest for guessing?"

An annoyingly infectious smile toys about his lips. *It's a legitimate question, Officer Herbal Tea, thankyouverymuch.*

"No, if you were under arrest, I'd need to have just cause, proof, and read you your rights. I'm here purely on personal interest. I want to know how you knew that there would be an arrow at the scene. The LAPD hasn't released that evidence to the media. No one knows but the crime scene investigators. Tell me how you knew."

Well, that's another thing I didn't see coming. I bite back an acerbic response. *Just answer the question, and he can leave and I can get back to my real work.* I delve deep to distill all I know and love about my favorite comic. "I mean, it's kind of a leap of imagination, but the picture I saw in the news looked so much like a panel out of a comic. *The Hooded Falcon.* Two goons trussed up on docks back-to-back. Classic superhero move. And there's this . . . I don't know . . . outline around the thieves that looks like a rabbit, which in the comic sometimes happened so the reader knew the goons belonged to Falcon's nemesis. So you can see how an imagination in my employ would jump to a fantasy of comic book come to life. In the comic, the scenes are always marked with a literal golden arrow sign, Falcon's signature."

Officer Herbal Tea looks up from his notes. "And this is a new comic? One your company is working on?"

I sigh. There's no way to package this conversation for a comic newb. Reboots are often beyond the comprehension of non-geek folk. "It's tricky. The original Falcon—based on Robin of Loxley—was written in the eighties and was less popular than his better-known *Justice League*–era compatriots: Batman, Wonder Woman, the like. Brilliantly illustrated—well, the originals anyway. They've been rebooted by a new artist since then. The new ones suck. I work on those," I add.

He's scribbling, and I note his furrowed brow, maybe at my candor about the current issues. Maybe I should learn to sugarcoat my words. But I'm just being honest.

"So, in the comics, the golden arrow is a what? A drawing? A pin? Only on bad guys? Does this Falcon character ever attack police, or is he simply out for crime fighting?"

Another tricky question, but I'm impressed by the level of his inquiry. If I were a Muggle policeman, I'd have listened to about three seconds of this before tuning me out. "Falcon and his sidekick, Swoosh, are vigilante heroes, fighting on the side of social justice. They often use the symbol of a golden arrow to mark their busts. Usually in the form of a golden arrow anchor running through the ropes holding the criminals, or the arrow—shot from his trusty bow—pinning the criminal to a wall. Was it *on* the criminals?"

"No." He glances up at me, then presses his lips together.

"It's a two-way street, this information thing. You're the one here asking for help."

"Drawn on the pier. Gold sharpie, maybe. And it wasn't even finished. My guess is they ran out of ink, or the wood chewed up the pen."

"And the outline thing, was that just in the picture? Like a flash or a glare or something from the camera? Did it look like a rabbit?"

The officer's lips narrow into a line, and I can't tell if it is amusement at my knowledge (or lack of) of photography or annoyance with being the questionee. "We noted a chalk outline, but I don't think anyone saw it as the *shape* of anything. Just a chalk outline. People just do morbid stuff sometimes." He sounds dismissive, but a thoughtful look flashes over his features, and he scribbles something in his notebook. I bet he is planning to reexamine the outline, which will probably be completely pointless.

Though there were similarities in the panel, to be sure, I figure that without the rabbit outline, I am back in tinfoil-hatsville. I'd been hoping for something more concrete when we started this conversation—a harpoon in the shape of an arrow tying the goons together or something. Not a measly scribble that could have been there for years before someone got the gumption to tie up a couple of passed out drug dealers or whatever. I'm not the only one with an active imagination, it seems, and as much as I love sharing my theories, it is time to come back down to earth. "So you think because someone drew *part* of an arrow on the pier in *sharpie*—"

"*Gold* sharpie." His full lips are now toying with a frown.

I ignore him and continue, "—that this *really* has to do with *The Hooded Falcon*? It's a stretch." And that's putting it mildly.

"I'm just following a lead and trying to weigh everything equally. You were the one who said the scene reminded you of this comic, and you knew the arrow was there," he responds, his lips pressed into a line again. I stare at them just a moment too long.

As much as my little heart desperately loves *The Hooded Falcon*, this line of thinking is useless. Real criminals don't mimic comics. This scenario is something that happens only *in* comic books, not everyday life. It's a good story, though. My brain is off and racing away with the new possibility. Brilliance strikes, and it punches straight through my writer's block. *It* could *happen in the project I'm working on. A copycat comic book crime scene. It's perfect.* And just like that, I'm feeling rather kindly toward this interruption. I could kiss Officer Herbal Tea.

I need to get back to my desk, stat. "LA is full of street artists. I suggest you go ask them who drew it. Now, I have a deadline and need to go. Is this all you wanted?" I don't realize I'm standing until I'm halfway to the door and catch the look of annoyance on his face. He's probably not used to other people calling the shots or walking out on him.

"Not really." He looks down at his notes then back at me with earnest eyes. "Rival drug dealers were cuffed with zip ties and then tied back-to-back with some packing materials from one of the crates on the dock. Our guys undercover say that there's a possible drug war brewing. Each side suspects the other and has threatened to kill the person who turned them in. Things could get ugly in a hurry, and it's my job to follow every lead—no matter how far-fetched—to keep that from happening."

I kick my hip against the door to the conference room. "I get that this is important to you, but to me it just looks like someone saw the criminals tied up and reads too many comic books. Thought they were being funny. Or it was already drawn there and it's a coincidence. There's no way that this is related to a thirty-year-old comic book."

"You said it was a current comic."

"Our latest issue had space aliens in it. The panel we're talking about is from the originals."

The last remark hits home, and he nods slowly, wheels turning the logic of it over in his mind.

I hold the door to the conference room open. With one more look at me, he tucks his notebook in his pocket, grabs his cup, and exits the room.

"Can I call you with any additional—"

"Email only. I don't do phone calls," I cut him off, holding up the business card I snagged off the conference room counter.

His eyebrows raise.

"Interrupts my creative flow," I state cryptically, ushering him out the door to reception.

Like a pack of hyenas, the guys in the office watch him leave. One makes a wolf whistle. I can't see who, or I'd already be using the rubber-band gun at my desk. "Shut up," I say to the room at large. "I left something at the coffee shop yesterday. He was returning it." I don't address the fact that I'm not holding anything except my coffee and slink to my seat.

But then I smile. Officer Herbal Tea didn't just bring me coffee; he brought me something even better. An *idea*.

CHAPTER 3

The smell of chemicals stings my nose as the chair swivels to face the mirror, and Lawrence's gorgeous dark face comes into view. I take a deep breath and let it back out, willing all the tension, all the stress and *baggage* I tend to carry around, out of my body. I have T minus three days to the green-light meeting that will make or break my promotion. I can't seem to stop seeing superheroes in every shadow. I'm obsessed with the news, hoping to catch a glimpse of a certain cop in the follow-up drug-bust stories.

"If loving the smell of hair dye in the morning is wrong, I don't want to be right," I say.

Lawrence makes a cluck of approval and runs his fingers through my short locks, finger-combing a part for the foils. "Don't I know it, *girl.*" He stretches the word out extra long in a way that's habit, even when he's not in costume. "How's work?"

I open one eye against the scalp massage. "Pass. Next topic, please."

"That good?"

"It's not bad. I at least made my deadline for sketches for our internal review. But work just gets me all . . ." I wiggle my head back and forth, unable to articulate how extra draining my job has been lately. "I'm hoping to get that promotion, and I think Casey Junior is going to announce it next week . . . but I've really got to nail my presentation at the exec meeting so the whole board can see that I'm the better choice. And, of course, Andy gets to approve my ideas for the executive green light—that historical reboot thing I told you about last week—and he doesn't like it. He said I could present it as is if I wanted but that he'd offer suggestions to change it if I was interested." I throw my hands up. "He doesn't even *get* what I'm saying half the time. I hate that he's my team leader and that we're both up for the same job." Lawrence was the first to get an earful when I found out months ago that both Andy and I had applied for the newly created art director position within Genius. I'd been giddy at the prospect of finally getting to be Andy's boss—the team directors would periodically have to answer to the art director. I'd be an executive at Genius, and finally people would have to take me seriously. I'd thought it was *perfect* . . . until I found out that Andy's seemingly lost sense of ambition had reared its ugly head and that he'd applied for the position too. Since then I've been paranoid that Andy is out to sabotage my ideas, just so he can appear the better candidate.

"Being fierce all the time takes its toll on you, honey."

"Preach, sister."

Lawrence steps away to mix the dye at the mirrored station in front of the chair.

I sigh, already missing his hands. "Seriously, L, you need to teach Trog how to give me scalp massages, and I'll never need another date as long as he lives."

Lawrence raises a penciled eyebrow. They're not as dramatic as when he is in full drag, but they're more than you'd expect a six-foot guy with a boxer's build to have. "Should the next topic be dating?"

My mind goes directly to Detective Kildaire's hazel eyes. "Hard pass."

A rumble of thunder outside shakes the windows to the tiny shop. I'm glad I called Ryan to see if he could pick me and the bike up in my car. Nothing's worse than getting your hair done and instantly having it ruined by acid rain. I'd been trying to get in to see L for a few weeks, but L's business has been going through the roof in the year since he was on *Drag Race*. RuPaul herself offered to help Lawrence franchise, but he still likes his quiet, slightly run-down shop, taking one customer at a time. He says it's *him* and that sometimes queens like to feel at home instead of like they're performing.

"How about religion?" Lawrence asks.

I raise my eyebrow right back at him.

He slathers the gel in my hair, wraps it with foil, and chuckles. "Politics? Or if you prefer the arts, I can practice my opening number on you." He bounces from foot to foot, aggressively humming something that reeks of Broadway. "You need to start making my new costume, you know. I'm thinking gold lamé *anything*. I don't care if those other bitches think it's outdated."

I laugh. I can never stay grumpy around Lawrence. He may be my singular most favorite human being on this planet. "I have some ideas I'm working on. Are you sure you're okay bartering colors for costumes? I feel like I'm getting the better end of this deal."

"Girl, my tips went up fifty percent wearing your stuff. Plus, when you're a world-famous designer, I'll sell mine for millions."

I nod and close my eyes, thinking about this possible promotion and how it smooths the way for me to do more costume creation for both movies and video games. For years I've been doodling my own takes on all the Genius characters. Flashy new revamps of their costumes. Sketches for cosplay adaptions. At first I thought it was my way of fleshing out my writing. But lately . . . well, I've been dreaming of doing it for work too, *without* the writing. Despite my distaste for following "traditional" stereotypes, I can't help loving costuming. The colors, the fabrics, even the sewing itself. It slowly turned from an augmentation of my "real career" to something I privately think of as my true calling. It's why I secretly applied to a fashion design competition specifically targeted at nerds, part of San Diego Comic-Con. I'm curious if I'm any good measured against "real" costume designers. But if I get this promotion, I'll get to have my cake and eat it too . . . I won't have to prove anyone right by quitting my job as the only female comic book writer at Genius to go design clothes. I'll be able to mold and shape my job into something I want. Plus, I'd be Andy's boss, and I'd finally win the long-standing stalemate of the difference of our ideas.

My eyes pop back open a minute later. "Actually! Speaking of politics, did you see that Edward Casey is planning a huge charity auction for the thirtieth anniversary of *The Hooded Falcon*? It's all over the Twittersphere today. It's going to take place at San Diego Comic-Con!" As much as I dislike the man, he does a lot for the fans of Genius, and this charity auction promises to hold some of the most monumental *THF* memorabilia that exists. I nearly rub my hands together in greed and issue maniacal villain laughter. At least *one* item will be mine.

"Mmmm." Lawrence makes a noncommittal noise and spins my chair to the side. It's not like Lawrence to clam up, and I turn my head, trying to see his face. I get one huge hand over each ear to hold me still for my trouble.

"*You* brought up politics," I grumble.

"I didn't know about the anniversary."

"Um, hello, I've been talking about it for months. In fact, I've told you three times about the gala you're attending with me. My boss says dates are *required*. I RSVP'd. I need you. Come on, come be my date, celebrate a comic that used to be awesome, and make my boss happy."

Lawrence pulls a face.

The only work events I can ever drag Lawrence to are ones involving *The Hooded Falcon* or ones with copious amounts of free food. This one would have both; it should be a slam dunk.

"So you don't want to be my date, or you don't want to make my boss happy?"

Complete silence from Lawrence.

"Come on, L. I know I make him sound awful, but he's not *that* bad. I know; I'll introduce you. Maybe he'll give us some insider knowledge about what's being auctioned."

The sour look on his face when I suggest introducing him goes beyond the typical bored-sympathetic look he wears when I rant about the patriarchy at work. I've told Lawrence stories about how I've been asked at every meeting for a year to take notes like a secretary or get coffee for the team. I know he doesn't love that Casey Junior can't seem to remember I like to be called MG and insists on calling me Michael. And he's always clammed up, but for years now I've just assumed he doesn't want to interrupt. That he is being a BFF by listening to me vent without judgment. This is the first time I've had the idea that maybe he's been clamming up about *something* and not just being supportive. But Lawrence is largely an "accept everyone as they are" kind of guy. He was once sabotaged onstage by another queen and proceeded to not only finish his act but use the ruined costume to his advantage—sincerely thanking the other queen afterward for helping raise his game. There's not a hateful bone in his body, so the slightly bitter look on his face takes me by surprise.

Lawrence is still silent, so I reach out and spin myself around. "I've already assumed you'd be my date. You or Ryan *always* come with me to stuff; it's too late to back out now." I study his face, which hasn't lost its look of pure distaste. "So it's my boss? You *actively* dislike my boss? I always thought you were just being supportively antisocial so I didn't feel awkward. L, you don't dislike *anyone*. Well, except that no-good Cleopatra Foxy."

"There's only room for one Queen of Egypt, and that's Latifah Nile," he says, followed by a characteristic hair flick, sans wig. "Now. If you'll face front so I don't wreck this mess." He turns me forward and pulls another foil. He's silent a long moment, like he's chewing on his words, then hesitantly offers an explanation. It's like a dam is breaking and these words have been stored up, waiting to come out. "I'll come, but don't introduce us. We've already met. He's always been a bit of an ass, so no, I don't like him. And he's not wild about me." L's mouth snaps shut, and he's got an "Oh shit, the cat is out of the bag" expression that makes me widen my eyes.

It takes a moment for Lawrence's words to register in my brain. Everything in my heart screeches to a halt. The way he said "we've already met" went beyond "we ran into each other at the artichoke dip at the Christmas party." There was a depth and a complexity there that spoke of true knowing. Which is beyond my comprehension since I've known L for *years* without him divulging that he knew my boss outside of my work.

"You know my boss? Like for how long?" I attempt a look over my shoulder.

"It's nothing." L forces my head forward and attacks my hair with a comb like the Hulk at an all-you-can-smash buffet. "I don't like or dislike him. I'm just saying I preferred his daddy. Now leave it and let me do my work."

I reach back over my own shoulders and grip Lawrence's broad arms, stopping them from their movement at the nape of my neck. I am most *certainly* not letting this go. "Whoa, whoa, whoa, you know this how? Like *preferred* preferred his daddy?" I spin back around, ignoring the yank on my hair, and quirk my eyebrows up suggestively. My mind is reeling. Do Lawrence and Casey have a lovers' past? Is that why he couldn't care less about other comic books? It would certainly explain him clamming up about my work woes.

"You are going to look the wrong kind of fierce if I don't get these foils in. You're a damn Tasmanian devil today." He finishes the processing in silence, then goes to the sink to rinse his brushes, letting me stew in my thoughts and chemicals. It is an unspoken pact between us that I don't pry into Lawrence's past. L accepts people as they are and expects the same from his friends. Some queens fiercely guard their real-world identities—understandable when some are high-powered lawyers or doctors afraid of losing credibility or business just because they enjoy performing drag. Lawrence isn't quite that tight-lipped, but he has always been cagey about his past. Of course, I've fished a few times. I asked him about where he grew up, went to school, all the normal small-talk questions at the gamer convention where I met Ryan—dragging Lawrence along against his will—at the Genius table and Lawrence was performing at an after-party. And a few times after our *Game of Thrones* drinking games (one drink for death, two drinks for boobies). But he always passed it off with good humor, saying he'd been "born with sequins and a tiara." It got to the point where I didn't even ask; I just accepted Lawrence as is . . . except this isn't something I can just set aside. This is *my* comic, *my* personal hero, and apparently one of *my* best friends is involved. Rule or no rule, I have to push.

"I'm waiting."

Lawrence gives me a look that says he regrets having said anything.

"*You* were the one that brought it up, L."

"Which I am regretting. It wasn't like *that*, though Senior was eccentric. He'd been known to wear women's underwear long before it was cool." A small smile flits across his lips before he meets my eyes in the mirror and his face closes off again. "I worked for Senior, case closed."

"You—what? You *worked* for Edward Casey Senior? The man who wrote *The Hooded Falcon*? The man who basically saved my life as a teenager? And you never thought to mention this in the *years* that you've known me?" I could understand maybe not telling me right away, but my feelings sting under the weight of how many opportunities L has had to divulge this information. I sure expounded on several occasions what the comic had meant to me as a teen.

The comic book store I worked in when I turned sixteen was the first place that had ever felt like home. Even though I wasn't allowed to run the register because I was a girl—*how 1950s can you get?*—I put up with it because I loved the stacks of adventures waiting to be read and the conversations about Falcon and Swoosh I had with customers while stocking shelves. It was where I dreamed about living the life I wanted instead of the life my parents dictated, the place where I made my first comic friends, both on the page and in real life. That was until my mother discovered my "retail" job had to do with the comic books she was trying to divest from my life and forced me to quit.

Without Edward Casey's comic, I never could have applied to work at that store. I'd never have dreamed of living my own life or had hope that my awkward teenage years could turn into something else.

Lawrence's eyes are focused on some point in the distance, and he seems lost in thought for a moment too. "Mr. Casey Senior was a good man."

The bell tinkles above the door as it opens. We both turn to see Ryan step in, his jacket held above his head against the rain spattering the sidewalk outside. I know by Lawrence's suddenly straight posture that we have to hold our conversation—for whatever reason, L is loath to let anyone else know that he worked for the Caseys. Something I'll respect, at least until I understand *why* it is some big personal secret.

Ryan is oblivious. "Hey, L." He waves, then takes in my foils. "It's a good look for you, MG." His own dirty-blond hair is tousled from the jacket over his head, but I'm the bigger person and fail to point it out.

I stick my tongue out at him but smile. "Shut up. And thanks for coming to pick me up. It's going to be a few minutes. I forgot to text you and let you know we are running late." L throws me a glance that says it's *my* fault for the monkey business.

Ryan looks outside at the driving rain. When it rains here, it means business. "I was going to go to a spin class for cardio day, but . . . I'll just stay and answer emails on my phone instead." He settles down on the uneven red pleather sofa in the corner near the ancient register and pulls out headphones. "L, I wanted to check if you still wanted to play in that *Assassin's Creed* tournament this weekend."

And there's why I love Ryan. He doesn't pigeonhole Lawrence or me into any box—comic book girl, drag queen, or otherwise. I'm finally free to be myself and am accepted in my own home. My cup runneth over; I really love my strange little family.

"I'm all in, and those bitches are going down. Could use the cash. I have an eye on a new microphone setup—those things are expensive." L wiggles his fingers like a pianist about to play. And he's serious too.

"You could start work for me next week, you know. I'd kick Dave right off the team." But he's smiling when he says it. Ryan keeps trying to get Lawrence to play video games for him as a professional. They rarely lose a tournament, which means good cash prizes, and now that Ryan is helping Genius Comics develop the newest Hooded Falcon video game—thanks to *moi*—he really could get Lawrence a job with his development company. Which L keeps refusing. Not all of Ryan's gaming friends are as cool with queendom as Ryan, and L loves being the reigning queen of wild color dye jobs in East LA. My friends have found their niches and success in their careers. I haven't. Not really, not until I get to wear that executive badge.

"I'm good," Lawrence responds, as always.

"What are you two girls talking about?" Ryan asks, picking up his headphones again. "Looked serious."

"We're talking about Edward Casey Junior," I say before Ryan can put on his headphones. Maybe L will tell him about knowing Casey Senior too, if given the open door. Seeing as Ryan recently started as a contractor for Genius Comics, I thought the conversational opening particularly suited for everyone involved and high-fived my dialogue-writing genius.

Ryan glances between us, then grunts, a sour look on his face too.

"What the hell. You two are being *so* weird today. It's like I don't know you." I throw my hands up as I watch Ryan clamp the bulky Dr. Dre phones over one of his ears.

"Men," I mutter.

"So have you done anything about that yet?" Lawrence addresses me, raises an eyebrow, and looks pointedly at Ryan. And by "done anything," he clearly means "hit that." I can tell he's trying to change the subject, which I don't want to do, but he's hit an Achilles' heel.

Lawrence has been hoping for a Ryan-MG ship for a long time. Which I get. On paper, Ryan would be perfect for me. He runs his own business, he nerds out with the best of them, he's not bad looking, he's not horrible to live with, and he's open-minded about his friends and clients. But. My feelings of my roommate-found-at-a-gaming-con situation possibly turning into something *more* led to a best friend. Not a romantic love. Lawrence just always holds out hope since Ryan and I are still single.

We've had this mini conversation a million times. "No. There's nothing that needs to be addressed. Look, I know we live together amicably and shared one *teensy* kiss, but I think that boat has sailed romantically. I love Ryan, just not in that way. In fact, last night he went out with a girl from his gaming group. I'm happy for him." I shrug, thankful that Ryan isn't listening, and try to shove the thoughts of Matteo out of my head. We need to get back to the matter at hand. Maybe a little humor will grease L's tongue. Sass *is* his first language.

"So. Casey Senior. Were you his colorist?" I'm teasing, but I'm surprised to see a flash of something haunted in L's gaze. It's an expression I haven't seen cross his usually jovial features.

His eyes flick to mine, and his shoulders sag an inch. I get the feeling that he *knows* I'm not letting this go. "Not his colorist. I was his security guard. You say he saved your life when you were a teenager? Well, he saved mine too, and he was a damn fine man for it. He got me out of a bad situation when he didn't have to, took me in, gave me a job, accepted me as a person." Lawrence's voice is quiet, and he avoids eye contact.

I sit back, letting that wash over me. I never knew. The million or so times I spouted off about *The Hooded Falcon* and he never said anything. For all the angst I have when people try to label me, I never considered Lawrence as anything but a lipstick-loving queen. *Security guard.* He certainly looks the part. I'd never mess with Lawrence in a million years, unless I wanted to get scraped off the street. The guy still worked out twice a day—he and Ryan went to the same CrossFit gym. His arms literally bulge out of the black tank top he's wearing today, and I saw him win a bet that someone could bounce a basketball off his abs.

There's so much story here, I don't know what to ask first. "Let me get this straight. You *worked* for Casey Senior? As a security guard? Why did you quit? . . . Oh." Edward Casey Senior died of a heart attack, amid rumors of a huge change in the plans for his comic book. Of course his job would have ended. "Lawrence, we have to talk about this. You have to tell me *everything*. How could you keep this from me?"

Again, a flash of something I don't understand crosses L's face. "Girl, sometimes the past doesn't need to be examined. Mr. Casey was a good and kind man, but he died on my watch, and I don't want to talk about it."

"But he died of a heart attack. No one can help that." I just reread the big *LA Times* article yesterday when doing research for my write-up on the thirtieth anniversary. Stress-induced heart attack.

Lawrence doesn't say anything for a moment. "Maybe." There's a shadow behind his word, but he moves on with a shrug. "Junior blamed me for it. For bringing trouble into their house, for adding to his father's stress. And Junior sure didn't appreciate my . . . extracurricular activities and dismissed me. I don't love that my life led me back to dealing with him, but I make it work. LA is a small town. End of story. Now, let's get you to the wash sink before your hair ends up like a trashed purple weave."

By the set of his shoulders, I can tell Lawrence is finished talking about his past, and this time I have enough to ponder that I let it drop. I wonder what else he's kept from me. It's nuts how complicated my life has become since Matteo appeared with his questions. I lean back over the sink and let the hot water and L's humming momentarily wash away my worries.

I snort at one of my own wayward thoughts. "Now at least I understand your willingness to go to Hooded Falcon stuff. I always assumed you just liked the spandex."

"I may not love comics, but I can appreciate the art. I loved the drawings that Casey Senior did in his journals. The messy ideas, the scribbles, the colors, the costumes." Lawrence shrugs, then meets my gaze in the mirror and gives me a small secret smile. "*And* the spandex. In fact, Senior gave me one of his journals right before he died. He knew I loved watching him work, drawing the characters. He'd said he wanted me to have it."

"Wait—like you have original memorabilia? And I don't know this." I'm a little jubilant, mostly deeply offended.

"I told you we were done talking." The blow-dryer clicks on, and we're forced into silence.

"Can I see it?" I ask the moment my hair is dry. Lawrence tries his best to hurry me out of the chair, but I'm not finished.

"It's just a journal. An *old* journal. Aren't we done talking about this?"

"If you show it to me, we can be."

"You're so stubborn."

"Back at ya."

Lawrence throws down the brush with a scowl, leaves me sitting in the salon chair, and trudges off to the back hallway without another word. I can hear him clomping upstairs to his apartment and . . . silence.

Ryan eyes me over his phone in puzzlement. He removes his headphones and motions to the back of the shop. "Are you done now?"

"Almost. Lawrence has an *original* journal from Casey Senior he's going to show me!"

Something sparks in Ryan's gaze, but his words are blasé. "And you care because . . ."

"*Ryan.* Seriously. Because I love *The Hooded Falcon*? Do you know me at all? You're working on the video game! Aren't *you* interested?" It takes all my willpower not to divulge the entirety of L's secret.

Ryan's lips press into a thin line, and something odd passes over his face. My friends are acting so *weird* today. He clamps the headphones back on his ears just as the creak of stairs announces Lawrence's descent. Lawrence reappears moments later and shoves a worn black moleskin notebook in my face.

I can't help myself. I squeal like a Whovian at the start of a new regeneration. "Lawrence, it's *real*!" I flip the pages, taking in the pen and ink sketches, the messy notes, the odd torn-out page. I have notebook upon notebook exactly like this of my own work. I recognize the thought process of a fellow comic book writer; familiar sketches call to me at the beginning of the journal—sketches from the last issue ever published. This is a *gold mine*. It's likely one of the last journals Senior ever drew in. I flip faster, wanting to see everything this treasure holds.

A scene near the back, fully and artfully wrought, especially for a sketchbook version, catches my eye. It's an all-black panel that spans two pages, the pen lines of a hatch fill in all the white, leaving just two lone figures in the center. It's the Hooded Falcon, kneeling before Swoosh and handing him his bow.

I do a double take and look again. I flip to the back, then forward again to the sketch. "When was this written?" I've never seen this sketch before, but its significance is undeniable, and it's *definitely* not in the canonical issues.

"Girl, don't you mess up my keepsake." Lawrence taps his foot. He reaches for the notebook, but I parry and spin the chair around, using his shins as a push-off point.

"I need a date; I need a date—ah-ha!" I find a little sketch that Casey Senior dated a few pages back, do a little quick mental math that only someone truly obsessed with the comics would know, and shake my head. "This isn't possible."

"It's real, if that's what you mean. He gave it to me himself, right after a meeting with his son." L sounds offended now.

I spin the chair back around and meet his eyes with my own wide gaze. "I believe you. But according to this, Casey Senior was retiring the Hooded Falcon. He was going to stop the Falcon series." I look around. "Can you copy these two pages for me? I promise I won't show *anyone*. I want to do some research if I can. This is the biggest news in the comic industry in *years*."

"But . . . the comic is still going, isn't it?" Lawrence looks confused and extremely hesitant to share his journal.

I catch my breath. "You said that Casey Senior argued with his son the night he died. What if it was about his plans to stop the comic? What if my boss knew his dad wanted to stop the comic and has been covering up and hiding the original creator's wishes? It'd be a *huge* deal if Casey Senior finished the series and his son hid the issues in order to capitalize on the franchise. I need to find out if anyone else knew about this."

There's a moment of coiled violence where I think Lawrence is going to rip the journal out of my hands. Instead, he takes a deep breath, and his shoulders relax a fraction of an inch.

"No one else sees this unless I say so." Lawrence takes the journal to the copier at the register and runs off two sheets for me. He's muttering about how I should just leave the past alone again, but I can tell he's a *little* glad we talked today. It takes a really good friend to dredge up your former life drama and maybe relieve a bit of misplaced decades-old guilt. Or maybe it's the thought of Casey Junior getting caught doing something wrong. Either way, I'll take it.

"I promise."

Without permission, my mind wanders to Officer Herbal Tea and his crazy theory centered around the same comic book. By some weird twist of fate, the original Hooded Falcon is in my life yet again. I can only wonder at what change he'll bring this time.

CHAPTER 4

"You have *got* to be kidding me."

My front door stands open the next morning, and there, like my own *Groundhog Day*, is Officer Herbal Tea. Trogdor yaps like mad, and I have half a mind to move the leg I'm using to block the door and let this guy's shins get nipped by my dog. I can't even hear OHT's response over the barking.

"Trog! Inside! Now!" I point and watch with satisfaction as his Wonder Bread corgi butt trots into the living room. Even after five years together, it still makes me laugh to watch his little purposeful stride.

My gaze runs over OHT.

"It's not the pizza! Or Lawrence!" I shout to Ryan in the living room before stepping outside and closing the door behind me. I would much rather have Lawrence at the door, but his afternoon appointments are running late, something about acrylic gel that sounded painful. Instead, OHT and I are nestled on my snug front porch, a little too cozy for my comfort, but what are you going to do in four feet of space?

"Am I interrupting?" he asks, trying to allow me room on the porch and failing miserably. His shoulders look the "lean and fit" type, but right now they *feel* like the "huge and hulking" variety.

"No, I often greet guests on my spacious veranda. I'm sorry the iced tea is still brewing," I say before I can catch the snark from coming out. "What? Now I'm under arrest?"

"No, of course not." He looks uncomfortable and plays with the cuff on his shirt. It's *not* cute, I decide. Not even a little bit. "I tried emailing you."

"It's a work email. I only check it on workdays."

"I have additional questions to follow up on. This case is extremely time sensitive."

"So you came to my house." I cross my arms over my ample chest. "You have thirty seconds to prove you aren't a stalker before I call the police. The *other* police, I mean."

"I needed to ask a favor. It shouldn't take much of your time."

I arch my eyebrow in clear indication of my dubiousness.

"There's been a development in the case I told you about. I looked up that stuff you talked about. *The Hooded Falcon* and the Justice Liaison."

"League."

"Yeah, League. I'm trying to find some of them to read—"

"Any newsstand will probably have the latest copy. Or Meltdown on Sunset."

"No, the ones you talked about. The older ones."

I laugh, my hands dropping to my sides. "Good luck with that. They're Bronze Age collectibles." At his look I add, "They've been out of print for years and years. Sometimes I have to sit on eBay for *months* to find one." I don't want to be accused of obstructing justice, even if "justice" is taking up an annoyingly large part of my tiny porch.

"So I discovered. Hence the favor." Sarcasm fairly drips from the comment.

In the interest of divesting my porch of said officer, I decide to play nice. "Okay, don't get snarky, Herbal T—er, Detective. How can I help you?"

"I've looked online, at the library, everywhere. I want to read the one with the scene you recognized, and Google says the only place I'm going to find one is in a private collection. I just happen to know this person who collects comic books *and* works at a comic book company . . ."

"A stunningly lovely purple-haired person that must be plied with copious amounts of free coffee in order to help you?"

A smirk starts at the corner of his lips and spreads into a quick smile. "So you know her too?"

I pretend to study my aquamarine manicure. Despite a small quickening of my pulse, smugness is most definitely *not* cute on his tan skin. Definitely not. Even when he's just agreed that I am stunningly lovely by omission.

"So can you help me?" His hazel eyes are wide and boyish. I find myself swayed by his gaze. Plus, free coffee.

I reach backward for the door handle. "Fine. I happen to know that Genius Comics has some of them in their library. I'll give you thirty minutes. Why you want to look through them is beyond me. I mean, it's not like there's someone out there in a cape and tights trying to be the Hooded Falcon."

When he doesn't join my laughter, I roll my eyes. "Oh Jesus, you think there's a man in tights and a cape." I lean inside the door, snag my keys off the hook, and yell to Ryan that I'll be right back.

The muffled noise from inside and the clank of sword fighting tell me he's forgotten about the pizza and has returned to playing video games. "In the zone," as I call it. Singular focus. He won't even notice I'm gone.

"All right, Detective, your vehicle or mine?" I motion to the old-school Schwinn bicycle locked to the outside of the porch, complete with bell and tassels.

He laughs, a good deep laugh with a wide smile that his face wears well. "You are quite the force to be reckoned with, aren't you? Are you sure *you* aren't donning a cape at night?"

"Let's not talk about my nighttime habits during official police business," I tease, shoving the keys into the pocket of my red skinny jeans. I'm amused to see a blush creep up his neck. Interesting again, OHT. Maybe there's some red-blooded man behind that altruism after all.

"To the police car," I say, giddy despite my dedication to remaining aloof. And I wiggle my hips just a little extra as I jog down the stairs, just because I can. I smile a self-satisfied smile when he joins me and I see the neck blush still in evidence. That joy falters as I see what vehicle we're walking toward.

"I thought you said this was police business?"

"I only drive a marked car for patrol. My car *is* a police car." There's a silent *thankyouverymuch*.

He opens the passenger door of a white Toyota Prius and helps me inside. First herbal tea, now this. If it were possible for this guy to be getting less and less my type, he's doing it in a hurry. Worse than a Muggle, he's a *vanilla* Muggle. An herbal-tea-drinking, Prius-driving, vanilla Muggle policeman with gorgeous eyes. I guess we all have our redeeming qualities.

"So what prompted the need for the comics?" I ask mostly to avoid sitting in silence. This car is *really* quiet.

"I got a piece of evidence back from forensics today, and something tells me that it's more than coincidence. Trust me."

"Cop's intuition?"

"Something like that."

I'd argue with him, but something inside me is enjoying this adventure, and I'm loath to cut it short, even if he's dead wrong. Soon enough we're hurtling with the speed of a turtle down the 110 toward downtown LA and Genius Comics.

We're back to silence. "A Prius, huh?" I look around the neat interior. Like brand-new off-the-lot clean.

"I don't actually think someone is running around in a cape," he says, his eyes still on the road. "And yes. A Prius. It gets good gas mileage."

"So does my bike," I say, looking out the window. Palm trees whisk by, hazy in the strong summer sun.

"I'd love to bike to work, but I live too far out of the city. It's not the distance but the traffic."

"Oh, I drive when I need to. And yeah, that's smart—I've seen a lot of wrecks where the bicyclist didn't end up on the upside."

"I thought you only had a bike?"

I shrug. "I wanted to see the inside of a cop car. I didn't *say* I didn't have a car. You drew your own conclusions."

Rather than get angry, he laughs again. It's infectious, and I find myself smiling back at him.

"So your boyfriend doesn't mind you leaving with a strange person?"

"Ryan's my roommate." I glance at him to gauge his intention. "My corgi, Trogdor, is the love of my life."

"You're really something," he says.

It doesn't sound like an insult, so I accept it as a compliment.

Usually people say that to mean that I'm *too much*—too colorful, too passionate, too smart, too dramatic, too sarcastic. It's what people say when they don't know how to categorize me, as if I should just fit into the social box of a woman who wants a picket fence and two kids, just like my mom.

I know from my failed attempts at dating that even when people *say* they are okay with my dyed hair and career choice, they usually aren't. After my last disastrous breakup, I decided I was going to stop letting other people's expectations bring me down. I was going to be full-tilt *me*, come hell or high water. I'd colored my hair a bright pink, the most shocking color I could imagine for my mother, to signify my dedication to being nontraditional and never looked back. Instead of being intimidated, Matteo seems genuinely . . . charmed by my quirks. It's been years since I've felt charming instead of like a spectacle. Charming is a nice change. Another two points for the detective.

I pause for a moment, surprised by my own next question. Officer Herbal Tea has intrigued me, which catches me off guard. I'm so used to fending off the overzealous comic-book-nerd attendees at con parties or actively avoiding the stuffy guys my mother tries to shove on me, it's been years since I've even wanted to fish about a guy's dating life. "How about you? Does your girlfriend know that you pick up strange women and drive them around in your car?"

His face remains passive. "I don't usually follow up leads in this way, and"—he shoots a quick glance at me—"I don't have a girlfriend to care that this one is a little . . . different. The case, that is. I live alone, I mean. I like the quiet." Again the red blotches appear under his collar, giving away that maybe this line of questioning isn't strictly business. I'm not willing to admit I enjoy getting a rise out of poor Officer Herbal Tea. And even if I do admit it, he's going to look at these comics, decide he's completely in left field, and go back to normal vanilla life. And I'll go back to focusing on the green-light meeting that could mean my promotion instead of cute neck blushes. The trade-off doesn't sound as good as it should.

I motion that he should take the next exit, even though he's clearly been to my office before. I'm a terrible side-seat driver. "Living alone for the peace and quiet. Sounds charming. I bet you have stellar houseplants."

"I do. And I bet my plants have better breath than your dog."

I pause. "Was that an actual *joke*?" I'm smiling again. I can't help it. Witty banter is my Kryptonite.

CHAPTER 5

I point to a lot on the far side of the building. "Park over there. It's near the off-hour entrance."

"Quite a few cars here for a Saturday," he says, turning off the car and unbuckling his seat belt.

"Creative work waits for no woman," I answer, slipping out of the car, then walk up to the side door. A quick flick of my ID badge and we're in like Flynn.

"Let's avoid mentioning the case, if that's okay?"

"Secrecy works for me," I agree.

The Genius building rises above us in the glass-and-steel style of every headquarters building in comics. Nondescript but impressive. Not quite Stark Tower, but we use seven floors of the total eleven, and that's saying something in a town where rent for a closet can be as much as a bedroom in other parts of the country. I know that fact personally. After quitting my first "real" job out of college—in a law office, just like my dad had wanted—to work at Genius and being cut off by my parents, I lived *in* a friend's closet for three months. If only my time in a cupboard had made me a wizard. I'm still bitter about that. I want a magic wand.

I hold the door to the back office open for him. I'm also an equal opportunity door holder, and I'm pleased to see that he lets me hold it for him without comment. "So anything in particular we're looking for? You never did elucidate."

Matteo's eyes dart around as he steps through the door. A few people walk through the almost-empty break area, probably working on last-minute deadlines. Something I'm familiar with. "Let's wait until I'm sure we're alone."

It's a cagey answer, but I understand why minutes later when I follow him off the elevator. I've been praying for zero peanut gallery, but no dice. I can see Kyle's feet propped on his desk as soon as we arrive on the fifth floor. During business hours we have our own floor receptionist to make it look fancy, though I like to think of our cubicles with the small bank of windows in the work area as the low-rent district. Smoke and mirrors up front, Walmart in the back. It's hard to believe that as *Office Space* as our corner of the universe looks, we produce some of the most colorful and dynamic media in the world.

"Shouldn't you be playing on your phone at home?" I glance pointedly to the phone in his hand where the *Sim City* app blinks—the guy is addicted. Kyle is wearing the male version of the office uniform: graphic tee, jeans that don't fit quite right, and some sort of grungy tennis shoes. I like to hold myself to a higher standard and at least always cover my tees with colorful blazers. Andy and Kyle perpetually look rumpled. Despite Kyle being my coworker and Andy being my supervisor for five years, it's like they roll out of bed surprised *daily* that they have to get to work—the fact that he looks the same on a Saturday proves my point. Kyle is the ultimate Peter Parker sans Spidey.

"Yo, MG. And . . ." Kyle swings his feet to the ground, his chronically broken chair tilting with a crunch of cracked plastic, then glances behind me. His eyes widen. Seeing the same guest twice is unprecedented in the years we've worked together. And I know exactly where Kyle's brain has gone when his gaze darts between us and a slow smile spreads across his face. Time to nip this in the bud. I don't have time to play the star-crossed lover or the lovely maiden or look like anything less than one of the guys in this office when I am up for a promotion. I work too damn hard to have it undermined by a man who drives a Prius. At least until after the "important announcement" scheduled for next week's executive green-light meeting, which I suspect is when my boss will tell us whom he's chosen for the newly created art director position.

"This is just—" But to my horror, Officer Herbal Tea crosses the room and holds out a hand to Kyle, leaving me standing like a sidekick with my mouth open.

"Matteo," he says, shaking Kyle's hand.

"Here, let me introduce you," I grit through my teeth. I can't believe this guy is running right over me. Doesn't he trust me not to blow his cover, as agreed? "This is Kyle, my coworker."

"Hey, man," Kyle says, doing the stupid guy thing where he puffs up his chest to act more manly around another dude. I hate when guys do that, especially since I know for a fact Kyle's favorite movie is *The Princess Bride*. And sometimes while he's working, he watches it on repeat on his iPhone for background noise.

"What did you do to your arm?" Matteo asks in a way that reduces them to thirteen-year-olds comparing fight scars in my eyes.

"Oh, um. An old lady. Hit me." Kyle forces a laugh.

I snort. "An old lady *hit* you? I thought you said you'd been doing parkour."

Kyle's face flushes briefly. "Oh yeah. I mean, I was. There's this old lady who does parkour with us."

"Whatever," I mutter. I don't have time for Kyle's weird stories. For a guy who writes and draws for a living, he certainly is a dollar short in the imagination department today. Time to cut bait and run while the going is good.

I struggle not to say "Officer Herbal Tea" out loud. Matteo's real name feels odd on my lips, like saying it makes him an actual person where he wasn't before. "Matteo is just—"

But *Matteo* has other plans and interrupts me again. "Hey, looks like the hydraulic lift on your chair is broken. Be careful. I'm guessing a free fall wouldn't be a good thing in your profession." He motions to the pens and paper scattered on the desk. Kyle is doing some final inking on a panel; I bet he's all prepared for our smaller team meeting this week *and* our bigger presentation next week, rumpled Goody Two-shoes. He's probably got three options, all fully fleshed and ready to go to the execs if Andy gives the go-ahead in our internal green light. It's the reminder that I need to get this little visit over with and go back home to work on my own stuff.

"Yeah, I've already done that once this week! It was *epic*." Kyle laughs and proudly points to an almost-finished panel ruined by a stray marker stroke across the entire page. Boys. Thankfully they stop short of chest-bumping.

I sigh, throwing my keys onto my desk to break up the man party and return the focus to why we're here. My bad luck holds out, and they slide between Simon's wall and mine. Just great. I bend to retrieve them, knocking the stack of papers on my desk onto the floor in the process. My research for the article on the thirtieth anniversary of *The Hooded Falcon* scatters like a game of 52-card pickup, further complicated by the pile of *crap* Simon has under his desk. I must have left the pages for the article on the edge of my desk without remembering, unless Simon has been snooping. He doesn't seem the type, but I *had* let it slip that I had a major idea. Maybe he got curious.

I frown at the rope, black hoodies, and clutter piled on the floor. Simon and Kyle must have been up to some sort of nerd mountain climbing for *Pokémon GO*, because who keeps this stuff under their desk? I sort through a small stack of dented cardboard, several wrapping-paper tubes, and duct tape. *Murderers. That's who keeps duct tape and hoodies under their desk.* Or nerdy ninjas who say they're learning parkour but are into team Pokémon bondage. My discovery of a pack of *Magic* cards, along with a pattern for homemade chain mail underneath the sweatshirts, seals the deal for me. Ninja Nerd City. I emerge from under my desk with a further understanding of just how far down the nerdom path my coworkers are. I remind myself to tease them mercilessly on Monday.

"I could look at it for you, maybe fix it." Matteo squats, peering at Kyle's chair with what I assume is a fake aura of professional capability.

"Cool." Kyle jumps off the chair, and they start all sorts of pointing and prodding. I do *not* have time for some pissing contest where they pretend to understand how a hydraulic whatever-it-is works. I am about to inform them of this when Kyle crows with satisfaction. There is *no way* Matteo actually fixed something that fast. Kyle's been fiddling with that chair for the better part of two months.

"Right on! I didn't think of rotating the supports that way! Thanks, man." This time when Kyle is back on his feet and shakes Matteo's hand, he's euphoric.

"No problem," Matteo says, pulling out an honest-to-God *hand-kerchief* from his pocket to wipe his fingers.

Kyle turns and gives me a grin and double thumbs-up. "Seems like a keeper, MG."

Everything's so effed up that I sputter something incomprehensible while Mr. Herbal Tea, Fix-It Man himself, walks back to my side and peers down at me with the most infuriatingly benign look on his face.

"Sorry about the delay. Didn't you want to look at something in the library?" Matteo asks. And dammit if there isn't a smile lurking in his eyes. This man is thoroughly *enjoying* watching me sputter. This man has my head spinning so fast, I'm losing track of what I'm reacting to. In fact, he's steering me toward the back of the office before I even realize that Kyle thinks OHT is my *special someone*.

I turn to defend my reputation, but OHT slides his arm around my shoulder and leans his lips near my ear. This maneuver is far more effective in stilling my protest than I'd like. My mind drops Kyle like a hot potato, and OHT's proximity takes precedence. I'm trying to remember just *when* it was someone had last caused goose bumps to rise on my neck in such speedy fashion.

"I don't want your coworkers to know I'm a cop, remember?" Matteo says in my ear. From Kyle's perspective, I'm sure it looks like sweet nothings.

I give him a look that clearly says, "No duh, I'm not a dunce."

With an adoring smile, he opens the door to the back hallway, ushers me through, and drops his arm from around my shoulder. The charade is up, and he steps a normal distance away from me, though I'm still calculating how long it's been since someone has whispered in my ear. Six months? A year? Probably since I dated Ryan's gaming pal for three months, before realizing he'd been vlogging all his dates with a "real hot comic chick" and uploading them on YouTube to gain followers. Complete with analysis of my physique, which superheroine had a rack like mine, and comparison pictures. Needless to say, it didn't work out.

I catch a glimpse of Kyle. He's grinning at me through the window in the door. It's going to take months of normalcy to regain my carefully cultivated resident-badass, no-personal-details-in-the-office, no-bullshit persona. I want to prove I'm ready for the promotion to art director. No one respects a boss who has office dalliances on a Saturday.

I welcome the space between Matteo and me. It allows me to regain my wits. "Let's go, *Detective*. The library is right through here."

CHAPTER 6

"So are you British?"

"What? No. Why would you even ask that?" I'm digging through the filing cabinet in the airless room that serves as our library of past work.

"You have one of those short dogs, and you have a picture of a telephone booth on your desk."

"First off, it's a TARDIS. Second off, Trogdor isn't short. Well, he is, but it's on purpose."

"A . . . TARDIS?"

I ignore him.

"Your desk and your card say 'MG.' You don't like your first name?"

"Is this twenty questions? How would you like it if you had a girl's name as a first name? I got called a boy all the way through elementary school. My first name *is* Michael-Grace. I don't have a middle name. Doomed to a life of stumping fill-in forms." I take a breath, realizing I'm dumping stuff on him that I usually keep to myself.

"No, I don't like my name," I say. "But it got me this job, anyway, because my boss thought I was a guy in the résumé portion. I guess all's well that ends well." I stop short of telling him that in my final interview with Edward Casey Junior, president of Genius Comics, he assumed I was a secretary. He actually asked me to get a pitcher of water and glasses for his meeting with Michael Martin, having missed the "Grace" portion of my name on my résumé. I've always wondered if the debacle contributed to my landing the job, and I spend every chance I can proving to him that despite my gender, I'm the best writer he has on staff.

"We're supposed to be researching your theory, remember?" *Not talking about my personal life.* I pull out the plastic-covered book and set it on the table. I slap his hands away from touching it, shove a pair of disposable gloves from a box on the table into his hands, and slide a pair on my own before carefully slipping the comic out of the protective wrapping. This is why I don't date non-nerds. I shudder to think of the skin oils that would find their way onto these beloved possessions—outsiders just don't *get* the magic of a pristine issue.

With a scent of the ink and paper, I'm swept back to the first time I held *The Hooded Falcon.* Some girls get moony-eyed about first boyfriends. First kisses. Me? The boys *called* me a boy but wouldn't hang out with me either. Well, at least until I was fifteen and the "girls" popped out. Then boys just wanted to hang out with my chest. No, for me it is comic books that make me weak in the knees.

I catch Matteo watching me. "Didn't you say there's a new development in the case that made you think of the comic book? Care to share it with the class so I know what I'm looking for?"

Matteo laces his fingers and leans his elbows on the table, bringing us closer together. "I need your help because I think someone here is in danger."

I'm not sure if the tingle running down my spine is because of his words or his intense gaze locked on to my own.

"Danger?" I try to play it off and force a laugh. "Thanks, Professor Trelawney, for your prediction. Now *you* sound like the one in the comic book."

"I mean it." His gaze doesn't change intensity, and another chill spills down my back. "I got the case file back from forensics today, and the note left at the scene? It references Genius Comics."

"That's crazy."

"Is it?" Matteo's eyes have a light of certainty in them, and it dawns on me how intimidating it would be to be interrogated by him. He comes off as this L.L.Bean catalog cover model, but there's this depth of conviction in him that is gripping at moments. Muggle waters run deep apparently. I squint at him. Maybe I'll upgrade him to Squib.

"You don't have to be a Genius to chase the White Rabbit," Matteo says.

I blink. "What?"

"That's what it said. The note left at the crime scene. The 'G' in 'Genius' is capitalized."

I see the Genius connection, sure, but my mind instantly jumps to the White Rabbit bit. The White Rabbit, a.k.a. the Hooded Falcon's nemesis. Surely this note couldn't be tying together drug dealers, my favorite comic book, and a White Rabbit–esque villain? *Not possible.* Okay, it's *possible.* But highly improbable. Comic books don't come to life. I know. I spent half my teenage years hoping for that very thing.

Detective Kildaire takes my silence as doubt. "See where I'm going? Genius Comics? You already confirmed for me that Genius Comics is the current producer of Hooded Falcon comics. And didn't you say you thought the chalk outline looked like a rabbit? I looked at it, and I'm not as convinced it's a rabbit, but maybe our vigilante is a lousy artist. Or White Rabbit could reference the street name for the specific brand of heroin these dealers are selling. Still waiting on lab results on whether or not it's the same designer drug formula. We've had a rise in its popularity recently."

My shoulders give an inch. *Okay, relax, MG. No need to see boogeymen around every corner. This theory makes a lot more sense than the White Rabbit outline indicating the* actual *White Rabbit, THF's nemesis.*

"Unless . . . you have other theories tied to the comic?" His gaze is shrewd. He leans farther forward, bringing his face close to mine across the table. Can he read my thoughts that easily? "These criminals are bad guys. I know you understand that concept. I don't want some overweight guy in spandex with a hero complex to get killed because he thinks it'd be fun to play superhero. Right now the drug rings are just pointing fingers at each other. And it could be that's it and that I'm chasing phantoms. But. If this is a real person trying to live out some superhero fantasy connected to this comic, I'm not sure how long that will hold if this masked avenger continues his antics. I'm trying to take the shortcut if this is a real person trying to tell us something using this comic."

I'm silent, a war raging inside me. It could be complete coincidence that the note mentions both the words "Genius" and "White Rabbit." More than likely it's what Matteo said: it's the coincidental street name of a drug. My brain can't even comprehend what would make someone play superhero with real villains. It has to be a coincidence, and the more time Matteo—*Detective Kildaire*—wastes on this crazy theory, the longer the bad guys are out there. Real people don't wear spandex and tie up drug dealers, do they? My mind flashes to Kyle and Simon and their injuries. Surely not. I can't picture either of them deciding to take down a drug ring instead of Jigglypuffs. This has to be coincidence or a joke.

"I still think it's a long shot," I say in all honesty. He's been quiet, letting me sort through his words while we lean over the comic spread on the table.

Eventually, Matteo sits back, breaking the connection of our gazes, and I feel the gulf between us. Like I've let him down. "Can you at least show me the episode that you recognized?"

His blunder brings a smirk to my face and a lightness back into the room. "It's an *issue*, not an episode, and yes. I think it's about midway through this one—one of my personal favorites, actually. THF was the first socially conscious hero that Genius published. Rather than fictional villains, he focused on *real* social crimes. Rape, drug production, addiction, corrupt politicians and cops, stuff like that."

I look at Matteo to make sure he's following me. He's nodding, so I continue, "This comic has two story lines coming together. It's a bit about THF running for mayor in his 'real' life, but it's also about his brush with a supervillain. This issue in particular is a real turning point in the Hooded Falcon's career. It's where he decides he'd have more power working *with* the law instead of outside it. You see, he'd caught these guys last issue laundering money and drugs already. They got off on a technicality, so he had to *re*capture them. He'd done his job, but the cops hadn't done theirs—what?"

OHT is staring at me with something like amusement on his face.

"Aren't you even paying attention?"

"You're so different when you talk about this. Like *The Hooded Falcon* is real to you."

That irks me more than anything else he could have said. I'm so *sick* of ComicsGate and everything this industry throws in my face about being a girl who loves comics. My mother said the very same thing to me at seventeen, two years into my *Hooded Falcon* obsession: "These aren't your real friends, Michael-Grace, and comic books won't earn you a living or bring you a husband. Go to school, make real friends, and meet real boys." Why does everyone assume I can't tell reality from fiction when it's my job to write? And isn't this *his* lunatic theory in the first place? Even though my geek heart would love a real-world vigilante superhero, I'm the one arguing on the side of logic.

I snap the comic closed, forgetting to be gentle with the copy.

He backpedals, sensing blood in the water. God help him if he tries to salvage this with a patronizing statement. "I know you know it's not real. I just meant it's nice to see you passionate about your work."

"Because I'm a freak show? A woman who loves comics, so I automatically can't tell reality from fiction? You're the one who asked me for help, and you're sitting here making fun of me. I think we're done here. You can just leave." I stand to excuse him from the room and am shocked at his audacity when he reaches across the table and grabs my arm with his gloved hand.

"I'm sorry, MG. Really. All I'd meant to say is it was really neat to see how passionate you are. Not because I'm surprised to see a girl reading comics. It's neat to see *anyone* passionate about this beautiful work. It's magical to you. I can see that. I don't get to deal with beautiful art or passionate writers in my job. That's it. I promise."

"Oh." A hot flash of shame fills my face with what I assume is bright red to match my glasses. After a minute, I clear my throat. I definitely gave him a dressing down he didn't deserve. It wasn't his fault that he chose the exact words that had galvanized my desire to prove I *could* make comics my life.

With a squeeze on my arm, he turns back to the copy on the table. "Can you show me the panel you thought you recognized?" Business it is. And I appreciate it.

"Um, sure." I sit back down and focus again on the copy. It takes me a few moments to find the page because my brain is buzzing from the fervor of my reaction. "Here it is."

I slide it across the table to him. He looks dutifully down at the page, a frown creasing his brow. "What am I looking at?"

"Okay, well, here is the panel I thought I recognized." I point to the lower left where a long panel shows a group of men tied at the pier. "In the comic, the guys are tied together with jesses—those are the leather thongs used to secure a falcon—and the golden arrow is the stake in the middle they're tied to." Not painted on the street. "The aura around them isn't actually there. It's something the author used to help the reader identify who the criminals worked for." I point to the white shining rabbit around the panel.

We both study the drawing. "I see the similarities, but it's not enough to convince me that ours was an intentional copycat." He rumples his hair with his hand.

I nod. "I can see it just being a drug deal that went bad, and one side tied up the other for the police, no crazy wannabe superhero needed." Or several vigilantes. My mind slips back to Kyle's wrist and the rope under Simon's desk, but I force it out of my mind. My writer's brain is taking this way too far.

The corners of Matteo's mouth are firmly turned down. "Out of curiosity, what happens in the rest of the comic?"

I thumb through the copy, letting the story come to me in snips and glimpses. "Well, these particular guys are laundering money. That panel shows him catching the thugs with the drugs, and then Falcon and Swoosh follow the ringleaders into a warehouse. This issue also deals with how the Hooded Falcon uncovers evidence that one of the other superheroes may be behind the drug operation and *may* be his nemesis."

"Kind of a Scooby-Doo ending?" Matteo is scribbling in his notebook, and I give a short laugh.

"Yeah. It's old Mr. Jenkins with a ghost mask. He's so helpful the whole episode, you should have seen it coming."

He snorts. Another two points: laughing at my jokes.

"Actually . . ." I flip forward in the comic and show him a panel where the Hooded Falcon and his sidekick are in full fight mode, complete with a dozen "KAPOWs." "There's this big battle scene. It turns out the rival drug lord knew all about the Hooded Falcon's plans to set him up. Since the Falcon's superhero partner was the only one who knew his plans, he figures out his own partner is leaking information to the gangs, like a double agent. Not only that, but the corrupt superhero plans to arrest both gangs and take over as the resident drug lord. He winds up looking like a hero for putting that many people in jail, and he gets to control a very lucrative, very illegal business. Falcon suspects his partner is not only a double agent but his nemesis, the White Rabbit."

"The White Rabbit."

I bite my lip. "It's the name of his nemesis in the comic book."

Matteo makes a note. "Coincidental?"

I shrug. "Or the chemist is a fan of comic books?"

"Maybe." Matteo doesn't seem convinced. He's still wearing a "thinking" frown. "Is that the end?"

I flip a few more pages. "Well, Falcon breaks into the double agent's lair and finds drugs hidden in his safe. Falcon tries to unmask the double agent and threatens to expose his real identity to the police, and they fight. Typical unbelievable crime-fighting stuff."

"Yeah, that doesn't seem plausible, does it? Though the tie-in with the street name of the drug and the dueling gangs fit. Maybe that's what the vigilante wanted us to find with the comics. That it's not just one ring; it's two."

"But you already knew that?"

He shrugs. "Yeah, but maybe our vigilante didn't know that. The rest of it with the superhero stuff is pretty out there." He sits back in the chair, and I replace the comic in the plastic cover and file it into the cabinet.

I agree. "Pretty far-fetched for reality, and nowhere to go with the story line, really. In fact, this is the next-to-last issue for the original line—Casey Senior died without completing the story arc."

It was a dark day in my young life when I found out I'd never get to see the Hooded Falcon beat the White Rabbit or win mayor of Space City. The new issues published after Casey Senior's death were wildly different and barely acknowledged the old series.

Yet White Rabbit is now a street drug, and someone's tying up competing drug dealers. Something wiggles in the pit of my stomach, dangerously close to belief.

We slip back through the now dark office. Kyle is gone, and I can't help glancing at Simon's desk and the pile of stuff beneath it. Perhaps a tiny bit of my own sleuthing is required to make sure Kyle and Simon aren't being vigilante idiots in spandex. Just on the off chance that Matteo is correct. Which he isn't.

"I'm sorry I wasted your time, but thanks for being willing to help," Matteo says as I climb out at the curb at my condo. I can hear Trogdor yapping from inside. I hope Ryan left me some pizza—it's our weekly nonhealthy food splurge, and I look forward to it.

I was anything *but* willing to help, but he put up with it admirably. "It was kind of fun to see the old Falcon again. I mostly read the new ones for work, and they're awful. I can't believe they're selling so well. Kids these days just don't appreciate good comics anymore." I'm rambling, and I sound crotchety. Am I nervous? My stomach *does* feel a little fluttery.

"See ya around, Detective Kildaire." He hasn't said I can call him Matteo, so I don't. He's watching me, and I swallow. "I had fun, actually. Sorry I couldn't help you more with your case." I have the ridiculous urge to ask if he wants to meet up for coffee sometime, but I stall so long, the moment passes. Some kind of brave new age woman I am.

He waves as he drives off in his ridiculous tiny car, and I turn to greet my ridiculous small dog. I'm maybe just a *teensy bit* sad that I won't see Matteo again. Or maybe, just maybe, fate has some fat man running around in tights and a tunic who will throw us back together again.

CHAPTER 7

I'm hopping on one foot, trying to jam my ballet flat on, when my phone rings. I hate Monday mornings. "No, no, *no*," I mutter, almost falling over. "I do *not* answer calls." I glance at the number. It's one that I don't recognize, so I push the silence button. Maybe my mother has signed me up for online dating again; that had been behind last year's rash of unrecognized callers.

"Bye! Have a good day at work!" I yell to the living room. Trogdor is already up on the couch, snuggled next to Ryan in his typical 8:00 a.m.–2:00 p.m. spot. The little traitor doesn't even look up. Ryan barely acknowledges me either, but I'm used to it.

Ryan briefly raises a hand, then shouts, "No, Dave, dammit, we can't have a hole here. It's the first thing someone will check! Add that to the list of bugs to fix this week."

I slept terribly last night, my mind working overtime on this *Hooded Falcon* thing that I keep trying to convince myself isn't a thing, and I slept through my alarm. I should have set two. I should have set *three*. I haven't slept through an alarm since college. Not only did I lie awake pondering the case, but Ryan and Lawrence had been out late all weekend with their tournament. I never sleep well with Ryan gone, and I'd basically been a zombie for two days. I hate an empty house—it's one of the reasons I got a roommate. Trogdor would basically show anyone who broke in where the electronics were kept, as long as they had food. Traitorous fluff-butt. So last night, with Ryan finally home, I guess my body went into hibernation mode. Not helpful.

I don't have time for breakfast, and I'm balancing my cup of crap Keurig coffee with my messenger bag as I dash for the door. Thank God I'd obsessed about this meeting enough to plan—a mustard-colored pleated skirt, black and white–striped shirt, and plaid scarf—days before and that pomade and short hair made my personal toilet less than a minute. I've spent *so* many hours in the last week perfecting my drawings, running over my less aggressive approach in my head, and imagining getting the promotion, I can't believe that something as mundane as sleeping through an alarm could put that all in jeopardy. I'm not just cutting it close; I might not even be there when the meeting starts. Most days it doesn't matter when I arrive. Today? Today matters, and of freaking course, my plan has been derailed.

I whip open the door and am immediately met with a wave of humidity. The sun breaks through a heavy mist, and it feels and smells like an urban jungle. I can hear a soft drizzle falling on the large broad leaves of the plants near the curb. I swear and swiftly turn around. I can't risk my pages, carefully placed in my bag the night before, getting wet. The messenger bag is waterproof, supposedly, but I'm not keen to put it to the test for an entire bike ride this morning. Not only that, but my hair would never survive. Bedhead can be masked. Drenched hair, not so much.

I reach inside the door, snag my keys, and hurry to my brown 1990-something Ford Aspire. "Come on, baby. Come on, baby."

I crank the key twice and am rewarded with the rich perfume of a flooded line but also the sputtering of the engine coming to life.

"One of these days I'm going to have to replace you." I pet the wheel as I pull out onto Santa Bonita Avenue and speed toward the freeway. That purchase has to wait until I pay off my college loans. Until then, it's the Hurtling Turd, as I affectionately call the Ford. I just can't warrant spending money on a car when I use my bike 90 percent of the year.

I'm lucky in avoiding too much gridlock, probably because everyone else is *already at work*. The car screeches into a parking spot outside my building—literally. I have to push the accelerator while I'm braking, or the engine dies. And that's when it starts raining.

I'm trying to gather up all my meeting prep and dash into the building, while pulling out my ID under the tiny canopy, when my phone vibrates and my cup of coffee topples off the top of the stack. I look down and see the splatter of my breakfast like a body laid out on the concrete.

"Dammit!" I yell, but there's nothing to do but heft open the door and get my bag and self in out of the downpour. I all but fall into the front entrance, where I find the group of executives I'm supposed to be meeting. They look polished. I look like Tinkerbell went through a car wash. Fan-frickin-tastic.

"There you are, MG! This meeting was supposed to start seven minutes ago." It's Andy, and he looks alarmed at my late arrival. Or maybe alarmed at my arrival in general, given my soaked and coffee-splattered appearance.

He's managed to tame his flyaway long curls and wears a suit jacket. He looks like a polished supervisor should, ready to present our team's work. I'm *never* late. I'm *never* anything but polished and together. Especially for a meeting with the main executives of Genius. It's what I *do*. It's who I am at work. Show no weakness, give no quarter, prove women are up to all tasks, not just getting coffee.

Except this morning.

I'm at a loss to explain myself with the truth, not without going into the lunatic theory of a real-life vigilante superhero or a thirty-year-old journal keeping me awake at night. I start to mutter something pithy about the rain and my prints and make my way through the open conference room door.

"Honey, you left your coffee in the car," a voice cuts me off mid-explanation. Already the executives are looking over my shoulder at the door behind me.

Andy's face registers shock, then something like . . . glee? "Oh. *Oh.* Hello again."

I whirl around because I have the sneaking suspicion that I'm going to find a tall, dark, and handsome tea drinker behind me.

"You—" I sputter, unable to form words. I'm infuriated he's witnessing my bedraggled situation and at the same time mortified to find I'm almost *glad* to see him. My gladness slips into nerves, eyes darting to where Simon and Kyle stand. Has Matteo somehow figured out that I've kept my suspicions about them a secret? Has he found out that I'm in possession of copies from a secret notebook? Maybe I'm under arrest. I do *not* love the slightly sexy daydream that plays out in my head entertaining that thought. I'm obviously delusional, paranoid, and desperately in need of my morning coffee. I try again to speak. "You—"

"Are too sweet. Yes, I know. Have a good day at work, pumpkin." He throws me a look that says he's apologetic about cutting me off, but then, to add insult to injury, he gives Andy a conspirator's smile. "I'm sorry she's late. Completely my fault."

The peanut gallery . . . no, my *bosses* titter.

Andy seems at a loss for words. "Um, yes, well, collect your things for the meeting, MG, and we'll see you inside." He hesitates, then *winks* at me. The group of executives, led by Casey Junior, heads toward the boardroom amid laughing and storytelling at my expense. My reputation is burning up and crashing to the surface like the USS *Enterprise* on Veridian III.

My fury from my morning implodes—detonation starting in T minus two seconds. OHT called me honey. In front of my boss. And pumpkin. And what the *hell*, also insinuated again that he and I are dating. No. More than dating. My mouth flaps open and shut. There are literally *so* many words I want to spew, they're stuck in the back of my throat. This man has cut me off for the last time. "The *hell* are you doing coming into my work?"

Matteo leans in while I wind up for the pitch and gives me a hug. His lips graze the sensitive spot just under my earlobe as he mutters, "You and I need to talk. It's important. I *did* try to call you."

I shove him backward. "I *don't* answer my phone, and you *didn't* need to make my bosses think I was late because we were . . . *you know*," I hiss back.

Matteo thinks a moment, and I can tell he's replaying the conversation in his head. The skin around his collar grows blotchy. "Okay. Maybe I could have chosen better words—*much* better words. I didn't mean to undermine you. I'm sorry. I don't usually have to contact our consultants like this, but it's time sensitive. I brought a peace offering?" He hands me a steaming-hot paper cup. I smell cinnamon. Damn this man and his knowledge of my weakness. My hand reaches out and takes the cup automatically. "If it's okay, I'll pick you up for lunch? We can talk then."

"No."

"I really think you'll be interested in what I have to say."

I hesitate. And finally nod my head. Then *he* gives me a wink and squeezes my elbow before amping up his voice. The man could be a damn actor. "Go get 'em, tiger." He gives Simon and Kyle a mock salute and walks back out the door.

Kyle and Simon have matching grins spreading across their faces. I am now the butt of every joke I never wanted to be a part of.

"I'll be ready in five minutes," I snap. And damn if I don't hear one of them laugh as I bolt down the hallway to the elevator.

Once the jokes die down, the meeting starts out well enough. Kyle, Simon, Andy, and I present green-light ideas for the smaller comic series we write individually. My pet project, *Hero Girls*, is the bestselling girls' comic book on the market. Unfortunately for me, comics aimed directly at tween girls make up the lower portion of the sales chart, a fact Edward Casey Junior brings up twice during my eloquent, insult-free speech. I've practiced my approach tirelessly. I'm not going to screw up this time; I'm as complimentary and politically correct as I can manage—the very epitome of what an art director at a major company should be. My presentation turns into a conversation about reducing my time on *Hero Girls* in favor of Kyle's more lucrative project while I lobby that the only way girls' comics will *gain* market share is to present more of them with relevant social topics. In the end, my brilliant idea for an offshoot limited-run graphic novel about origin stories is completely shot down. I avoided using the word "douchenozzle," which was on the tip of my tongue, and I deserve a damn Tony for that performance. But this is what being a leader is, right? Sure, sometimes I get a tad combative about my ideas because I'm passionate, but this morning it can hardly be considered my fault. Yet I refrained. I won this round . . . well, not really *won* but avoided catastrophe. And the next part of the meeting is what will make it or break it for me. I've groomed the *Hooded Falcon* idea *just* for Casey, and I am sure he is going to love my historic reboot.

I tuck the *Hero Girls* pages back into my folder, deflated but not surprised. Casey Junior has hated *Hero Girls* since the beginning. The only reason he lets me keep working on it is the interest Netflix has in a possible TV spin-off. I leaf through the pages and catch sight of the *Hooded Falcon* sketch. It's gritty, loose in all the right ways. It shows action, and it uses many of the vintage stylings for text and action tags. It's the perfect cross of the modern hero and all that makes vintage comics popular. My heart lifts again. *This* is the idea I had while talking to Matteo, and my gut says that it's going to put me on the board.

It's still drizzling outside, and I fight to keep my mind on the meeting. It's the kind of day when I like to curl up and daydream plot ideas or sketch costumes, but this morning's encounter with Matteo has me rattled. I keep thinking about his voice in my ear instead of focusing on the single most important meeting I've had in a long time. It's unlike me. Instead, I fill my head with possible story lines for my historic reboot. Maybe I'll pitch a few to show Casey Junior just *how* prepared I am. To show him *how* dedicated I am. My mind runs down a rabbit trail of stories, and I scribble madly on the side of my notes, nearly cackling with personal pleasure at the sheer genius I'm channeling at the moment.

It takes a moment of silence around the table to draw my attention back to Andy. He's stopped talking, and everyone is staring expectantly at me. My brain flies into overdrive, and I try to piece together the last words I heard.

"I agree," I say as firmly as I can. Authority is good in an art director, right?

Edward Casey Junior sits forward and steeples his fingers on the table. "I'm glad you agree with Andy's proposition that you go first. So would you like to present your ideas for *The Hooded Falcon*, or would you like us to come back to you?"

Thor's hammer. I mentally shake myself and gather my professionalism around me like a cape. I can do this. Small bobble. Back on the horse, or the speeder bike, or whatever. "Yes, of course." There. Perfect delivery. Professional. Not at all apologetic like I've been daydreaming.

I flick copies of the panel I drew last night across the table. Andy catches sight of the panel and shoots me a look. This is the idea he didn't like. I do, though, and if I'm going to be art director, I have to learn to take risks. Champion my own cause. March to my own drummer.

"The current direction of *The Hooded Falcon* differs from where the comic started, what originally made it popular. I'm proposing a historic reboot. A story line that would take us back to the roots of *The Hooded Falcon*, away from the c—" I stop myself short of calling what we've been currently writing crap. "—current story line with the alien overlord and back to social justice. We can reawaken the love people had for the first series, especially those that have stopped reading the comic because it's so different. I want to bring back an old story line but in a unique way, using current crimes to copycat the Falcon's iconic battles."

Edward Casey Junior frowns, shifts in his seat, then tucks the panel into his notes. It's a death knell. "I don't see how that would tie in with the current story line."

Ah. I prepared for this. "It wouldn't have to be in canon. It could be a time to use a special issue—"

Casey Junior waves his hand, not even hearing me out. "I want to keep continuity, especially with the video game coming out." He looks at me, his gaze inscrutable. "Someone up for an art director position would need to think globally about marketing, product branding, and momentum."

Was that a dig at my proposal or my application for promotion? Or both? Dammit, I was prepared for this, and he didn't even *listen* to me. Everything I rehearsed, the story lines I brainstormed. All wasted.

There's a rustling of paper as the other executives follow suit and tuck my beautiful rendering of a modern *Hooded Falcon* into the notes from the meeting. I've been dismissed. Color me Batman in *Knightfall*. I'm fighting the good fight but getting my rear end handed to me. How does this keep *happening*? My ideas are *good*, dammit.

"But—"

Casey Junior has already moved on and looks at Andy expectantly. Instead of moving ahead and presenting his own green-light proposal, though, Andy glances down at my drawing.

"Retro is in these days," Andy starts, as if he knows *anything* about what is "in these days." The guy thinks Hawaiian shirts are the height of fashion. "Everyone is into reboots. *Star Trek*, *Sherlock*, *Batman*. We'd be missing out if we didn't capitalize on what's popular."

I snort. Hadn't I just said that? Sure, I said we needed to move away from the current story line, but what I meant was adding a retro flair.

That was obvious when I said historic reboot. Historic equals retro. Retro is popular.

I expect the same rebuff, but Casey Junior nods thoughtfully at Andy.

Andy sees the nod and continues, patently avoiding eye contact with me. "Jumping off MG's idea, what if we did a reboot celebrating the thirtieth anniversary of *The Hooded Falcon*? A limited-run graphic novel. It wouldn't have to be in the main story line. Something fun like the Falcon solving the same kind of crimes from the original series. Get people thinking about the good old days of comics—nostalgia? It would tie in perfectly with the anniversary, and we could keep continuity in the canon for the video game."

What. The. *Hell?* That's *my* idea. No, my *ideas*. The limited-run graphic novel from *Hero Girls*, mashed with *my* idea for the classic reboot and the copycat crimes. Mine, mine, *mine*. Sure, Andy somehow managed to make it sound flashier than I had in my presentation, but surely everyone at the table realizes that Andy just presented my idea *again*. The idea they'd just shot down. The idea he shot down last Friday. My mouth flaps open then closed. "Jump off MG's idea" my ass. "Switched a few words and served it up" was more like it.

Casey doesn't bat an eye. "I like that. We could market it as limited edition, crank up the price. It will appeal to our major market." Casey Junior drums his fingers on the glass-topped table once, then bangs his hand down, making the glasses of water and coffee jump. "Done. Have your team move forward on it. Good thinking, Andrew."

I can't just let this pass. "Sir. I—" Half the heads swivel in my direction. I don't even know what I'm going to say. Accuse Andy of stealing my idea? Rail against them for giving Andy the time to respond to his criticism and not me?

Andy sees the look on my face and knows I'm about to out him. He also can probably read in my face that I'm gearing up to make a scene worthy of a comic book panel: *KAPOW—MG slugs her newly minted nemesis across the table*. I push myself out of my chair so fast, I startle the man next to me.

Andy's Adam's apple bobs frantically, panic etched on his face. "Thank you, sir," he says, whipping his attention back to Casey Junior. "But it wasn't just me. I mean, MG had the idea for the limited edition."

He might have just saved his own sorry butt. I relax backward, just an inch, as he prepares to continue his confessional. Maybe Andy had just been trying to help me defend my project?

Casey Junior doesn't let him finish, though. He waves his hand. "Spoken like a true director. Of course it's a team effort, but it takes a special someone to take the individual strengths and ideas and put them into one cohesive plan for the product. It's something an art director would do. Now, I hope one of your remaining team members has a good suggestion for the next arc for the current Falcon story line?"

"Team effort, yes. Exactly that," Andy parrots back and gives me a small smile like that's going to soothe my soul. The soul that at this very second is burning with such ferocity, the Human Torch would be jealous.

Not only has he *stolen* my ideas; he's getting praised for stealing them. It also sounds suspiciously like he's getting *my* promotion because of *my ideas*. It's unacceptable. I won't stand for it. I'll stay after the meeting and talk to Casey Junior privately.

Kyle and Simon are sinking in their seats; they know I'm about to explode. They were privy to the conversation in our team meeting when Andy told me my idea was boring. Andy suggested we bring in one of the other superheroes for a team storytelling arc, like Superman versus Batman. Which would be great if that hadn't been done by our competition three times last year.

In fact, that's the very idea that Simon presents—which, of course, Casey eats up. Andy must be feeling *pretty* good about himself. Jerk. It fuels my fire just thinking about him getting promoted, and I don't even listen to Kyle's presentation. I'm too busy stocking up my defense arsenal in my head.

Casey Junior says he has an announcement, but when it's not about the art director job, I quit listening again. Something about a new vice president of marketing. I look around as everyone else in the room rises with Casey. They're all gathering into some sort of receiving line. We've never done this for a new VP before, but I'm okay with it. It means I can get to Casey Junior without seeming pushy or overbearing.

"I'd like you to meet Lelani Kalapuani, our new vice president of marketing. She'll be attending the team meetings from now on and will be helping us select the art director." Casey claps Andy on the shoulder in unofficial congratulations as he says this.

Fury nearly blinds me. I'm near him now, at the back of the group of executives gathered around the main door to the conference room. "Sir—"

Casey glances at his Apple watch, then up at me. "I have another meeting in here in five, Michael."

I grit my teeth and push onward. Do or do not; there is no try. "Sir, I need to talk to you about the ideas I presented. It's important."

Casey sighs, and his gaze meets mine for the briefest of moments. "Yes, yes. I realize that I may have been a bit unfair in the meeting today."

That shuts me up. *Really? It was that easy?*

Casey pushes through the crowd to the door, and I elbow through behind him. He turns over his shoulder to speak to me. "I know how much you girls like having your own comic books. So go ahead with the limited-run graphic novel spin-off. If sales are good enough, we'll consider more projects like it in the future. I wouldn't want to be accused of being sexist. Girl power, right? That's what Lelani's here for."

It's gone so wrong so fast that I don't even respond to his patronizing smile but instead follow his gaze and catch sight of our new VP through the dwindling crowd. Casey's words sink in. *She'll* be at team meetings. Andy fawns over a slim woman, expertly dressed in a tailored white suit that somehow doesn't look out of place against her flawless mocha skin, dark almond eyes, and cascade of black hair. *A woman.* Casey has hired a woman executive, finally. Maybe, just maybe—if one disregards his girl power comment—things are changing around here. I hope this is more than a show to placate the affirmative action people, though I wouldn't put it past my boss. Maybe my influence has finally been felt. *Michael-Grace Martin, gender equality superhero!*

Casey is almost out the door, pushing past the remaining pack of executives. "Oh, and Michael? My next meeting is with an investor. Can you please take these water glasses with you to the kitchen when you go back upstairs? And have the secretary bring new ones in. Thanks."

Or not.

CHAPTER 8

"Did you have a good meeting?" Matteo asks when I walk into main reception. I'm expecting a smug smile, but instead he looks anxious.

"No, I didn't." *And it still stings.* I cross my arms, and the receptionist looks up to glance between OHT and me. More fodder for the peanut gallery.

"Let's go outside." I don't look to see if he follows me but stalk through the door and into the humid afternoon. It's not raining anymore, but it feels like it could start again at any moment. Just like my mood.

I whirl to confront him. "Do you want to explain yourself?" We're standing between his Prius and my brown Aspire. From the building, it could look like we're trying to decide where to go to lunch. *I'm* trying to decide where to punch him first. It could be that I'm keyed up from my horrible morning stuck in an office with three people who refused to make eye contact with me. Or it *could* be that *someone* embarrassed me right in front of my bosses and threw off my mojo.

"I realize that this morning was awkward."

"Awkward? Do you have any idea what you've done?"

"Other than my job, you mean?" He's confused now, a furrow between his dark eyebrows.

Everything is jammed inside of me, rattling around like Pac-Man in a block jail: the continual internal abrasion of Casey's dismissal and how I have to try twice as hard as Andy to be taken seriously. Andy's ability to sell *my* ideas better than I did. And while he *is* a douchenozzle for stealing my ideas, I'm just a teensy bit afraid that he's getting the promotion because he's better at being director than I am. That Andy *actually* presented my ideas better, and I hate it. Also rattling around is the fact that Matteo let them think I was late because I'd lost track of time with my boyfriend, insinuating I'm not serious about my job or at the very least that I'd throw over a meeting for a man. I've become the butt of the office jokes. Add in Matteo's breath on my neck and how it makes me secretly *want* that reality to be true, and the little block jail can't hold all my thoughts and grievances anymore. There's no room for Matteo if I want to keep everything contained. I don't have time for dalliances. I need to focus on my job.

Matteo patiently watches me chew through all of this, his eyes infuriatingly concerned.

"You just don't get it, and you never will."

"Condemned without trial, it seems." Delivered offhand, with a ring of simple truth . . . and somehow that statement seems *sexy* instead of patronizing. I'm getting internal whiplash from how fast I seem to swing from wanting to punch OHT to wanting to kiss him. I blame the "hot cop" trope that is shoved at us from every crime show ever. I shouldn't be fantasizing about kissing the cop that could arrest me for what I'm keeping from him: Kyle's and Simon's injuries, Lawrence's background with Casey Senior, the journal pages.

Matteo's hand sneaks up and rubs the back of his neck. I've made him a little nervous, even though his gaze is unwavering. "I'd like to explain myself?"

I raise an eyebrow. This is new territory: I'm not used to levelheaded discourse when I yell.

"I brought you a drink, hoping to catch you before work. Then I saw you drop your coffee. When I went to see if you needed help, it was obvious that your boss was mad you were late. It's the first thing I thought of. I did all of that because I tried to call you and you didn't answer."

"I *don't* answer calls." But I realize that *perhaps* I'm using him as a scapegoat. He threw me off, sure . . . but the rest of the meeting was a creature of my own making.

"I needed to actually *talk* to you about the case. I can't write down what I need to show you in a text. *Or* an email." He's caught my caveat before I can even say the words.

That stills the string of retorts that I have. "Did something else happen?"

He glances toward the building, then back at me. "Yes. If you're okay coming to the station, I'll bring you back after lunch hour?"

My stomach plummets. He found out about Kyle and Simon. Or the journal. "Am I under arrest for real this time?"

He laughs, and I'm glad for it. "No, MG. Although I kind of feel like *I* should be read my rights for upsetting you so much. This is just to ask you some more questions about a new development."

"Oh." His half apology smooths some of my ruffled feathers, and I make a concerted effort to lower my hackles. Recovering a little of my normal spunk, I blow out a breath, ruffling my purple bangs. "You may proceed. To the station, Alfred."

"How was your meeting, really?" We pull onto palm-lined First Street. White arched windows, red roof, and gorgeous front lawn mark the historic downtown headquarters of the LAPD. Behind it, glinting in the sun, sits the glass cube and impressive gray metal building that houses the new station. Horrendous traffic for years while they completed it, but now it's a building any comic hero would be proud to defend.

I shoot Matteo a glance. He's got an adorable worried crinkle between his eyebrows. I shrug, not up for explaining Andy's deceit. "It wasn't your fault my meeting went badly. It's mine. *They* thought your little stunt was funny."

Matteo's gaze is serious, though I tried to be lighthearted with my delivery. "Either way, I'm sorry. I kind of lost my head when I saw you. Struggling with the door, I mean. I apologize if I came off as unprofessional and for making you look unprofessional too."

My heartbeat picks up, and I want to roll my eyes at myself. No matter which gorgeous lips, with beard-scruffed cheeks, are doing the apologizing, "no apologies" is my number-one rule, so I'm baffled as to why I find this apology sexy. Matteo waves his badge at the guard as we pull into a parking lot full of police cars and park along the side of the building. The tallest part stretches up into the sunshine, past the tops of the swaying palm trees.

I stare up through the windshield, first at the building, then covertly at *Detective* Kildaire. The full weight of his job and why we're here hits me like a punch from *The Thing*. I've now yelled at, thought about kissing, and threatened the physical well-being of an officer of the law. Without the station and the car, he's just a cute, slightly annoying guy. Now, watching him climb out of the car, throw his suit jacket on, and check to make sure his badge is in his pocket . . . it's *real*. I fight back a groan. I've made a pretty awesome idiot out of myself. My palms are sweating, and my nerves resurface. Keeping things from Matteo seems logical. I'm protecting my friends. Keeping things from *Detective Kildaire* at the *police station* seems like less of a good idea. Maybe it's time to come clean.

"MG?" He's peering into the car again, concern wrinkling his forehead. "Are you getting out?" I love and hate how familiar my name sounds on his lips, as if we've known each other for years and it's normal for me to be interrogated on my lunch hour for funsies.

He ushers me from the car and through a set of glass double doors bearing the insignia of the LAPD. I'm so busy gawking at the people surrounding me in the lobby, I barely register when I'm handed a guest badge at the front desk. Clerks are carrying stacks of papers, officers typing reports into computers. And a few . . . saltier people are sitting in chairs lining the wall near the front desk—a homeless man with two suitcases and three coats, a teenage girl passed out with her hat over her face.

"We'll go back past intake, and it'll be quieter." He leans close for me to hear over the din. "We have more than three thousand officers on the force. It can get pretty noisy in here."

We weave through a labyrinth of short halls and open work spaces until we reach a bank of rooms with glass doors. They're comfortably furnished with tables, chairs, and sofas. Not exactly the dingy single-pendulum-light-fixture rooms from TV, but my palms still start to sweat.

"Right in here. You can put your coat on these hooks if you'd like. The air-conditioning is out today. The last brown-out fried something. Gotta love this city." But I can tell he does.

After he closes the door, it's deafeningly quiet in the room. And warm. I shrug out of my black blazer and hang it on the hook next to his suit coat. It looks cozy—too "his and hers" for my taste, like I'm admitting that we fit together, so I take it down and toss it across the back of the sofa. No need to remind me of my parents' house where everything is monogrammed, matchy-matchy, gender specific, and *just so*.

It's the embodiment of my parents' stuffy-if-comfortable marriage. My mother gave up her true passion as a nurse to be a "lady of the house" and raise privileged, polished, perfect children. Think Emily Gilmore without the quaint East Coast charm. It's everything I don't want in a relationship. I want depth, breadth. I want messy and color-ful. I want sitting on a couch and watching *Star Wars*, not sitting at a fancy dinner with sixteen forks. Matteo gives me a weird look when I move my coat, but I ignore it.

He sits in a chair across from the sofa and slides a glass of water across the oversize coffee table toward me. "I ordered you lunch. Is a veggie pita okay?"

"Yeah, sure." Rabbit food. Probably without dressing.

He notes my displeasure, though I try to hide it. Is he this obser-vant with every person of interest or just me? My blood sings a little, contemplating the possibility. Maybe he feels the same fascination that I feel when I'm with him.

"I just assumed you were vegetarian. You know, being fit and riding your bike to work . . ."

I laugh. "No, I only ride my bike to work because I'm allergic to other forms of exercise. I hate the gym. I hate treadmills. I hate yoga. I love biking, so I can eat whatever I want." I eye him a little askance. It's rare that my slightly curvy form is considered the epitome of "fit." In fact, I don't even own a scale. My personal philosophy is eating in moderation; feeling good over numbers; and if I don't enjoy an exercise activity, I'll never repeat it. Not exactly a poster child for workout-aholics. I'm afraid he's up to that false altruism again, but the gaze he sweeps over my figure is appreciative, and it buoys my pride enough to allow the rabbit food to slide.

"I'll split my BLT with you, then."

I smile. "Deal."

He fiddles with something that looks like a voice recorder. "So what do you want to believe?"

The question takes me completely off guard. Had I spoken when I hadn't meant to? About my pondering an attraction to him? About the information I know? My heart races under my breastbone, and I feel my own neck grow hot. "W-what?"

He's still studying the recorder. "Your shirt. It says 'I Want to Believe.'"

First a surge of relief, then a tingle. He's referring to the "I Want to Believe" T-shirt I changed into after the meeting. The shirt with the words across my bust, which I now realize he had to be staring at to ask the question. I can feel my ears growing hot, a telltale sign that I'm blushing. "My eyes are up here," I joke. "It's from *The X-Files*."

He shuffles a few papers in a businesslike manner. "Why else do you put words on a shirt if you don't want people to read them?"

True. It's a legit question, but there's that telltale blotch at his shirt collar, so I have to wonder if I wasn't *a little* right about it too. Look at us. Matching his-and-hers blushes.

Matteo clears his throat. "Are you okay if I record this? There's a video recording for the room, but I wanted a copy for my use as well. This comic stuff can get complicated." Now he's all business, and it's a little disconcerting. *Detective Kildaire* is back.

"That's fine." I swallow twice and perch on the couch facing him.

He goes through a list of statements: today's date, my full name, his name, a case number that sounds like gibberish, and the time of our interview. Then he reaches across and pats my arm. "It's okay. You don't need to be nervous. It's just you and me talking. You look like you're going to throw up."

Yeah, that's what they tell all the prime suspects on TV right before they catch them in the lie that seals the case.

"Oh good. Glad that's on tape." It's my best attempt at levity.

His lips quirk up, and it does funny things to my stomach. I nearly toss my cookies with the added jolt. I have *got* to get a handle on myself.

"All right. Michael-Grace Martin, can you confirm for the record that you have not told anyone of our previous conversation?"

It's weird to hear my whole name come out of his mouth. It's even *weirder* that it doesn't sound weird. I hate my name; from him it sounds normal, like he says it every day. The familiarity eases my tension, and I resign myself to being interrogated—even if kindly. He is *good* at his job.

I lean toward the recorder and say, "No," in a clear voice.

"The recorder can hear you fine from the couch."

"Oh. Okay. Then, no. I didn't have a chance to tell anyone I met you. I mean, not that I had a reason to . . ." I'm flustered, so I scrunch up my face. "No." There. Pretend like it is an office meeting. Clear, concise answers. It's good practice for me.

"Can you tell me where you were Saturday night?"

I think. *Not good.* I'm *that* person on the TV show—a lame alibi that can't be proven. "At home, in bed."

"And can anyone verify that?" Cue color blooming under his collar, but he remains the passive professional.

"I was sleeping alone." *Thankyouverymuch.* "So unless you can interview my *dog*, you're out of luck—oh!" I snap my fingers. "Wait! Trog! He went out around eleven, and my neighbor yelled at me to get him a bark collar. So, yes! My neighbor can confirm that I was home." Victory.

He takes down her name and address. "And your roommate?" I may be imagining it, but Detective Kildaire's voice becomes steelier when he mentions Ryan.

"He and my friend Lawrence were at a video-gaming tournament. They played all night."

He nods, makes a note, and sits forward. "Have you noticed anything unusual around your office? People doing something they shouldn't?"

My mind goes directly to Kyle and Simon. I swallow hard. "I—uh—" I stall for time, trying to figure out a way to tell Matteo without telling him what I suspect. Is it cool to make your coworkers major suspects in a vigilante drug-busting case before you know for sure they're behind it? "Unusual like what?" *Rope, duct tape, black hoodies, and bruises?* I'm so wound up; my head is about to start spinning around like R2-D2.

Matteo runs his hands through his hair. "I'm not sure what we're looking for exactly. I brought you in because we're worried about your office. That note that I told you about at the first crime scene? Someone leaked its contents to the drug ring."

"You can't be serious. So the drug rings are stupid enough to think that someone from Genius is running around and tying them up? They're smarter than that, surely?" I bite my lip, mind churning through what he said. One word stands out to me. "Did you say this was *leaked*?"

"Yes, we're still trying to figure out what happened."

What he's not saying is that a *leak* means a cop told the drug dealers what is on that note, whether intentionally or by accident. One of Matteo's own is possibly a double agent, and I watched enough *Castle* to know that rarely works out well.

"And now you think they're going to come after Genius Comics? Just because of some note?"

Matteo doesn't answer. Instead, he reaches for a tablet on his side table and opens it while I watch with eyebrows raised. He flicks through video files, then sets it on the table in front of me.

"We've been following a few different leads. Someone stopped a purse-snatcher Friday night, though we can't confirm it was the same person. Only interesting because it fits your theory of a social-justice vigilante. However, Saturday night there was another bust. This time it was some middle-ups. Our superhero tracked them to the warehouse district, and a security camera caught some footage."

A grainy black-and-white video plays on the tablet, and I squint. "What am I looking for?"

"Just watch."

A few figures come into frame, and I scan the screen intently. It's too far away to make out any identifying features. I'd be hard-pressed to even determine gender and height, much less identify someone in a lineup. Is someone from Genius recognizable in this video?

"I still don't see—" My breath catches in my throat. Something flashes across the camera. Something that looks suspiciously close to a figure *flying* through the air.

Matteo's mouth presses into a line when I glance up. The rest of the video is useless. The figures on the street move out of frame, and the flash doesn't reappear. I reach forward, swipe my fingers left to run the video back to the flash of dark movement I saw. I stare at the screen in shock, and the last vestiges of my resistance crumble like the shield around the USS *Enterprise* in every mid-episode fight sequence. "That looks like a person *wearing a cape*, flying through the air."

Matteo skips the "*I told you so.*" "The problem is, now both drug rings are looking for this person, and they think they're connected to Genius Comics. We haven't seen a feud like this brewing since the massive drug busts in the eighties. It isn't a good thing for an untrained civilian to be involved in."

This guy doesn't look untrained to my eye. He looks like he's *flying*, and he captured the bad guys. My brain stutters. There's actually someone out there in a *cape*. Someone I might know fighting crime.

Matteo's words strike me too. *Drug feuds. Possible double agents.* The past and the present rattle around together in my head. It seems like this comic book is everywhere I look: drug wars, just like in the original *Hooded Falcon.* The discovery that Casey Senior had planned on ending the comic but his son kept it going. Then there are my coworkers. Kyle or Simon is potentially in bodily danger for some ill-placed role-playing, if that's what they've been doing. And to top it all off, there's the possibility of a dirty cop—a story line straight out of the vintage *THF.*

"We need to talk," I say to Matteo. He's been silent, letting me stare at the tablet, where I've frozen the blur into a smudge of black suspended on the screen. First the bust on the docks. Now a bust in the warehouse district. The cape. The similarities between the comic book and reality are too much for me to deny any longer. Someone is out there masquerading as the Hooded Falcon, following a drug ring that seems to mimic the original books. But can I trust Matteo? Would he tell me there is a dirty cop if he *is* the dirty cop? Doubtful. I refuse to admit that I make snap judgments about people, despite what Lawrence says, but I will admit to having fantastic instincts about people. And all my instincts about Matteo say he's as true-blue as Captain America.

I blow out a breath. He's not going to be happy when I tell him I've been keeping stuff from him. No way out but through. I open my mouth to spill my inner demons when we're interrupted by a knock at the door, and Matteo motions in a younger officer carrying a white paper bag.

"Ah, here's our lunch. Ms. Martin, I'd like you to meet our youngest narcotics officer. Officer James, our comic book consultant for the case, Michael-Grace Martin."

I smile at the sandy-haired officer, but he doesn't return the gesture. He simply shoves the food at Matteo and mutters something about not being a delivery driver. Oh, how I can identify with that. I *am* Officer James at my office. The fetch-and-carry kid.

"He seems nice."

Matteo rolls his eyes. "He's in a hurry to make detective and doesn't take kindly to things he sees as beneath him, but he's good at his job. Uncanny instincts when it comes to drug dealers. Now, what were you saying before?"

I tell him about everything—from Kyle's and Simon's sudden interest in a nerd fitness group to Lawrence's journal—as quickly as I can. I feel a pang of remorse about betraying L's confidence, but I stop short of mentioning that I have copies of the journal in my possession. I told L I wouldn't *show* anyone else; I'm simply letting Matteo know it exists. Technically I'm keeping my promise.

To Matteo's credit, he doesn't break his calm and professional demeanor while listening to my list of confessions but runs his hands through his hair and over his stubbled chin. When I finish, he closes his notebook and sits back. "This is likely someone you work with—maybe Kyle or Simon. Someone who knows the comics as well as you do. Someone with either something to prove or a misplaced Robin Hood complex. We've got to stop whoever this is before they get themselves killed."

"But why can't you just be glad someone handed you some bad guys, throw them in jail, and go your merry way?"

"Because this person is ahead of us. And while it works in comic books, it doesn't work in the real world when citizens take the law into their own hands. Truly, I'd like to figure out who this masked avenger is, find out what they know, and either work with them or take over. I get the feeling there's a reason they're tipping off the police instead of making a report. It doesn't seem to me like this is your average backyard role-player."

I raise my eyebrow, impressed that he even knows those words.

He ignores my incredulity. "It's close enough to what you're telling me about the comic to drive me mad—we're looking at a road map but don't know how to read it. These criminals are not nice people. I want to keep our vigilante from getting hurt, so we need to find him."

His serious face is doing serious things to my insides when I should be more concerned that *I'm* the one they hope knows how to read the road map.

Matteo continues to study me. "Are you still willing to consult on this case for us, assuming, of course, that your alibi checks out? I'm sort of breaking procedure by bringing you in so early, but time is of the essence with this case."

The chance to watch a real-life comic book plot unfold and help save my idiot coworkers from repeating history and stirring up a drug feud that could land LA on its backside? Not to mention the apparent capes and costumes in play? A *real-world* superhero. It's like my entire life has led to this. My name is Inigo Montoya, and I've just found the six-fingered man.

"I wouldn't miss this for the world."

He freezes me with his gaze, and a zing of electricity shoots down to my toes. It isn't a quick once-over or the analytical scan of a cop looking at a suspect. This is deeper. Matteo takes stock of my *person*—everything from my ballet flats to my sarcastic quips, sizing me up as a partner. The way he inclines his head in an indistinct nod gives me the impression that I haven't come up wanting in his appraisal. "I have some paperwork for you to fill out while you eat your sandwich."

His next words have a ring of finality to them. They sound suspiciously like the opening lines of a comic book introducing a new hero: "Welcome to the LAPD, Michael-Grace."

CHAPTER 9

Matteo pulls up to Genius Comics, and I'm surprised when he parks in a visitor's spot and turns off the engine instead of just dropping me off. "I know this is awkward to ask."

My heartbeat zings in my chest. Is he going to actually ask me out? I'm shocked to find that I'd readily accept. I'm slightly desperate to put my finger on just what intrigues me about this man. And bonus points that he doesn't seem the type to secretly tape, analyze, and try to market dating a geek chick like some of my more recent relationships.

He keeps looking ahead, fingers fidgeting on the steering wheel. He's *nervous*. My body responds in kind, releasing a horde of dragons into my stomach.

"I need you to keep the fact that you're helping us a secret." He leans forward.

I'm waiting for the other shoe to drop. "Okay, but what do I tell everyone?"

And now he looks *really* uncomfortable. "You said your coworkers already think we're seeing each other. We could let them draw their own conclusions and just not correct them? That way we don't have to out and out lie. You can help with the investigation if need be, and I can just drop in if I need to?"

So he *is* asking me out, but only as a cover. My little stomach dragons blink out of existence. It makes sense—he'd gain access to my coworkers, be able to come by the office without alerting anyone to the fact that the police are watching Genius. But it doesn't mean I'm happy about it. "You will *not* distract me at work. You will text any and *every* time you are coming, whether or not I agree to your scheme."

He slides out, opens my door, and insists on walking me to the lobby.

I try to tell him every which way to Sunday with my eyes that it's *not* necessary. That it's chauvinistic. That I won't be attacked in the one hundred feet to the main door, but he insists by ignoring me pointedly.

"So is that a yes?"

I eyeball him, trying not to note how good he looks with his work shirt rolled up at the elbows and his noon-o'clock shadow. I've got a lot going on right now, and I hate to admit that maybe, just *maybe*, my feelings are hurt about being only a pawn. A work tool. Not to mention the fact that there may be a double agent out there. Though it's unlikely, it *could* be Matteo. My instincts don't seem to be firing right around him, muddied by the electricity I feel. If I play along without doing my own bit of sleuthing, I could be leading the bad guy right to my friends and coworkers.

"It's a 'we'll see.' I don't have time for a boyfriend, fake or otherwise. Especially not one who drives a Prius. My friends would *never* buy it."

He ignores the Prius dig. "Can I stop by the office and look at the new comics? We need to get a feel for where we think this is headed, now that we know more about what we're dealing with."

"You *could* buy them yourself. I have a lot of work I need to do this week. Not only am I writing a new issue; I have to try and figure out how to get this promotion. I thought my boss was announcing it today, but he didn't, so there's still a chance. And there's this huge gala thing we're hosting for the thirtieth anniversary in a few weeks." A ball of stress forms in my stomach. As much as I said the words to make an excuse, I really *don't* have time for a boyfriend right now. Or a pretend boyfriend.

"But I need you to look at them and tell me what you're seeing. You're the expert." He's wearing that damn look on his face that makes me think of puppies.

"Fine." I hold up my finger before he can crow with victory. "But not at work. You've already shot my week to hell. You can come over to my house later this week and look at mine. I work from home Thursdays." This way I can keep him away from my coworkers and boss . . . but then he'll be in my house. I'm not sure which is worse.

"Deal."

I pull open the large glass doors, and of course, my full team—Kyle, Simon, and Tejshwara—are gathered in the front lobby, so they see us walk in.

"I'll see you later," Matteo says.

"Yeah, okay." I give a half wave and turn to flee to the safety of the elevator, but not before my coworkers muck up the situation even further.

"Hey, Matteo!" It's Kyle, and he's crossing the room to the main door before it can close. I note a fresh bandage on his wrist. From his newest escapade swinging in over a warehouse in his Spider-Man pajamas, perhaps? "We were thinking about having a movie marathon this weekend, and we wanted to invite you and MG. Saturday, at my house. From eleven to eleven."

My mouth actually falls open. This is unprecedented territory. I don't get invited to work parties. Other than Christmas, but then I just bring Lawrence or Ryan with me and hang out by the artichoke dip for four hours.

Matteo doesn't look surprised. He looks infuriatingly calm and *normal* about this. He says, "Oh, that's so nice of you. I think we could make—"

At the same time, I say, "No."

The peanut gallery looks between us.

"I thought you had that *thing* on Saturday?" I say through gritted teeth. This is getting out of hand. I didn't realize we'd face the pretend dating thing directly after our conversation.

"I think I can move it around, that is, if *you* want to go? Doesn't it sound fun? Movies with friends?" Innocence. Pure innocence.

And now I'm the bad guy if I say no. Frickin' brilliant. "Can I see you over here for a moment?" I grab Matteo's solid arm and pull him closer to the door. It's the first time I've grabbed him instead of the other way around, and I don't like contemplating asking him how often he has to work out to be a detective. It must be often from the feel of his muscled arm beneath my hand. My palms are sweating again. *Fake* relationship, MG. *Fake relationship.* I can no longer deny my attraction to Matteo. But now he's my partner? Boss? There are rules against these things. "Are you *trying* to undermine me at every turn, or is it just a particular talent you have?"

Color appears at his collar, either from my accusation or the fact that I'm still touching him. I release him like I'm holding molten steel, accidentally brushing his hand with mine as I retract my arm. I pull my hands into my chest, likely resembling an off-balance *Tyrannosaurus rex*.

"It might be the perfect opportunity to look into your coworkers. Get to know them." I know he's thinking about the bandage on Kyle's wrist, and I have to admit, I'm curious too.

I've stayed silent while Matteo has interrupted me too many times, and the gloves are coming off. "Then maybe do you want to *ask* me instead of barging right through and trying to control my life?"

He looks suitably ashamed but meets my eye. "Can we go to your work party?"

It's at this point that I realize we're being watched by all of my team. They might as well have popcorn, they look so entertained. Here I am, a novelty again. This one of my own making, though. Surely it won't be that bad to go hang out for a few hours in the name of helping solve this case. I'm hoping the "greater good" works out better for me than for Dumbledore.

I address the peanut gallery first, "Thanks for the invite. I think we'll be able to make it." I lower my voice and address Matteo, "As long as *someone* behaves themselves, capisce?" My world. My rules.

Matteo nods once in agreement to me, then waves to Tej, Kyle, and Simon before heading out the door. Why, when this comic has helped my life for so many years, is *The Hooded Falcon* wreaking such havoc this time?

CHAPTER 10

No matter how hard I try, I can't get Ryan or Lawrence to vacate the house on Thursday. Ryan's office day moved to Friday, so it's to a full audience that I open the door before Matteo can knock.

I need to keep this meeting brief, especially since we're going to be relegated to my bedroom instead of the living room. "I'm giving you thirty minutes."

He takes in my bright-blue cheetah yoga pants and black T-shirt. "Looks like a real ballbuster day at the office."

I will *not* laugh. We're serious work partners now. This is a business meeting. But I smirk, and he sees it and looks satisfied. Every time I try to put him into a box, he goes and gets all witty and charming again.

And dammit, he smells good. Who wears . . . I sniff . . . awesome-smelling laundry detergent to a work meeting? Look at me, weak-kneed from laundry detergent fumes. I definitely have been dating the wrong people if clean clothes are a turn-on.

"I *am* working," I say, closing the door behind him.

"I don't doubt it. You are a woman of your word." He reaches down to take off his shoes, and it's oddly intimate to see him in stocking feet in my entryway.

"Thirty minutes," I say again, and I turn to lead him into my room when I come nose-to-chest with Lawrence. And Ryan. Holding Trogdor.

"This is your big work meeting, huh?" Ryan looks at Matteo like he just stepped out of a spacecraft from Jakku. There is no skirting this introduction.

"Matteo." Matteo leans across me, easy as can be, and holds out his hand to Ryan and Lawrence. He doesn't even wince when Lawrence gives him the squeeze of a lifetime, his signature "don't mess with my girl" move. He also doesn't bat an eyelash at the bedazzled paisley headscarf Lawrence has wrapped around his head today or the bright-silver polish on his nails. Two more points for him.

"Ryan," my roommate offers in return, then continues to stand there.

The intro doesn't budge Ryan or L, so I let out a blustery sigh. "What's with the third degree?"

Ryan feigns innocence. "No interrogation here. We're just being friendly, MG. Where are your manners?" says the guy who grunts instead of forming words while he's gaming. Unless, of course, they're curse words. Those emerge perfectly and often.

I want to keep *everyone* away from Matteo, especially Lawrence. What if Matteo mentions that I've told him about Casey Senior's journal? "You've met Ryan. This is Trogdor and Lawrence." I motion to each of them in turn, then look at Ryan. "Satisfied?"

Now Ryan's got some sort of smirk on his face. Great. "Supremely."

"So glad I could entertain you," I say dryly.

"Trogdor. Like *Homestar Runner*?" Matteo asks. I whip my head around and eye him. I know he has no idea who Trogdor is. He must have googled it after he met Trog last time.

"Yeah." Ryan turns the dog over, little stub legs in the air. Like a man possessed, he starts doing our personalized imitation of the Trogdor dragon video, altered for the dog. "First you draw a loaf of bread, then you draw anodder loaf of bread, and then you draw two pizza slices on the head for ears . . ." Trog licks Ryan's face.

"Not to break up the comedy act, but we have things to do in my bedroom."

I close my eyes as both my friends chortle and Ryan says, "*Things*, huh?"

"Move it or lose it, Ryan." I shove past him. "That's not what I meant."

He closes rank behind me and blocks Matteo in the entryway. He's still smirking, but now he and Lawrence remind me strongly of two big brothers; I'm more than mortified.

"So what do you do, Matteo? Are you with Genius too?" Ryan sizes up Matteo's button-down shirt. It's not normal Genius fare, and I want to smack my own head. *Work meeting*. Right. Matteo would have to work with me for it to be a work meeting.

Matteo clearly picks up the same vibe I do but handles it like a pro. Completely casual. "I went to school for architecture." He hangs his head sheepishly and looks at Ryan and Lawrence. "Actually, this isn't for work. I met MG in a coffee shop. She and I got to talking, and I told her I wanted to read some comic books, so she invited me over to give me a few suggestions."

Lawrence's and Ryan's heads swivel to me in tandem. It's *creepy*. I know how implausible this seems. I *never* invite guys from the coffee shop to my house to show them comics. My home is my sanctuary, and Ryan and I have a strict no-hookup policy in the house. My mind spins, trying to figure out how to tell them about our work without spilling the beans. Maybe Matteo won't mind if my roommate knows about the ruse.

Lawrence busts up laughing instead of questioning Matteo further. "I bet she did."

Somehow they are buying it. After giving me a good once-over, Lawrence opens his arm to let Matteo past. "Best not keep a woman waiting, son." He goes so far as to clap him soundly on the shoulder.

"It's nothing. Seriously, guys. Just go do whatever you were doing." I comport myself with every ounce of dignity I can muster until Matteo and I are safely in my room. I leave the door wide open.

"*That* went well," I mutter, glancing around my room. In my head I'm cursing myself for not cleaning up. I didn't really plan on bringing him in here. I see the rubble of my room with fresh eyes. Not too much laundry. The bed is half-made. Some papers and drawings on the floor and on my nightstand. I walk over to the dresser, stuff a pair of undies back in, and shut all the drawers.

Trog trots in and hops on my bed with a jingle. The white duvet is peppered with the copper-and-white hairs that incessantly fall from my dog, and when he lies down, a cloud of them fly into the air.

Matteo must decide that looks like a good idea because he walks over to my bed and sits next to the dog. I'm left to fend for myself and end up sitting awkwardly facing them in the wooden chair that holds a plant near the window.

"Now what?" I ask, looking at the man and dog on my bed. Matteo looks far too at home with my dog. On. My. Bed. Can I even count the months—nay, years—it's been since I've had a guy in my room other than Ryan or Lawrence? Voldemort—the guy who filmed our dates for profit—was the last one, so two years? Quite the dry spell. I have the insane urge to push him back onto my bed and sink my hands into those artfully disheveled locks of his, fake relationship or no.

"I guess we could always do what your roommates are expecting and . . ." Matteo purrs as if reading my mind. For the briefest of seconds, something sparks in his gaze that looks suspiciously like desire, but it's gone in a blink. "Look at comic books?" he finishes.

I let out a small chuckle, and it breaks the tension, though my stomach has yet to unclench from my vision of us rolling around on my duvet.

"Fair point. Work. The case." My closet is a disaster area, and I want to shield him from too much of the mess, so I open the sliding door farthest from him and reach in to look for my stack of comics. "They're here. I just have to find—whoops." I knock over a stack of watercolor sketches. I'm not the most neat and tidy of women. I cultivate the "creative chaos" style of housekeeping.

I dig for a few more minutes. "That's weird. I swear I thought I'd put them in here." I look around my room in hopes of inspiration and spy the comics on the top of my bookshelf. I guess I moved them at some point. Yet I could have sworn I put them in my closet. Maybe Ryan wanted to look at them as reference material for the video game? He's the only one who ever comes in here. I shrug my unease off, anxious to get to the business of looking through comics so I can stop sneaking glances at Matteo petting my dog on my bed.

Nabbing the comics off the shelf, I sit in front of Matteo. Trog is now on his back, laying it *all* out for the world to see. He has zero modesty.

"So this is the first of the new ones, and I thought we could look at where Casey Junior picked up and Senior left off. Show you the difference between the two comics just so you have an operating knowledge of the series as a whole."

It's incredibly awkward for me to turn the comic book halfway between us. We're both craning our necks at angles that aren't comfortable, and I let out a huff of frustration before picking up the stack of comics and plopping myself between Trog and Matteo. My hip presses into Matteo's, but I imagine a stone wall there. Partners don't focus on how aware they are of other partners' legs, right?

I look up and our eyes meet. I should say something about the comic book. I reach for another, and instead, I end up sliding back a fraction of an inch when my weight lands on the issue instead of grabbing it. Something flicks in his eyes, a switch going from cool to hot. He helps me to sit up again, heat searing through my shirt sleeve where his hand rests like a lightsaber. He's close. He's *too* close. Matteo leans forward, his eyes on my lips. It feels like I'm standing on the edge of a cliff, like this is something *big*, exciting, and suddenly scary. My heart stutters to an absolute halt in my chest. Frozen. It's Castle Black in there. Something thaws, a trickle at first but picking up speed until it's a torrent. My body automatically returns his lean. Matteo is so close, his face is blurry. Then his breath is on my cheek, and . . . he reaches right across me and grabs the framed picture off the bedside table.

I'm getting whiplash. First I think he's going to ask me out; then he asks me to pretend to date him. Then an almost-kiss, but now he's studying this picture frame like it's a clue to the damn mystery. It's a picture of Ryan, Trog, and me at Halloween. Looking at it through his eyes, I realize how cozy we look. Like I fancy my roommate, even though to me he's family. Aren't you allowed to have pictures of your family next to your bed?

I swear the muscle in his jaw tightens ever so slightly.

"It's my favorite picture of Trog," I say by way of explanation. It's probably best to get back to business. "Anyway, this first issue of the new reboot is the only issue that addresses the old story line with the smugglers and the double agent—"

"Is Trogdor in a box?"

I blink. "Yes."

"Is that another one of the jokes I don't get? Like a Japanese cartoon thing? Or an online meme?" He says "meh-muh," and I stifle a laugh.

"It's anime, and a meme," I say, correcting his pronunciation. "And no. That was his costume. He was a box."

"A box of . . ."

I shrug. "Just a box. This year he's going to be the demo-corgan from *Stranger Things* . . ."

Matteo throws his head back and laughs, interrupting me. Trog gives an indignant snort and sneeze, wiggles on his back, then slides off the bed and trots out the door. Fuzz-butt traitor. "So you're saying that you're a comic book writer, have purple hair and a million inside jokes from movies and books I've never seen or read, and that your dog was a plain ol' box for Halloween?"

"I thought it was funny." I'm defensive now, and not a little put out.

"It *is* funny. You just keep surprising me is all." His face is warm, open, and inarguably magnetic right now.

"Oh." I refuse to return his grin. We're dangerously off the rails here.

I open the comic and scan the pages. Instead of the beautiful yellows and greens the originals were drawn with, these are an in-your-face, gratuitous riot. I love me some colors—just look at my hair—but after years of having rainbow-hued locks, I've learned an important lesson: *judicious* use of color is key. "Here," I say, pointing at a page. "This is where they return to the warehouse and fight with his partner. And here"—I open the first of the new issues—"here's where it moves away from the old story line. It's also where they find the secret portal to the alien planet, and . . . Are you listening to me?"

Matteo replaces the picture on the table and leafs through the stack of drawings. "Did you draw these? And yes, of course I'm listening. They find the lair, tie up the double agent. And I have a question about that. But I also want to know if you drew these."

I reach out, snag them, and stuff the drawings for L's new costume into my desk drawer. I'd rather have him rifling through my underwear. My drawings are *private*. "Yes, I drew them. And why don't you go ahead and ask your question about the comic book and leave off snooping."

He wears an innocent look that I'm not buying. "Fine. Touchy. I thought you said the other day that we didn't know what happened to the double agent." The words "double agent" send a tingle up my spine. A dirty cop. Brewing drug wars. White Rabbit. There are too many odd coincidences these days between *The Hooded Falcon* and real life.

I wiggle forward so my feet dangle off the edge of my bed, trying to extricate myself from the force of gravity that Matteo's larger person exerts on my smaller frame. I fail miserably and seem to only draw attention to the fact that we're pressed together in the middle of the bed for no reason now that Trogdor is gone.

"That's what I'm getting at. The story line was basically dropped in the new series. In the old ones, it's set up as a big reveal. They find the drugs. Falcon is going to unmask him. They're going to expose him to the public. Then the new ones"—I flop my hand around, searching for a word—"tie it up in a matter of pages. They simply go to a warehouse owned by the double agent, find the stash of drugs, and capture him for the police. They never reveal in the comic who the superhero was to Space City, even though we're told he was a double agent. We know he was *someone* important to the book. This cliffhanger has always bothered true followers of the Falcon. And now we know why. Casey Senior died before his final comics could be run." I pause, still feeling guilty about revealing L's secret to Matteo. "Lawrence's journal proves that Casey Senior planned to unmask the double agent, end the comic, and retire the Falcon."

"But the new one didn't."

"No."

I'm starting to recognize the super intense gaze as Matteo's thinking face. "Why change the new one so drastically?"

"I suspect because either Edward Casey Junior didn't *know* what his father had planned or more than likely didn't care. I told you that it was in this episode that they launched the new cycle. New villains, new weapons. Even the costumes changed drastically. Being a Robin Hood character isn't cool anymore; kids aren't interested in social justice. If you don't have aliens and stun guns, you aren't selling, I guess. Really the only thing he kept was Swoosh, the sidekick, and the fact that the Hooded Falcon uses a bow and arrow."

I bite my lip, a thought occurring to me. "You don't think that Casey Junior . . ." I can't even finish my sentence. Son killing father certainly isn't an unheard-of story line in comics.

Matteo frowns, picking up my thought anyhow. "Hurt his father to keep the comic running? Possibly. Your friend Lawrence said that Casey Junior was pretty bent out of shape about his father's death, right? I don't really see him murdering his father in cold blood, but we'll have to add it to our list of possibilities. I'm not sure that we have enough to question him yet, though, anything to tie him to the *real* reason we're investigating these comics." He rubs his hand over his stubbled chin, making a rasping noise.

"I guess," I say, not convinced. Casey Junior is my number-one suspect, internally. Kill your father in cold blood to keep him from ruining the empire he's built and take it over to reap fame and fortune? Add a few capes and some spandex, and it seems like a Hollywood blockbuster plot to me.

"It doesn't help my theory if the story line never really got finished for our masked avenger to replicate or follow." Matteo glances over the comics, then up at me. "Can we go over the order of events in the issue that we're loosely following? Let's try to get ahead of our misguided superhero before he gets killed in the crossfire."

"Yeah, sure. I think I have that one, actually. Well, half of it. It's old. It fell apart years ago." I dig around in the pile I brought over and hand some papers to Matteo to hold while I sort through issues. My copy is battered compared to the pristine one in the work library, but I love it just the same.

I flip to the page. "Okay, so if I were to guess about what were to happen next? It would be something in a warehouse. Or on a boat. We already know that our suspect was in the warehouse district. We could guess he tracked these guys to where they stash their drugs, either when they get them in or when they're being sent out."

Matteo nods, flicking through the papers I handed him. He's not paying attention *again.* "Warehouse or boat. I'll look into those. Can I borrow that issue from you?" He's still focused on the pile of papers, frowning like he's looking for something right in front of his face.

I'm kind of offended that he's brushing off my predictions. That's the whole reason he's here, right? I'm starting to think that maybe he has superhuman powers to focus on two things at one time, and he's *very* interested in my papers for some reason. I hesitate. He's not asking for the original series, but it's still against my rules. "Yeah, no problem. Just get them back to me."

"What is this?"

I eyeball the pile of papers. "My research for my article on the thirtieth anniversary of *THF*." It's about the LA heroin war that framed the backdrop for the rise of *The Hooded Falcon*'s popularity, and I can tell the eerie similarity to the comic isn't lost on Matteo. He flips to the next papers in the bunch. "And these?"

My heart flip-flops, recognizing the acceptance letter I received in the mail. I still can't believe it is true. "Information on San Diego Comic-Con. I entered a costuming contest held there." I stop short of telling him all about *the* biggest geek-girl fashion design competition in the country and how excited I am. Matteo seems to inspire conversational tangents, making me want to prattle on like a schoolgirl. I have to keep course correcting my brain if this is a business meeting. I am an LAPD consultant now, after all.

"*This.*" He sits up straighter and nearly throws the paper at me. "This we can go in with."

"What on earth are you talking about?" I pick up the folded print-out of the list of memorabilia for the charity auction. Casey Junior's face smiles from the too-polished-to-be-candid picture of him sitting at his father's desk in their LA mansion. "The charity auction?"

"No, the picture."

I study it, then glance up at him, still baffled.

"Beside the desk," Matteo nearly crows.

I look back and do a double take. It's a glass cabinet tucked into the corner of the room housing a perfect replica of the Hooded Falcon's costume—cape and all.

"You think . . . my boss?" I can't imagine Casey Junior running through the streets in a cape.

Matteo shrugs, but his eyes sparkle. I'm pretty sure it's the same look I get when a great idea strikes me at work. "It's enough to question him. Let's see if your friend's information holds water. Thank you for your help, Michael-Grace. I'll be in touch about the interview with Casey and let you know if I find anything on the warehouse front."

I pad to the door behind him. He slips on his shoes and heads outside with a wave. A second later he sticks his head back in. I'm still standing there, fighting the insane urge I have to run after him like I don't want him to leave.

"Oh, but I guess I'll see you this weekend. I'll call—er, *text* you about it. I'm looking forward to meeting your coworkers." He winks.

I smile, relieved that this isn't fully goodbye.

CHAPTER 11

I shut the door behind him and turn to find Ryan and Lawrence standing in the entry again. These guys are *sneaky* for large men.

Lawrence's mouth hangs ajar. "He's meeting your *coworkers*?"

"It's not like that." Then I realize that it *is* like that and that I sound stupid. "Well, I mean, he's already met them."

I might as well have announced I'm selling all my electronics and living an unplugged life—Ryan looks *that* weirded out.

"He already met them because I left my wallet at the coffee shop, and he returned it to me at my office. Then he fixed this chair, so Kyle has a man-crush on him now and invited him to a movie thing. It's not a big deal." I'm being disingenuous about more than just the wallet. I *like* Matteo. He's funny and smart and makes me laugh, and even though he's not my type, he just . . . sneaks up on you. I remember the flash of heat in Matteo's eyes and wonder if after all this hoopla dies down, maybe I *should* invite him out for a drink. Sure, he wouldn't know Trogdor from Smaug if they bit him in the butt, but he sure *is* cute. And now I'm thinking about his butt. *Stop it. Stop it. Stop it.*

Maybe it's time to change the type of guys I date. I haven't had such great luck with the geek crowd. The last con party I attended, a guy walked up to me five or six times before finally telling me my Codex outfit was "neat," then followed me into the bathroom, resulting in me threatening to beat him with my papier-mâché staff.

Ryan stares at me as I mull through my thoughts, then calls me on my bluff. "Right. No big deal. Because you always invite people over to read comics in your bedroom when they return your wallet at your office."

Lawrence doesn't look put out like Ryan does. He looks *gleeful.* "Girl, that man is Atlanta, Georgia, in Ju-ly, and he can come and build me a tower anytime."

"Oh come on, give me a break. We'll probably never see him again." *Lie.* I seem to be lying to everyone these days.

"You didn't see how he looked at you." Ryan crosses his arms.

My pulse quickens in my veins, but a familiar anxiety washes over me, breaking down the hope spawning in my stomach. Dating a non-geek means they might want to normal-fy me. I am terrified of someone constantly telling me my shows or comics are dumb, wishing I'd "tone down my hair a bit," or asking me to give up my job like my mom. I did the normal-guy thing once. It took a botched engagement to wake me up. No, it is better to continue flying solo, and far fewer entanglements for the police case this way.

I shove my reaction back into the padlocked box it belongs in. "Let's all go back in the living room. I have something I want to show both of you."

I reemerge from my room several minutes later with a stack of papers, which I present like a trophy on the coffee table while standing in front of the TV.

"You make a pretty crappy window—aw, sonofa, L! You're supposed to kill the aliens, not our team members!" Ryan leans around me, and I hear the sound of video game gunfire at my back. More specifically crossbow fire.

"Well, I *wouldn't* if somebody wasn't standing in front of the television."

They both throw their controllers down and grumble.

"You guys can go back to killing imaginary—"

"We're working on a real project. This is my *job,* MG." Ryan still sounds like a petulant four-year-old.

"I know. I'll keep this brief. But I want to show you what I just finished filling out." I hold out a paper to Ryan.

"Congratulations, you learned to fill out a form." Ryan barely glances at the paper as he takes it. This drives me crazy about Ryan and is why I can't date a gamer. His job is all-consuming at times. It's like pulling teeth to get *anything* out of him when he's focused. And how much he identifies with his gaming heroes verges on unhealthy. Like a lot of guys who game, I feel like he wants to be heroic in real life but decides it's safer to be a hero in a fake world rather than face judgment. Plus, the regulations for crossbows are murder, I hear.

Lawrence, thankfully, isn't acting like a toddler and takes the sheet of paper. "Girl, is this what I think it is?"

"Yes! I got in!" I can't contain myself any further. "And, L, I would so be honored if you would be my model. I only have two months to come up with *the* best costume design of my life."

Ryan finally glances up and grabs the brochure off the top of the stack of papers on the coffee table. "San Diego Comic-Con, Miss Her Galaxy," he reads out loud. Realization dawns on his face as he flips through the pages. "Oh, this is that fashion show you were talking about entering."

"Yes. And thanks to L's encouragement and my drawings for his costumes, they've accepted me! More than fifteen hundred applicants, and they only select twenty!" This couldn't have come at a better time. I entered on a whim, but now I need to see if I'm *really* any good at fashion and costume design. If I win, I'll get a deal designing for Hot Topic stores . . . I wouldn't have to get the promotion. I could give a one-fingered salute to Genius . . . but that is a big if and something I don't want to bank on quite yet.

As good as my ideas are, my presentations at work *haven't* been going so well. The more worked up I get about them, the worse they get. I am the better writer—of this I am certain—but *maybe*, just maybe, Casey's favor of Andy doesn't have everything to do with the ideas themselves. I'm concerned that even if I *try harder*, nothing will change. That this is how Genius is, take it or leave it. And I'm contemplating leaving it, which is something I never thought I'd do.

This contest would be something just for *me*. If I win, I'll become a household name for geek girls everywhere. I'll support my fellow femmes and rub elbows with the best. It's time to take a risk on myself and possibly on my future.

"MG, that's really impressive." Ryan looks up, all trace of toddler gone. "Seriously. I thought you weren't even going to apply." He stands up and scoops me into a hug. It's so warm and comfortable, I forget any weirdness between us.

Lawrence is next and swoops me up. MG sandwich. My absolute favorite spot in the universe.

"So you'll do it, L? I'll make you look fierce."

"Will I be the only queen?"

I shrug. "I think so. Cleo definitely won't be there; that's for sure."

"I'm in."

Excellent. L is the Fezzik to my Inigo, and I need him there with me. "And we'll need our cheering section. How about it, Ryan? I brought you all sorts of info." I cut off Ryan's response before he can roll his eyes. "I *know* you hate cons. I get it. But this one isn't a gamer convention. It's just general geek merriment. I think Jean-Luc Picard is going to be there."

Ryan's eyes gain a hint of interest. "I'm not promising anything." But he takes the brochure from me.

"I have a color at eleven," Lawrence announces, stretching up and touching the ceiling. "I need to go open the shop. Ry, I'll see you at the gym later."

Ryan grunts in agreement. It's their guy-love language, though I don't understand how one grunt can say so many different things. It's one of the things that makes Ryan and Lawrence closer to an old married couple than friends.

Ryan was originally L's roommate but ended up moving out because a spiteful lover had dumped a bottle of wine on their PlayStation when L beat him at *Call of Duty*.

Ryan didn't mind L's eccentricities—L was the first person who befriended Ryan at the gym after he'd moved to LA, and Ryan seems to have something dark in his past that makes him shy about meeting people. We don't talk about it much; he clams up big time whenever I ask. Maybe it's why he and L get along so well: they have that in common. He always says that he has a fresh lease on life here and that he's making amends for his past any way he can.

Lawrence slips his shoes on, and I note the letter "L" written in sparkles on the black leather. That bitch has been bedazzling without me.

I blow him a kiss as he leaves, lock the door behind him, and walk back into the living room to sink onto the cracked pleather couch. I prop my feet over the end, grab one of the woefully mismatched couch pillows, and settle into Ryan's side.

Ryan's answering grunt means I'm clearly inhibiting his ability to make a living today. "Hang on, everybody. I'm going to mute. MG is back." He pulls the headset off and looks down. All sorts of horrible commentary starts pouring from the TV as the other gamers in his group start catcalling and suggesting video game–based sexual positions. I catch the term "paladin missionary style" before Ryan manages to silence the channel.

"How's work?" I ask.

He raises his eyebrow, and his eyes say that it would be going better if I stopped interrupting, but he decides to be diplomatic. "The job is more challenging than I could ever have imagined. How about *you*?" He draws out the syllables, obviously fishing for the reason I'm back on the couch instead of working like a good girl.

Two of the characters on screen pretend to do a striptease, and Ryan runs his avatar forward to knock them over.

"My big presentation didn't go as well as I wanted." I tell him about Andy basically stealing my idea.

"You have so many talents. So many skills. You can smell a story a mile away. Fastest brain this side of the galaxy. But maybe this isn't your superpower. Maybe you're not General Leia. Do you even really want to be a team leader? Less time on your own work? More time with the executives? Maybe this isn't the only solution."

My glance must give away my skepticism because Ryan rolls his eyes to the ceiling. "For instance, if Andy gets the promotion, wouldn't there be an opening for team captain or whatever? You'd still be Kyle and Simon's boss."

I contemplate that. "True." Before he can crow with satisfaction, I hold up my hand. "*But* Andy would still get to be executive, *and* I want the promotion so that I can do costume design."

"I get that, but . . . surely if Andy gets the promotion, you use that genius brain of yours to figure out another way to do what you want to do? And maybe it will be better than your plan A?"

I press my lips together and meet Ryan's brown eyes. His hat is on backward over his blondish hair, so he looks like a teenager, but the words coming out of his mouth are surprisingly grown-up—and almost exactly verbatim what I've just been telling myself. When did Ryan turn in to the adult of this relationship?

The players in the game are now testing what look like vials of potions on one another, and Ryan leans forward to yell into the mic. "Quit that, you guys. We need to test those against the alien horde . . . Aw, dammit, Lee, now you've attracted the band of rogue archers, and you know they're still glitchy."

"I'll leave you to it." I hop back off the couch and smirk. Ryan is already completely immersed again, his fingers flying over the controller. Something has shifted, though. Ryan seems older, wiser. Have I missed something in his life while I've been sidetracked with the case? Must be that girl he's been seeing. "Love you, Ryan."

He smiles, still staring at the screen. "I know."

CHAPTER 12

It's Friday morning just after breakfast. I've already walked Trog and have the television on, hoping to hear something related to my case.

"The Golden Arrow strikes again. This seems to be the latest in a recent string of vigilante justice . . ."

I turn from the sink, glass of water halfway to my mouth. It can't be. The Golden Arrow? Is that what the media has decided to call our masked civilian? I roll my eyes at the general public's lack of creativity with naming superheroes, seeing as our competitor already has an "arrow" superhero with a different-colored moniker.

"Moments ago we got word that this warehouse had been chained shut by persons unknown, and an anonymous call was placed to the police claiming that they would find more than just criminals inside. We suspect a drug bust of large proportions. Police have surrounded the area with crime scene tape, so we can't get any closer, but it looks like teams are arriving to transfer dangerous individuals to the police station." The reporter is gleeful, her red suit standing out against the grays, blues, and rust hues that make up the warehouse district alleyway. I recognize the building they're standing in front of. It's the same one I saw in the video at Matteo's office.

My phone buzzes. I can't tear my eyes away from the screen where the news feed cuts to a chopper view of the warehouse near the docks. A brilliant gold arrow painted across the front of the building and doors, at least twelve feet long, gleams in the morning sun. The bold gold glitter paint makes me think of Lawrence. This is a hero right up his alley.

My phone buzzes again, and I glance at it. It's a text from a number I don't recognize, but I'm not surprised by what it says.

I'm going to call. Answer your phone, we need to talk.

A smile tugs at my lips. Matteo's learning.

As I read the lines, the screen transitions to the active call icon, and I thumb "Answer."

"I see it. On the news," I say without preamble.

Matteo doesn't waste time on formalities either. Chopper noise beats in the background of his call, indicating he's already at the scene. "I'd like you to come look. When can you get out of work?"

My heart starts to thud a staccato rhythm in my chest. "I guess around three?" This is *real*. It's insane, but *real*. My very own comic book come to life.

"That's late, but it'll have to do." He hisses out a breath. "I'll let you get ready for work. Call me when you're out. You're going to want to see this." Then he's gone, leaving dead air between us.

"I'm glad you made it. Traffic is horrible today. Everyone is a lookie-loo." Matteo holds my car door open for me as I climb out into the smoggy, nasty air that is LA's inversion layer. I sputter on the smell of too many cars, too many fast-food hamburgers, and the lurking scent of wood decaying in the water. It's why I avoid the Santa Monica piers like the plague. Everyone always lauds the "fresh sea air." For me, I'd rather be at home with my air filter.

It's three o'clock on the dot, and I did everything short of faking sickness to get out of the office today. Everyone wanted to talk about the upcoming gala and the Golden Arrow on the news.

"What do I need to bring with me?" I shove sketches into my Genius messenger bag, then reach in the back seat to grab the original *THF* issues I smuggled out of Genius. They would *kill* me if they ever find out. I have to hope I keep them pristine and use them only if truly needed. The new ones can be replaced. The originals can't.

Matteo leans in and pins a media pass to the lapel of my jacket, and I go still. I am inordinately fascinated with his fingers fastening the pin, though it takes no more than fifteen seconds. My heart careens in my chest like a Mario-kart around a curve.

Matteo, on the other hand, looks cool as a cucumber. All business. This is a crime scene, after all. "There, you're all set. Come on, let's get you across the line. We've been trying to keep the media out all day. I think reporters are about to start rappelling in from the next building to get a look."

I raise my eyebrow at him.

"I like *Mission Impossible*. I'm a gadget guy."

I can see that about him.

He flashes his badge to the patrol officer standing near the street. "Kildaire, narcotics," he says by way of greeting.

What am I? *Martin, superhero consultant? Comic specialist?* At the patrol officer's nod, Matteo holds the yellow tape up, and I duck under, resisting the urge to snap a picture of myself and post it to Instagram. I'm *inside a crime scene*. Just call me Temperance Brennan. And Matteo is *so* Seeley Booth. He's wearing a brown felt fedora today over his dark locks and sun-kissed brown skin. It looks very twenties throwback. Very noir detective. Very, *very* sexy. I mean, I'd find Worf drinking prune juice attractive if he put a fedora on. Be still, my twenties era–loving heart.

Thinking about *Bones* brings me to my only worry about the crime scene.

"The people inside aren't dead, are they? I do *not* do dead bodies."

"No. They're all alive and in custody. I'm not sure they'll be appreciative, given the jail time they're facing."

The afternoon sun shines directly in my eyes, and I squint. Perpetually wearing glasses means no sunglasses. I'm also afraid I've overdressed for the weather. I wish I'd worn a hat, and I'm regretting the navy-blue coat over my "Don't Let the Muggles Get You Down" graphic tee. It's my silent homage to the person who's quickly becoming my favorite Muggle. I couldn't help myself today when I saw the shirt in my closet. I thought of Matteo and had to wear it. Would it be inappropriate for a crime scene investigator expert to wear just a tee, though? I decide to swelter it out in my jacket for a bit, even though I already feel a drop of sweat sliding between my shoulder blades. Ah, Los Angeles. I hate being hot, but I hate being cold more. And as hypocritical as it is for me to hate this city and love it too, there it is. I'd never live anywhere else.

Matteo leads me over cracked and rutted asphalt, around the corner of a metal building, and to the front door of the building I recognize from the news. The golden arrow looks spray-painted, and a few other police in uniform still work to photograph and document it.

"Ah, Detective Rideout, Agent Sosa, this is Michael-Grace Martin, the comic book expert I was telling you about." Matteo ushers me forward, his arm behind my back, toward two people in suits standing by the far end of the building.

"Hi," I say. I reach forward for a quick handshake from both, used to leading out. God help the man if he does that limp-finger "lady handshake" thing.

"Detective Rideout assists me with the LAPD narcotics portion of this investigation."

By the look of him, this Rideout guy's not thrilled I'm here, but at least it's a firm shake.

Matteo then gestures to a dark-haired agent wearing a bright-blue coat. Her hair is cut short into a stylish but severe page cut that would feel like shackles to me. All that maintenance, no movement, no creativity, just morning after morning of the same smoothing and straightening. "Agent Sosa is from the DEA and is evaluating whether or not the FBI needs to share jurisdiction. Copycat crimes aren't common, so Detective Rideout and I are leaning toward asking for a federal profiler to help out as well."

I snort. "Well, it's not like it's often that someone pretends to be a superhero."

"Actually"—Detective Rideout levels a gaze at me—"it's not unheard of. What's uncommon about *this* case is that they're good at it. I saw it before on patrol. Isolated incidents, and because bad guys don't have moral compasses, the would-be hero is beat to a pulp in four seconds flat and ends up at the hospital in an embarrassingly tight spandex suit."

Matteo shades his eyes and glances toward the building. I follow his gaze. My eyes wander over the golden arrow, lingering on the lower part of the door where more graffiti is partially obscured by a crate and a pile of crime scene tape.

"Should we show the lady comic book expert the stuff we found inside the Lair of Justice?" Detective Rideout gives me a once-over that clearly shows he's interested in two assets of my person in particular, and not the smarts. He leans over, under the guise of opening the front door, and says in a low voice, "That's a reference to *The Hooded Falcon.*"

My brain flashes back to my conversation with Ryan. I need to be a professional here. A team player. I don't want to default to insults. But years of this treatment while working in the comic book store and at Genius cause an automatic stiffening of my spine. Mansplaining comics is literally *the* most annoying thing in the world to me.

I halt at the door to the warehouse, and the group turns to look, a smug smirk on Detective Rideout's face. He thinks he's made his point. I'm about to make mine.

"No, you shouldn't show me inside. First off, I currently write for Genius Comics and have worked in the industry for ten years—I think that far outweighs your weekend trips to the comic book store." Matteo looks horrified, though a little fascinated at my outburst.

I can't help myself. The words just tumble out of me, just like they do in my meetings when I get defensive. "Secondly, the *Hall* of Justice refers to the *Justice League*, which is a competitor's property. Falcon's personal hideout was called the Glen, until the new series when they changed it to the Falcon's Nest, which personally I think is a dumb name, but whatever. I wasn't there for that vote." I take a deep breath, fully aware of the uncomfortable set of Detective Rideout's shoulders.

"And thirdly, no, you shouldn't take me inside because you are about to walk straight past something important. Do you see that graffiti there? To a *true* comic book expert"—I can't help but add the dig—"that mark tells us who these criminals were selling to, or who the Golden Arrow *thinks* they're working for."

They turn in unison to look at the graffitied white rabbit, and I bite my cheek to keep from smiling.

"And *that's* why she's here," Matteo confirms.

I walk over to the heavy metal door, kneel low where kids have been tagging the building with several colors of spray paint, and point to the outline of a white rabbit.

"The Easter Bunny?" I don't even have to look to know it's Rideout's dulcet tones.

"You see how this looks as fresh as the golden arrow? I don't think it's a mistake. This is the White Rabbit."

The DEA agent frowns and looks at Matteo.

"You mean the Hooded Falcon's nemesis? As in a real person?" Matteo asks. "Are we chasing *two* vigilantes now?"

I chew on my lip, unsure. I decide to go with my gut because that's what I'm here for. "I don't think so. I think it's a reference *to* the White Rabbit, but it's hidden. It's like our suspect—the Golden Arrow, I think they're calling him—didn't want just anyone to find it." A prickle rises along my neck. Is this meant for *me?* Is it a warning? Matteo said that these drug cartels wouldn't think twice about killing someone to keep their silence. And here I am, willing mouse chasing a cat in a game with ever-heightening stakes.

I continue with my explanation, though Detective Rideout looks like he's about to glaze over. You can always tell a true comic book fan by their knowledge and love of a good origin story. Falcon's is the best in my opinion, and Rideout has sunk lower in my estimation for his failure to latch on to the tie-in.

"In the origin story of the Hooded Falcon, he's an average Joe who stumbles upon a drug deal at a dock. Instead of walking past, he calls the police to stop it. The drug dealers see him, abduct him, stow him in the ship, then ultimately leave him on a deserted island where he has to fend for himself for months before a ship comes back. It's where he hones his hunting skills to survive. The same smugglers come back to the island to pick up the stash. He sneaks aboard and ends up commandeering the ship, steering it into the port of Space City, and turning over the entire ship, crew, and drugs to the authorities." I point to the rabbit. "The rabbit is the sign of his archnemesis—the White Rabbit, a Chinese drug lord. It's accepted as a reference to China white, or a slang term for heroin."

I look around, and all three of them are blinking at me. Suddenly I'm not so sure. "Didn't you say that White Rabbit is what the street drug is called?"

"Yes." It's Agent Sosa who answers. Her mouth has puckered like she's sucking on a Sour Patch Kid. "We did the field tests, and it's positive for heroin. Possibly other elements, though more than likely that's contamination from the scene. We have yet to do a full scan at the lab. It's more likely that this drawing is in reference to the street drug."

I bite my lip. Other contaminates like a designer drug? But . . . Occam's razor. I suppose it's possible I'm stretching this too far. I look at Matteo, who shrugs. We're all in the dark here. Until I am sure that the Golden Arrow is trying to identify a specific nemesis, I should keep to the simpler explanations. "Probably."

We tour the rest of the crime scene, but I don't see any further indication of hidden messages or Hooded Falcon trivia. Towering stacks of boxes and crates, most of which are being sorted through, cataloged, and photographed by officers, fill the warehouse. The warehouse stock sheet says there are twenty bays of other goods to inspect, everything from books, magazines, and comic books to KitchenAid mixers, machine parts, and—I laugh—cereal. Crates and crates of cereal.

"Maybe they're putting heroin in Cap'n Crunch. I've suspected it for years." My joke earns a smirk from Matteo but not even an eye roll from Rideout. Great. He's grumpy *and* he has no sense of humor. *Detective Dursley* it is.

Matteo points to the largest group of people in the warehouse, gathered around a small stack of crates on the floor. "We discovered the uncut heroin. Agent Sosa here has explained that more than likely it's from Mexico, since we're so close to the border and it's not unheard of for illegal shipments of drugs to come on small boats from Tijuana."

I frown. That doesn't line up with the White Rabbit from the comics, but I'm still not sure how literal to take the story line. "Could it be from another country, say China?" Just the other week, Ryan pointed out an article online about the rise of the designer drug culture in LA. It said that countries like China, Laos, and Vietnam were hotbeds for synthetic drug production and that US port cities were starting to see more of them. Now *that* could be a nod to the White Rabbit in the comics. Something moves deep in my subconscious, and the image of the boat from the panel with the people tied to the dock surfaces.

"Could these drugs possibly be readying for *export* instead of going to other states?"

Agent Sosa squints at me.

"Well, it's just that the initial drug bust was down by the docks, and in the scene it reminded me of from the comic, the drugs were being loaded onto a boat, not off."

Agent Sosa flicks a glance at Matteo, then sweeps her dark page cut behind one ear and gives me a small smile that looks a *teensy* condescending, like she's humoring a kindergartner. Which I practically am, since the most I know about drugs is that Tylenol Cold & Sinus wipes me out for three days. "We're going to proceed as if it's a standard drug trafficking case until proven otherwise. In my professional opinion, that's what we're dealing with."

"It's just . . . it's a lot like the plotline with the White Rabbit in the series. Enough that I think you should look into it?"

Agent Sosa narrows her eyes at me, and I feel like I'm overstepping my bounds on my first day at work. "This is cut-and-dried. We'll test it and send a report to the narcotics team, but it's your basic pure heroin. Next it would have been cut, packaged, and trucked out to the surrounding area. I don't even think it's what the street teams are labeling White Rabbit. The lab will have to tell us. We're wasting our time in this warehouse looking for clues, past testing the product."

"One of the dealers from the first bust is with a notorious Mexican cartel," Detective Rideout adds. "And I agree that the connection to the comic book is weak. We should move forward with the cartel theory."

I'm *not* convinced. Or my gut isn't. I shoot a look at Matteo. "The Golden Arrow is obviously a fan of the comic book. What if he's trying to tell us something? In the comic, it has to do with China, and it has to do with shipping."

Matteo nods slowly. "I agree that it's too soon to dismiss the idea. That's why we have MG here. She's the expert. If she says there may be a connection, let's follow up—no matter *how* out-there it sounds, Detective." Rideout was muttering under his breath but stops short when Matteo calls him out.

"As I was saying, there's no harm in checking which ships were in port the night of all the busts. See if there's a connection. Agent Sosa, just test the sample, and let us know if there are any anomalies that would point to this *not* being Mexican cartel for whatever reason."

Rideout could double for Cyclops, his laser gaze nearly slicing Matteo in half.

Agent Sosa looks likewise displeased to have her *authority* questioned in such a manner. "Fine. Whatever. I'm telling you to leave it alone. You're wasting your time."

Leave it alone? Her acidic tone gives the distinct impression that I've made an enemy, or *two* if I count how Rideout's lip curls up right now. Yet something pools in the depths of my stomach, buoying my spirits. Matteo heeded my thoughts. He stood up for me to his partner. *He* thought what I'd said was worth following up on.

Something in me says I'm on the right track here, even if in their professional *opinion* I'm off my rocker. If this lines up and we are literally chasing rabbits, then we are also looking for the crooked cop. My head moves as if on a swivel to take in first Rideout, then the group of police working over the crate of drugs. How easy would it be to fiddle with the crime scene? There are so many cops, it would be hard to pin it down . . . but the note from the Golden Arrow was leaked by a member of Matteo's team. So Rideout; that younger officer I met, Officer James; or Matteo. Or any one of the other fifty cops here involved in the case. I'm not even sure how widely known the note's contents are.

My eyes narrow as I recognize Officer James among those bagging evidence. He slips one of the baggies into his coat pocket, and my hackles rise. It could be coincidence, or it could be tampering. I open my mouth, about to ask Matteo to watch James, when I see Agent Sosa approach James. They exchange words, his hand fishes back into his pocket and produces the tagged evidence, and they both bend their heads over it. Sosa nods and puts the bag into her own pocket. No drama. No other cops shouting or pointing. No sirens, and *no* Golden Arrow swooping down to say, "Aha! I've got you now!"

I thank my lucky stars I haven't blabbed to Matteo yet. *Apparently* I'm seeing the comic book everywhere. Poor Officer James. How would he like to know that I suspected him as a dirty cop just because he is the low man on the totem pole?

Agent Sosa moves off to meet with the other teams inspecting crates while Matteo takes me to the area where the men were locked up. It's a large utility closet housing mechanical equipment—nothing tying that to the books.

"Do you have pictures of how you found the men? Were they tied with rope again?" My brain jumps to the pile of rope under Kyle and Simon's desk. I'm looking for anything that will point me in a direction. Any direction. Why draw a rabbit? Is it really *the* White Rabbit, or is it in reference to the drugs? It may just be more lunacy, but I feel like I know the Golden Arrow. Like he or she leaves these clues for *me*, and I'm not smart enough to decipher them.

"They were handcuffed with zip ties and chained to a large welded pipe," Matteo answers, pressing his phone's camera on and showing me pictures of the scene this morning. I flip through, looking for anything that catches my eye. I feel useless here; I add questions instead of giving the cops any direction at all. In fair imitation of my work presentations, my one thought about the source of the drugs has been shot down, and it seemed simple: our vigilante wanted to alert us to drugs in this warehouse. Maybe end of story. No need to look further.

"Wait. Wait. Scroll back. This one here. Do you have any other pictures of him?" My stomach lurches as I catch sight of something on one of the guys' hoodies. It's slightly obscured by another person chained to the pipe, but I see enough of the white to think it may be a rabbit.

Matteo frowns and flicks through the pictures on his phone. "This is a little better, but not great."

It's enough. My eye for lines helps where Matteo's eyes fail. It is the exact same rabbit we saw outside. "This guy has the same rabbit on his hoodie."

Matteo shoves his face closer to the screen to verify my claims. "So what would this mean?"

"I don't know yet." I bite my lip, thinking.

"Well, we took everyone in for questioning. I'll find out who he is. Maybe he's the leader and our suspect marked him. Or maybe he's a graffiti artist who spray-painted the same image from his hoodie onto the building."

Again my gut tells me it's more than coincidence, though I don't know what it means . . . yet. I'll get there. I feel like I'm *this close* to getting it. Getting what the Golden Arrow is playing at. And my writer's sixth sense says the story isn't done; there's another act coming. We just have to figure it out before someone gets killed.

Daylight mingles with twilight by the time Matteo walks me back to my car.

"No matter what my partner says, we have lots to check in to. You saw stuff that we would have missed. This is getting serious. If the cartels suspect that this dude landed their whole stash of pure heroin at the PD, it won't go without retaliation. We need to do some digging to see if your coworkers have costumes. Anything that would suggest research on drugs in LA. Rope, gold paint, stuff like that, and the party is the perfect opportunity. Do you want me to pick you up? That way we can discuss the case on our way there. Make it look more like we're seeing each other if we arrive together." He shoves his hands in his pockets and scuffs his shoes. Honest to God shuffles his feet. I feel an answering blush stain my own cheeks.

Then I think about Lawrence, and Ryan, and how I don't want any more questions because I don't want to lie to them any more than I have to. "How about I meet you at your house?"

A look of surprise crosses his face, then curiosity, then acceptance and something that looks like amusement. Like he's figured me out. "I'm all for equal opportunity driving, so sure."

"Just text me your address, and I'll be at your house around nine?"

"Sounds good." He pauses and looks at the sky, then back to me. "That was pretty impressive back there, Michael-Grace. I think you definitely proved your worth as a teammate today."

My heartbeat zings a little in my ears, and I smile back, opening the door to the car. "I did kick a little ass, didn't I?"

I start my engine, and the headlights cut a swath through the gathering night like Captain America's shield deflecting enemy fire. I watch Matteo walk back toward the crime scene, a feeling of isolation washing over me. The media frenzy has died down, the reporters have gone home, and a blanket of eerie silence covers the street. Not a car in sight. It rained while we were in the warehouse, a late-afternoon squall that has heightened the smell of gasoline and rotting fish. I roll down my window, trying to ventilate my car, and glance out at my now clearer view of the alleyway.

Is that the flapping of a cape up there on top of a warehouse? My heart stops in my chest.

I squint, sure I am seeing things in the dying light of the evening. But no, my eye catches it again. The flap of fabric on the rooftop. The Golden Arrow? Come to watch us piece together the puzzle?

Immediately I throw my car into reverse, hardly looking behind me as my tires squeal on the pavement in my zeal to back up. I *have* to get my headlights to illuminate more of the alley. When I think I'm far enough back, I throw caution to the wind and get out of my car, cell phone clutched in my hand. If I can get a picture of him, we'll have something to go on. I race forward, eyes on where I last saw the fabric. I can now make out the form of a person, but it looks . . . wrong as I approach. The Golden Arrow isn't moving. He isn't *on* the roof; he's dangling from it.

I gasp and run forward, hand at my throat, disregarding the drizzle of rain pattering on my head. The figure doesn't move at the sound of my approach, but I finally see why. The dim light of my headlights reveals a stuffed dummy, hung by its feet off a fire escape. A cape dangles down toward the street below, a huge golden arrow stuck straight through the chest. The words "You're next, Batman" are written in black paint on the cape. Or at least I hope it's paint. A shiver runs down my spine. The warning is clear—the drug dealers know that there is a civilian defender involved, and they're threatening the well-being of whoever is interfering with their business. Too bad the Golden Arrow could be someone I know, and *I'm* stuck in the middle of this mess, and Matteo too. It's the first moment I realize that I could seriously get hurt helping with this case—what if the drug dealers are hanging around waiting for someone to leave the crime scene who would be easy to kidnap? I punch Matteo's number before sprinting back to my car. I don't want to be caught anywhere near this ominous sign. I tell Matteo what I've seen and hang up the phone.

This is no cat-and-mouse game; this is life or death comic-book style, and since the rest of the team seems to be refusing my advice, it's up to *me* to figure it out before someone I know ends up like that dummy.

CHAPTER 13

A peppering of sand hits my car as I cruise down the lonely desert road. The address that Matteo texts me is outside the city. *Way* outside the city. I'm feeling like I could take one wrong turn at a cactus and end up on the planet from *Dune*. In fact, when I pull up to the modest walled house that Siri insists is the right one, there's not another building in sight. In any direction.

I would have pictured Matteo in a trendy downtown loft drinking sangria on his rooftop garden patio with his neighbors. It's so quiet out here, my steps on the gravel sound like something out of a badly produced horror movie.

"Glad you made it!" Matteo stands at the front door across a courtyard landscaped with a plethora of rocks, colorful blooming cacti, succulents, and tall spiny grass—a little capsule of the best of the desert. An oasis. "Come on in. The gate is unlocked."

"Paranoid much?" The gate swings open on silent hinges, even though it weighs at least twenty pounds, and I close it behind me with a clang. Although if it were just a tiny gate between me and endless desert, maybe I'd be paranoid too.

He shrugs. "I bought it this way, and it keeps out the coyotes."

"Coyotes?" I shoot a trepidatious look over my shoulder. I'm all for small, fluffy, lovable dogs, but I'm not a wildlife lover. It's why you don't *ever* catch me at the beach. Or in the pool. In addition to my translucent pale skin that burns in the merest suggestion of sunlight, I may or may not also be convinced that sharks can and will live anywhere. For instance, in swimming pools.

Matteo laughs. "They're not out right now. They're mostly nocturnal." He turns to go inside. "I mean, unless they have rabies."

I skitter up the path to the porch. "Yeah, that makes me feel better."

"Hence the gate," he says with a wink, sweeping the front door wide.

The house is simple and contemporary on the outside and wide open, daylit, and clean on the inside. We stand in a living room filled with square gray furniture, a glass fireplace flanked by huge windows with views to the desert, and an art deco lamp. To the right sits an open kitchen—simple, modern—and to our left is a short hallway to what I assume is the bedroom and the bathroom. It's so neat, clean, and contemporary, it looks like I walked straight into a design magazine. The magazines I like to glance through, not the ones dripping tassels and jacquard. Sleek and professional. Grown-up. I slip off my bright-yellow flats and set them next to his leather shoes.

"Come on in. I'm about to make some coffee. Not the fancy coffee shop stuff, but it's not too bad."

"It's okay. I'll take a cup. I can't believe you live all the way out here, on purpose."

He busies himself in the kitchen, putting an actual kettle on the stove. I haven't seen a real kettle since I left my mother's house.

"For five years," he confirms.

Five years driving this far out of the city to go home? No way. I'm too instant-satisfaction. If there were a transporter available, even if it were only questionably safe, I'd be the first to use it.

He catches me looking at him and frowns. "I know it's not glamorous, and most people live in LA for the city and the nightlife, but I like how quiet it is out here. I like to think."

"Think about . . . coyotes?"

Humor sparks in his eyes again. "Mostly my job. I take work home, review cases. I find answers and make connections I can't make while I'm in the office where it's busy. Sometimes I think about the universe. You are reminded how small you are out here in the desert. I like that. Puts everything in perspective after a tough day."

Spines ebb and flow beneath my fingers as I run my hand down his bookcase. Even the books are neat, orderly, and I think even organized alphabetically and by category. The architecture section is particularly prodigious, and I read the titles *The Small House*, *The Sustainable House*, and *Desert House*. "So you really did go to architecture school?"

"Mm-hmm." He's pouring the water into a French press, so I keep looking at the books.

"Did you design this house?"

He laughs. "No. It's midcentury modern by a local architect really into passive solar design. Not too many people want to live this far out, so I got a deal on the place. Really, no one recognizes what a work of art and science a house like this is. Or not many people. But someday I'd like to design my own house out in the desert."

"It's like camping every night."

"You say that like it's a bad thing."

"I've been camping exactly once. Let's just say we refer to it as the Great Misadventure of 2012. It involved carrying a thirty-pound cooler with no handles more than two miles, a pillowcase with my clothes in it, a lopsided tent that trapped every mosquito inside, and Lawrence being mistaken as the suspect in a carjacking and arrested in the parking lot on our way home. We didn't repeat it."

Matteo snorts. His hair is a little more tousled than I've seen before. He's relaxed in jeans and a new button-down shirt, his cheeks clean-shaven, his dark eyebrows furrowed over the task of placing the mugs and saucers on the counter in a neat line. It's . . . *adorable*. And that odd sense of intimacy hits me again before I'm ready for it. Like I'm peering into his soul without his permission. I turn back to the books, afraid of what he might see on my face if he catches me looking this time.

The rest of the bookshelf is filled with psychology books, crime scene investigation books, and a big fat tome of federal codes, which holds zero interest for me, so I wander into the kitchen.

"How did you end up being a detective if you went to architecture school?"

He pauses, and I can see the internal debate about how to answer. "That's a long story. I didn't know it until I was grown-up, but my mom had been a drug user. She missed her family in Mexico, felt alone and bored. It's not that uncommon for housewives, actually. It made me want to help prevent others from making the same mistakes she did. So I joined patrol, and then when I discovered I was really good at narcotics, I put in for the promotion to detective."

From the shadow behind his eyes, I'm guessing there's more to this story, but I don't pry because we haven't exactly crossed the gulf between pretend significant others into the realm of "Tell me your deep dark childhood secrets." Even superheroes guard their origin stories in comic books.

"We have to wait until the timer goes off," Matteo says as I slide onto a barstool. The concrete counter is smooth and cool under my elbows as I prop my chin in my hands awaiting liquid sustenance.

A chiming sound emanates from my pocket, and I pull my phone out. It informs me that it's searching for a signal and that I'm currently roaming. No joke; it's a regular safari out here. It's apparently been searching for a while because I can practically see my battery charge draining.

"Do you need to make a call?" He's eyeing my phone as he pours the coffee into cups. The rich aroma fills my nose, and my mouth actually waters. *Coffee, coffee, coffee.* The song of my people.

"No, my phone is just searching for a signal. It's draining the battery."

"Service here can be tricky. I have a landline if you need." He motions with a spoon to the corded blue telephone attached to one of the stained wood columns that separate the kitchen island from the living room.

"You have a *land*line?"

The spoon clinks as he swirls something into each cup then places mine in front of me. He doesn't answer because, well, duh, he just told me he did. After a quick scan, I don't see a television either. Definitely no towering stack of video games like *my* living room—thank you, Ryan—or any of the memorabilia junk that fills my friends' houses. Or any of the typical accoutrements of router, modem, and cables.

"You don't have Wi-Fi." Beyond judgment, I'm in the horror zone.

"Nope." And he seems entirely unperturbed about his caveman status. He licks the spoon and tosses it in the sink. "Now, I made you a breakfast blend with coconut oil and a sprinkle of cinnamon. Don't knock it until you try it."

He laughs at the face I make. Hipster status fully reinstated. "Coconut oil?" Though the scent of cinnamon tantalizes my nose.

"It makes the coffee taste even better. Would you like a biscotti?"

I nod my head. What man even has *biscotti* in his house? Double hipster points awarded, even if they are *awesome* hipster points. I can't think of any other way to phrase it, but Matteo is the *adultiest* adult I've met in a long time. He's a real grown-up. Fully in the man category, unlike some of the borderline perpetual teenagers I seem to meet.

If my life is *Firefly*, my crew consists of these forever-young people— they're playful, they're geeky, they're always up for a marathon of *Arrow*. But in a way, it's refreshing to meet someone who made the leap—Matteo's the novelty in my world. Usually I am repelled by the thought of dating an adult. I picture being a grown-up as stuffy, no room for play, fun, or *color* in life. It's "go to the office, kiss wife on cheek, read the news, go to bed, repeat until you die," as modeled by my parents. But Matteo . . . His version of adult is different. It's polished, sophisticated, and sure, he owns more than one pair of shoes and a couch made from something other than plastic, but he seems *alive* still. Maybe it's his job, that he brushes shoulders with danger. Maybe it's that he seems to not only accept my quirks and my hair and my comics but is charmed by them. Or maybe it's just him.

My eyes stray to my yellow flats sitting next to Matteo's shoes on the step. Out of place, but a welcome relief against the gray background. Like his house needs my splash of color. The thought takes my brain all sorts of places and gives me a pang of wanting I shouldn't feel with my *work* partner. I mentally pull myself back from the edge.

"But what do you *do* out here?" No online gaming. No Reddit. No Instagram. No Netflix.

"I read. I sit out on my patio and listen to the desert. Work on my cases. Think."

"So you work, and then you come out here and you work. But don't you get—" I snap my mouth shut, realizing how personal and inappropriate my question is going to be.

"Lonely?" He thinks for a moment, then sips his coffee. "Yeah. Sometimes. And I know everyone else loves the city, but it fills up my head. I get this wired energy, and I can't relax. I *can* relax out here, and I need it. I'm not a great person otherwise. I've met that Matteo. I don't like him." He looks . . . wistful? Bitter? Resentful? His eyes find mine, and we sit in silence as the steam from our cups rises between us. "But yeah. Lonely sometimes."

It sounds like an admission. A *personal* admission, like maybe he feels less lonely with me here. My stomach does a flip-flop. He hit the nail on the head with how I've been feeling lately. Wired up and pulled in a lot of different directions. Maybe I need some time in the desert too. Complete with a bodyguard to protect me from coyotes and all the bad guys who suddenly sprang to life in my world.

But no Netflix. That seems extreme.

I take a hesitant sip of my coffee to fill the thoughtful silence that's fallen. It's . . . good. Better than good. This is the best damn cup of black coffee I've had in ages—no milk, sugar, or caramel needed. Just like Matteo, it's simple, straightforward, and unique. I moan in delight.

Humor is back in his eyes now, the flash of vulnerability and heat gone. "I *told* you it's good." He takes another sip to make his point. "So if we're supposed to be dating, I should probably know more about you. What exactly is it that you do for work?"

I shrug. "Perhaps I'm a woman of mystery."

He looks out the window, so I can't tell if he's teasing. "You most certainly win that title. I know you know a lot about comics. But what do you *do*?"

"I write," I say simply. "In big comics it's often split up into two pieces. The art and the writing. Some people get to do both. Quite a lot of the commercial stuff is published so fast that it's easier for one person to do one, and one to do the other. I lay out a general story line and break it into pages and panels. Then the artist draws what they think matches with the story. Sometimes it's a two-way street and they feel really strongly about a panel they want to draw, and I adjust the story or the structure of the page for it."

We lapse into silence. I can't quit contemplating my damn shoes at his house. Like a splatter of yellow paint from a dropped brush on an otherwise pristine page of line drawings. A puzzle to figure out, like there's something to put together. The feeling his house has been *missing* my shoes.

"Were you ever married?" My words fall out before I check them.

"Going right for the big guns, huh?" But he doesn't look upset.

"It seems like if we're supposed to be dating that I would know."

"I was engaged for a few years."

"Oh. What happened?" I want to smack myself. "Wait, you don't have to answer that. That's really nosy."

I catch a flash of white teeth as he laughs again, and my spirits buoy. "It's okay. And you don't need to be sorry. I'm glad I figured out it wouldn't work before we got married and had kids. She was an actress—"

"Ah. No need to explain further. They are a breed apart." LA is swimming with wannabes, almost-wases, and has-beens. Neck-deep. Can't throw a rock without hitting one.

He smirks. "She wanted to live in the city and constantly be out for exposure. When I sold my place in LA and moved out here, she didn't like having to drive in for auditions or shopping. She was wonderful and vibrant and fun. Cliché as it sounds, she was like an exotic flower. She didn't fit in the desert, which is where *I* fit."

My mind goes directly to his lush courtyard full of exotic-looking vegetation. Did he plant them just for her? An oasis for his love? I'm admittedly a *little* jealous of said exotic flower, but I push it down. I get what he's saying. It resonates deeply, like a chord struck in me. "Dreams have to match up. Or at least be compatible side by side." I'm not sure what else to say, but it seems to be enough.

He nods. "How about you? Ever married?"

"God no." I snort. Then I feel bad. He's told me about his; I can at least return the favor. "I was almost engaged once when I was too young—my first year of law school. He didn't 'get' me, and I had the good sense to end it before we made each other miserable. There hasn't been time after that. Or anyone who seems pleasant enough to deal with for a lifetime."

There haven't been a pair of shoes that could sit next to mine in a doorway for more than a few months. Tom worked for my dad while I was in law school. My first *real* love, forever trying to change me. The night he asked me to marry him—two kids in love who had no idea what they wanted in the world—he told me that if I said yes, I "wouldn't have to write those comics anymore—not work at all when we had kids." It was my moment of reckoning, looking at a future just like my parents'. No fun, no color, no passion, no room to be crazy into geek fandoms. Tied down. Boring. Typical. I didn't *want* to be typical. I wanted to be a superhero. I told him *no thank you*, dropped out of school, colored my hair the next day, and never looked back, even after my parents told me they wouldn't give me another dime if I didn't finish law school.

Enter the Hurtling Turd, my new crew, and the job at Genius I landed after three years of freelance writing that had finally made my dream come true. But here I am thinking that just *maybe* something has been missing. Maybe I like how my shoes look next to Matteo's. He intrigues me, makes me feel a way I haven't before in my life. Longing for stability. For permanence. For partnership, where before I was a content party of one. Pretty heavy stuff.

"I've been thinking about the case," I say, not taking my eyes from his face. "And I read some of my old comics last night looking for the White Rabbit." I want to see how crazy he thinks I am away from the crime scene and away from his partner.

No sign of a smirk. "And?"

"I can't help but feel like this bust is more than what it seems on the surface. Everything has lined up with the comic books, maybe too well. This person, the Golden Arrow. Why not just call the police, report drug activity, and call it a night? It's like they're trying to indicate that they're following a certain person or story line. It's like trying to read tarot from a normal deck of playing cards—like I'm looking for something that isn't there. But. My gut says it's worth following the *story*, not just the crimes. The connection. The presence of a drug war, then and now. The heroin in a warehouse. It's going to sound crazy, but I'm a writer, and I draw off of real life all the time. What if Casey Senior wrote about a real drug ring? And somehow the Golden Arrow figured it out?"

Silence.

"But why would the crimes repeat themselves if they already happened thirty years ago?" Matteo takes another sip of coffee and mulls over his next words before speaking. "Right before Casey Senior died, there was a huge bust of the biggest heroin rings in the city. The streets were cleaned up. I'm not saying you're wrong. It's just how would we ever go about proving it's all related?"

I let out a breath. His willingness to listen frees up my mind to start piecing story threads together. That bust he's talking about—the city was rid of its most notorious criminals. But maybe *someone* has survived and had their pickings of a marketplace conveniently cleared of competitors. "In the comic, the next steps are catching smugglers on the boat and chasing the White Rabbit. I think we'd be smart to look at the shipping logs. Stake out the warehouse. Search to see if there are connections to China."

Matteo nods slowly. "As it stands, I'm set to interrogate the man from the warehouse who had the rabbit on his hoodie. It *was* painted on. We just need to figure out why, or if he saw the person responsible. If all this is more than coincidence, we're also possibly looking for a double agent. Maybe *that's* why our Golden Arrow can't come to the police," Matteo adds.

I give one nod, unwilling to comment. It's true. If we are following this story to its extent, we are also looking for a dirty cop. I keep thinking this seems designed for . . . well, *me*. Like the Golden Arrow expects *me* to put together these clues, and it's unsettling.

Matteo shrugs. "I'm just glad you stumbled upon me in the coffee shop to help us out. We'd have no clue without you. We'll call it divine providence until we see a reason to think otherwise. Ready to go?" He drains the rest of his cup, and I follow suit.

"We'll review what you know about your coworkers in the car. Yours or mine?" He pats his pants pockets, looking for the little notebook he carries everywhere.

"Let's take mine," I reply. But as we walk briskly to the door, I can't help but feel oddly sad about leaving. Though this whole case is complicated, my thoughts feel more in order here, in this quiet place with this quiet man. There's something serene that would possibly become addictive. I can picture sitting with Matteo, each of us with a book in front of the fireplace . . . and I slam the door shut on that vision. Again I am reminded that Matteo isn't just some guy I keep hanging out with. We have a crime to solve, and we are both in uncharted territory.

CHAPTER 14

"So we're looking for a costume, a cape, anything that would suggest knowledge about drugs and crime, and Hooded Falcon *anything*," Matteo reminds me on the doorstep of Kyle's house.

"Roger that. I hope you're ready for geek immersion."

As the door opens, I school my features, trying to look like I'm not snooping in my coworkers' lives in order to solve a drug-related crime spree. We make it perhaps two feet inside before we're attacked by geekery. A small herd of people descends on us wielding wands and a large floppy brown hat—bringing forcefully to mind the time I was attacked by geese at MacArthur Park. I hate nature.

Before I can defend myself, the large floppy hat lands on my head, covering my eyes, and the darn thing starts to *sing*. When the hat ceases its wagging, it crows, "*Better be . . . Hufflepuff!*" much to the delight of those standing by. I recognize Kyle's sarcastic snort.

"I would have bet Slytherin." Most definitely Kyle. I lift the brim.

"You'd better be glad I don't have my rubber-band gun, Kyle. Plus, what a lame welcome. I'm *obviously* a Gryffindor. I demand a retrial."

A titter of laughter ripples around the group, and the hat is replaced on my head. It does its jiggly dance, and I stand patiently until it crows, "*Better be . . . Gryffindor!*" More laughter as it's pulled back off and transferred to Matteo's head.

He ducks so that a tiny elf of a girl can put it on him, ever gracious even while wearing a clear WTF expression.

The sight of the large pointed sorting hat on Matteo's head causes dragons and glee to bang around my ribcage in a death match. "I don't know about this one . . . I think he might be a Squib."

Matteo knows he's been insulted and throws me a playful dirty look.

"Better be . . . *Ravenclaw!*"

I'm already clapping. "Yes! That's perfect! You are *so* a book nerd!"

He still looks baffled. "What is a Ravenclaw?"

The same woman who put the hat on his head holds out her hand. "It's your Hogwarts house! You may now enter the party! I'm Nina, Kyle's fiancée, and a Hufflepuff. We've heard so much about you, Matteo. And you too, of course, MG. I'm so glad you could make it!"

Her perkiness goes beyond normal irritation and into the realm of . . . infectious. I find myself smiling back. "Thanks for inviting us." I lean over as if I'm telling her a secret in a stage whisper. "Matteo is new to a lot of this."

She squeals and claps. Kyle wanders up behind her and throws his arm around her shoulders. "MG. Matteo. Welcome!" He points to the kitchen. "The house-elves are in there." He points over to a large living room where five or six people are sitting, already engrossed in conversation. "*Star Wars* marathon starts in about ten minutes in there." He opens a door directly to the right of the entry, which reveals stairs. "Downstairs will be a mix of *Settlers of Catan* tournament and random episodes of *TNG*. There's a Charmander nest down the street for those in the office *Pokémon GO* competition, and"—he glances at his Apple watch and finishes off with an announcement at large—"pizza will arrive at four p.m.!"

I give a mock salute, and Matteo follows me like a puppy into the kitchen, where the masses have descended.

"What do you do, Matteo?" Nina munches on a baby carrot.

"I went to architecture school," Matteo responds with his pat answer, and I pray for a diversion away from his job description because while *he* can hold it together, I can't lie to my coworkers that well. Any diversion. Some kung fu vampires to pop up from a grave who need slaying. Anything.

"He's an *architect* and he fixed my chair in two seconds flat," Kyle responds. Total bromance.

I clear my throat. "How about you, Nina? What do you do?"

"I'm an actress—theatre, not movie. *Hamlet*. Neil Simon. Stuff like that. And then I help do some production management stuff to actually pay the bills." She laughs.

"That's really neat. Actually, I've always wanted to do costumes for theater but have never pursued it."

"You do costume design?" She looks impressed.

"I take a few commissions. Mostly drag shows right now, but I want to get into art direction so that I can help design superhero costume adaptations. Maybe do costume work on the side." I bite my lip and cut a look at Kyle, hoping I haven't said too much. This is why I don't attend work parties. I suck at playing politics.

Kyle doesn't even bat an eyelash at my work comment but dives right in about the costumes. "That's really cool. I didn't know you did that. You'd be great at costume design. Your costume sketches are the best on our team." His straightforward vote of confidence nearly bowls me over, especially given my role within the team is usually the dialogue, and his is usually the panel art. He shoves chips into his mouth and turns toward the Crock-Pot.

"Stock up. This looks like serious business," I say to Matteo, eyeing the spread of a humongous Subway sandwich bar and several home-made-looking sides. My stomach literally growls as I spot a huge bowl of my favorite artichoke dip from the Christmas parties.

"So, MG, if you do costumes . . . can I talk to you about something?" Nina moves closer to me and drops her voice. Her eyes dart to the Crock-Pot as if attempting to gauge whether Kyle can hear her.

"Sure, what's up?"

"Well, Kyle will kill me for asking, but I know he and Simon have been doing this extracurricular stuff, and they need to make it official. With costumes. I was going to try to hack something together myself, but . . . Well, if you're a professional, we could just hire you to do it."

My heart races, and I channel my mental energy into *not* gaping at her like a fish. I didn't even have to snoop! Proof that Simon and Kyle are two superheroes in want of costuming! On one hand, I'm shocked they've managed to elude police thus far, but on the other hand, I'm glad that this mystery can finally get solved. They can just *tell* us what they know about the White Rabbit. I school my features. "Oh, yeah, um, of course. I'd love to. What kind of costumes are we talking?"

Nina eyes the floor. "Well, you're a fellow geek. I'm sure you'd understand, but I need chain mail."

I blink. "Chain mail?" Wouldn't that be a little heavy when scaling the side of a warehouse?

"Well, a whole knight costume really. I know it sounds silly, but they are having so much *fun* learning to sword fight."

"Sword fight."

"It's this whole LARPing group they joined to keep fit. Sword fighting, metal working, rope making, stuff like that."

Live-action role-playing. I've heard of it. Never done it myself, but I don't hold it against anyone if they want to nerd out in costume. But this negates what I thought would be a big break in the case and possibly means Kyle and Simon are up to nothing more than hitting each other with wooden swords. Or cardboard tubes, like the ones under their desk. I inwardly groan. I need to tell Matteo.

The man in question now leans so close to me, I can smell his aftershave. It's a heady scent, and my brain swims with his closeness. Is he playing up the dating thing? Is he possibly going to kiss my shoulder? Or give me a hug from behind? I am so lost in *that* role-playing fantasy that when he speaks he takes me by surprise.

"*What* is a pufflehuff?"

I snort. "*Hufflepuff.* It's another Hogwarts house, from Harry Potter," I whisper back, reveling in his aftershave awhile longer.

"Is that the wizard thing?"

"It's a person. And yes, he's a wizard. Why do you ask?"

Matteo nods toward Andy. "That guy over there said that he'd thought for sure I'd be in that Hufflepuff house. I told him it sounded girly." He lowers his voice until just I can hear him. "Plus, I need to be making notes about your coworkers, so maybe you can introduce me?" I bite my lip but nod, and we shuffle around the kitchen until we're in a corner between the sandwiches and the artichoke dip.

I keep my voice low, anxiety pooling in my belly. It's normal that I introduce everyone to my guest, right? *Act natural.* I point in turn at the people in the room with us. "That's Andy. He's essentially my boss. He presents our team's work to the executive art directors at Genius. He really doesn't seem the type to chase anyone, much less bad guys, but that's your area of expertise." And the guy who steals my ideas to get *my* promotion. Even if he did do a *teensy* bit better job packaging my ideas. I'm not quite ready to forgive him, though, so I'm going to just continue to studiously avoid him today.

"Next is Kyle, who you met. He's an illustrator, and he works on the new *Hooded Falcon* and whatever other current Genius comics are tying in. There's Tej over there; he's the most charming guy you'll ever meet. He works on adaptations for films, coordinating with developers, marketing, press releases, that sort of thing. He's not always a part of our work team, but he's awesome." He's also gorgeous, geek or not. Mocha skin, dark hair always updated with the trends, immaculate clothes, and black plastic-frame Clark Kent glasses. He's laughing in the living room with a woman I assume is his girlfriend or wife. I'm newly ashamed that I don't even know if my coworkers are married.

Simon steps into the kitchen, so I introduce him, hoping it comes off as natural. "And this is Simon. He's the illustrator I work with the most. His desk is right next to mine, and he's helping me with *Hooded*

Falcon and *Hero Girls* right now, although I hear tell that he's going to be pulled onto a revival of *The Green Monster*. Version six hundred million."

"Version six hundred million and *one*," Simon corrects, reaching out to shake Matteo's hand before pointing to the girl deep in conversation with Nina. "And that's my wife, Isabella—no relation."

Matteo looks thrown. "No relation to . . ."

"*Twilight*?" Simon smirks. "Sparklepires?"

"Let's not destroy Matteo's perfect and pristine mental canvas with that," I say, looping an arm around Matteo. His middle is solid, and I can't keep myself from wondering if he has a six-pack like the cops on TV have. A moment later I let it drop, unsure if the contact is appropriate.

"You've never heard of *Twilight*?" Simon asks.

Matteo gives an affable grin. "Unless you mean the Zone, no."

Simon studies Matteo the way a scientist studies a curious specimen. "So what fandoms *are* you into?"

"Fandoms?" The word is obviously foreign in Matteo's mouth.

"It means, What are you a fan of? What do you watch? Who do you ship?" I pop a baby carrot in my mouth, devilishly relishing his squirming under the question.

"Ship?" he asks finally, rubbing the back of his neck. He shoots me a look that plainly says, "Help!"

"Ships are couples. Shorthand for 'relationship' originally, but now just means two people you want to see get together." I really should help him. Really, I should. Simon watches us with naked glee on his face.

Matteo frowns. "I liked that Arwen lady and Strider? Is that a ship?"

I struggle not to correct him that Arwen was an elf and not a lady. Though kudos to Matteo for being able to even name Arwen from *LOTR*. I try to hide my distaste. Those books are long and boring, with a few exciting dragon chapters followed by long and boring.

Simon nods. "Ah, so you're a fantasy geek. I can dig that. Sorry it's not *D&D* downstairs."

"Don't you like *The Lord of the Rings*?" Matteo asks me, puzzled.

"Not my favorite. I'm more of a space geek. *Trek*, *Wars*, *Battlestar*, *Firefly*, *Doctor Who*—science fiction, space opera. That sort of stuff." I turn to Simon. "He's new to all this."

"So there are *types* of . . ." He probably wants to say "geeks," but I can see he's afraid of offending Simon.

Tej leans in around Simon and dips a chip into the French onion dip. "Geekdom? You betcha. I am a fellow fantasy geek." He executes a mini bow. "People come at geekdom from different directions. There's the Japanese anime lovers, like my wife. Then there's the band and music geeks—"

"Guilty as charged." Andy waves a hand. We've attracted everyone's attention apparently. "I played oboe." *He would.*

"Music geeks like to dabble. A little of this, a little of that," Simon finishes.

"And then there are the space geeks," Tej adds.

I raise my hand. "Although every once in a while, if I've had some wine, I do like *Game of Thrones*. Or should I call it 'Death and Boobies'? Brienne of Tarth is my Patronus."

Tej cracks up. "Yeah, you need to drink for that show."

At this point, Matteo has his arms crossed over his chest and is staring between us like we're speaking a different language. "What on *earth* is a Patronus?"

"Well, technically our animal counterpart when you use the *Expecto Patronum* spell. But it can also mean a character you love. Or admire. It's pretty standard in the geek world. For example, if you ever need to *find your people*, it's totally legit to yell out, 'Who's your Patronus?'" Simon makes it a point by yelling the last words. It's a game we play in the office from time to time.

"No one could possibly be prepared for—" Matteo is cut off by a chorus of answers from various rooms in the house.

"Giles from *Buffy*!"

"Katniss Everdeen!" This from Nina, who looks pretty fierce for a wee one.

"Neil deGrasse Tyson!" Simon answers his own question with a smile.

Kyle steps into the kitchen and taps Matteo on the shoulder. "Hey, do you want to play *Settlers* or just hang with the lady friend and watch the movies? I can sign you up if you want." He holds up a clipboard.

"Absolutely Ron Swanson from *Parks and Rec*," Tej answers.

"Dana Scully," Tej's wife calls.

I offer her a fist bump. "Word. Dana Scully is amazing."

Matteo turns to me, wide-eyed. "How do I know who *my* Patronus is? Can you look it up somewhere?"

This brings a wave of laughter from everyone gathered.

"Okay, okay. Nothing to see here. Move along." I try to fight my own laughter. "Babe, we'll visit Pottermore sometime. For now I think"—I tap my chin—"Wash from *Firefly*."

Kyle arrives back in the kitchen carrying the *Settlers of Catan* box. "Okay, I'm headed downstairs after I start the movies."

After the spirit animals conversation, Matteo sticks to me like glue. I'm his life raft in this sea of awesome. "Oh good, I'm curious about these *Star Wars* movies. I've heard about them a lot since meeting MG."

You could have heard a pin drop.

Kyle sucks in a breath. "You've never *seen Star Wars*? Like, *ever*?"

"Never seen them, no. Is that bad?" Matteo has failed his entrance exam to my world. *Never seen Star Wars.*

"We've got ourselves a *virgin*!" Kyle grasps Matteo's shoulders in his hands and shakes him back and forth with enthusiasm. "Don't worry. We'll be gentle. Well, at least I'll be gentle. The jury is still out on MG."

I cough to cover the rush of heat spreading on my face, and beside me, Matteo's hands spasm.

"Where on *earth* did you find him?" This question is to me, and I can tell that Kyle is baffled I'm dating someone so far outside our world.

"You'd never believe it," I say with a smile. I turn to Matteo, having a bit of a hard time meeting his eyes after the virginity comment. "Shall we?"

I escort him into the living room. This should be more than interesting. I've never seen *Star Wars* for anyone's first time.

Matteo pops the bottle cap on a beer and takes a swig. "Let the beatings begin."

"We will watch these movies in the only order that should ever be presented," Kyle announces while slipping the first Blu-ray disc into the player. "Today will be episodes IV, V, VI. Next weekend I, II, III, and *Rogue One*." There is some mild booing from the crowd at this, and Kyle waves his hand. "I know. We all have to deal with Jar Jar together, but I'm a purist, and we can't skip them. And *then* we'll watch the new ones, starting with *The Force Awakens*."

Matteo leans over. "Why would we watch episode IV before episode I?"

"So much to learn have you, young Padawan. It's the historical release order."

Matteo's eyes dart to the side, then back to mine. His tone is confessional, his eyes furtive. "I wasn't expecting this to be so much . . . fun. It makes it hard to do my job. Your coworkers are a blast."

I'm having fun too, and Matteo makes it hard for *me* to focus on the case. He's *too* good at playing boyfriend. I smile and bump his shoulder with mine. The fun is just starting. "Just wait until you see the movies."

I've seen these movies at least twenty times, and I'm used to making snarky comments and pointing out filming errors. I haven't watched *Star Wars* without a liberal dose of cynicism since I was ten years old.

But something funny begins to happen when we start *A New Hope.* The words scrawl across the screen, and Matteo reads them out loud, and a shiver runs down my spine. This whole universe is about to be opened up to him, and I'm the one who gets to introduce him to the marvels of the *Millennium Falcon.* And R2-D2. And I'm seriously hoping this is the old cut with the non-remastered Jabba. I realize I'm giddy. It feels magical. Like the first time I saw them myself and got caught up in the wonder of it all, instead of wondering where the stormtroopers got so much PVC to make their armor in space.

And it's not just me. The enjoyment level amps up across the room. No one goes downstairs to play *Settlers.* Everyone is up here because it feels new and exciting. Instead of being on the outside, I can feel Matteo being encircled by my coworkers, and it fills my insides with warm fuzzies. I snuggle onto the couch, trying to walk the line of looking like a couple without crossing professional boundaries. I settle for legs touching, but no cuddling.

"These aren't the droids you're looking for" launches a whole conversation—which requires pausing the movie—between Matteo and Tej about the Force. Kyle jumps in, explaining the finer points of robotics in the Empire. I sit back and watch all of this unfold, feeling like a spectator on several levels. I'm grateful that my coworkers invited us and teased Matteo a little but then welcomed him into the fold. They didn't *have* to do that. Heck, I don't think *I* would have done it if the tables were turned. How many guys have I dumped after the first date because they just "didn't get" my life or my geek culture references? I didn't have time to educate people. Matteo kind of forced my hand, but he's *into* it. My own universe expands a smidge.

Matteo laughs at the right times, sits forward at the right times. He's not just pretending. I catch myself watching him more than the movie, my heart beating in my throat, pulse pounding in my body. This is *sexy.* Instead of being repulsed by his non-geekdom, I'm inarguably attracted by it. A wave of heat suffuses my face, and I sit against the back of the couch, needing a breath of air, a small moment to gain my composure. My heart is pounding like I've just run a mile.

"You okay?" Matteo leans his head into mine as the movie hits a quiet spell. He pats my knee in a way that is meant to appear classically affectionate but ends up shooting spirals of energy right through my middle. I'm having an internal meltdown because he *touched my leg*. How *thirty going on thirteen* can I get?

"Yeah. Of course. You?" *If by "okay" you mean "melting inside."*

"I'm having a great time." The words sound affable and normal. But our eyes meet, and there's *something* that catches there. Something that sparks in his gaze to mirror my own unguarded reaction. His hand stops patting and holds my knee, his long fingers nearly encircling my leg. The gesture is no longer a play at affection. It's a searing brand on my leg. The heat between us isn't make-believe. In this moment it's real and palpable. Our gazes lock in the slowly waning afternoon light. It's the first moment that I know for certain he feels this crazy pull too. The crazy pull that we can't do anything about because we're solving a crime together.

The sounds of scuffle—Obi Wan disarming the ruffian threatening Luke—return us to reality, and we turn to regard the screen. Matteo's hand falls off my knee, and he sits back, intentionally putting distance between our bodies. I don't blame him. My own chest is rising and falling faster than sitting on a couch warrants. That was some sort of intense moment, and I know we need to focus on why we're here, not give in to my urges to make out on the couch.

"So do you guys do this every weekend?" It's a casual question for Matteo to ask, but I sense he's going somewhere with this, like he just read my thoughts. Are we that in tune?

Kyle grabs a pillow off the couch, presses pause on the remote, and leans against the coffee table, Nina snuggling under one arm. "Nah. Once or twice a year."

"It seems like there's so much I need to learn," Matteo says, eyes still glued to the TV. "What did you watch last weekend? I need to start keeping a list." Matteo not only has an ulterior motive, but he's a skilled professional when it comes to gaining information and feeling out alibis.

Kyle laughs. "We'll get you squared away. We actually didn't watch anything last weekend. Nina had her fifteen-year high school reunion, and I took work along for the hotel."

"It was so romantic," Nina intoned, not batting an eye.

Matteo muffles a laugh with a cough. "I bet. Was the hotel nice, at least?"

"Holiday Inns aren't too bad. Good Wi-Fi."

Nina ignores him. "We were in San Diego. The weather was awful, though. Kyle actually left the party really early and drove back up here because he worried about moving his artwork around in the rain."

Only I see Matteo's attention snap to Kyle. Because I can read *him* now too, I know he's wondering if Kyle was up in LA in enough time to get to the warehouse district. But has he *seen* Kyle? The guy couldn't wrestle a squirrel. He's shorter than me, wiry, and about as nonthreatening as Trogdor. Not to mention that I found out about the sword fighting, which shoots my theory to hell.

"It's my *job* to care about my art," Kyle says, rolling his eyes. "Now quiet. This part is *so* great."

"Maybe you were late for a sword fighting lesson?" I ask sweetly, batting my eyes at Kyle.

"No—wait. How did you? Nina, did you *tell her*?" Kyle eyes Nina with mock horror.

"I asked her to make you and Simon costumes, so relax." Nina rolls her eyes, shoves a chip in her mouth, and turns back to the TV.

"It's no big deal," I say, "but it sure puts my mind at ease about why I found cardboard tubes under my desk the other day. But what do you need duct tape for? I assumed it was something kinky. Now I'm assuming it's something dorky." I hope Matteo's picking up my intentional mention of the clues.

Simon's face has turned red now too. "The duct tape holds our cardboard armor on. I didn't realize you saw that stuff."

"Cardboard . . . armor?" Matteo looks between Simon and me, completely baffled.

I make a show of turning to Matteo. "You see, it turns out that Kyle and Simon are learning to sword fight and make ropes and draw pictures like medieval times. It's called role-playing."

Matteo turns to Kyle, comprehension dawning on his face. "You said an old lady hit you. Is this actually what happened to your arm?"

Kyle chugs the rest of his beer in what I take as a ploy to look more manly. "Sword fighting. Yeah."

Simon cackles with glee. "It really *was* an old lady. Kyle got his ass handed to him."

"Hey, man, you have to partner with her next week, so shut up." Kyle tosses the empty can onto the coffee table.

"So you guys have been fake sword fighting with old ladies." Matteo looks part gleeful and part disappointed. Exactly my feeling. No lead on the Golden Arrow, but a damn fine story.

Simon scoffs, acting offended. "Sword fighting is *hard*. And we do other stuff too. We're learning to write with quill and ink, illuminations, stuff like that. There are guilds and crafts, and it's all very historically accurate. Scientific, even."

This doesn't mean that Kyle or Simon *can't* be the Golden Arrow; it just makes it less likely. I'm relieved but bummed. I never wanted Kyle or Simon to be the vigilante, but here we are back at square one. At a dead end with no promising leads.

"Can we go back to watching the movies, please?" Kyle shoots Nina another dirty look and presses play just in time for my favorite scene: Han in the cantina.

I usually roll my eyes about the alien-Muppet costumes, but this time is better because I get to watch Matteo recognize young Harrison Ford. And again, I get the distinct impression that he's truly *enjoying* this, even if he's also finding a way to question each of the couples about their past few weekends. When he gets up to use the restroom after the first movie, I wonder if it's to make notes.

"You guys are cute together." By the accent, I assume it's Tej's wife behind me. She went to the door to grab pizza between films.

I smile. "Thanks."

"I've seen you before at work functions and at the office Christmas party, and you always seemed so reserved. Focused on work. I don't know you well, but I can tell you're different around him."

She may not know me well, but she's hit the nail on the head, and that freaks me out. I *am* different around Matteo. Where I'm usually too busy to take time away from furthering my career, Matteo is a breath of fresh air in my life I didn't even know I needed. Something to turn me on my head and give me a fresh perspective. I always tell myself how happy I am with my party of one, but tonight I've glimpsed a version of me that would hang out for movie marathons with coworkers. He's opened my eyes to some of what I've been missing to uphold my persona at work. I'd never have come except for Matteo, and I realize just how lonely a party of one can be sometimes. How can one person affect me so much in a matter of a week?

My phone buzzes in my pocket, and I seize the opportunity to escape. "I'm sorry. I have to go grab this." I hold the phone to my ear even though I received a text message, say "Hello?" loudly enough to be heard, and step out the front door.

The text from Matteo is short:

Come upstairs.

I wait a few moments for effect, then head back inside, shooting a quick glance to the kitchen, where the pizza is quickly disappearing. No one will miss me.

I find Matteo in a bedroom upstairs standing at a closet. He's not just taking notes; he's *snooping*.

"Isn't this illegal?" I hiss, poking my head back out the door to make sure no one followed me upstairs.

"I got lost on my way to the bathroom. Come look at this."

I stand beside him and peer into the closet. Costumes of all types line the wall. Including a Hooded Falcon, complete with hooded cape. I chew my lip. "We go to a lot of conventions. It's a part of the job."

"There you guys are. The second movie is starting," Nina's voice comes from the doorway, and I jump about a mile high.

"Oh, um, we were just . . ."

Nina gives me a bawdy wink. "It's fine. I see you've discovered our costume closet. We just got that Hooded Falcon one last week off eBay. I thought it would be fun for Kyle to go as the Falcon for the anniversary gala, although I'm going to have to do some sizing work. Maybe you could help with that, MG. Right now Kyle would trip and fall on his face, the cape is so long. Are we going to get to see you in costume, Matteo?"

I shoot Matteo a look. "Oh, I, um, I've already invited my friend Lawrence." I haven't even thought about inviting Matteo to my work party. Silly me, as I didn't *have* a fake boyfriend two weeks ago when I invited Lawrence.

"Maybe I'll just have to change her mind about that. I look dashing in a cape, or so I imagine." Matteo plays the ever-doting boyfriend and pulls me against his chest. My heart does somersaults. I bet he *does* look dashing in a cape.

"Second movie is starting!" Kyle yells from the living room.

"Come on, let's go. I don't want to miss anything." Matteo grabs my arm, and we follow Nina downstairs where we settle back onto the couch. I end up leaning against the armrest, my feet across Matteo's lap. It's cozy, and some of my ruffled feathers settle. I'm fairly certain Kyle isn't the Golden Arrow. He and Simon never seem particularly *up* for fighting crime in the real world. They're more fit for the Dork Squad than the Justice League. The case remains a mystery. My gaze returns to Matteo.

Watching the second movie is just as endearing as the first, even as I mull over the case in my head. And my fake boyfriend. I'm a little afraid he's taken my heart by surprise and not just my mind.

CHAPTER 15

I bang my head slowly on the desk in hopes of reawakening all my carefully cultivated brain cells. Ever since the work party this weekend, my mind has been a gooey mess of crime stories gone wrong, developing L's costume for Comic-Con, and hot cop fantasies instead of focusing on the circus of deadlines parading through my week. I still haven't started my *Hero Girls* pages, and the rough outlines are due to Andy by Wednesday. I'm still fiddling with the ending for my *Hooded Falcon* pages—those are headed to the printer for a test run on Friday, come hell or high water. And speaking of, I still haven't said a word to Andy, even though it's 2:00 p.m. on Monday and we've been in the office all day together. My mind feels stuck, swirling, and I blame it all on Matteo. So what if I like him? More than like him. No biggie, just solve something the DEA and LAPD can't crack; then I can ask him out. There's no reason for this creative stagnation and romantic angsting. Especially since I've heard *zero* from Matteo since I dropped him off at his house after the party. He's obviously not pining personally or professionally. No updates on the clues. No updates on the warehouse. Nada.

I've been drowning my woes in sewing sequins . . . something that normally drives me batty but has been like a life raft for my fingers, which have been itching to pick up the phone.

"Yo, MG. You all right?" This from Simon, who has removed his headphones and can hear me banging my head.

Show no weakness. Give no quarter. "Yep." I continue to bang my forehead.

He pauses. "You don't look okay."

"You've obviously never seen creative genius at work." I sit up and slap my palm to the desk, sick of my own mental waffling. Would Buffy just sit home and wait for a vampire to show up? No, ma'am. She'd strap on her favorite halter and go patrolling. It's time for stomping boots. I'm going to get my work done. Then I'm calling Matteo to ask for an update. Yes, *calling*.

As if summoned by my thought, my phone buzzes, and Lawrence's face pops up on my screen. One of the only people I ever answer for; God help me if I ever take a call from my mother again. I forgo formalities because he's my bestie and I know why he's calling. "Sorry I didn't deliver those costumes last night. I ended up restitching that cummerbund. Twice. I'll get everything to you Friday before the show, I promise."

Silence greets my words.

"L? Did you pocket dial me?"

"Did you come to my house last night?"

"I—what? No. I didn't get a chance to drop off the costumes. Why?" A chill of foreboding makes its way down my spine.

"I don't know. I think someone was in the shop. It's very strange. A few things are moved, but all the money is here."

My mind goes back to my room, where I felt the exact same sensation. My stuff had been moved, but nothing taken. Surely this couldn't have anything to do with the case? That would be ridiculous. Yet . . .

I probably should come clean to Lawrence. Tell him about the case, about Matteo. About how I told the police about Lawrence's journal. Could Matteo be the one who broke into Lawrence's? Can cops even do that? Or maybe the dirty cop is responsible. Or . . . the Golden Arrow. My paranoia's amping up because it seems like I am at the center of this somehow. That the Golden Arrow is watching me and those I love. Watching the case. Watching but waiting for . . . what? Better to ask Matteo first then talk to Lawrence.

Time to throw some shade, even though it kills me to do it. Stall tactic. "Do you think you're being paranoid?" I don't; Lawrence is probably spot-on. But what if Lawrence ends up like that hanging dummy? I need to talk to Matteo, stat.

"Maybe." Lawrence doesn't sound convinced.

"I'll see you tonight, right? We can talk more about it then. Just . . . make sure to double-lock your door. Maybe it was some homeless person who got in and took a nap on your couch again." I force my voice to be bright and cheery.

I hang up just as a text message comes through. As if called by my bat signal, Matteo's name appears.

> Scheduled interview with your boss at the station. Can you be here around 3 to watch on closed circuit? You might have to prompt comic book questions if it's needed.

I punch my affirmative reply and straighten my shoulders. I'm Janeway. Captain of my own destiny. I have things to do, friends to save, and gold lamé hot pants to finish before the show tonight. That thought lifts my doom and gloom a smidgen. Sometimes glitter and men in drag are exactly what a girl needs to be set right again.

And sometimes all it takes to make your day is seeing your jerk of a boss in an interrogation room at the police department. The satisfaction I feel watching him nervously sip the water on the table makes up for a lot of the grief he's given me over the years. I'm heady with power as I realize I can have Matteo ask him *anything* I want. I fight the urge to do a villain laugh. I will use my powers for good, but I'm going to watch him sweat first.

Literally. Casey Junior is a big-boned man, and I can see beads of sweat forming at his receding hairline. He keeps his head buzzed to hide his balding, but the dark stubble forms a wicked widow's peak. Otherwise he looks comfortable in his navy suit and brown shoes. Always together. Always the boss. Even when he's nervous.

"Thanks for agreeing to speak with us," I hear Matteo's voice before I see him on the compact TV screen. He tucks his tie as he slides into the chair across from Edward Casey Junior.

I'm in the next room but could be watching this anywhere. Rideout is supposed to be watching with me to pass along any questions I have, but so far I haven't seen him. Not that I'm too bothered by it. We already had a small powwow and decided Matteo would question Casey alone, unless he thought he needed a "bad cop" to play against.

Casey gives Matteo a winning smile despite his moisture. "Anything for the LAPD. Though I can't think why you would need to interview me, I'm happy to give my time." Add "always the politician" to his list of attributes.

"Well, we have a fascinating case on our hands that seems to be something in the way of your expertise. We could think of no one better to ask advice from."

"Oh. Ask away." Casey Junior's shoulders relax instantaneously. His face gains color. Matteo's methods are spot-on; even I know that a relaxed suspect shares more information. Let him think we're on his side then *wham-o*. Got your nose.

"I'm sure you've seen the news about this Golden Arrow?" I can see only part of Matteo's face—the camera is aimed mostly at Casey—but by the set of Matteo's shoulders, he's watching Casey as closely as I am for any hint that he knows more than he should.

Casey barely covers up a snort of derision. "That lunatic probably makes your job hard to do these days. Damn shame, but it's driving up Genius business, so I can't complain. How can I help?"

"Well, we think the Golden Arrow may be taking on the persona of one of *your* superheroes. We're hoping you can shed light on why they may have picked this particular comic book."

"I'll do what I can, of course, but there's no point in trying to figure out why someone who is mentally unbalanced does whatever they do. They could have picked any superhero."

"We think there's more to it than that. That's where you come in. The vigilante has been busting drug dealers and re-creating panels from one of the last *Hooded Falcon* issues your father published before he died. Do you know if your father wrote about any real crimes at all? We're looking for a connection between this drug ring and the comics your father wrote."

This question stops Casey dead in his tracks. He swallows noisily and sits back, jovial manner gone. "I, uh, that's an interesting question to ask. Certainly he was inspired by real events. Constantly poring over the newspaper for inspiration. But what does that have to do with what you're investigating?"

The warning light in my head flashes. There's something *more* here.

"Here's the thing: the media isn't reporting this because we haven't released the information, but there was a note at the first scene that indicated a connection to Genius Comics. At the most recent warehouse bust, there was a white rabbit spray-painted both at the scene of the crime and on a suspect. We're trying to determine if there's a *real* White Rabbit out there, and you are one of the only people who would be able to help us with that, Mr. Casey."

Dead silence. I didn't expect Matteo to take this tack at all. It raises the hairs on the back of my neck. He hasn't asked about a costume or an alibi. He's gone in with my suspicions and gone in swinging, presenting them like fact and not wild speculation. Calculated, professional, to the point. This is Detective Kildaire in all his glory, traces of "my" Matteo gone.

"I . . . You're sure?" He doesn't seem surprised. His ashen face looks closer to *terrified*.

Matteo leans forward, and I can just see the compelling and serious expression on his handsome face. "Deadly sure. It's why we need to get to the bottom of this. The drug lords are after this wannabe superhero, and they've picked up on the comic book connection too. They could target your staff and your building if we don't shut this down. If you think you know something, I suggest you share it."

"I-I was younger when my father wrote it. Dad didn't discuss everything with me, but yes. Honestly, I think he wrote about something real."

"What makes you think that?"

Casey takes a deep breath, holds it in for a long count, then lets it back out slowly. He raises his eyes to Matteo's face. I know that look. I see it in the boardroom monthly. He's taking Matteo's measure. His fingers cease fidgeting on the table, and Casey seems to take hold of himself. From my vantage point, it looks like he's about to be truly honest with Matteo.

"My father *did* always use the newspaper for inspiration; that's true. And the drug culture in LA in the eighties was insane. The comic book was his way of trying to change the ills of the world. I mean, he was constantly trying to help out kids from bad situations. He'd hire them or mentor them when he could, but it was more than that. My father saw *himself* as some sort of superhero." The last came out with a note of bitterness.

Matteo doesn't respond, allowing Casey room to continue. I shift on my feet, heart pounding. It's a good thing I'm not in there. I'd be halfway across the table to get answers.

Casey continues after a sip of water. "Something about that last story line was different, though. My father was *different*. Gone a lot. Lots of . . . questionable personal decisions. At the time, I thought he was going senile, that he finally thought he *was* the Hooded Falcon . . . We were fighting more. But I think he'd based his last comics on

142

something real that he was investigating. He didn't tell me about it, and if he told anyone about it, it would have been the equally crazy kid who lived with us—he was trouble. There were other kids he'd hire for odd jobs—helping with his typewriter or gadgets or whatever. But this one . . . got to my father the way no one else had, and he used him until the day he died. I told my father that every chance I got, even though my father wouldn't listen to me."

My stomach turns over. The kid who lived with them. He has to mean Lawrence. There's true bitterness in Casey's voice. If he's involved in this case somehow, could *he* be the one to have broken into Lawrence's place? *My* place? Could my boss *be* the Golden Arrow?

Rideout picks this moment to burst into the room where I'm standing, sloshing a cup of coffee all over the floor. He mutters an expletive as he jams a headset on and tries repeatedly to get the earbuds inserted properly. He shoots me a look like it's *my* fault he's been getting coffee and missing the interview. "Kildaire, ask him about the arguments. Possible motive."

Before Rideout even finishes speaking, Matteo's voice—quiet, calm, and without a hint of being prompted—comes out from the TV screen, "You were fighting. Fighting about what?"

Casey Junior shrugs, and for a moment I glimpse the younger man he must have been when his father was alive. Not the big bullish businessman but the awkward teen. "I was fifteen. We fought about everything. His comics. His eccentricities. How embarrassing it was to have me invite friends over and have him show up in a cape and tights. About this kid he had live with us for a little bit. He just brought people in off the street and fed them and stuff. It was stupid and dangerous. Though he'd never invited any to live with us before. I had to nip it in the bud."

Rideout watches the TV screen like a hawk now. "Use the journal," he growls. We talked about Casey Junior possibly being the culprit, but my stomach clenches at the fervor in Rideout's voice. He's like a hound on a scent. If this is how Rideout questions people, no wonder Matteo does the interview first.

Matteo gives an almost imperceptible nod. "And did you fight about how he was ending the comic?" Matteo's words slide home, and Casey Junior's jaw tightens.

"What do you mean, 'ending the comic'?" Casey Junior's face has shuttered, his features completely controlled.

"We found evidence that your father planned to end the comic after the current story line. Did that make you angry?"

"You found—how could you know that?"

"We found a journal for an issue of *THF* that shows the Falcon retiring."

Casey Junior's face floods with color, and his hands move to grip the table. "You found a journal? Show it to me." It was an order. A demand.

"We can't share evidence—"

"If you want me to say another word, you show it to me." Casey's face is a dusky red, his voice shaking. I've never seen him unhinged like this. He is . . . furious? Scared? I can't tell which.

Matteo doesn't say a word but rises from his chair and exits the room.

My heart races a mile a minute, and I know Matteo is coming in here even before the door opens.

"We need that journal. There's something here. Something he knows. Something he's not willing to share for some reason."

"It's at my friend's house," I stammer. I hate using L's name right after he was mentioned in the questioning.

"I'll send an officer to go get it."

Oh crap, oh crap. Not only have I *not* told Lawrence about the case or about telling Matteo I've seen the journal; now Matteo wants to go get it by *force*. My best friend won't be my best friend anymore if that happens. I need to fix this. Lawrence would end up a suspect, and it would all be my fault. My mind flies to my messenger bag where I tucked the copies.

"How about the copies I have?"

Matteo's eyebrows draw together over my withheld information, so I plunge ahead with my explanation. "We can just tell Casey that we can't show him the whole journal, but this will prove we have it. I'll ask to borrow the journal tonight and bring it to you tomorrow."

Matteo thinks for a moment, then nods and accepts the copies before walking out the door, saying, "This will work in a pinch. Thanks."

I wait with anxious breath for him to reappear on the TV screen.

"Interesting how much inside information you keep coming up with," Rideout comments, not removing his eyes from the screen.

My stomach plummets. "Happy coincidence," I manage to respond, following his lead and keeping my eyes on the screen.

"There are a lot of happy coincidences where you're concerned—" Rideout continues but is interrupted by Matteo's arrival back on the screen.

I didn't miss the veiled accusation from Rideout and just pray he is the only one who thinks I am involved further. Matteo *must* know there's no way I could actually *be* the Golden Arrow.

"Here are a few pages from the journal." Matteo hands the photocopies over to Casey Junior, who studies them.

"Where did you find this? I've been looking for *years* for my father's journals. Where are the rest of them? I need to see them. All of them."

"We only have one. Are you telling me there are more?"

"Yes." Casey Junior rubs his hand over his head so hard, he'd yank out hair if he had any. "Yes, and I need them. Where did you find this? It's important."

"Why have you been looking for the journals? To hide the fact that your father planned to stop a comic that put millions in your pocket?" Matteo drops the bomb like it's no big deal, but Casey Junior explodes.

He stands up, knocking over his chair, and I think for a moment he's going to rush Matteo. "I loved my father, and I didn't know he was serious about ending the comics. I could never find his notes after he died to wrap up the story line. But this!" Casey Junior returns to the table and grabs the photocopies. "This proves that he *had* notes. Detective, you have to find them. The other journals. I don't know how this ties in to your current case. Really and truly, I don't. But these journals contain the identity of the person I think killed my father."

Goose bumps race down my arm, and I gape at the TV screen. *Killed his father?*

Rideout, on the other hand, is in his element. Calm. Steely. "Chase it, Kildaire."

"Murder? Mr. Casey, your father died of a heart attack."

"That's just what the police report says." Casey Junior has regained some composure and sits back in his chair. "I'm sorry I didn't tell you this at the beginning. It just sounds so ludicrous. I don't expect anyone to ever believe it, but it's my firm belief that my father was killed by the man he was following. The man he intended to write into his comic book as a villain. I've been searching his belongings for *thirty years* to find clues."

Rideout grimaces. "Kildaire, this is starting to sound implausible. I suggest . . ." Then he throws the headset at the TV because Matteo has taken out his earpiece and leaned toward Casey.

"You believe your father was murdered? For writing a comic book?"

"Yes."

"And that the police covered it up?"

"Yes."

"And you think these journals hold the notes including the identity of the person who killed your father?"

"Yes."

"Mr. Casey, I have to ask . . . If you suspected murder, why didn't you file a report?"

"I-I think it was a double agent. A cop he saw dealing drugs." Casey runs his hands over his head, then places them back on the table. His eyes harden. "He was going to publish the cop's real name when he unmasked the other superhero in the comic, but I could never prove it. I heard my dad and the kid arguing about it once, and I was afraid of coming forward without an identity or proof. In case . . . you know."

"In case the cop who took over was the double agent and killed you too?"

"Yes." I think I hear a note of relief in Casey's voice. Like he's just removed a splinter that has been a pain in his ass for thirty years.

"Okay. If we can find this kid, we'll bring him in for questioning. We'll do what we can, even though the time to search for him would have been right after your dad's death. Can you give me a name?"

"I've tried to find this guy for years. Never knew his last name. I only know his first name is Lawrence."

Fear curdles my stomach, forming a pit of doom. Lawrence not only worked for Casey Senior; he was a part of the shenanigans that got Casey Senior killed. At least that's what my boss believes. I guess I'm not the only one keeping secrets, but this could get Lawrence sent to jail. Or killed by the drug lords if they figure out he is involved. I frown. Unless Lawrence *is* the Golden Arrow and is avenging Casey Senior's death, but wouldn't he have told me that?

Matteo clears his throat. "Lawrence. Okay. Description?"

"We were both pretty young, but he would probably be a big black guy these days. Over six feet probably. That's all I know. I don't know why someone has been following drug dealers or making reference to the White Rabbit. Maybe the White Rabbit was a real person too. We won't know until we find those journals. I've looked everywhere in my father's belongings for them. Will you please let me know if you find more?"

Matteo's face doesn't give anything away, but I'm already dying inside. He jots in his notebook, then tucks it into his shirt pocket.

"Thank you, Mr. Casey. I appreciate you weighing in on this. We'll take your counsel seriously in this matter. Would you mind giving a written statement?"

Casey Junior hesitates. "Is it necessary?"

Matteo sits forward in the chair, bringing him within inches of Casey Junior's face. "Mr. Casey, I assure you this case is my number-one priority. The safety of citizens is at stake, the safety of *your* employees, and now possibly the solution to your father's death. I need a written statement."

Casey blows out a breath. "Okay."

"Excellent. In light of your new information, may I also have permission to look at your father's office?"

"Sure. I've looked through there a million times, but be my guest. I hope you find something I've missed."

Matteo shakes Casey Junior's hand and stands up to leave. He tosses a look at the camera that is clearly meant for me. "Stay where you are; we need to talk" is written *all* over his face.

He arrives shortly and shuts the door with a click behind him. Rideout starts yelling about how Matteo removed the earpiece, but Matteo has eyes only for me. "MG, did you know about this?"

"Of course not. I had no idea he thought his father was murdered."

"That wasn't what I was talking about. I'm talking about your *best friend* being a person of interest in this case."

I chew my lip. "Not really. Lawrence did say he'd worked for Senior. It's why he had the journal, but that's it. I didn't know the rest. I promise."

"We're going to have to bring him in for questioning."

"Can't we just—"

"MG, he's a *suspect*. You should be thankful I'm not saying we need to arrest him." He pauses to study my face. "Do you think he knows more than what he told you?"

I shrug. "Maybe. I didn't even know to ask. Matteo—he's not the Golden Arrow. I *know* him." I'm outwardly vehement, but . . . do I really know Lawrence? Look at all I've learned in a week about my so-called best friend. Talk about secrets and lies on all sides these days. I bite my lip. "But . . ."

"But." Matteo looks less than thrilled.

"Well, it's just that Lawrence called me earlier and thought maybe someone had been in his shop. And, well, the day you came over to my house? I thought maybe someone had been in my room."

Matteo's mouth presses into a line, a clue to his suppressed fury. "And you're just mentioning this?"

"I-I didn't think about it before." Which is stupid since Matteo increased patrols at my house and I've been feeling for a week now like the Golden Arrow is taking my involvement personally.

"Was anything taken from your room?"

"No, maybe just some comic books moved around. And really, I'm not even sure about that. Lawrence said the same thing. If nothing was taken, it's not a big deal, right?"

"What if someone is trying to find out what you know about the case? Or found out about your friend's journal and suspects that he has something to do with the case too? Did you think about that?"

I frown. "Well, *now* I'm thinking about it."

"That's why you're not a cop," Rideout says with a pointed look at Matteo.

Matteo runs his hands through his hair. "And keep me in the loop next time, will you? We need that journal. We need to question Lawrence. And now that I know that someone could be watching him, it may be safer to take him into custody."

My hands make fists of their own volition. This has gone sideways so fast. "Don't do that. Don't put him in custody, Matteo. He hasn't done anything wrong." I hope.

Matteo looks unconvinced. He glances at Rideout, who gives him a shrug that I read as "It's your own funeral." "Fine, we won't put him in custody unless something comes out of the questioning. But we *are* going to bring him in to the station. He's a bigger player in this than we thought."

I nod, but inwardly I'm dying. If the police show up at Lawrence's door before I can tell him what's been going on, I'll never forgive myself. Also, I want to see the entire journal before the police have it. What if the crooked cop loses it on purpose? A plan hatches in my head. I need to get to Lawrence before the police.

Rideout seems oblivious to my plight. He's staring at the TV screen with a scowl that would make any comic book villain jealous. "This just keeps getting more complicated. Now we're trying to solve a thirty-year-old possible murder as well?"

I chance a look at Rideout, then address Matteo, "I think it's all related. The last issues, including the journals. The drug dealers. The White Rabbit. We just have to put it all together. We're getting close. I can feel it." Even if it looks like my friends—no, my *family*—are involved and their lives are at risk.

Rideout makes a sound of derision in the back of his throat and pushes the TV screen and cart into the corner of the room before stalking out into the hallway. He grabs the arm of the younger officer, Officer James, the one I saw pocket evidence at the crime scene. I recognize the thinning sandy hair. He and Rideout have an intense discussion, and my interest piques. The younger officer looks angry about something, and I can't help my brain from going back to the warehouse. Two more officers walk by in the hall. One looks vaguely familiar too. This is the problem with my paranoia. Until we have a way to pinpoint the double agent, it could be literally *anyone* at this police station with knowledge of the case.

Matteo's fingers snap in front of my eyes, and I'm brought out of my thoughts and back to the interrogation room. "Hello? Get your coat. You and I are going to go look at Casey Senior's office while your boss is making his statement. I've told Officer James to take a *very* long time to complete this task so that your boss won't know you're our informant. Casey mentioned he's shipping many of the items in the study for a charity auction tomorrow, including the costume. It's likely our only chance." He motions to Officer James, who still looks cranky, but now I understand the heated exchange with Rideout. I would be upset too if I had to stay at the precinct and do paperwork while my partners went to search a suspect's office.

Rideout sticks his head back in. He barely gives me a glance and addresses Matteo, "Let's get this show on the road. We only have an hour tops before this guy heads home."

"Oh goody," I mutter under my breath. Instead of a cozy conversation in the car, I get to enjoy the dulcet tones of Detective Rideout singing all the verses of *subtle jabs about why MG shouldn't be here*. All the better for me to stew about Lawrence on my own.

Lawrence didn't just work for Casey Senior. He was a confidant. He *lived* with the man. If Casey Junior is right and his father was murdered, odds are Lawrence has seen his killer. Not only that; if there *is* a leak in the LAPD, it's only a matter of time before Lawrence becomes the number-one target. We need to wrap this up yesterday.

CHAPTER 16

The manor sits like a refined older gentleman—elegant, slightly sprawling, with the air of being worn in and relaxed—atop a hill overlooking a private greenbelt outside of LA. On one side, Griffith Observatory looms atop the same scrubby hill looking down on us, and on the other three sides, there isn't a house to be seen. Deep woods obscure the view of the nearest neighbor, and I contemplate the possibility of them being my favorite movie star.

"Rough place to grow up," I mutter, climbing out of the sleek dark sedan, a real undercover car this time. No Prius in sight. This is a serious investigation at this point. All it took was a flash of Matteo's badge in front of the camera on the front gate, and it opened straightaway. Now, a figure in a conservative black suit comes down the stone steps toward us. My parents may be rich, but they aren't "front gate with a camera, butler at the front door" rich.

In short order, we are escorted inside the spacious foyer, classic and distinguished with checkered black-and-white floors and a large arrangement of flowers. At first glance, it's the opposite of who I am. I expect to hate this house, to feel the overpolished, stuffy, overpowering feeling of Casey Junior in every room. Instead, it feels oddly like . . . coming home.

There's an aura. I *feel* the presence of a man I've never met, in this the birthplace of my favorite stories. He's everywhere. The old-fashioned brass light fixtures that come off as charmingly retro instead of tacky and outdated. A huge bust of a superhero cast in bronze and attached over a doorway like he's flying through the wall. The row of paintings between that door and the stairs that have the eyes cut out. I assume it's so someone in the room can look through them—it's classic comic fodder, kooky as all get out, and I love it. I not only feel Casey Senior's presence; it's like the house welcomes me. Sighs with relief that I've come. I shove away the thought that Casey Senior's spirit *wants* me to solve this case. That's crazy, right?

It also shows that Casey Junior has *not* redecorated in the thirty years since his father's death. I frown, thinking through his impassioned interview. Perhaps this house is the very proof I need to show that Casey Junior *really* loved his father. Wants his presence to linger.

"Are you coming?" Matteo's voice comes from the staircase in the foyer.

I realize I've been staring around the room and have completely missed all of Matteo's conversation with the butler.

"Oh, um, yes, of course."

Matteo turns to follow the butler up a curving staircase—quiet, with a worn and soft red velvety carpet runner. I make my way up the stairs behind him, taking in the house. *This* is the perfect superhero lair. Comfortable. Impressive. Homey. Huge enough to hide a batcave in the second living room. Heck, Casey Junior even has an Alfred.

"I know what you're doing," a voice comes from behind me, and I jump about a mile in the air, my mind going directly to ghosts, goblins, and the specter of Casey Senior's murdered corpse. Instead, it's the all-too-real, unpleasantly corporeal Detective Rideout.

"Climbing the stairs? You must have graduated top of your class."

"No, I *know*." His hand grabs mine on the railing, and the touch sends creepy crawlies straight to my soul. I yank my hand away and turn to face Rideout, careful to stay a full step above him and his impishly smirking face.

"Know *what*?"

"I'm not stupid. First you happen to meet Kildaire in the coffee shop. Then you *happen* to see those white rabbits that no one else saw. Then you *happen* to just have these journal pages on you, and your best friend is the key to finding the murderer. Kildaire may be blinded by your"—his eyes wander down to my chest, then back to my face—"finer assets, but I'm not fooled."

This man must have come from Mordor, and I wish he'd just go back to Mount Doom and the fires that birthed him. I turn my back to him and start up the stairs again. "I don't know what you're talking about."

"You're the Golden Arrow, and I will prove it. I don't know what you're doing messing with the case, but I'm going to figure it out."

I whip around so fast, I almost lose my balance. "What? Are you *insane*? I'm helping with this investigation. I'm the only reason you've figured anything out. Without me, you guys would have no idea."

Rideout shrugs and mounts the stairs with a relaxed manner that just sets all my creep monitors off. "Our profiler gave me the report today. He thinks it could be a woman we're chasing, not a man; the original thugs were drugged, not beaten . . . a woman's tactic. Intelligent, educated, well steeped in geek culture, and with a way to keep tabs on the police investigation to avoid being caught. Sound like anyone you know?"

I decide on bluffing outwardly. "You're barking up the wrong tree, Watson." But, inwardly, I'm panicking a little. It *does* sound like me. Could the Golden Arrow be trying to frame me for all of this?

Rideout's mouth presses into a line. "I'm watching you."

I let him get far enough ahead of me that I have the landing all to myself. It's back to quiet and comfortable, though I'm still shaken. If Rideout isn't just being an ass, if he *really* thinks I am the Golden Arrow . . . well, I could be in *real* trouble.

At the head of the stairs, I pause. I could have sworn Matteo and Rideout went to the right, but I hear a noise to my left. The house seems to pull at me, so I wander down the worn path in the deeply padded wine-colored carpet to the set of large double wood doors that takes up the entire left end of the hall. Casey Senior's study entrance is no less impressive than the house itself.

Matteo and Rideout are on their mission; I can already hear them knocking around in the study. I didn't think I'd gotten that far behind them, but then again . . . this house kind of sucks me in with its quiet and creative energy. I can feel the stories here, picture Casey Senior plotting and sketching, drawing on the ethereal ideas floating in the air. Something about the atmosphere in this house speaks to my writer's soul. I feel a bit like I've crossed into a fairy ring—one hundred years could have passed in a day, for all I know.

I pad up to the door and push down the brass lever. It's hard to open against the thick carpet, and I push my body weight against it. The hinges squeak slightly, and I pause, realizing I didn't hear that squeak when Detective Rideout and Matteo went in. Maybe the second door is more oiled or something. From inside the room, the noises stop.

I press again, and the door moves forward under my weight, swinging into the room . . . where I come face-to-cape with a figure who is *not* Detective Rideout or Matteo.

The yell that erupts from me is half scream, half war cry. For a brief instant, I think maybe I've interrupted a servant dressed in an odd uniform. But this figure is dressed all in black, wearing a *mask*, and a large golden arrow shines across the chest of the person's spandex suit.

I stumble backward at the same time the figure whirls around. I fall back, hitting my head on the wooden door, and land in the hallway. I scramble to my feet, but by the time I make it back into the study, Matteo hot on my heels, I glimpse only the edge of a cape as the person *jumps straight out a second-story window*. No hesitation.

"Matteo, it's *him*!"

"What? MG, are you okay?" Matteo's hands are on my shoulders, probably trying to see if I'm hurt.

There's no time to examine the splitting headache already developing from my fall. "Matteo, he's here!"

"He who?"

I'm frantic at this point, pushing Matteo's hand from my neck so I can get to the window. "The Golden Arrow. The Golden Arrow was right here in this room when I came in. And he just jumped through the window. He's *out there*, Matteo!"

Matteo gives me one quick searching glance and rushes to the window. Rideout puffs into the room seconds later, his eyes darting between Matteo and me.

"Jesus, what happened in here?" Rideout asks. "You yelled loud enough to alert the entire county to the fact we're here, and what the *hell* did you do to this office?"

I cut a look around the room, noting for the first time that it's been carefully ransacked. There's no other way to describe it. Everything has been pulled off the walls and arranged in orderly piles against the baseboards. The desk drawers are sitting out.

I blink up at Rideout, then look at Matteo. "I—he—Matteo, tell me you saw that. Saw him jump out that window."

Matteo returns from the window and crouches in front of me. "There's no one out there, MG."

"Interesting." Rideout regards me as if I'm Poison Ivy herself. His words echo in my head. *I'm watching you.*

In response to his silent accusation, I spit out a retort: "This room didn't do this to *itself*. And definitely not in thirty seconds." I want to yank out my hair. How did Matteo not see the Golden Arrow?

"No. Probably not." Matteo and Detective Rideout share a loaded glance, and my blood pressure increases. It's obvious they're having a conversation without talking.

"Well, aren't you going to go *look* for who jumped out that window?" I'm practically yelling again, and I don't care. Rideout has obviously gotten to Matteo with his stupid theory. Only it doesn't hold water because I just *saw* the Golden Arrow, and it wasn't in a mirror.

Matteo considers me for a moment. "I'll go look around outside, okay?" He shoots a look at Rideout. "We could be dealing with a possible B and E." Matteo makes a move to leave but pauses just short of the door, turning back to look at me. "Are you all right?"

"I'm *fine*, just startled having come face-to-face with the person we've been chasing."

After a brief pause, he nods before disappearing down the hall.

I stand in silence.

Rideout leans his shoulder against the wall and crosses his arms, watching me. "I have to hand it to you: this was complicated to organize. You had no way of knowing you'd have time alone in the study. What were you looking for?"

"What on earth are you talking about?"

"Getting us to bring you here but sneaking in to search by yourself first. Or give your accomplice time to get away. Pretty brilliant. What were you looking for? Evidence that would name you as the Golden Arrow? And then pretend like you saw someone? Bravo." He mocks me with a slow clap.

What. A. Dick. I throw my hands in the air. "I didn't do this. Do you really think I could have taken everything off the walls in thirty seconds? That's crazy, and you know it."

We wait in silence for Matteo to reappear, though I have a sneaking suspicion I know what he's going to say.

Matteo's face says it all before he opens his mouth. "Nothing. No cars left the gated driveway." He pauses, then continues, "The security cameras were experiencing some technical *difficulties*, and nothing from the last twenty minutes recorded."

Rideout grunts. "Heck of a coincidence."

"Yeah."

We're all silent for a moment. At least Rideout can't think I still did this, right? I bite my lip. I've had time to glance around the room while Matteo's been gone. There's order to the chaos; the room isn't just torn apart. The knickknacks that sit in neat lines are intact, no books pulled off the shelves. Mostly it's just the paintings yanked off the hooks, exposing the walls. The Golden Arrow was systematic.

"I think I know what he was looking for," I say to the room.

Matteo pulls on a pair of latex gloves and sets about taking pictures with his phone.

"Interesting that you *know*. But fine, elucidate," Rideout answers, raising my ire. Even Matteo makes an annoyed grunt.

I decide to just ignore him. "You know the issue we looked at? How they discovered clues to the identity of the double agent in the wall safe? I think the Golden Arrow is looking for the journals. Or something else that Casey Senior would have kept to identify the double agent or the White Rabbit. I think he was looking for a wall safe."

A chill chases down my spine, and I feel the house whisper an assurance to me. It's a *great* story line. One any comic book would be proud to own. One I'd be proud to write, and if there's anything I think I understand about Casey Senior at this point, it's that he loved a good story. Even if it's his own story. "What if this is what it's all about? Identifying the double agent? Or the White Rabbit? What if the Golden Arrow has figured out Casey Senior was murdered and that his killer is still at large?"

Rideout gives a full belly laugh. "This is ludicrous. Kildaire, you can't possibly buy it. This guy died of a *heart attack* thirty years ago. Old news. We work narcotics. You and I know that big eighties bust put all the big dealers in jail. White Rabbit guy included, if he ever existed. These rings are all brand-new, and no drug dealer runs a ring for thirty years unless you live in Argentina or Mexico. We are chasing a thirty-year-old wild goose, and we're losing the trail of the real drug guys by following this *girl's* false trail."

"What if we find a wall safe?" I ask. "What if the journals are in there?"

Rideout sneers. This guy is *not* the good-cop half of their team. "Okay, then, show us. Show us the proof."

I press my lips together, willing Matteo to feel what I feel in this room. Something in my head clicks into place. Call it intuition. Call it Casey Senior's spirit from the past. Whatever it is, I feel surer about this than I have anything about this case so far. I'm letting the story lead me, not the facts. Exactly how I write my comics. I get a nugget, a vision, then chase that story down its own path. I don't try to box it in. I'm open to wherever it wants to lead. Facts are Matteo's part of the investigation. Comic stories are mine.

I look around the room, my attention lingering on the painting behind the desk. "I interrupted the Golden Arrow before he could take all the art down. We need to look behind it."

Rideout snorts. "If this was an attempted burglary, this room is evidence. We can't move anything."

That figures. He asks for proof, then tells me I can't look.

Matteo turns to Rideout. "We'll wear gloves. We're here to look at the office and look for the journals."

Rideout mutters a string of words I can't hear before finishing with "It's your funeral."

Yahtzee. I accept the pair of latex gloves from Matteo before crossing to the desk and grasping the side of the ornate frame. It's almost as tall as I am. I recognize the panel drawn in the frame as the one I saw Casey Junior lounging in front of for the charity promotion article Matteo and I saw when we were looking through the comics in my room.

Matteo lines up on the other side of the frame. "All right. We'll lift it enough for you to look through the crack in the side. On three: one, two, three . . ."

Something inside the frame shifts as Matteo and I awkwardly lift the painting up and slightly away from the wall. My heart races. I'm convinced we've broken the antique frame, but it holds together enough for me to lay my head against the wall. It's an awkward angle. Even with my nose literally touching the frame, I can't see the wall clearly.

"I need a flashlight," I say.

"Rideout, if you wouldn't mind."

"Of course I *mind*. I'm a narcotics detective, Kildaire." But I hear rustling, and a cell phone with a flashlight appears near my head.

"A little farther down, more toward the wall—yeah . . . right . . . right *there*. Matt—*Detective Kildaire*, there's something on the wall behind the painting." My head pops up, nearly sending Rideout's phone flying.

Matteo studies me like I'm a puzzle, but after a moment he nods. "Okay, let's take down the frame. Let's look at what's behind there." We lift, but the five-foot frame is awkward and hard to manage. I don't think the Golden Arrow could have removed this one by himself, at least not in one piece. It explains why it's the only one remaining on the wall. Something clunks inside the frame again as we shift it wildly, trying to unhook the wire from the mounting device.

"A little help here, Rideout," Matteo calls. Rideout mutters about how this is "all a part of my plan" just quietly enough that I don't think Matteo hears. I'm so excited to be right at the prospect of finding the journals, at being one step ahead of the Golden Arrow, that I ignore Rideout's ridiculous allegations.

Finally the frame leans against the wood-paneled wall, and I behold in triumph a small safe in the wall behind the desk.

"Just like in the comic books." Call me Professor X. I'm a brain-*ninja* to find this.

"It could be coincidence," Matteo says, taking a picture of the safe with his phone.

"Or the perfect place to keep journals that contain the name of a drug lord and a dirty cop in league together." I study Rideout from the corner of my eye. Maybe *that's* why he's so unsettled. Prickles dance on my skin as I consider the very real possibility that Detective *Dursley* could be the dirty cop. And that he's annoyed with my clue-finding abilities, looking for a way to pin this all on me.

Rideout doesn't seem to notice me staring. He's talking over my head to Matteo. "You do realize that the journals can't be in there. Casey Junior said he's been looking for *thirty* years."

I cross my arms. "Maybe he didn't know the safe was here."

Rideout rolls his eyes at me like the teenage boy he is. "After thirty years? You don't think he knew his dad had a safe in here?"

Matteo watches us like a tennis match. "Chances are he knew it was here, *and* there's no way for us to unlock it without a warrant and a special team . . . Oh."

"Oh what?" I hold my breath. I know this is the answer. *This* is what the Golden Arrow wants. This is the key to the story.

"It's open." Matteo studies the wall safe, then extracts his pen from his pocket. He slides it up the side of the door, and sure enough, it swings forward. "It's been disarmed."

We all crowd around to be the first to glimpse whatever is inside the safe. Except it's empty. Completely. Well, that just takes the freaking cake.

"What now, Dexter?" Rideout's dry drawl comes from over my left shoulder. I hate that he's using nicknames like I do. Just because I use my knowledge of comics to catch a comic book criminal doesn't make me Dexter.

I ignore him and turn my face to Matteo's. "We need to find those journals." I beg him with my eyes to believe me. To believe *in* me. These journals are the key.

Rideout crosses his arms again. "If our vigilante is after the journals, we need to figure out how the Golden Arrow even knows about them.

I suspect help from the inside." He looks pointedly at me, and Matteo grunts.

"Funny, I think the same thing," I shoot back, not bothering to hide my glare from Matteo. Rideout is the one breaking the rules of professionalism here.

"Rideout, drop it. MG, he has a point. Who knows about these journals?"

"Lawrence showed one to me. I showed it to you and Detective Rideout, and you showed it to Casey Junior." A very short list. My stomach turns over again. All jokes aside, Rideout is a jerk, but possibly right too. How would the Golden Arrow have known to even look in this office if he didn't know the journal existed? Was he just going off the comic books? I press my lips together. It seems unlikely. It's like the Golden Arrow sees everything I do, and *that* idea gives me the willies. Am I under surveillance? Does the dirty cop on Matteo's team also feed information to the Golden Arrow? That idea seems more unlikely than the last. The Golden Arrow knows the case, that the journals exist, and has reason to want to find them. If it isn't Casey Junior, there's only one other common denominator.

Matteo nods slowly, his mind obviously chasing the same path as mine. "We'll need to inform Edward Casey Junior about what allegedly happened here today and see if he wants to make a report. It's possible that he left the room like this going through his father's office for the auction. But maybe not. And we need to talk to the only other person who seems mixed up in this."

I swallow hard. Lawrence.

CHAPTER 17

Cars clog the Hamburger Mary's parking lot by the time I pull the Hurtling Turd into a spot. A good sign. Everyone loves a full crowd, and an early-summer Friday night is prime drag show time for the locals. I reach in my back seat, gather the pile of fabric into my arms, and hurry across the lot. Usually I'm giddy about coming to a drag show, but tonight my stomach is a ball of nerves. I'll let L perform; then I'll have to spill the beans. So many beans. And hope he has beans to spill right back that will solve my case. And keep L out of jail.

I wind my way through the crowd as quickly as possible. I hope I can get back in enough time to snag a great table. I'm almost to the back of the house when I see a familiar face. Kyle's fiancée, Nina.

"MG!" She yells my name like we're old friends, and my heart instantly warms a little, easing my anxiety. Her enthusiasm is literally contagious. She waves me over.

"Hey, Nina. What brings you guys here?"

She takes a sip of the large drink in front of her. "Bachelorette party!" The girls all whoop. It wouldn't have been hard to guess, given the large tiara on Nina's head and the sash that says "BRIDE" slung across her middle. I'm a terrible human, I'd already forgotten that she and Kyle were getting married soon.

"Congratulations," I say, smiling. The group is already tipsy. They're in for a good time once the queens start performing.

"Kyle said no strippers. He didn't say anything about drag queens."

A girl after my own heart.

"What are *you* doing here?" Nina eyes the pile of gold lamé.

"I'm dropping off a costume I made for my friend. In fact, I'd probably better get back there so I can still get a table after."

"Nonsense, you'll come sit with us."

"Really?"

Nina grins. "I insist! We nerd girls need to stick together!" She leans over to me and whispers dramatically, "These are theater friends. They get it. They'll be happy to have you too!"

My heart warms just a bit more. Nina does seem cool, and Kyle never outright backstabbed me the way Andy did. Maybe a friend of the female variety would do me good. Again this case has pointed out to me that I've been alone on my own isolated island. I can't even remember the last time I reached out to my friends from college or my cosplay group. I suddenly miss them. "Okay. I'll be back."

Backstage *sounds* glamorous, but at a drag show, it's pretty much one tiny room stuffed full of panty hose, cosmetics, and men in wig caps. I stand at the door and try to locate Lawrence among the group of men. Someone is yelling about lipstick on the mirror, and someone else snips back, "At least it's not on your teeth like last time," but I don't hear or see Latifah Nile anywhere.

"L!" I wait, no answer. I snag one of the queens right by the door, a plump Filipino who I've seen several times do a great postwar-era pinup routine.

"Can you find Latifah Nile for me?" I hold up the pile of costumes.

He turns and shouts into the room, "Hey, queens! Has anyone seen La-tee-tee? You bitches just need to shut it for one second so that—"

Lawrence emerges from behind a dressing rack in the back corner of the room, one eye already done up in gold glitter, Cleopatra cat-eye style.

"Girl, you look *fine* tonight," he says, taking in my own penciled purple eyebrows, glittery purple lipstick, and chunky skull-and-crossbones necklace. "You're going to make these queens jealous. Is

Atlanta here with you?" The mention of Matteo both gives me but-
terflies and kills them with a ball of anxiety. L is a suspect, and it's
all due to my meddling.

I flush. "No, just me. And a friend here for a bachelorette party. I
needed to refabulous myself. I wilted a little this week." I lean in like
I'm telling him a secret. "I learned from the best."

And it's true. I learned the art of super-dramatic makeup from
Lawrence. Shockingly, there aren't many places I get compliments on
my Violet Femme purple lipstick. Yet another reason I love drag shows.
No one appreciates drama or makeup quite like queens.

"Well, my drag mama would be proud. And, girl, you're never
anything less than fabulous. You just wear it different sometimes."
Lawrence gives me a squeeze, then pounces on the fabric I have in my
hands. He's already wearing the foam padding around his rear, reined
in by layers of panty hose to make the look complete.

Outwardly Lawrence is completely normal, seemingly unfazed by
his recent apartment scare. I'm trying to follow his lead, but inwardly
I'm at war with myself. I want to talk to Lawrence, but there are so
many queens around, I don't dare do it here. "Do you want to try it on
in case I need to adjust it? Maybe the bathroom could give us enough
room if we need to pin it." At the very least sans eight queens.

Lawrence beams at me, then makes a shooing gesture. "Nonsense.
You just go get yourself a table before one of these queens steals you
from me. One of these bitches can help me if I need to pin something."

I nod, swallowing my panic in an awkward gulp.

"Girl, what's wrong? You feeling okay?"

I open and close my mouth, unsure of how to approach this. *No big
deal. The police are going to show up and question you, and I'm worried you
might be playing superhero.* "Just something I wanted to talk with you
about. It's nothing . . ." I turn to leave but think better of it. I need to
know. Rip off the Band-Aid. "Actually, where were you today? Around
five o'clock?"

Please have an alibi. Please have an alibi.

Lawrence pulls back, looking surprised. "Did something happen?" He taps his chin. "I think around three I was out getting lashes for tonight, but I'd have to check."

So . . . nothing solid, but my shoulders relax. There's nothing in Lawrence's face that suggests he's lying. Maybe I'm all bent out of shape with my suspicions for nothing. Yet there's still the police stuff to tell Lawrence.

L reaches out and rubs my shoulder. "Seriously, girl, are you okay?"

I almost divulge the whole story right there in the backstage area. I want so badly to come clean to L, but the plump Filipino queen sidles up to us and leans over the gold lamé.

"So *this* is your secret weapon, La-tee-tee!" The queen flicks a nonexistent wig and gives me the once-over. "Girl, your costumes are on fleek. I need a new one next show. Any chance you take food stamps?"

The nearby queens laugh at the joke, and I crack a smile.

"Sorry, I only deal in lifelong indebtedness and firstborns, but I'll let you know when I start accepting Visa."

"You will *not*," L says firmly.

This isn't the time or place to discuss matters with the show about to start. I highly doubt Matteo is going to show up and pull L offstage mid-act, so I decide to let L perform without worrying. I pat Latifah on the padded rear before I leave. "Maybe we can chat after you're finished. We'll go to IHOP and have pancakes. Right now, you go show them how it's done."

I make my way back out to the table, where the girls are already enjoying another round of drinks. I slide in next to Nina and sigh, leaning my head against the booth back. The end of the night looms over me, and I hope I'll be able to enjoy the show. But I keep reliving opening that study door, catching a glimpse of the person in black. Ruminating about what the Golden Arrow knows and what he or she is looking for, trying to figure out just how I can help solve this case, especially now that Rideout seems to be gunning for me as a suspect. I need to start at the beginning. If this is all about Casey Senior, I need to start there.

Which is where Lawrence comes in.

Just as I finish this thought, my phone buzzes. It's a text from Matteo. We need to talk about the case. New development.

With an apologetic look at Nina, I type back, Not a good time. With some friends at Hamburger Mary's. Can I call you later? I have *got* to explain to my best friend why the police are after him first.

We're plunged into darkness as a voice booms over the loudspeaker, "Ladies and gentlemen, welcome to Hamburger Mary's famous Drag Review."

A spotlight pops on, and there's Latifah Nile standing center stage, hip thrown back, gold sparkly heels perfectly apart in a dramatic stance, and one ridiculously fantastic sequined top hat pulled down over her eyes. The sequined tailcoat I designed fits L perfectly.

"I am your host for the evening, Latifah Nile." L repositions the hat dramatically atop the afro wig, and the crowd cheers and catcalls like crazy. "And we have quite the show for you tonight. You can see we're doing some updating." L sweeps a hand in suggestive curves over her gold lamé and sequined bodysuit down to the gold sequined skirt and panty hose–clad legs. She looks like a mix of vintage twenties, sexy temptress, and a nod to Egyptian style with her signature eyes. "And tonight I'll be"—L produces an old-fashioned cane from somewhere behind her, cracks it on the floor, leans over it to better show her taped cleavage over the top of the bustier, and pouts—"putting on the Ritz."

The girls at my table yell and wave money in the air even as the music comes out over the loudspeaker for L's number. She's slow stepping, sashaying, and generally shaking what God—and foam padding—gave her to a cabaret-paced "Puttin' on the Ritz."

The crowd cheers as she makes her way slowly down the stage, mimicking bawdy versions of most of the lyrics. She pantomimes money, bends over a little, and snaps up like someone spanked her, much to the delight of the front row. L actually *sings*, which is unusual at a drag show, her voice smoky and seductive.

I holler with the rest of the girls as L stops with a drumbeat, waggles her hips, and pouts. It's a genius routine. At one point Latifah wanders over to us and puts her sequined top hat on my head while she leans on the cane and addresses Nina.

"Are you sure you want to get married, honey? There are so many men and so little time!" Shimmying her shoulders to the heavy drumbeat, she does a Ginger Rogers slide and makes her way back up to the stage.

"We have so many good acts tonight, and I can tell you are the *perfect* audience." She winks, and someone calls something from the audience. "You all behave now." She waves her hands and does a grapevine with the cane out in front to exit the stage.

I'm beaming, and I can't wait to give L a huge hug and a high five. No matter the case and all the shade going down, Latifah is *damn* good at her job. I turn to Nina, unable to contain myself. "What do you think?"

"The glitz, the glam, the costumes, the *eyelashes*. This is so much fun!" Nina laughs and fans her face. "This is the best bachelorette party *ever!*"

I laugh. "Yeah, not too many straight men come to these events, but when they do, it can get really hilarious."

Nina cracks up like she's about to fall off her seat. Boy, she must be really in her cups; she can barely catch her breath. "MG, isn't that your boyfriend over there? He might need saving. It looks like there are four or five gay men fighting over him."

"What?" I whip around, and like my eyes are powered by magnets, my gaze meets Matteo's. I feel it like a physical jolt all the way down to my feet. Then waves of nerves come crashing down on me. Is he here for L? Maybe he's come to pull L offstage midperformance and drag her down to the station. My heart hammers in my chest.

"Um, I'll be right back. I thought he was . . . working."

I make my way across the room to where Matteo is politely telling a tall gentleman in a crop top and a pink wig that he doesn't drink. I offer the tall man a smile, then turn narrowed eyes on Matteo. "What are you doing here?"

"You told me where you were, so I thought I'd just come . . ." He looks around, bewildered. "Where *are* we?"

"Hamburger Mary's."

The next act starts, and I pull Matteo back toward the table with me. "I can see why you're good at your job."

"I need to ask you about a suspect. The guy in the hoodie."

"So ask."

"Can we sit? It won't take very long, and then I'll be going back to the office tonight to follow up."

My shoulders relax. So this *isn't* about Lawrence. I sigh. "All right, come on." I drag him the rest of the way to Nina's table. If the show follows its usual pattern, we won't see L for at least three or four numbers.

The girls at the booth go gaga over Matteo and giggle to themselves while making room for him. Nina won't even let me apologize for crashing her bachelorette party and goes back to attacking her hamburger with glee.

Once Matteo and I are as alone as we can get, I turn to him. The faster we get this over with, the faster Matteo can leave. "Okay, Scotty, give her all she's got. Let's hear it."

I try desperately not to think about how I'm squished up against him, the thigh of my tight black pants against his slacks. *Bigger fish to fry, MG.*

"Scotty?"

"Never mind."

The next performer's music starts, and Matteo tries not to seem like he's staring, but who *wouldn't* stare at a five-foot-five Filipino hottie who literally just burst out of a clamshell? A campy mash-up of *The Little Mermaid*'s "Kiss the Girl" with Katy Perry's "I Kissed a Girl" booms over the speakers. The performer's forties, victory-rolled hair and sexy pink kimono-style maxi dress are perfection.

Matteo blinks. "I just expected hamburgers." His genuine confusion undoes some of the tension I've been feeling. Matteo is just here to talk. No ulterior motive. He didn't know this was going to be a drag show. Or that L is a performer.

"You do seem to have a habit of arriving at interesting moments. Is it something you come by naturally, or do you have to practice?" I take a sip of my beer.

He rubs the back of his neck. "Honestly, it just seems to happen around you. I can't find my feet sometimes."

He gives me a look far more searching than could be labeled "professional interest." My heart stutters in my chest. His gaze drops to my lips, and mine to his. It amazes me how fast we can go from my paranoia to banter to crazy sexual tension. His admission that he can't find his feet around me does impressive things to the dragons in my stomach.

The urge to kiss him overwhelms me. *We can't, we can't,* my brain chants. *Do it, do it,* my hormones insist. He's fighting the same battle. I see it in his face. *It's a bad idea. We work together.* Another part of my brain points out that it's dark, and no one would see one *tiny* little kiss . . .

Then Nina *screeches* inches from my ears. The finale of the song washes back into my reality, and Matteo and I lean apart. I study Matteo, not for the first time feeling like I'm on a roller coaster where he's concerned. Striking a balance between the case and my personal feelings gets harder and harder to manage. If he were a normal guy, I'd definitely invite him as my date to the work thing later this month. Matteo in a cape? Oooh, yes, please.

"You're a million miles away. What are you thinking about?" Matteo's face is still far too close for professional conversation.

"The gala at my job." I take myself by surprise by admitting this. I need to get him out the door, not talk about this right now. It's as if Matteo's presence continually inspires my candor, whether I want it to or not. I am far more truthful with him than practically anyone else in my life, save Lawrence and Ryan, at least until this case fell in my lap.

"Okay . . ." He frowns, not following.

"I think it would make more sense if you came to my work party."

Matteo's eyebrows rise—I've taken him by surprise with the change in direction too.

The can of worms is open, so I decide to roll with it. "It will be fun, I promise." Okay, maybe I'm trying to convince myself as well as him. "Costumes, capes, contests, all the free booze you can imagine. I mean, of course it's so you can check out more Genius folks, now that we don't think it's Kyle or Simon."

Matteo taps the table with his fingers before replying, his face looking strangely torn. "Are you asking me to come with you to your work party?"

"Yes, Captain Obvious. I just said that."

Matteo searches my eyes in that "more than professional" manner again that makes my heart turn to electric goo. "No, I mean, are you asking me to the work party for *you* or for the case?"

Applause fills the air around us as yet another act finishes up. I haven't even heard the song or seen the performer—the world always falls away when I'm with Matteo. I'm also not sure how to respond to his question. I'm not going to lie to myself; I want Matteo to come with me. I want to see him in a hot comic-inspired costume. I want to dance with him, laugh with him, do a normal couples-type thing with him . . . Only we aren't a normal couple.

We're a pretend couple, and we're trying to solve a thirty-year-old mystery. Unless I make a move. My thoughts distill. This may be my opportunity to change the pretend part, even if we have to wait until after the case is over to follow through. That's assuming we all live through this and no one gets arrested. I am *not* wearing a jumpsuit; orange clashes terribly with my hair.

I put on my big-girl panties and answer him honestly. There's that candor thing again. "Both."

He lets out a breath, and I see relief mixed with another emotion on his face. Anxiety? He reaches over and puts his hand on my knee like he did while watching *Star Wars*, and he gives it a small squeeze before returning it to the table. "Deal."

My heart stutters in my chest again. He's glad I asked him for me and not just for work.

"Wasn't that wonderful, ladies and gents? Another round of applause. You're really going to love this next one too, but first, I wanted to say a special hello to my dearest friend . . ." Gold sequins glint in the spotlight, and my attention is drawn to Latifah as she struts back onto the stage . . . and the double take she does when she lays eyes on Matteo. *Uh-oh. This is definitely not when L usually reappears. Not the night to go off script. This could be bad. So, so bad.* Here I am trying to keep these two apart, and Latifah is literally going to land in our laps. I can only pray that Matteo doesn't recognize Lawrence in drag.

I smile grimly as a vision in gold sequins sashays across the crowded floor in our direction. "I guess you're about to meet my friend, Latifah."

I see understanding dawn on his face the moment before he turns in the booth and comes face-to-bustier with Latifah. I say my prayers.

"Hello, sugar," she purrs into the microphone. "It seems my sweet girl here has brought Atlanta brisket for dinner instead of a hamburger." The crowd roars with good-natured laughter as Latifah makes a big show of sizing up Matteo's shoulders.

She holds up one hand, showing off her long golden nails. "Don't you know this is a bachelorette party? You are being very naughty by crashing it. Should I send you to my room?"

She winks at me, then squeezes Matteo's shoulders one more time before doing a dramatic shiver and wandering back to the stage. "Whew, I am burning *up* in here. This man sandwich is *hot!*" She throws another wink back at me. "You just let me know if you need help with it, sugar." She sashays back up to the stage.

Matteo is beet red now; I can even tell in the dark. Even as much as I'm freaking out, this is *hilarious*. I try not to laugh, but it's difficult when the table literally *shakes* with the mirth of the other girls.

"You should see your face," Nina says in gasps. Then she reaches around me and grabs Matteo's hand. "But you are such a good sport about it."

He really is. I offer him a small smile. "Okay, now we might be even for you crashing my evening." I relax just a *little*, realizing that Matteo doesn't recognize Lawrence as Latifah.

He rubs a hand over his hair and over the scruff on his cheeks. "You drive a hard bargain."

I shrug and sip my beer. "If you don't pay no tolls, you don't get no rolls." And at his baffled look I set down my beer. It's time to get Matteo out of here before Latifah comes back. "Sorry. *Men in Tights* reference. And didn't you have case developments to discuss?"

He shoots a look over my shoulder to Nina, who is clearly involved in counting her money with the rest of the table to figure out how much they have to tip the performers. He scoots in closer to me and bows his head so he's closer. To anyone else, it would look like a lovers' tête-à-tête. I shake off another ridiculous pang of longing over our *pretend* status.

Matteo doesn't seem likewise conflicted right now. He's back to business. "It's about the suspect with the painted rabbit on his hoodie. He didn't see the person who did it—dressed all in black except for some sort of cape. We ID'd the suspect, but it took a long time to find any reason the Golden Arrow would have marked him as different. We were looking, but nothing stood out. No priors, clean record, not even a parking ticket."

"That's it! He must have help on the inside. No one has a clean parking record in LA."

Matteo rolls his eyes. "Anyhow, I just finished looking through his family's records, and I came across something interesting. Do you recognize this name? It's his father."

I lean over and glance at the phone screen Matteo has pointed in my direction. "Song Yee?" I ponder this. "No, never heard of him. Yee, is that Korean?"

"His family is from China, all legally immigrated in 2012. Midfifties, married, teenage son named Huong."

The White Rabbit. I *told* Detective Rideout and Agent Sosa I thought there was a connection to China. My Spidey sense tingles. It's more than just a coincidence. I don't understand the drug part; that's Matteo's wheelhouse. Maybe this kid isn't just a drug dealer. Maybe his family *produces* the drugs. Ships them in to the dad or the son, who deals it. This would certainly fit the White Rabbit's story line. Maybe the Golden Arrow has tagged *the* White Rabbit; maybe it's that cut-and-dried. Over and done.

"Should I have heard of Song Yee?" I ask. There must be a reason Matteo is asking. Some connection to our case other than China.

"Not necessarily . . . except Song just bought into a printing company. He only owns a small portion, all on the up-and-up. Nothing shady about buying in, but I happened to look into the company's clients, and—"

"A printing company?" I'm confused.

"Marvelous Printing."

I sit back and think. My gaze meets Matteo's as it finally dawns on me. "They print some of our comics. They print *The Hooded Falcon*."

A beat filled with hooting, hollering, and "Uptown Funk" stretches between us as I absorb the information. I sit back and take a sip of my now warm beer. I bought it only to nurse something while I watched L, but I really wish it was something stiffer at this point.

"Could this be how the Golden Arrow discovered Yee, or as I'd bet, the White Rabbit?" I ask.

"I hoped your creative genius could figure that out."

"Flattery will get you everywhere." I pull off my glasses and tap them on the table while I think. "This has to be what the Golden Arrow knew about Yee's son. Too coincidental. But I'm still puzzled how this ties in to any of the other stuff. Maybe Huong or his father could simply be *the* White Rabbit we're looking for. It's not exactly like the comics, but they could be importing drugs from their family in China and dealing them out of the warehouse. But . . . how could this kid being a drug dealer relate to the printing of *The Hooded Falcon*?"

"We questioned him this afternoon—Huong Yee, the son. He's still in custody and had some interesting information to share in exchange for a plea deal. He told us that there *was* a cop working with his ring. And he'd give the identity in exchange for us dropping his charges. Not only that, he didn't think the drugs came from Mexico like Sosa's theory. We've arranged to speak with a judge on his behalf. I'd like you present when we question him again, for the plea deal. We've asked Agent Sosa to review the tape of the interview and be present for the next one too. She knows these bigger rings better than I do."

"The dirty-cop thing plays right into the comic book story line, but how could the Golden Arrow have known that?"

Matteo shrugs. "Maybe he didn't. Maybe you're right and the Yees are the White Rabbit, and that's all he meant to show us. But it sure seems more than a coincidence. *The Hooded Falcon* crops up yet again."

I tip the half-empty beer to the side, then let it fall back to the table. What I wouldn't give for my red ball and a desk wall to think right now. "But that doesn't make any sense. What does a printing press have to do with the drugs?" My mind works a mile a minute, looking for the thread of the story. Even if one of the Yees is the White Rabbit, neither of them seems old enough to be the same White Rabbit Casey Senior was chasing.

"I don't know, but we're going to add surveillance to the printing press until we figure it out."

Matteo jumps slightly as his phone buzzes in his hand. Frown lines crease his brow as he flips through a message. He shoots me a look, then glances back at his phone.

Nina leans over my arm and sloshes a drink toward Matteo. "You guys look *waaaay* too serious. This is a party." She executes a cute little wiggle in the seat next to me. "And, MG, your friend Lawrence was *so* good tonight. Your costume was divine!"

Matteo's eyebrows draw together, and I realize he's put two and two together. "Your friend . . . Lawrence." I can literally see comprehension dawning.

I sip my beer and try to look innocent.

Matteo sighs. "Well, I don't have time to talk to him, er, her, right now. Probably tomorrow by the time this all gets wrapped up, but I'll tell Rideout I located him. Her. Lawrence." He motions to his phone, picks up his water, and salutes the table. "My apologies, ladies. I didn't want to crash the party, just stopped by to say hello. MG, I'll catch you later?"

I spin to face him, relief and curiosity warring for dominance in my heart. "You're leaving?"

"Yeah, that was work." He stands, straightening his tie. His eyes slide past me, and I can tell he doesn't want to say anything in front of our audience. So I follow him out the door and to the parking lot.

It smells like a summer night just before a storm; a wet heaviness hangs in the air, and the clouds seem charged.

Matteo vibrates with an anxious energy. "There's a ship off schedule that just pulled into the dock outside the warehouse. It could be nothing, but patrol has been watching specifically for something like this."

"But you think it's something?"

He shrugs. "I'm not sure. Detective Rideout and Agent Sosa think we're chasing our own tail and wasting resources monitoring this warehouse. The drug operations know it's under surveillance, so Sosa thinks they'd never continue to use it." Matteo runs a hand down his face.

I chew my lip. "I can see her point." I hesitate. "But . . . the dock. The warehouse. The rabbit, then the boat. It's all the progression in the book. I think the ship thing is our best bet at following the Hooded Falcon. At least until we figure out the printing press angle. If you stop watching the warehouse, what happens if we miss the next clue? What happens if we miss the White Rabbit himself?"

"That's what I'm thinking too." He tucks the phone back in his pocket. "I'll call you if I find anything."

I cross my arms. "What if you miss it? The clue, I mean. You would have missed the white rabbit without my help."

He shoots me a look. "You're not coming."

Oh yes. I am.

"I didn't say I'm coming with you. I just asked what if you miss a clue." I watch enough true crime TV to know that he can't take a civilian along, but if I just happen to feel like strolling in the warehouse district of LA at night, well, then he couldn't stop me from exercising my basic rights.

He studies me, sensing a trap. His phone buzzes again, and he starts walking to his car, pushing the unlock button on his fob. The lights flash on a dark sedan that I gather is his undercover car. "I'll call you once I'm there and see what's going on."

"You should probably get going. Toodles." I wave at him and turn, making a show of walking back toward Hamburger Mary's.

"Michael-Grace . . ." Matteo can tell something's up.

"What? I already said I know I'm not going with you."

Of course I'm going. Just not *with* him. I'm the Captain freaking Janeway of my own destiny, and if he thinks I'm going to let him or that jerk Detective Rideout screw with *my* crime scene, with the masked avenger masquerading as *my* favorite hero, when it's *me* who tipped them off in the first place? Not to even mention the fact that Rideout thinks it's *me* working with the Golden Arrow? Forget Captain Janeway. Trekkies unite and all due respect, but she has to play by Starfleet's rules. I shove aside the niggling thought that I should play by the rules. I need to be a rule*breaker*. A vigilante hero of my very own. I am the Han frickin' Solo of my destiny now.

CHAPTER 18

It takes me a moment to debate. If I stay, I could catch L before the police talk to him. If I leave, I won't get a chance to talk to Lawrence until *after* my midnight stroll in East LA. I don't have time to dither, and Matteo is already at his car. My come-to-Jesus meeting with L is going to have to wait.

I yank my phone out of my purse as I run, ricocheting off any number of men, women, queens, and the rainbow in between as I go. Normally I'd apologize. Right now I have to get to my *Millennium Falcon* and get to a nunnery—er, warehouse.

I'm texting and running, a huge no-no, but manage to get one sent off to Lawrence.

> Something big came up, had to go. You were wonderful. Need to talk after your show, will text you later.

I'm startled when the phone buzzes not a few moments later. Usually L is MIA during a show. L's message makes me laugh out loud. Well you wouldn't want it to be small, would you? Have fun, I know I would.

Oh, L. Only he could make me truly belly laugh in the middle of chasing a police detective chasing a masked avenger chasing criminals unknown. L better still love me after I explain the mess I've gotten him into.

I skid in my heels on the pavement as I run down the poorly lit aisle toward the Hurtling Turd, now thusly dubbed the Millennium Turd. I am, after all, Han Solo. I catch sight of a set of taillights pulling out of the parking lot and breathe a huge sigh of relief. The lights belong to a dark new-model sedan, and I'd bet dollars to doughnuts that Matteo is behind the wheel.

I slide into my car and pray over the steering wheel, *Please, oh please, oh please, start.* The engine cranks on the first try, and I crow in triumph. Oh, how I'd give my left arm for light speed at this moment.

It's only several moments more before I too am out on the main street on my way to the warehouse. In fact, it's not too long at all before I can see the dark sedan ahead of me in traffic. Okay. I can do this. This is about stealth. I need to stay far enough back in traffic so he can't see—

My phone rings.

I don't need to look to know it's Matteo, but I look just so I can see his name on my phone. "I don't answer phone calls," I announce to my passenger seat, where the phone flashes. I reach over and send it to voice mail.

Surely he can't see me. There's no *way* he can see me. I intentionally let a huge pickup truck cut me off.

My phone rings again, and again I send it to voice mail. *"I don't answer calls."*

Matteo didn't say the words "You cannot show up at the crime scene" to me. He just said I wasn't going *with him*. Big difference. He must have figured out my loophole.

My phone dings my text message tone. Smart man. But I'm smarter. I glance at the phone, where Matteo's name is lit up on my display. There's a one-word text underneath: No.

"Oh, I'm sorry, Matteo," I say in my best stewardess voice, picking up the phone. "I don't text and drive either."

I click off the phone, toss it back on the passenger seat, and proceed in a blessedly quiet car toward the coast.

I decide I can't quite shadow Matteo directly to the warehouse district. Traffic thins. I get off an exit early and weave my way through dark streets, picking up my phone again and using my GPS to guide me.

"Okay, no big deal. Remember? I'm Han Solo." I throw the Millennium Turd into park and switch off my lights. Except now I remember that Han was supposedly frozen in carbonite for a *year* before his rescue, so maybe not the best battle cry.

I'm about a block east and a block north of the warehouse, and it's dark. Like the inside of Dexter's mind dark. Patches of low clouds block any moonlight, and surprise, surprise, the streetlights in this part of the city work only every so often. I reach over and grab my phone, wondering if I should predial 911. I mean, it's not like there are just people lurking on every corner looking to grab the next person that walks by. I don't want to be paranoid. But I also don't want to be stupid. I already know there might be some legitimately *bad* people in this area getting ready to move hundreds of thousands of dollars' worth of illicit substances.

I debate only a moment longer. Somewhere out here is a masked avenger. I'd bet my near-mint copy of *The Black Canary* number 1 on it. The heels of my shoes crunch as I step gingerly onto the gritty, cracked pavement, and I close my door as quietly as I can . . . which feels like the decibel level of approximately 6.7 air horns. I need desperately to get a new car. The Millennium Turd is just not a stealth vehicle. Speaking of, I'm not really dressed for stealth myself. The dark colors that happen to make up my outfit are sparkly as well. I'm about as well hidden as a disco ball at a flashlight festival.

I scoot across the street and into the deeper shadows afforded by the taller warehouse. Then I creep up the block. I jump out of my skin only once when something skitters away from me into a broken window, and once when a car door slams farther down the street. I see one other person hurrying in the opposite direction. I stay where I am, stock-still, until he passes. Not a few seconds later, a car engine roars to life, and headlights spill against the metal buildings.

After what seems like an eternity, I ease around the corner of the warehouse I'm looking for. A large semi idles in front of the huge bay doors, a shipping container strapped to the flatbed trailer. A crew of maybe eight men pack the container in an efficient manner, though I can't identify the crates from this distance. I wish I owned binoculars. I'm hoping against hope that this is the White Rabbit's crew. All of this will be over, and I can move on with my life, and my best friend and I won't have to be the number-one suspects in a crime Lawrence knows nothing about.

I peek around the corner again. This time I catch sight of a group of men moving toward the end of the building where I'm halfway hidden. One tall and slender, the other two built like refrigerator boxes with legs. Comic book criminals if I've ever seen any. I chance one more glance to confirm. They are most definitely headed in my direction. *Well, bantha fodder.* What am I going to do now?

Scanning the wall isn't much help. It's a metal building with windows higher up. But it's dark. Maybe I can just suck in my tummy and stand in the shadows and hope they don't turn the corner? I channel "Grecian Urn" with all my might, as if every warehouse has a sparkle-clad statuary that I'm blending into. My heartbeat accelerates to a slow gallop. *This* is probably why it's a bad idea for me to be here.

And then I see it. The little cove of a door along the wall, shrouded in inky darkness. It's a perfect hiding spot, thank the stars above.

Not one second too soon, I skitter on tiptoes to the doorway, and just as I catch the barest glimpse of the men round the corner, I step back into the alcove and let the shadows swallow me.

I land against something softer than a building, something that gives an audible grunt when I step on its foot. That something slips a hand around my face, covering my mouth, muffling my scream.

"You are in *big* trouble," a voice growls in my ear. My pulse beats so wildly, my head swims. I scrabble at the hand trapping my mouth and attempt to bite it at the same time. I am rewarded with another grunt and a slight lessening of the pressure. I squirm and wiggle, trying to get even a fraction of an inch of space to maneuver.

I was at a wedding once where a drunk bridesmaid accidentally drove her stiletto heel clear through another girl's foot on the dance floor. I might not make it all the way through the arch of the foot beneath mine, but I'm hoping if I replicate the move, I'll cause him enough pain that he lets me go.

I gather my strength, lift my foot, approximate the location of my captor's limb, and do a quick countdown in my head. Three, two . . .

I catch the slightest scent of cinnamon.

"Matteo?" Only there's a hand over my mouth, so it comes out "Mmm-mmm-ohmmmm?"

"Shhh." I recognize the voice this time. "I'm going to let go. Don't scream, okay?"

I nod against his hand, and it drops from my mouth. He shifts me slightly to the side like we're hugging, and we melt into the alcove together, my heart hammering for several reasons. Most pressing is definitely the footfalls I hear on the pavement maybe twenty feet to our left. What if they are looking specifically for *this* door? The other reason is definitely Matteo's proximity. We're pressed together from thigh to shoulder. It's better than I imagined.

Matteo seems to have the same thought and shifts his body against me. My cheek presses against a hard material under his jacket. It's Kevlar, unless I miss my mark. I love a man in uniform—well, costume. I'm thinking now of expanding that admiration into hot space-cop tropes. The point still stands that Matteo is in Kevlar, and here I am parading around in pleather. I've *really* misread the situation's danger level.

Footfalls approach, and Matteo lifts his hand to his side. It's hovering just above where I assume his holstered firearm is. I hold my breath as we watch the group of three men walk past the alcove without even a glance. They're talking about their next delivery and joking quietly about mundane things. Drug smugglers wouldn't be telling dirty jokes, would they? They'd be searching every nook and cranny for cops. I almost give a mirthless laugh; right now they'd definitely find one.

They continue along the street, and I can feel Matteo relax a little bit. He takes a half step back, allowing me to right myself from the uncomfortable angle I've been standing in pressed into the corner.

"What are you doing here?" I ask, keeping my voice low.

"I'm out here looking for you since I knew that you'd be here." He doesn't bat an eye. A foregone conclusion that I'd risk my own neck. "I should ask you the same question. Why are *you* here?" He sounds mad. I glance up at him, and his face is carefully blank. Professional Detective Kildaire at my service.

"I went for a pleasure stroll? At night? In a crime-infested neighborhood?"

"And what was your plan if you happened upon an unsavory character?"

"Who says I *haven't* come across one? I had a plan." He's still basically blocking my body in the alcove, though I can't hear anyone else. His nearness intoxicates me. I can't control my breathing. I feel half-panicky, half-giddy, like I'm on the best and fastest ride at the carnival.

"You did bite me," he says, his voice close to my ear. Less mad this time. I hear a faint tone of amusement.

"That was part one. *This* was part two." I place the heel of my stiletto where I assume the arch of his foot is and jump half my weight onto it. "Only harder than that. I don't want to hurt you. I've seen a stiletto go straight through a foot."

A strangled noise escapes his lips, half pain, half laugh. Matteo scoots back in surprise, eyes wide as he looks down at me. "Only you would use fashion as a weapon, Michael-Grace Martin. You are singularly the most infuriatingly fascinating person I've ever met."

I chance a look up at his face because I can't tell if he's angry or amused. What I find there takes my breath away. He's looking at me . . . *really* looking at me. I'm hyperaware of our close proximity, the darkness of the alcove, the racing of my heart, and the mere inches that separate our lips.

"You are compromising my case." His voice is husky. I hardly hear his words because I'm too entranced by his five-o'clock shadow and the movement of his full bottom lip. Once the words do register, I'm not sure if he means I'm compromising *him* by our close proximity or the case by the fact that I'm chasing down criminals on my own when I should have been letting the police handle it.

He leans an inch closer, and I can sense the war within him. The inevitable gravitational pull our lips have against the sense that this is a very, *very* bad idea.

WWJD—What Would Janeway Do? She'd probably have a diplomatic answer. Screw her. Diplomacy is overrated. What would Han do? He'd kiss the girl. So that's exactly what I do. I reach out, slide my hands up his jacket, twine them around his neck, run my fingers through the slight curls at his nape, and pull his lips to mine.

The world bursts into color as my lips meet his. He's not hesitant to follow my lead. It goes beyond chaste first kiss. Instantaneously searing, the product of two people who have been dancing around this contact for weeks. I've never had one simple kiss undo me in milliseconds. His hand wraps around my waist and pulls me to him, firmly, possessively, the buckles on the Kevlar digging into my own chest. I want the vest off. I wish I felt his heart pounding against mine. I want more.

The sky behind my eyelids bursts a brilliant and ferocious orange and magenta. Thunder rolls across the sky. I'm breathless and flying through the stars, my body alight with a fire that stems from the point where my body meets Matteo's.

That is, until I realize that the fireworks and thunder aren't just in my head. They've actually happened.

Matteo and I jump apart, realization dawning at the same moment.

"W-what was *that*?" My voice shakes as I draw a deep gasping breath. Maybe because I'd just had the most intense first kiss of my entire life in the alcove of a warehouse? Or because things are exploding and the man I was just kissing is already holding a gun?

Matteo grazes my cheek with one hand. "You stay here, okay?" His gaze lingers on my lips for just a moment. He leans in, brushes my lips ever so briefly with his, then dashes out of the alcove, while I'm a little slower on the uptake. My brain still fights with the intense wave of lust that crashed through me, my head still spinning from the kiss, but my eyes are searching the street outside, looking for danger. And my ears are straining to put a label on the rolling, thundering noise I heard.

With one good mental slap, I'm back on my feet, all senses firing together. I don't want to stay *here* all by myself while someone's bombing the neighborhood. I feel vulnerable and alone without Matteo's solid mass beside me. He's already sprinting up the street, and I follow at a safe distance, constantly glancing behind me to make sure I'm not being followed. A plume of smoke and fire rises above the warehouse district. What looks like an explosion only a few blocks away.

Other people are running up the street now, but they don't seem to be chasing either one of us. The fireball in the sky even draws the crew loading the crates. I don't have much time to scan the faces because I'm already sprinting up the street after Matteo. *Don't trip, don't trip, don't trip* beats a staccato in my head as I run. One errant rock and I'd have road rash.

"What's going on?" I wheeze as I flop to a stop next to Matteo's dark sedan. He's already halfway inside, the key in the ignition, the radio in his hand.

"Jesus, MG. Do you ever listen to me?" He runs his hands through his hair in frustration, then seems to shrug it off. Bigger fish and all that. "I don't know what's going on. I'm listening to the scanner."

I fall quiet. Well, as quiet as an out-of-shape girl who hates running—much less in stilettos—can be. Which isn't very.

The fire's intensity already diminishes, though enough of it still burns for me to see clouds of smoke filling the sky. Even here I can smell the faint hints of burning wood and an acrid smell that reminds me of fireworks.

Matteo says a string of gibberish into the radio, letters and numbers that mean nothing to me. Matteo looks concerned. No, he looks pissed. A garbled response immediately, and somewhere in the distance a chorus of sirens lifts into the cloudy night.

"Get in." Matteo reaches over and pushes the passenger door open.

"I—what?"

"Get in the car, MG. Please." All business. "I need to respond to this. I don't know what's going on, and I'm not leaving an unarmed civilian here alone."

So now I'm not Michael-Grace. I'm hardly even MG. I'm an "unarmed civilian" he needs to protect.

His face softens. "I'm not leaving *you* alone. Not here. I need to know you're safe. Get in, please."

I cross quickly in front of the car, slide in the passenger side, and the car lurches forward before I even have the door shut. I glance over. Matteo clicks his seat belt, and I do the same. There is zero conversation as we speed along the street. At each stop he flips a switch for his lights and we fly through the intersection. A mess of static and different voices fills the radio. Some must be dispatch, and some are officers responding to the scene we are headed toward.

I catch a word I recognize among the gibberish. "Did they just say Marvelous?"

Matteo's face is grim, focused on the road as he drives. "Yes. There's been an explosion and a fire. While I was requesting backup at the warehouse and talking with the Coast Guard and . . ." He trails off, and I *know* he's reliving our kiss. My stomach drops through the floor of the car. "While I did all of that," he continues, "we guessed wrong. Not only were those guys loading crates *into* the warehouse; we missed the Golden Arrow. We chose the wrong lead, and it literally blew up in our faces."

We. At least we are still a team in his mind.

"What do you mean?" I rock violently from side to side as we fishtail into a parking lot filled with police cruisers and a firetruck. The sign that just flashed by my window confirms my suspicion.

"I mean"—Matteo throws the car into park and is halfway out the door before he turns to me—"the Golden Arrow just blew up Marvelous Printing."

He shuts his door with a slam, and my mouth falls open. How could he possibly know that? I start to open my door when I see it.

I know how he knows.

The fire inside the building has all but burned out, but on the lawn, just off the quiet commercial street where Marvelous Printing resides, there's a fire still burning. Artfully drawn with some sort of long-lasting fuel and set aflame, an arrow burns bright in the darkness.

CHAPTER 19

The smell of acrid smoke stings my nose and eyes the moment I'm out of the car. "Oh my *God*, it's a golden arrow."

"No. Absolutely not. MG, you get back in that car right now, and that's an order." He returns to where I stand outside the car, reaches behind me, and reopens the door to the sedan.

I cross my arms. I want to see this building. I want to know what's going on. This is my case too, dammit. And *my* friends are suspects, and Rideout thinks it's me, and someone killed my boss's father over it.

I swear a vein is about to explode in Matteo's head. He grits his teeth, looks swiftly around, then reaches for me. He drags me forward two steps until we're so close, I can smell his soap again, even over the scent of fireworks in the air. My heartbeat races wildly, thinking he's going to kiss me, right here, in front of everyone. Instead, he leans his forehead against mine, takes a deep breath, and speaks very quietly. "Michael-Grace, for the love of all that is good, will you *please* get in the car? I need all of my attention focused on figuring out what's going on, and I can't *do* that if I'm worried about you." He cuts off my argument before I can even make it. "I'm not saying you're not capable. I'm saying this is *my job*. You are not trained for a crime scene, and there may be other explosions. This case is important to you. I get that. But right now I need to make sure you're not complicating things further and that you're safe, okay?"

I snap my mouth shut. His sweetness sops up my usual vinegar, and my hackles lower. Fire crews make their way across the parking lot and cautiously into the building. It wouldn't be just my neck I'd be risking. If someone had to come looking for me, it'd be their neck too. It would be Matteo's neck I'd be risking. Without another word, I slide into the car and let Matteo close the door behind me.

He jogs off into the smoke, and I feel a twinge deep down in my stomach. Guilt? Over kissing him? Anxiety for his safety? Worry that our feelings are a complication to this case? Fear that I won't get a repeat of the singular most amazing kiss I've had in all my years on this planet?

I sit and listen to the radio, which chatters incessantly. There are so many buttons, I wouldn't even know how to turn it down. A few minutes later, Agent Sosa and Detective Rideout arrive.

My phone buzzes, and I jump. I guess I'm a little on edge watching all these police milling around. It's Lawrence. I look at the time and groan. It's already well past midnight. And rather than sitting at IHOP with Ryan and Lawrence, I'm sitting in the passenger seat of an undercover cop car listening to static about 10-30s and Code 10s.

Just checking on you. I hope your hot date is going well! Don't do anything I wouldn't do. Xoxo.

I chuckle. That wouldn't leave much off the table. I bite my thumbnail, then reply, You have no idea. I'm safe and sound, call you tomorrow. We need to talk first thing. My anxiety reappears full force. I got lucky diverting Matteo tonight.

Almost immediately the dots appear that show me L is typing back. It can't be going that well if you replied to my text. Get back to that hunk of man, and I'll talk to you tomorrow.

If only it were that easy. I tuck the phone away, lean my head back against the seat, and close my eyes. Guilt over sharing Lawrence's journal with the police and Casey Junior has me sinking in my seat. I broke my promise; now L is a suspect. If there's a dirty cop involved, Lawrence going in for questioning could be trouble. There's a murderer on the loose who could kill him for his journals. Or for that matter, kill me for putting it all together. Solving this case could very well mean saving my friend's life. Or my own.

An idea starts to form, a way to protect Lawrence. I sigh and stare at the ceiling of the car. If I execute the plan, it will mean lying *yet again* to Matteo and the police. I'm caught in the perfect storm of lies, truth, and thirty-year-old ghosts.

After what seems an eternity, Matteo climbs back into the car. I stifle a yawn, rub my eyes, and sit up from my seat a bit. He appraises me for a full beat in the relative dark of the car, but even so, I can tell his eyes are bloodshot from the smoke. He's brought the smell of burning campfire into the car with him. "Were you asleep?" he asks.

Despite being bloodshot, his eyes soften as they take in my appearance. That odd sense of familiarity passes over me—the feeling I've known this man for much longer than I have. Like he's seen me half-asleep in my Wonder Woman pajamas for a lifetime and still thinks I'm adorable. It's the first time I've given credence to past lives; maybe Matteo was more to me in another universe too.

"Mmmm, maybe dozed off a little." I sit up straight, wiggling my toes. I'd taken off my shoes in an effort to sit more comfortably, and now I regret it. "What's the word?"

He shimmies out of his jacket, then awkwardly out of the Kevlar vest. The shirt beneath is filthy, pressed to his chest with sweat and soot. One yank has the button-down shirt pulled over his head, leaving him in nothing but his slacks and a white T-shirt that clings to his shoulders. I'm suddenly *very* awake. Yum.

He tosses those in the back seat, then reaches forward, cranks the engine, and begins driving.

"The explosion was well contained in the front lobby. A lot of flash but not much structural damage. It looks like it was meant to attract attention rather than destroy the building."

"Like fireworks." I remember the acrid smell that wafted our direction.

The look he gives me is odd. "Yes . . . *exactly* like fireworks. How did you know that?"

"I didn't *know* it. I guessed. But it's good that the building is intact, right?"

"There's a fair amount of smoke damage, but yes. Largely, it could have been worse."

I sit back against my seat and stare out at the dark streets streaking past my window. "So . . . why would someone do that?"

Matteo looks tired. He draws a hand over his face. It's a thinking face, but more than that, it's a frustrated thinking face. "I don't know. I have theories, but each seems as unlikely as the next."

We're almost back to the warehouse. I vaguely recognize the street we shot down on our way to the fire.

"Do you think this is the Yee connection? That somehow someone found out?" I ask.

Matteo is silent.

"But why would he burn Marvelous Printing?"

Matteo eases up behind my car and puts the sedan in park. "Again, I don't know. It seems like it was for attention. Either way, I missed my mark tonight. And Detective Rideout isn't happy with me. He can tell I'm . . . distracted right now."

I've mucked things up more than that. No matter that it was two sets of lips doing the kissing, it was most definitely my idea to close the gap.

Matteo watches my face. Reading my mind. "Michael-Grace, I wouldn't have traded that kiss for anything. It's just . . . you could have gotten hurt. I let my feelings take precedence over my job, and my job, this case, is the most important thing right now, you know? Detective Rideout was right to call me on it. He also thinks that you somehow convinced me to be at the warehouse on purpose tonight. I don't know why he's so convinced that your motives aren't pure, but tonight didn't help disprove his theory. I told him he was crazy, but he's threatened to bring our . . . involvement up to the captain."

My face falls.

"MG, this case won't always be between us. But we need to figure out what's going on, and right now that's more important than how I feel about a kick-ass girl I met in a coffee shop, okay?"

All of a sudden it feels like the end of a date. And not the good kind. Matteo is quiet. He looks spent, and I don't doubt it's been a long day for him. I fight the impulse to reach across the car. To reestablish the connection I felt earlier.

"Okay," I say, making a production of putting my shoes back on my feet and jingling my keys.

Matteo takes a breath in, holds it for a few counts, and lets it back out. "MG?"

I turn to face him, keys in hand.

"You *didn't* have anything to do with tonight, did you?"

I hate that he has to ask, and my heart falls further. "No."

"And you don't know who set the fire?"

"No. I would have told you."

He nods slowly. At least I feel like he believes me, but he looks back up, and I can still see the smallest shred of doubt in those dark eyes. "Okay. It's just that this is serious business. After today it means charges of breaking and entering. Arson. This has gone beyond tame wannabe-superhero stuff. It's outright dangerous for everyone involved. There won't be a slap on the wrist. This means jail time. Even if it ends up being one of your friends."

I swallow and nod. Lawrence. Or one of my coworkers. Or major charges against *me* if someone—Rideout, the Golden Arrow, whoever— is trying to frame me like Matteo suggested. Serious business indeed. Suddenly the Golden Arrow seems scarier than the White Rabbit. More tangible. Closer to me, breathing down my neck. When did my super-hero become a villain?

"I'm going to make sure your car starts." *Detective* Kildaire is back.

"I guess you'll call me when you have more information?"

He nods. "I'll be in touch. Don't say anything to anyone until you hear from me, okay?"

I open the door and step out into the night. After being ensconced in the car for more than an hour, it's chilly in the damp quiet of the sleeping city. I have the strangest urge to lean back in and tell Matteo it's going to be okay. My gut still says there's something tied to the warehouse. Something we missed tonight because the Golden Arrow had other plans.

True to his word, he waits until my car sputters to life. Rather than refreshed, I feel like my damage bar is lower than ever. My shields are down. My heart is battered. This Friday night definitely has not turned out at all like I thought. And somewhere out there, our masked friend still runs free.

CHAPTER 20

Lawrence buzzes like a bee, cleaning up the station where he trimmed my hair while I'm ensconced in one of those bubble-orbit hair dryers with my foils. It's too bad I'm here to ruin Lawrence's day and maybe our friendship. It's been three days since the fire at Marvelous Printing. The media has covered the fire as suspected arson and hasn't publicly announced the Golden Arrow's involvement. That doesn't stop pictures of the burning arrow from showing up on Twitter or blog posts the police probably don't want published. The Golden Arrow is gaining quite the cult following, truth be told. I've seen more than one post praising the person for "doing what the police couldn't" and a few about people trying to contact the Golden Arrow to see if he needs a sidekick. People aren't just fawning over him; they are contemplating following his example. Exactly what the police are hoping to avoid.

Radio silence from Matteo since Friday night, though I know Lawrence is on his short list. I've been on pins and needles, waiting for Matteo to show up at any moment, or at the very least call me to tell me he's arresting my bestie. Finally, I couldn't stand waiting. I told L I want to get a new color for the gala, and here I am. Lies of omission.

We're just finishing making my hair Power-Up Blue, and I couldn't love it more. Just shy of navy, and it screams superhero. Superman wishes he had hair this awesome.

I pretend to read through the new issue of *The Hooded Falcon*. The fire has set back production at Marvelous Printing. Nothing major damaged, but all the machines needed to be cleaned over the weekend. I got a call from Andy early this morning informing me that our limited run of *Hooded Falcon* origin books was lost in the fire. He dropped off a new test copy, straight off the press, just this morning, and he needs everyone on the team to sign off on the test copies *today*. It's the only way the issue will be released in time for the thirtieth anniversary.

"Weight-of-the-world-type stuff?" Lawrence catches me staring out the window into the waning late afternoon light. The Monday rush hour is winding down, and the roads are quieter. It's my favorite time of day—pensive. Not quite dark enough to need light, not quite light enough to see well, everything made of part shadow, part reflection. If I were a superhero, this would be the time of day I'd go crime fighting.

I sigh. "More like fate-of-the-world-type stuff."

L arches one perfectly drawn brow at me. He sets down the broom, spins the chair next to me, and settles in it. "This sounds serious. Is there a shortage of sequins for my dress?"

Despite my anxiety, laughter bubbles out of me, and I instantly feel better. "No, I have all the material I need for your dress, you tall drink of water."

"Is it Hot-Lanta?"

"Part of it."

"Your date didn't go well? I've been wondering why you haven't texted gushing. Bad kisser? Fish lips?"

I think back to the "date" where we saw a drag show, kissed in an alcove, and missed catching the person who set off an explosion at a printing press. "It's complicated. I like him. And he likes me. But the timing isn't right." Like we are just two normal people who met in a coffee shop. I sigh. Rip off the Band-Aid. "But that's not what's got me in a funk. Well, not all of it. L, we need to talk."

"Girl, you're not breaking up with me for that tramp down the street? He wouldn't know navy from cyan."

"No, definitely not. You're still my best friend, but . . . I may not be yours after this."

"I doubt you could make me hate you, M. What's up?"

I bite my lip and toss the test copy of *The Hooded Falcon* onto the countertop with L's styling tools. "Do you remember the journal you showed me? Well, I kind of broke my promise to you. I showed the copies to someone."

Lawrence frowns at me, an expression I see so rarely, it makes me swallow in nervousness. "You showed someone the copies I gave you?"

"Yes. I'm sorry."

"Michael-Grace, I knew you'd end up showing one of your nerdy friends. It's not a big deal. I still have my journal, and you got your research."

I close my eyes. "It wasn't a nerdy friend. It was the police."

"You . . . *the police*? Why on earth would you need to show sketches to the police?"

Go big or go home? If I'm going home, I'm going home big because everything tumbles out in a rush. "Because I've been helping investigate a rash of copycat comic book crimes. Matteo is a narcotics officer, and my boss was in for an interview. Matteo showed him the copies, and Casey Junior is convinced the new crimes are linked to drug dealers his dad was following before he died and that he was murdered by a crooked cop." I swallow, nearly tossing my cookies onto the floor. "And you . . . were there. Casey Junior said you were involved. And you have a journal, so now you're kind of a person of interest in the case, so I need to ask you some questions before the police show up to take you in for questioning."

We both look at the door. I half expect to see Matteo marching into the little shop, furious that I'm interfering *again*. That would probably be the nail in the coffin for us romantically, and Rideout would *definitely* have his proof that I'm meddling in the case.

I refuse to look in the mirror or at Lawrence. Long moments pass. I shut my eyes, contemplating becoming a praying woman.

"That's a lot to handle." No sass. No character. Pure unfiltered Lawrence.

I open one eye. He's still in the room with me and hasn't bludgeoned me with a curling iron, so that's a minor success. "I know."

"You've had *all* that going on and you haven't told me?"

My long-held breath explodes out of me. "The police told me to keep my involvement secret. There have been threats made against people involved in this case."

"I see." Sarcasm drips from his words. "Thanks for letting me know I'm involved." Cue internal eye roll.

"I'm really sorry, L." My voice sounds a little quavery. I will *not* cry.

He stands up, lets out a deep breath, and wipes his hands on his pants. "I guess what's done is done. What do you need from me?"

"Are you mad?"

"Beyond pissed."

"Are we okay, though?"

"We will be, eventually. Let's work on keeping my ass out of jail first, shall we? You owe me some damn fine costumes for at least a year to make up for this."

I offer a small smile that doesn't extend much past my lips. "Deal. I need to know if you have any other journals, and . . . well, the police are going to ask for the journal, and I want to see it before they have it. I think we should copy it in case the crooked cop gets his or her hands on it."

He moves off, removing his color-guard apron and tossing it on the counter as he goes. "I'll go grab it. Come with and ask me whatever else you need to know."

"Okay. Do you have any more journals or know where more of them are?"

"No, I was just given the one by Senior as a gift. Maybe he gave the others away. I don't know. He was pretty eccentric. Maybe he hid them in a safe or something."

That confirms my suspicions, but at least L is a second voice for that. I follow him up the narrow stairs in the back of the salon to his apartment. It's cluttered with what I can describe only as bachelor queen kitsch. Pieces of costumes, wigs, piles of workout magazines, and dirty dishes scattered around a one-color-palette living room dominated by a TV and gaming system. "Okay. I also need to know about your relationship with Edward Casey Senior. I know you said you worked for him and he helped out, but his son seems to feel like it was more. Not in *that* way, but as in you guys spent a lot of time together?"

Lawrence digs through a box on the kitchen counter, muttering to himself. "I didn't give you the journal, did I?"

"No, you made copies and took it back." A tingle starts at the base of my spine.

"Maybe I put it in my closet up here." He opens what should be a second smaller bedroom door to reveal his personal walk-in closet. Rows and rows of queen costumes. I rarely come in here; he keeps his current stuff downstairs. Lawrence has amassed an impressive collection of fabric.

I'm in awe, looking at a history of my costume design skills. I spy a hastily sewn drapey white evening gown with a stitch so crooked, my fingers itch to rework the entire thing. My first costume for L.

"L, do you keep *all* my costumes?"

"Of course I do. They're works of art. Listen, I mean it. When you're winning awards for costume design, I'm going to sell these for millions. MG originals." He's digging through a stack of papers on a side table.

It touches something inside me. I forget the case for a moment and run my hands along the fabric. This is why I love design. Each of these costumes allows the wearer to step into another skin. To be whoever they want for the night. It's part of what I want to do with my job, and I bite my lip thinking about the promotion I may or may not get. As written right now, it doesn't out-and-out include design time. I'd still be in limbo. If I, by some miracle, get the job, do I still want it?

"Do you think the queens were serious last night about paying me to make costumes?" My mind also flashes to Nina's offer to hire me for Kyle's costume. And her offer to introduce me to the theater costumers. Maybe there's a simpler way to do what I want. If I'm willing to give up wanting to be an executive at Genius.

"You are *my* secret weapon," he jokes. "Even if I'm pissed at you currently."

"I'm serious. Do you think they'd hire me? If I quit my job or went part-time?"

Lawrence studies me from over a half stack of papers. "You want to talk about this now?"

"Yes."

He shrugs. "You've been turning them down for years now. Most of them would jump at the chance. But you'd have to do mine *first* and then the others'."

Isn't this what Ryan was talking to me about? Being creative with my own solutions instead of hammering a square peg into a round hole? Who says I can't do both? *I have been.* If I can costume part-time and write part-time, I won't *have* to get the promotion. I won't have to massage the job description. I can continue my work as a writer on the projects I love, continuing to look for opportunities at work, but not let that stop me from designing. Suddenly the Miss Her Galaxy competition holds new meaning. It's not a test anymore. It's the inaugural flight of my new decision. Let Andy have the promotion and kiss executive ass. I'm going to do what *I* am good at. I'm going to go into business for myself and design things I love for people I adore.

"It's not here. Bedroom," Lawrence says.

A dash of cold water on my thoughts. My fashion future needs to wait. We're both moving quicker now, sensing something is off.

Lawrence may be bachelor-messy, but he's not careless. Especially not with a prized possession.

Lawrence practically tears through the box under his bed, tossing items onto his pillows. "I wouldn't have put it somewhere else."

"L . . ."

"Maybe in my closet." He heads over there and paws through the junk on the floor. Old tennis racquets, a medicine ball, layers of glitter-camo *something*.

"Lawrence. You know last week how you thought someone had been in your apartment?"

Lawrence stops digging and turns to me.

"What if the Golden Arrow got your notebook?" I finish.

"Girl, this is bad. How would he even *know* that thing existed?"

I hesitate. "I told the police, and Casey Junior *did* say he thought his dad was killed by a cop."

A shadow passes over Lawrence's face. I wait for it to lift, but the gloom stays put. "That was thirty years ago. But if Junior is right and this is about his father, this is bad. Like *really bad*. And if the police are in on it, or in on it again . . ." He trails off, rubbing his hands over his face. "Did your boss really say he thought Casey Senior was murdered?"

The weight of that idea hangs on Lawrence's frame, heavy as a millstone.

"Yes. He said he thinks the heart attack ruling on the police report was a cover-up."

"I'd *suspected*, but of course, I couldn't come forward. I was a homeless high-school-dropout drag queen. I figured everyone would think I was crazy." He runs his hands over his face again and looks at the ceiling. "Casey Senior was definitely playing superhero on his own time. I just never knew that it was what he put in his comic books or that it got him killed."

I sit on the bed in the purple-tinted sunshine streaming through the sheer paisley curtains, the roller shade beneath hanging lopsided and broken. Lawrence comes to sit next to me, and we both bask in the warmness of the sunshine for a moment, lost in thought.

L's voice breaks the silence. "I was always a good kid, but my parents didn't take kindly to me coming out. My dad was head of the psychology department at a state college, and my parents had dreams of me becoming a professor or a lawyer. I failed all my classes in school except theater. I've always known it's what I wanted to do. Long story short, they kicked me out when I told them that I preferred men to women. I didn't have anywhere to live or a way to pay for school, so I started doing drag shows. Back then it wasn't as popular as it is now, and it took me a while to meet my *real* drag family. I fell in with a bit of a rough crowd at first—drugs, meaningless sex, sabotage—but it was a place to live, and I loved the stage. Anyway, one of the things they'd have me do to earn my rent was to steal stuff for them to sell. I didn't love it, but I didn't really have any options."

"Lawrence, that is *awful*."

He nods. "It wasn't good. So there I was in this ritzy neighborhood, supposed to break into this house where the people were on vacation. I broke into a window, crawled in, and came face-to-face with Casey Senior. You can imagine my shock. I'd gotten the wrong house. I think he expected me to pull a gun or something, but I've never been made of material like that. So I apologized profusely, made up some ridiculous story about how I was dog-sitting for these people, forgot my key, and broke into the wrong house by mistake." L gives a humorless chuckle. "He knew I was lying, of course, but he invited me to sit with him like I was a *guest* and not some skinny black kid who had just busted his window. He asked me my name, and I told him my real one, and when he asked what I was *really* doing, I told him the truth too. All of it. My parents, the queens, the drugs, the stealing. How we'd hit several houses in the neighborhood. I can't explain it. The guy had this energy around him. He made you want to trust him with your story."

"I get that." It's what I could feel in his house. His spirit was still there for sure.

Lawrence takes a deep breath, then stretches his legs out in front of him. "Anyway, after hearing my story, this guy I'd never met offers *me* a place to live. He says he likes my story and that lots of superheroes have tough beginnings. He tells me that I'll have to work for him, help out with watching the house for break-ins from my old crew, and help around the house, but that if I did that, I could stay until I had enough money for college. So I did."

I put my arm around Lawrence and give him a squeeze. "I had no idea."

"I don't tell many people."

"So do you think the queens you lived with are the ones we're looking for? Do you think they could have killed Casey Senior?"

"No. But if that's what really happened, I have an idea who it could be. And . . . if it is them, then Casey Senior's death *is* on my hands."

I shift on the bed as a car door slams outside. I throw myself backward on the mattress and yank up the shade on the window over L's bed to see the street below. A quick glance assures me it's not Matteo, so I turn back to L and motion for him to continue.

He nods and continues, "Casey Senior was horrified to find out that there was so much crime going on right under his nose. You know, I believe he really did think he was a real superhero. Anyway, I told him about how we'd been stealing items from the houses and giving them to various drug dealers in exchange for drugs—all types. Heroin, weed, cocaine. I didn't even use the drugs, but I was the fetch-and-steal boy to support everyone else's habits. So after hearing my stories, Casey Senior decided that he was going to make a formal complaint to the police department and that I could give them all my inside knowledge so that they could crack down on the problem and stop it cold. It was a great idea, until the police officer arrived and I recognized him as one of the drug dealers I'd stolen stuff for."

"Yikes." My pulse speeds up. I've been right to worry about crooked cops. Lawrence has already had brushes with them in the past. Maybe even someone who is recognizable today.

"Yeah. I managed to make enough hand gestures that Mr. Casey realized there was something up. I slipped out of the room, and he ended up just reporting that someone had attempted to break in through the downstairs window, and the officer left. Mr. Casey got kind of . . . excited then. He loved a good story, and a dirty cop, in his mind, was the best kind of story line. He asked me all sorts of questions and . . . well, we sort of started following the drug dealers around."

I can see where this is going. "You followed them around, and he wrote about it."

"I guess he did. At the time I thought it was a game, sort of like my job working security was also my job to rid the neighborhood of my previous friends."

L tells me about some of their escapades, many of which ring eerily true to the comic. Following a dealer to a warehouse in LA. Watching boats unload cargo into the warehouse. How they followed dealers from different rings and how Casey Senior suspected that the rings were planning a showdown. Everything falls into place in my head like a huge game of *Tetris*.

"Lawrence, this is huge. You guys should *not* have been out there tailing these guys."

"I know that now. At the time, though . . . it just seemed *fun*. Mr. Casey would come back from these trips so excited to work, and before I moved in, I guess he'd been really down in the dumps, feeling like he didn't make enough of a difference in the world writing comics. I never paid attention to *what* he wrote. I just knew that spying on bad guys was fun."

"You were Swoosh."

"Who's that?"

"The Hooded Falcon's sidekick."

"I guess so."

I contemplate all that he's just revealed. "But after he died . . . surely you could have said something then. Especially if you thought maybe he got killed for investigating these guys."

"Mr. Casey had told me that he prepared evidence for the police. Now I think maybe he'd found proof of the cop's involvement, something the cop couldn't deny, though at the time I just thought it was general 'we followed drug dealers' stuff. He was going to seal it in an envelope and send it to three different detectives so that he could be sure it got addressed. When he died and that big bust happened, I just figured that he'd done what he promised. That his information had put all of those men in jail and that his spirit could rest well knowing he'd done what he'd set out to do."

"That's really romantic."

"It's stupid is what it is, if you're saying that these guys are still in business. I don't know how they avoided that bust, but it's apparent they'd kill to keep their secret."

"And you don't know where the information went?"

"Like I said, I thought he sent it. Then he died, and Casey Junior resented me. Thought I'd brought trouble into his house—and he was right. So then I got fired, and here I am." Lawrence stands and brushes his hands on his pants.

"Thank you for telling me, Lawrence." I stand and follow him down the stairs into the shop. Still no sign of Matteo, which is good. But now I have so much more to weigh in my head.

He turns to give me a brief hug. "Don't ever lie to me like that again, okay?"

"Deal. Thanks for the dye job. I'll just grab my comic and head to the office to sign off for Andy." But I pull Lawrence's apron off my proof copy and stop dead, staring at the front page. This is definitely *my* copy. There's the telltale splatter of coffee on the back cover from my breakfast that I ate in the car, so it's not like someone snuck in and put a new cover on it. This is the cover that came out of the test-print run, but it's *not* the cover I saw Andy send to the printer. I must have looked only at the back cover when I brought it in. Someone *changed* the test-print file after I'd seen Andy send it off. I flip forward to the second page—it's exactly as I remember it, but the first page is a single panel, which we never do. Not only that, it's not a finished drawing. It's a sketch. A sketch I've seen before.

It's the Hooded Falcon and Swoosh kneeling in the middle of a dark panel, one holding out the bow to the other. It's the same panel I admired in Lawrence's journal.

"This isn't the end . . ." written in bold comic script and the words "I know" are sketched in the Hooded Falcon's dialogue bubble. Underneath the panel are four typeset words I didn't see earlier. I read them now, and the bottom falls out from beneath my feet. "And I'll find you." It's signed with the drawing of an arrow.

I'm eyeing Lawrence, the sense of impending doom as thick as the scent of dye and shampoo in the air.

I hold up the comic and point to the panel signed by the Golden Arrow. "I guess we know who has your journal."

Lawrence mutters a string of curses a mile wide.

I pull out my phone to call Andy right this very moment but catch sight of a familiar car parking on the other side of the street. *Crap, crap, crap.* And a familiar gorgeous, hazel-eyed cop driving it.

"L, is your front door locked?" Usually when he has only one client, he locks it to avoid the homeless visitors.

"Yeah, why?" Lawrence picks up my frantic vibe and cranes his neck to see out the windows.

"Matteo's here." I do a bad impression of an army crawl, hit the one light switch that's still on, and get back to my feet. "We need somewhere to hide!" I grab Lawrence's hand and pull him along toward the back hallway.

"From your boyfriend?"

I chance a look over my shoulder. We have maybe ten seconds before Matteo can look in the front door. We'll never make the stairway.

"We need somewhere where he can't see us!" I'm hysterical now. "I'm *not* supposed to be here, and I'm definitely *not* supposed to be telling you everything I know about the case."

Lawrence grabs me around the waist, opens the door to our left, and all but throws me in. He whips the door almost closed behind us, then stands along the wall so he can peer out through the crack.

"Did he see us?" I pant the words, collapsed on the floor against a rack of clothes or coats. I can't tell in the dark.

Lawrence is silent for a long minute. "He looked in, knocked. Now he's going around the back." I can see only a sliver of his face. The room is pitch-dark otherwise. "Did you lock your bike up back there?"

"Yeah." Inwardly I groan. "Maybe he won't notice."

"Maybe." Lawrence sighs, shuts the door, and flicks on the light. "If they have a warrant, we can just say we didn't hear them knocking. You were helping me sort my costumes or something." He peeks back out. "But I don't think he saw us."

My mind goes directly to the warehouse. Last time we spoke, Matteo mentioned that they were dropping surveillance. But L needs to know what he's getting into. "If we do this, things could get sketchy. It involves breaking and entering. And perhaps narcotic smuggling."

"Average Monday night for me."

I laugh. "I shouldn't get you involved."

"Honey, that's what *real* family is. They're the people you call when the bodies pile up."

I hesitate again. I want him to be fully aware of the dangers. "There's a dirty cop. Someone leaked case info already. I'm really worried that if you go in for questioning, someone bad may recognize you. I think you should take a work vacation. I'll see how the investigation is going. See if I can figure out who's leaking info."

"You want me to evade police?"

"Not evade exactly. Well-timed trip to visit your drag mom?"

Lawrence thinks for a moment. "I can lay low. I've done it before."

I sigh. "Okay. Let's do this thing. We'll call anything related to this ridiculousness . . . Operation Janeway, okay? Like a code word."

"You know what this means, don't you?" Lawrence has his usual gleam and sass back, seeming more *excited* than worried about this whole fiasco.

"That we're both terrible decision makers and likely going to end up in jail for this, but at least we'll have each other?"

"Better." Lawrence flashes me a big smile. "It means that we need to go through my closet. We are going to be the fiercest, most fabulous crime-fighting duo this town has ever seen."

CHAPTER 21

Worrying about work should be illegal while your best friend is in hiding, your *pretend* boyfriend keeps asking if you've heard from him, and you're analyzing every fact you know about a thirty-year-old murder in your spare time. I've spent most of the last three days avoiding Matteo. I think he's convinced it's because of what he said after our kiss and the fact that he's trying to track down Lawrence to question him. I *know* it's because I'm lying to Matteo. Not that I know where Lawrence is *exactly*, but the fact that he's missing . . . that's all me. Instead of sketching, I've been researching obsessively about the drug culture surrounding Casey Senior's time of death.

I made some really interesting discoveries. Namely that Detective Rideout's father had been questioned in connection with one of the drug busts right before Casey was killed. He was cleared of all charges by the police chief, but it gave me a little tingle of foreboding.

There's a story here.

The fact that Rideout's father and the police chief were chums isn't lost on me. The chief, Tony Munez, became the star of Los Angeles for pulling off the biggest drug bust in LA history. Several rings, several head honchos, all at once. There was a freaking *parade* in his honor. So when he vouched for Rideout's father, the city dropped the charges. Rideout's father retired, but the Rideout I know trained directly with Tony Munez until the older man retired as well. Talk about hero worship.

"Paging Dr. House."

My head whips up, and I come face-to-face with Kyle. The red ball I've been throwing at the wall bounces away across the room. I forgot I was even throwing it.

"Sorry, was I bothering you?" I ask.

Simon's sarcastic reply comes from behind me: "A slightly better noise to work to than jackhammering, but not much."

Whoops. "I'm sorry, guys. I've got writer's block."

"We can tell." Kyle's annoyed expression melts, and he reaches forward to grasp my shoulder. "We've all been shaken up. This week has been crazy with that lunatic running around burning down buildings."

It's easier to agree, so I nod. "Yeah. That's it. I think I need some fresh air. I just can't get this villain right for the *Hero Girls* issue."

"Well, if you're stuck when you come back, let me take a look."

Usually I'd respond with an "I got this, no problem," but I am s-t-u-c-k *stuck*, and my brain can't seem to come up with anything original. New MG thinks that just *maybe* having Kyle help won't be so bad. My shoulders relax just a hair. "Okay. I'd like that. *If* I'm still stuck."

I head out the office door and toward the elevator. I don't know where I'm going exactly, but I have this constant need to move right now. Anything to alleviate the feeling of anticipation. Like the other shoe is about to drop and I'm not going to like it.

With a ding and a hiss, the doors slide open. I step inside, only to realize that Lelani already occupies the car. She's cool and poised in a tweed skirt suit. If Casey Junior hired her for affirmative action, at least he hired someone who looks the part of an executive.

"Hello, MG."

I offer a polite smile and turn to face the front. She may not be warm, but at least she doesn't call me Michael. "Ms. Kalapuani."

We wait for the doors to close, and I lean forward to press the "Close Door" button, even though it doesn't hasten any movement.

The awkward silence stretches, though it appears I'm the only one who feels the *awkward* part of that. "So, uh, how are you liking Genius Comics?"

Lelani smiles. I note that her smile is made up of small even white teeth. The effect should be charming, but something about her smile reminds me of a shark. "I like it very much, thank you."

I can't help myself from prying. I really want to know why Casey Junior hired her. Was it just to have a skirt among the pants? "So did you work for a comic business before this? How does Genius compare?"

Her smile doesn't falter. "No, I've never worked on this side of the industry. Before this, I acted in and helped market superhero adaptations for movies."

"So you were an actress?" No surprise there; she's gorgeous. But it's an unusual résumé for a marketing executive.

The elevator begins to move. Thank God. "Among other things. I've been meaning to come find you and check in about your *Hero Girls* issue. I have some ideas."

"Oh yeah?" And now she wants to meddle. Fantastic.

"Mr. Casey isn't the most fond of it, but I'd like to become an advocate. We girls need to stick together, right?"

I study her face. She *looks* sincere. She sounds sincere too, but I can't shake the feeling that Lelani's Cheshire smile doesn't reach her eyes. That she's calculating. Maybe she's sizing me up as much as I am her. Touché. "Right."

The elevator seems to be taking forever to descend five stories. I don't know that it's ever felt this long. It's on par with how I feel reading a *Sentry* issue.

Lelani breaks the silence first. "You're a good writer, MG. The best on your team."

I'm surprised at the straightforward compliment. Two points for no womanly, manipulative mind games. "Thanks."

"But you tend to isolate yourself."

Or not. *Ouch.* Has she been talking to Casey about our promotion? "Um . . ." is all I can manage. I'm not sure how to respond.

"Your characters, I mean." She offers another smile that has me thinking she may have a hidden agenda. "I'd like to see *Hero Girls* play more with some other characters. Maybe get them into a few of the special team issues with our big hitters. Stuff like that, maximize their exposure. It makes it harder to nix the project if it's not all by itself out on a limb."

Nix the project? I'm taken aback. Partly at what might be a veiled threat and partly at the genius of her idea. It's so simply stated, so . . . *spot-on*, that I can't believe I've never thought of it before. And her comments about being a team player. Either she's been reading my mind, or she's incredibly insightful. Eerily so. Didn't I just have this conversation with Ryan?

"And your villains. I think if we changed up what you're doing just a little, we'd have more commercial success."

And just like that, my hackles are back up. "My villains don't need to be 'changed up.'"

The elevator dings, the floor sways beneath my feet, and the doors open onto the polished marble floor of the lobby. I start to step out, planning on making a hasty excuse and exit, but Lelani's cool hand on my arm stops me cold.

"I've upset you. I didn't mean that. I only meant to say that your villains, your *world*, are so black and white. Good guys and bad guys."

I huff, resisting the urge to shake off her arm. Who cares if I write Supes instead of Bat? Sure, the Falcon is a bit of a rogue, but he operates within the law . . . usually. *He* certainly has never set anything on fire like the Golden Arrow has. And while I love a good Han Solo in my love life, this is *my* writing we are talking about. "Well, of course there are good guys and bad guys. That's what comics are all about." She has to know that, being an actress and all.

Her lips press together slightly, and she shakes her loose long dark hair over her shoulder. "That's what the *old* comics are about. I'm talking about the new breed of superheroes. The new breed of villains. The gray area. I think you need to broaden your views and your writings to think that your superheroes may not always be good and your villains may not always be bad."

My mouth snaps shut. Again Lelani's insight cuts through more than just my work persona. It goes straight to the core of what I've been struggling with on the case. The Golden Arrow. The White Rabbit. The dirty cop. Me. More shades of gray than I'm comfortable with. Good guys who are bad guys. Bad guys who aren't all bad. It's *not* my usual fodder. I'm a comic book purist. *But* Lelani has a point. The gray-area stuff makes a damn good story.

Her hand drops off my arm, and she walks forward into the lobby. With a little wave at someone near the front door, she turns to look at me again. Appraising. "Take my suggestions or leave them. I am simply suggesting giving your *Hero Girls* villains a more contemporary appeal. Let readers see a complicated villain that they can identify with. Let them explore the idea that every good guy makes mistakes. Does whatever it takes to get the job done. That every antagonist has his or her own story."

With that, she walks off toward the front door. I watch her go, stymied by the insight. By the laser-point focus that woman has. She nailed every problem on the head and gave me a way to work through them. She is a freaking *genius*.

Lelani rises on tiptoe to kiss the person she's meeting on the cheek before they head out. But I know that cheek. That brush of blondish hair under a backward hat. The person she's meeting is Ryan. My Ryan. I watch as they make their way to the parking lot. Seeing "a girl from the gaming group" indeed.

I stare after them for a long moment before performing an about-face and pushing the elevator call button again.

So Ryan and Lelani are a thing. *Interesting.* Ryan and I obviously haven't been talking enough lately, but I plan to jump on him about that tonight after work. Lawrence mentioned that Ryan had a date . . . but *Lelani?*

I shrug and step back on the elevator, no longer stuck for direction with my work. Lelani is worth her weight in gold as far as I'm concerned. She's given me lots to think about, and more importantly, she's given me the seeds of a story.

Date night. Or it would be if Matteo hadn't drawn our professional line in the sand seven days ago in a parking lot lit by a burning arrow. I've spent this entire last week throwing myself at my work and L's costume. I've caught up on all my *Hero Girls* sketches and have used every free moment to work on my design for Her Galaxy—anything to keep my mind from wandering to that kiss. Matteo made it clear he likes me. His lips certainly didn't lie. But until this case is solved, we can't be together, and if Rideout somehow convinces him I'm a suspect, I may lose Matteo for good.

At least Andy and I are back on speaking terms. The moment I realized that the Golden Arrow had planted the sketch into the test print of the comic book, I went straight to Andy. Screw the promotion or what going to Andy could do to my chances; this sketch *couldn't* get out to the general public. The drug lords would come after Genius for sure. I told Andy I'd screwed up the test proof and inserted a sketch from another project by mistake. We corrected the file with Marvelous Printing and ran the prints the next day.

I feel *awful* keeping something like this from Matteo, but if someone on Matteo's team is dirty—and my suspicion can't help but land on Rideout—I don't want them knowing the Golden Arrow has the journal and is trying to publish it. Best I can figure, the Golden Arrow set the fire with the express purpose of diverting attention so he could change a file on the printing press. Another connection. Another puzzle piece.

The news has also gone quiet; the Golden Arrow seems to have gone underground. The case is in a holding pattern while the arson team sorts out the fire and the burglary team sorts out Casey Senior's office. Agent Sosa is also reviewing Huong Yee's interview. On TV the justice system works so much faster than it does in real life.

I lean over the mirror, applying mascara for the second . . . third time? I've screwed it up at least twice now because my mind keeps going to Lawrence's story and wondering *why*, if all the drug ringleaders were busted in the eighties, it is coming back around now. Had someone gotten out of jail wanting revenge and the Golden Arrow got wind of it?

There's a knock, and I swallow hard, heat rising to my cheeks and the tips of my ears. When do I ever get nervous for a date? No, a *non-date* date. When it's with the most gorgeous man I've ever seen, who kissed me like he was heading into epic battle—that's when. I smooth the black lace of my bodice and hurry from the downstairs bathroom. I kick aside the black-tulle, green-sequin mess that is the scraps from L's Comic-Con bustier and nearly trip and fall into the door.

Matteo stands on the other side, ever dashing in his button-down shirt rolled at the cuffs. "I didn't think flowers would be appropriate, but I come bearing coffee." He holds out a paper cup to me, the scent of cinnamon in the air.

I take his offering and give him a small smile. The man knows me. I'd *much* rather have coffee than flowers. Much more appropriate and appreciated. A gift for all occasions.

"You look . . . really nice." Matteo's eyes burn as they travel down my length and back up. My heartbeat speeds up, faster than a speeding bullet. Despite my concern about how many secrets I'm juggling, Matteo is irresistible. I give in to the temptation to flirt. "What, this old thing? I've had it for years, and I just thought it needed to get out beside a suit for the evening." I give a slow twirl, letting him appreciate the costume. The way the black-lace sheath dress hugs my generous curves. I spent hours updating my old Ms. Genius costume from a con, replacing the skimpy leather leotard base of the costume with a forties-era lace-bodice dress. I added my homage to Ms. Genius's lightning bolt to the top of the dress in glimmering gold satin, and at my hips lies Ms. Genius's signature scarlet wrap. Comic book chic.

He watches my slow twirl, and I revel in satisfaction watching him watch me. Any guy who loves a dressed-up geek costume is okay in my book.

I make a show of asking him to do a twirl of his own in my entry-way. "You, however, are *not* dressed properly for the gala. Matteo, this is a costume ball."

He shifts uncomfortably. "I brought this." He holds up a black plastic Zorro mask, complete with a single elastic band to hold it on his head.

"No."

"What do you suggest?"

"I was prepared for this too." I lean down and grab a plastic bag sitting by my feet near the door. I hand it to him, and he raises his eyebrows at me.

"My costume, I presume?"

"It may not fit perfectly, but it will do, and we'll go together with our forties-throwback stuff. You can only be one superhero. This is one of Ryan's. I made it for him a few years ago. Navy paratrooper pants. Navy army-inspired jacket with the insignia, and"—I back away a few steps and pick up the cardboard shield I made for Ryan—"*tada!*"

Matteo looks like he might argue with me, but he shrugs his shoulders and heads toward the downstairs bathroom. "When in Rome."

CHAPTER 22

We arrive at my office building twenty minutes late to the party, and I already can't focus. Matteo makes a really *hot* Captain America, and we touched-but-not-touched the whole car ride here. Every time I snuck a glance at him, I swear he was just turning his head from watching me. If I were a betting woman, I'd say he's just as hot and bothered as I am, judging by the sheer volume of times he's adjusted the neckline of his costume. So much for a calm professional front tonight.

The building glitters, lit up like the Eiffel Tower, from strings of Tivoli lights on the trees and strung up outside the main entrance. It's magical, surreal. A huge banner hangs in the lobby declaring the thirtieth anniversary of *The Hooded Falcon*.

We join the queue for coat check, and I nearly break my neck trying to see everything at once. Food stacked high on trays, carried by black-tie waitstaff. Buffet tables scattered around the perimeter of the large open lobby—I immediately spot my favorite artichoke dip. The very air in the room shimmers, from the lights strung across the ceiling, to the lights onstage where a live band assembles, and to the cocktail tables set up around the room with sequined tablecloths. A funky sixties-style chrome bar is set up for the occasion, flanked by two ice sculptures of the Hooded Falcon—one the original, one the current reboot. In short, it's magical, and it fills my geek heart to see hundreds of people in mostly Genius-inspired costumes turned out to celebrate my favorite fictional character.

When it's our turn, I hand the girl my long velvet coat with the maybe-real-I-don't-want-to-know fur collar—a treasured find from a thrift store. I fought Lawrence over it and won. The attendant hands me back a ticket. Then Matteo and I turn to face the room, shoulder to shoulder, Ms. Genius and Captain America among our caped compatriots.

It's all I can do not to grab his Captain America–clad hand and drag him to the dance floor to join the crush of people. The urge to be close to him distracts, though I know that Matteo is a professional; he's dedicated to keeping this about work tonight. I'm almost relieved as we push through the crowd to the bar. I need to keep my own head on a swivel. There's been no word from the Golden Arrow all week, and I can't help but *feel* he or she might be here tonight. This is, after all, a gala for superheroes.

The line for the bar is a million leagues long, so we settle in for the long wait. It gives us a good vantage point and a good reason to people-watch—how I like to label "spying on my coworkers" to myself. The guy in front of us wears an impressive adaptation of the original Hooded Falcon. His brown forest cape is draped expertly over one shoulder, and a quiver of *real* hand-fletched arrows sits on the opposite. I'm admiring the detailed stitching when I realize that I know this stitching. I *did* this stitching.

"Ryan!" I reach forward, grab the man's shoulder, and spin him around.

"Oh hey, MG!" Ryan's gaze flicks from me to Matteo, back to me, then across the room. He offers his hand to Matteo with a "Hey, man." We all stand awkwardly for a long stretch. I haven't had a chance to talk to him about Lelani. We've both been so busy this week. In fact, I've hardly seen Ryan all *month*. He's watching Matteo with a hostile look that makes me think I know why Ryan's being weird. I've never let a guy come between us before. It's a rule in our house. Yet for all he knows, I met this guy in the coffee shop and pretty much dropped off the planet.

Matteo clears his throat. "I see a colleague of mine. I'm going to go say hello. I'll be right back, MG?"

"Yeah, okay." No need to ask me twice. I want space to talk to Ryan.

Ryan's face jumps to life the second Matteo leaves. "Did you bring Lawrence? I need to talk to him, and he's not returning my calls."

"No, I—uh—think he went to visit his drag mom, right? He'll be back soon. I think he told me a week?"

Ryan frowns at me. He can *so* tell I'm lying. It's why I've avoided talking to anyone about Lawrence. With all I'm carrying around, I'm about to come apart at the seams, and Ryan knows me best.

"What did you need to tell him?" I ask.

Ryan studies my face for a minute, then glances around the room again. He looks back to me, and something odd happens. I realize that Ryan is deciding about whether to say something. Ryan, Lawrence, and I are *always* honest with one another. How has our relationship gotten to this point? I'm keeping secrets from him, and it looks like he might be keeping a secret of his own. Lelani.

I nearly hit my head with my hand. Of course, *Lelani*. He wants to talk to Lawrence about her, and he's not sure how I'll react because she's my boss. My shoulders relax.

"It's okay, Ry. I know what you've been keeping from me."

He looks startled—his eyes fly to my face, and I swear color drains from his cheeks.

I motion my hand forward. Jesus, the guy looks like he's about to have a heart attack. "About Lelani?"

Ryan still looks like I could knock him over with a feather. The line shuffles ahead, and I grab Ryan's arm and drag him up with me. "It's no big secret. I saw you guys leaving for lunch the other day. It's okay if you're seeing my boss."

Instantly Ryan relaxes. He shakes his hands slightly and blinks. "Oh . . . You saw that, did you? Yeah." He runs his hand down his face, then places it back on the thick leather belt that wraps over his cloak and costume beneath. "We're seeing each other. I'm sorry I didn't tell you."

"That's okay. I know it's a delicate situation."

Ryan's face hasn't regained all its color yet and still has that hesitant, watchful quality. He leans in closer to me. "Listen, while we're being honest, I looked into your boyfriend."

Ryan and his damn hacking.

I make some sort of noncommittal grunt. This shouldn't surprise me. Ryan and L are protective, but it *still* violates my privacy. Not to mention what he probably found out. Secrets revealed indeed.

"He's a cop."

I square my shoulders; no need to take this lying down. "Yeah, I know. I knew all along. He doesn't like telling people." It's as close to the truth as I can get in this setting. I should have been honest with Ryan from the beginning, saved us all this trouble.

"I can see why. He's working on that Golden Arrow case."

Ruh-roh. "Yeah, I guess." Time for distraction measures. "So what are you going to order? I'm thinking about getting a whiskey sour."

"MG." Ryan's hand isn't gentle on my arm, and he forces me to face him again. I'm eye-to-cloak with his costume, more specifically the large golden pin in the shape of an arrow that holds his cloak closed. Either Ryan has leveled up in his costume creation, or someone else has been fiddling with *my* costumes. Lelani. My thought derails when Ryan gives me a small shake. "This is serious. That case is dangerous."

I sigh. "I know. Ryan . . ." I glance around at the people near us in line. Almost everyone is on their cell phones, no one paying attention to us. "I've been helping a little on the case. It's how I actually met Matteo." There, closer to the truth without all the bells and whistles.

Ryan moves back a half step, taking me in. "You sure that's a good idea? The news reporters say that the drug lords are threatening anyone even *involved* with the case now. That's you, in case you're missing my point." That's Lawrence; that's Matteo too. It's probably even Ryan since he lives with me. I bite my lip so hard, I wince.

The line shuffles forward again, and I glimpse Matteo making his way back toward us. "I can't stop now, Ry. We're close to solving the case."

"But—"

I don't let Ryan finish. I paste a cheery smile on my face and reach a hand out for Matteo. "Oh good, just in time for a drink."

Matteo gives me a quizzical look but puts an answering smile on his own face. "How about that martini, then? Shaken not stirred?" He does a James Bond impression, and I like him just a *little* bit more for how bad it is.

Ryan looks between us, back stiff, face cold and impassive. "She doesn't like martinis. I think I've lost my date. I'll catch you later, MG." With a swirl of his cloak, Ryan melts into the crowd on the dance floor.

Matteo openly frowns at Ryan's back now. "What's that all about?"

Nothing is going my way tonight. "*That* was my roommate telling me that he found out I've been lying to him about you being a cop."

"Oh. But how did he—"

"Don't ask. Ryan has his ways." I will *not* get a second best friend arrested while I am still trying to protect the first. "Either way, he's mad at me, and not you."

"I'm sorry, MG." For a moment it's *Matteo* looking at me, not Detective Kildaire. "I've made things complicated."

I sigh. "Let's just catch the bad guy so we can move on, okay?" We step up to the bar, order our drinks, then turn to survey the room. There are so many people to watch, I don't even know where to start sleuthing.

"I guess we can go talk to Tej. He's the only other member of the team we haven't looked into. I can introduce you to all the marketing people."

We take a quick tour of the room and find Tej at a cocktail table eating Swedish meatballs with his wife. I let Matteo steer the conversation. I feel like I'm recovering from a one-two punch in my life: first, Lawrence has been forced into hiding because of *my* choices, and now, my other best friend is pissed—for good reason—that I lied to him about my boyfriend. And he doesn't even know the half of it.

With only partial attention, I listen as Matteo casually questions Tej about his alibi for the night of the explosion, then about the afternoon when I saw the Golden Arrow at the Casey mansion. I don't know how he sounds so *normal* asking people these things, but Tej and his wife are all smiles, sharing their alibis without a second thought. I can tell when Matteo starts using platitudes like "Maybe we'll see you next weekend for the movie marathon" that he's ready to move on. I look around for a suitable reason to drag Matteo off and find our next victim.

"I'm sorry about the promotion," Tej says, snapping my attention back to the conversation.

"Sorry?"

Tej's eyes widen, and he looks a bit like he wants to eat his words. "Yeah. Um . . . I guess they're going to announce it formally on Monday, but I thought they would have told you at the same time as Andy."

My eyes fly across the room to where Andy and Casey Junior are laughing over drinks. Most definitely celebratory, bro-hug, good-ol-boys-club, no-girls-allowed drinks. All around the table, everyone is frozen, watching my reaction. And I wait for the wave of anger, of injustice, of *anything* to crash over me. But it never comes. In my head, I'm clinging to the life raft of Ryan's words. And my conversation with Lawrence. I'm shocked to find I'm a little bummed, but . . . that's it.

"Andy was a good choice," I say carefully. "And sure, I'm bummed, but I guess this means that there's an opening for team leader now, right?" I shoot Matteo a look to gauge his reaction. He looks almost . . . proud of me. That's one I'm not used to seeing on my dates' faces.

The band strikes up a jazzy swing tune just as the conversation wraps up, and Tej's wife grabs his arm. I can tell they're looking for an easy way to extricate themselves from the awkward conversation, and I don't blame them. "We *have* to dance at least once. Come on. Maybe MG and Matteo will join us?"

In a complete reversal from the day in the lobby where he accepted the movie invitation without asking me, Matteo is hemming and haw-ing while I throw out a cheery "Sure, we'd love to." I know there's no other way to get Matteo on the dance floor, and the music drags at me. I want to just forget about Andy's promotion for a minute. I don't have the time to add that to my list of internal grievances right now, and dancing is the perfect way to achieve that.

"Come on, it's just one dance. We can scope out our next target while we're out there. And this music is perfect for our costumes." It may be a nerdy statement, but it's true. I can imagine no better music for our characters to dance to.

He protests but follows me out onto the floor, where he grabs my hand with one of his and my waist with the other. Slightly old-school, but I can dig it. We find a jazzy rhythm, and I shoot a shocked look up at him. "Matteo, you can *dance*."

"Why are you so surprised?" He frowns, and I can tell he's trying to keep this *professional*. It's starting to push my buttons because in this moment, I *dislike* Detective Kildaire. He's stuffy and focused on the case. Which is what I should be, except I'm swept away by the capes, the costumes, the jazz music, the dancing. I can't help myself. The story thread I'm picking up tonight is deeply *romantic*, in the old-fashioned sense.

I want Matteo back.

"Why am I surprised that you've got rhythm? You drive a Prius, and you drink tea."

He throws me a good-natured scowl, a piece of his dark messy hair falling across his forehead. My heartbeat accelerates. Not only is he a man in uniform tonight; he's a man in costumed uniform. I don't know that I've ever seen anything so sexy in my entire life.

"Are you really okay about the promotion? I know you really wanted it."

I think for a moment before meeting his gaze. "Yes, I think I really am. I've got some other pretty awesome things going on in my life right now, and it just seems kind of . . . small. Something I can work around."

His hand tightens on my back, and he pulls me just an inch closer. This case still stands like a wall between us, but Matteo and I are drawn together like magnets through it. If the case were over and I could finally be honest about everything, well, there wouldn't be *anything* between us anymore. My mind goes to all sorts of scenarios with nothing between us, and my face grows warm.

"Don't you look at me like that," he warns, a friendly smile plastered on his face. He spins me out, then back in, letting our bodies crash together just a smidge too much for propriety before setting me back on my feet. "We have work to do."

"I don't know what you mean. *I'm* looking for clues," I say, playing along. The music and the dancing and Matteo's hands on my waist are making me *giddy*, the heady atmosphere of the party not helping either.

"Sure you are—" Matteo drops my hand suddenly and looks over my shoulder. "Agent Sosa. I didn't know you'd be here."

"Apparently."

I turn around, schooling my features into a pleased surprise. "Oh, hello again. We met at the warehouse."

"Yes, I remember. You're consulting on the case." Her voice is chilly. There's the reminder. I can tell she doesn't approve of Matteo's conduct.

"Are you here as a guest? Or are you also here for research on the case?" I make sure to add a sweet smirk to cover my pointed explanation of *why* Matteo is here with me.

"I'm here with my husband and father. Purely pleasure tonight, I'm afraid." The corners of her lips go up in an approximation of a smile, but it doesn't reach her eyes, and her tone makes it clear she doesn't qualify our dancing as "business." I can't picture her coming from a family of comic book nerds, but you never know about people. I try not to let my judgment show.

Matteo gives a cough. "Glad you're here anyhow. MG—er, Ms. Martin has made some really impressive headway on the case this week. A possible connection from the time the original *Hooded Falcon* was written. I can catch you up on Monday if you'd like."

"Yes, I suppose I can make the time." Wow, she's *cranky* that Matteo is here. Her eyes flick to me. "I'm surprised you're still working on the case. Detective Rideout seemed to think there was a—ah, what words did he use?—conflict of interest? Don't let me get in the way of your . . . investigation, if that's what you're calling this."

Well, that just throws a bucket of ice on the only fun I've had all night. Agent Sosa moves off toward the front of the room, and Matteo and I follow suit, the fun gone from the brief moment of letting go. My heart sinks. I've obviously lost the respect of Agent Sosa by acting so unprofessionally and made her think less of Matteo as well. We don't talk about it. We just grab new drinks and snag a table near the front of the room to watch the speeches. A few friends from other departments stop by, and I introduce Matteo, but he's distracted.

Not five minutes later, the lights dim off and on, and the general din of the room drops as people move to the cocktail tables. Casey Junior appears on the stage, dressed in a stunning black tuxedo.

"MG, your roommate Ryan, how did he know I'm a cop?"

I turn to him, surprised. "The speeches are about to begin." I do *not* want to discuss Ryan's illegal activities.

"I'm serious." He has that look on his face like he's piecing together a puzzle, and I don't like it.

"Why? What are you thinking?"

"Well, he would have access to your stuff and Lawrence's, right?"

I frown. "Yeah, I guess."

"And he'd know the cops working on the case if he were . . . involved in the vigilante field of employ."

Nausea threatens. "Matteo, no. That's not it at all. Ryan's a hacker. Please don't tell him I told you. I don't want *both* of my best friends in trouble with the law."

"But you said he's smart and good with computers." Matteo is on a roll now, an aha moment written all over his face. "Able to disable a security system maybe? And he obviously loves the comics." He holds up a finger. "*And* didn't you tell me that he's got costumes, capes, and tights, the whole lot?"

"So does every nerd in this place. You saw Kyle's closet. And don't you think I'd know it if my own roommate were parading around this city in tights and a cape? Well, other than tonight, I mean. *Everyone* is in tights tonight." I'm indignant on behalf of Ryan, but I'm also a little rattled. Matteo's words sink in, and my mind runs a mile a minute. Ryan *is* all of those things. Matteo has a point.

"You're forgetting what your profiler said, though," I say slowly, my mind rewinding to the words Rideout threw at me on the stairs. "They think you're chasing a woman. Well educated. Ties to the comics industry. Ryan is a guy, high-school dropout, and works in video games."

Matteo doesn't look convinced, so I rack my brain further.

"I mean, you can ask him about it yourself, but I'm pretty sure Lawrence and Ryan were at a gaming competition for at least one of the Golden Arrow crimes."

"They could be working together." Matteo leans in now, his voice hushed but passionate. I recognize the fervor I feel when something clicks for me in my stories; only this time Matteo is off his mark.

"*Neither* of them fits the profile. Plus, Lawrence was at the drag show the night of the explosion, remember? And . . ." I struggle to recall Ryan's schedule. I snap my fingers. "Lawrence mentioned that Ryan was missing the show because he had a date."

"That could just be a cover-up." Matteo sounds *victorious* now.

"No. Not made up. She's right over there, and she'll tell you herself. I saw them going out to lunch again this week. They're a real couple." I motion over to Lelani, and beside me Matteo goes still. His shoulders slump slightly. He's gone from victorious to . . . defeated? Wow, my argument must have been excellent. I've won this round, thank Thor.

The room hushes. I catch a flash of dark hair near the front of the stage and crane my neck to catch sight of Agent Sosa standing just off the front of the stage, drink in hand and sour face still in evidence. Standing beside her and schmoozing with several of the Genius executives is someone I recognize as one of LA's government officials . . . city manager maybe? I don't pay attention to politics when I can help it, but his face and name *do* seem familiar. Which puts to rest my curiosity about her coming from a comic book–loving family.

Casey Junior is checking the mic on the podium, and I turn to watch, glad we've settled the Ryan issue. Casey Junior leans forward and addresses the crowd, "Welcome, and thank you all for sharing this night with me. I wish my father was here to see how many came to celebrate." Usually I'd roll my eyes at this, assuming he's tugging at emotions to gain customers, but now I *know* he's serious. Suddenly I'm like the Grinch who grew a heart. I hardly recognize myself these days. Casey Junior gives a short account of how his father started the comic and how he's proud to carry on the family legacy. No mention of the controversy. No mention of his father's possible murder or crooked cops. I'm distracted and miss Casey Junior introducing the next speaker, but suddenly the crowd around me claps as Junior walks offstage and an older gentleman takes his place at the podium, his steps measured and careful. He uses the podium for balance, his wrinkled hands less than steady, even gripping the sides.

The crowd rustles like a celebrity has joined us. To me, it's just a guy in an old-fashioned captain's uniform. Apparently, to everyone else, this guy is *someone*. It finally dawns that I'm seeing the celebrity police captain I've read about in my research, in the flesh.

"Thank you, thank you," he says, waving down the applause. "I'm happy to be here to celebrate. I accepted the offer to speak tonight because while some people call me a real-life superhero"—he pauses again for more applause—"we all know that Edward Casey was the real superhero. He was a visionary, a man before his time. His comic inspired social change, and I can speak personally to that. But Edward Casey didn't just write about people fighting social injustice; he was a friend to the Los Angeles Police Department. Just before his unfortunate death, he had given a statement specifically to help end crime happening in his very own neighborhood. Edward Casey Senior is one of the many reasons we were successful with the biggest drug bust in LA's history. May we continue to honor his memory by supporting social justice, supporting our law enforcement, and encouraging those we love to wear a cape now and again." He continues to speak, and the crowd eats it up. He's charismatic despite his age and apparent frailty. There's a wave of laughter, and I look at Matteo. He's basically got stars in his eyes. This man is one of his heroes the way comic book superheroes are for me. I expect to be overtaken by the same wonder as everyone around me—this guy is as close to a real-life Superman as LA has ever had—but something prickles in the back of my head. Something that feels like the hints of a story. My Spidey sense.

The beginning of his speech has my mind wandering. The climate of the comic and the climate of LA were unbelievably similar. A drug war. A big bust. And in the comic, the reveal of a *superhero* who went rogue. A superhero, or a *cop* manipulating the drug war for his own benefit. A *superhero* who would benefit by having his competitors in the drug trade removed and who would kill any man who tried to unmask him.

Ice forms in the pit of my stomach. "How old is he?"

Matteo still claps, watching the older gentleman exit the stage. "What? Who?"

"Anthony Munez."

Matteo's brows crease in annoyance, and he answers in a hushed whisper, "I don't know. Seventy-five? Eighty?"

That would make him forty-five when he was police chief. I drum my fingers on the table. The puzzle pieces start fitting together, even though I don't love the picture they're painting. I need to make sure my hunch is correct. And I need to get back in that warehouse to conduct my own search before the White Rabbit realizes how close to him I am and disappears, or worse. My safety, Matteo's safety, and L's safety all depend on *proof*.

Applause rings out. I've missed the rest of his speech, and now the crush of the crowd threatens to keep me from acting on the idea I just had: Lawrence had seen the dirty cop all those years ago.

"I need a picture," I say to Matteo.

"Of?"

"Anthony Munez. Come on. Come take a picture with your idol." I reach into my small bag and produce my iPhone.

Matteo lets me shove my way through the crowd that has formed at the bottom of the stage. Captain Munez has just reached the last step, and we're only second, next to Agent Sosa, in his receiving line.

Matteo nods to her. "Agent Sosa. And I assume your husband?" Matteo shakes her hand first, then reaches for the hand of the gentleman next to her. "Ah, yes, it's City Councilman Sosa, right?" They must have assembled to greet Anthony Munez like, it seems, the entire room is on its way to do.

Ah. Councilman. I knew I'd seen his face on a bus stop somewhere. I shoulder away several of the gray-hairs who have convened to pay court to Munez. He's started down the line, first pausing for a picture near Agent Sosa and her husband.

I wait until after the flash of the camera has cleared from my eyes before lunging forward slightly, hand on Anthony Munez's arm. "Can we get a picture too, sir? Detective Kildaire is a huge fan."

"I hardly think that's appropriate." It's the acerbic tone of Agent Sosa's voice. Her husband's face is a similar mask of disapproval. What are they, the propriety police? They can get pictures with the fabled police chief, but Matteo can't?

Munez settles the stalemate with a gracious half bow. "Nonsense, nonsense. Happy to help. My public misses me, and I miss the spotlight."

Gotta get while the getting's good. "We'll be quick about it!" I shove Matteo toward Anthony Munez and step back to take the picture.

"One, two, three!" My cell phone hates the low light, but I manage to get a blurry one that should work. "Detective Kildaire, this should go in your office. Thank you, sir. It was so nice to meet you." I spin on my heels, texting Lawrence as fast as my fingers can fly over the keypad.

Meet me at Genius right now. Come alone. Operation Janeway.

Matteo grabs my arm just as I reach the line of people arriving at the coat check. "Hey, MG, stop. Hang on. Where are you going?" He drags me around to face him, perfect in his costume. How I wish I could spend the night dancing under the glittering crystal chandeliers with him. Except in this moment work is *really* between us more than he knows.

My hunch grows, and if I'm correct, the White Rabbit already knows or will soon know we're on his trail. Matteo will be in the line of fire. I'll be in the line of fire. I need to keep my next moves secret, even if just to protect him. After this is all over, I plan to kiss him silly for days.

I wrench my arm away. "I forgot about something I need to go do." I reach the coat queue and dash my hands through my hair because the line is *so* long.

"What? That's crazy." Matteo elbows into line behind me. "We're here to work."

"We are; we were. But I need to go." I grasp his arm, willing him to believe me. The crowd surges around us. I recognize Nina and Kyle, dressed as Wonder Woman and the Flash. I see Ryan over in the corner, deep in heated conversation with Lelani. *This* is where I wish I were staying. This is where I want to be. At this fancy party with Matteo in his hot costume, with my awesome friends. I feel an intense wave of longing that nearly knocks me off my heels. It's odd how I feel like I belong with these people when I've spent so many years building up a wall. All it took was one hazel-eyed narcotics detective to turn my world on its head. But I have a killer and a drug lord to catch. And there are too many damn people gathered around this coat check.

"You stay here, okay? Free booze. Check into my coworkers. Steal the canapes. Lots of fun to be had. And look, there's Ryan with my boss Lelani near the coat check. Maybe they're leaving too. Quick, you can go meet her. Ask her about the date. Do your thing."

Matteo's face is frozen and impassive. "I know who she is."

"You do? From researching Genius?"

Matteo clears his throat. "No, we were engaged."

It's like a punch in the gut. Engaged? Let's go ahead and rain on my parade with my *boss*, who is my roommate's girlfriend and hopeful alibi, is Matteo's ex-girlfriend, and happens to be goddess-model hot and super-brainy smart.

Matteo clears his throat again. "I, uh, didn't know she'd gotten a job here. I probably should go say hello."

It's as if everyone freezes for a moment as I absorb this, while inside my emotions run wild like Storm is wreaking havoc with my internal weather. What if he still has feelings for her? He might not be over her. She dumped *him*, right? And he planted an oasis for her at his house. And now I'm dealing with a wave of uncharacteristic jealousy. I don't have time to deal with my complicated reaction to this. Better to stuff my feelings into a padlocked box and focus on my mission. I turn toward the coat check. If nothing else, Matteo talking to Lelani will buy me time to meet Lawrence. "Yeah. You go do that." I'm going to go catch our killer.

Matteo hesitates, then takes a few steps toward Ryan and Lelani. My throat constricts—the locks on that padlock in my brain must not be very good. I can't watch—my gorgeous Matteo standing next to gorgeous Lelani. They would have stupidly perfect children.

I turn, push through the line of the coat room and up to the front, where a different girl is now dutifully tearing off tickets. "I lost mine," I announce.

"Some of us are in *line* here." An elderly woman in a truly spectacular forties-era pantsuit tries to push in front of me.

"This is an emergency. A life-or-death one," I say. That stops the pushing. A tad dramatic, but oh well.

"Do you remember what your coat looks like?" The girl chews her lip and looks unprepared for an *emergency* at the coat check. "I'm not supposed to let people back, but—"

I don't even wait for more permission. I skirt the table and head for the door to the conference room that masquerades as the coat closet. Not two seconds later, the door opens again, and Matteo nearly falls into the room behind me.

"Jesus, it's dark in here," he says.

"The coats don't seem to care." I click on my phone flashlight to add meager glow to the few amber-colored downlights turned on in the room. How would anyone find *any* coat in here? Of course, mine is long and black, just like the hundreds of long black coats hanging against the walls. I start checking collars. Fewer fur collars, so that should help.

Matteo's presence distracts me. I keep thinking about him with Lelani. It has me all tangled up inside in a way that terrifies me. We're not even a *real* couple. I have no claim on him. I'm not the jealous sort. So why am I all bent out of shape just because Matteo's ex is about as close to my opposite as the world can get?

Matteo's voice emanates close to my ear, and I jump. "Where are you *really* going? You're not off on another dangerous adventure without me, are you?" He intends it to be a joke, forcing a lightheartedness. I don't laugh. "Seriously, MG. Is this about earlier? The dancing? Or the case?" He sounds hurt, but I don't have time to sift through my emotions or his. Double-strength padlocks. I need to go. Now.

As if summoned by my thoughts, my phone buzzes. Lawrence. **Five minutes out. I'll swing by the front?**

I punch in the thumbs-up sign and continue searching.

Coat Check Girl enters with a pile of coats over her arm. "Find it?"

"Not yet!" I try to sound cheery instead of panicked. She gives me a weird look and exits again, while I grin like a maniac.

Matteo watches me search in silence. Finally I find my coat, in the darkest corner of *course*, and yank it off the hanger. I turn to leave the room, only to find Matteo standing behind me.

He's too close. I can't think straight. The scent of him—cinnamon and probably his hair gel—is an aphrodisiac to the part of me that wants *us* to be real. The part that wants to throw caution to the wind, tell him where I'm going, what I know, and who I suspect. I have to restrain myself from melting into him. It's an urge I need to resist. Until this drug lord, this *killer*, and this vigilante are behind bars, Matteo won't stop. It's his job to find them. And it's my job to help him.

"Michael-Grace, you're obviously upset. Can we talk about this?"

"I'm not upset. This is business, remember? No reason to be upset." Maybe I'm a *little* upset. Okay, a lot upset. The fact that I've just realized how invested my heart is in this fake relationship, how invested *I* am in this case, leaves me rattled.

"MG, look at me."

"I need to go."

"Look at me."

I do so defiantly. If it will speed up the process of me getting out of here, fine.

His hands reach out for me, fingers closing around my waist. He pulls me to him, though I fight for a few steps. "Michael-Grace Martin, come *here*."

I am at war with myself, but my full name on his lips is my undoing. I move forward until I'm nestled against his Captain America insignia.

"I know why you're upset. I know we said this was business, but it's clearly not just business." He sounds pained and unsure. Like he's not one to usually be vulnerable. It's hard for him to admit; I hear it in every note of his voice.

Clearly not just business. Our proximity allows me to feel his heart thudding a mile a minute, and I'm losing my resolve to run out of here at about the same pace.

I need to keep my mind on my plan. Leave. This is a distraction when the case may be going cold as we speak. "It's not?" I get suckered into the conversation. Emo MG wins this round.

"Not for me." He takes a breath. "Look. I'll lay it out there. I know this is messy. And I know there's the case. MG, I'm not good at this." His grip on my waist becomes stronger, more sure, like he's reached some decision. "I probably put work first too many times in my past relationships too. But you're different. I want you to know that." He licks his lips, and there's a small quiver in one of his fingers before he tightens his grip more and pulls me even closer. His voice gains surety, and I revel in his breath on my cheek. In our closeness. "If working this case means you're walking out on . . . us, whatever we are, I'll resign from it. I'll let Detective Rideout finish up. I'll take away the thing that's keeping us apart."

My heart hammers in response. He'd give up a case for me? Forget a one-two punch; this is a total knockout. One that leaves me weak-kneed and dizzy. I've *never* had a man offer to do something like that before. I'm used to boyfriends using me. There was the guy capitalizing on our dates. On a broader stage, the years I've felt undervalued by the executives at work. All the guys at cons who were interested only in my "finer assets," as Rideout said. Yet here's Matteo, knight in shining armor, willing to give everything up for *me*. It's something I thought

I'd never want, but I'm awash with how amazing and scary this feels. Because it's real.

Real. Reality crashes back in as I contemplate how *real* the case is too. I can't have Detective Rideout head up this investigation. Not only did he train under Anthony Munez and could very well be *the* dirty cop, but he'd have me in jail in less than twenty-four hours, guaranteed. Offering to give up the case proves Matteo is true. Honest. The double agent would never give up control, and I need an honest cop at the helm of this, no matter what happens.

I reach out and put my hand on his chest, right over his true-blue heart. "I want you to stay on the case. I want us to solve it. And no way you're letting Rideout lead this. The guy already thinks I'm the Golden Arrow. I'd end up in handcuffs for sure." The darkness presses in on us, and I run my hand up his arm. "I—I really appreciate you saying those things. You're worth waiting for, however long this case takes." The last words come out in an almost-whisper. I mean them to the very bottom of my stiletto heels and all the way back up again.

Matteo looks like I've given him Christmas. Then his lips are a breath from mine. "MG, I can't stop thinking about you." His wrists circle mine, and he lifts our hands above my head and presses me back into the pile of coats.

Our kiss isn't soft. We grasp at each other as if we're drowning. We fall into the coats, and I grab the bar above us to keep from falling all the way through. We shouldn't be doing this, but *oh* we should be doing this. I'm made for this kiss—costumes, coat closet, and all.

Matteo's breath is ragged as he drags his hands down over my coat and back up underneath, his hands hot against the lace of my dress. He leans down, kissing the pulse beating wildly at the base of my throat, and I nearly pass out from the sensation. My head swims, blood pounding in my ears. I can't get enough of this man. He's gotten under my skin, in my brain, and stolen my heart.

Coat Check Girl chooses this very moment to reappear. A triangle of light from the door falls across us, and she clears her throat in a loud and well-rehearsed manner. "Did you find your coat, miss?"

The coat rack nearly collapses beneath Matteo and me, and we part on a laugh.

"I—uh—yeah, I found it. Right here. Thanks for checking on us." *Not.* I push to stand, grab my coat where it has sagged to my elbows, and pull it back over my shoulders.

She throws me a look that says she's partly sorry she had to interrupt us. "I have more coats to hang," she says with one last appreciative look at Matteo. "Be back in a sec." The triangle of light disappears.

"I feel like I'm fifteen," Matteo says, his forehead coming to rest on mine.

"If you were kissing like this at fifteen, you needed to teach lessons." My phone buzzes again. "I really do have to go. But I'll call you later, okay?"

Matteo's hands settle back around my waist. Then he snuggles my coat around me further, buttoning the top button. He pulls me in for a sweet peck. "If you must."

Something in the pocket of my coat sticks into my side, and I frown. I haven't put anything in my pocket.

"What's wrong?"

"I don't know. There's something poking me in the side."

"I didn't think it was that obvious." Matteo gives a bawdy wink, and I laugh.

"No, I'm serious." I dig in my pocket. There's definitely something in there. Something like a book. I definitely didn't put a *book* in my pocket. I extricate it with difficulty and hold it up to the meager light.

It's a softcover journal.

It's a *black* softcover journal I've seen before. *Dammit, dammit, dammit.*

Matteo's eyes widen as I flip quickly through the journal. "Is that what I think it is?"

I snap the journal closed and shove it back into my pocket. "My journal of ideas? Yeah. I forgot I had this with me. Ideas for the new *Hero Girls*." But it definitely isn't my journal. It's Casey Senior's missing journal, the one whose sketches showed up in my test copy of *The Hooded Falcon*. What the hell? Who snuck this journal in my pocket?

Matteo knows something is up. I can see the light of suspicion dawn. "Are you *sure* that's your journal? Because if it belongs to someone else and you took evidence, you'd be a suspect and off the case."

The warning is clear. Come clean now and stay on the case. Lie and risk losing my freedom and the man offering me so much more. But he didn't see the note at the back of the journal. A note to *me*. It simply said,

MG, Rabbit in the Glen. Tonight, 11 p.m. Follow the arrows.

If I turn this over, the journal pretty much frames me as the Golden Arrow or, at the very least, an accomplice.

I offer a small smile. "I guess that would be one way to solve the problem between us?"

Matteo grits his teeth. "I can't *date* a suspect either."

My phone buzzes, reminding me of my appointment with fate, and now with a warehouse. I don't wait to see if he's hurt or angry. I'll deal with that fallout later. I square my shoulders. I give him a swift kiss on the cheek. "Then I guess it's a good thing I'm not one."

CHAPTER 23

I race out of Genius Comics as fast as I can without looking like I'm fleeing a fire and find the Millennium Turd in the parking lot, lights on, Lawrence at the helm. Thank God his drag family was close enough for him to make it up here in under an hour.

"What's shakin'?" Lawrence calls as I throw open the passenger door and fling myself into the car.

"A whole lotta shade," I respond, putting my arm over my eyes. So much has just happened, I don't know where to begin. "We need to carry out Operation Janeway tonight."

"Like right now?"

"Now. Well, right after I show you this." I fumble through my purse and retrieve my phone. My fingers slip on the device in my haste to pull up the picture I took inside. "Do you recognize this man?"

I hold out the picture, realizing now *just* how blurry it is. Photographer I am not.

L rubs his jaw and looks at the picture. "Maybe?"

I throw down my phone in frustration, and L shoots me a look. "What, MG? That picture sucks. Who is he? Why should I know him?"

"He's the old police chief. The one who was in charge when Casey Senior died."

"The one who cleaned up the streets in the eighties, single-handedly reduced crime rates, and took LA into a long stretch of peaceful living?"

I grit my teeth. "Yeah. That one. I think he's the White Rabbit. I wanted to see if you recognized him as the cop from Casey Senior's house or any of your superhero stuff."

Taking the phone from me, Lawrence studies the picture again. He gives a noncommittal shrug. "I mean, maybe. But it's hard to tell. And anyway, MG, are you *really* going to accuse someone like *that* of being the White Rabbit?"

"Not without proof, no."

Something occurs to me, so I snatch the phone back and navigate to an internet browser.

"What are you doing?"

"Googling."

"Girl, we don't have time for that—"

"L, you said that picture sucks, and I'm trying to find a better one. This guy was *all over* the news in the eighties. There *has* to be a better picture." The silence stretches as my phone maddeningly halts on the load screen. Stupid dead zones. "Come on, come on, come on."

Lawrence sits in silence maybe a full thirty seconds. "I thought you said we needed to be quick."

"We do!" I growl in frustration. The few pictures that have loaded are articles about tonight's gala, nothing about the younger Munez. I'm facing having to start the search over. Maybe *'80s Munez?* But what if all that come up are articles *about* the drug bust? I literally beat my forehead with the phone in frustration.

Lawrence sighs, watching me. "Even if you could find it online, this dude is so old. Highly doubt he's donning a cape and spankies."

"What if he has a protégé? L, I've been thinking. Rideout's dad worked with this guy. Munez got Rideout's dad out of some serious charges. Then Rideout trained with him for years until he retired. Maybe Munez is the original, but my hunch says that we're dealing with a younger cop, still on the force, and someone in Matteo's inner circle. Someone who took his ideas and runs the same operation. Maybe *this* is what the Golden Arrow is trying to tell us."

"That's a lot to prove, MG."

I give up and throw my phone—still stuck loading the fourth and fifth pictures on Google Images—into my lap. I'll have to try again later. "Yes, thank you for your assessment. Now let's go before Matteo comes out. He already suspects that I have the journal, and if he sees me with you, well, I'll be off the case for sure." His warning said as much. If he finds proof that I've taken the journal the police are looking for, I'll probably be arrested for impeding an investigation. I catch L's startled look at my mention of the journal. "I'll tell you about the journal on our way. We need to get to the warehouse by eleven p.m."

Lawrence shifts the car into drive, though we can't move forward yet. We have to wait for several people to meander across the road toward the party at an infuriatingly slow speed. Too late, I recognize Agent Sosa and her husband walking through the parking lot. I will her not to notice me, but my car's wheezing exhaust system is pretty noticeable in the sea of luxury automobiles. She catches my eye. I can't look away, even as they make their slow way in our direction.

Agent Sosa stops just outside my window. It seems intentional and threatening, even though I've done *nothing* to this woman but be polite tonight. "Leaving so soon, Ms. Martin?"

"Business to attend to," I answer through my open window. I make a move to roll it up. Having it down was a *big* mistake.

Her eyes slide to Lawrence, then back to me. Lawrence does his usual "haters gonna hate" ignore-them routine. I wish I could be as good at it as him. Instead, I reach across the middle of my car and grasp his hand with mine. I'm fighting off a strong case of the heebie-jeebies along with a ball of anxiety that would make Black Lightning nervous. I'm positive he can feel my hand shaking, and he squeezes back.

Her sour smile has turned into something of a Cheshire grin, and it doesn't sit well with me either. "Well, it was nice to see you again. Maybe we'll see you and your friend around. Lawrence, isn't it? I thought someone inside was asking about him. Have a nice night. I'm sure we'll be seeing both of you soon." She and her husband continue around the car, but I'm frozen in my seat.

"L, did she just use your name?"

"Yes. Shit. She doesn't seem friendly."

"She knows Matteo is looking for you." Dread seeps into my pores like one of Lawrence's ridiculous gel facial masks. This gets more *real*, more dangerous by the minute. "We need to go. She knows who you are. I'm with you, and I'll bet my spandex that she's going to tell Matteo. You could get arrested for evading police, and I could be arrested for obstructing justice. On so many counts." I think of the journal in my pocket. My heart sinks, and I fight a wave of nausea. But my job right now is to keep Matteo safe, keep L safe, and solve this crime so I can beg forgiveness. No way out but through. Sometimes you just have to go into the fight and throw a lot of elbows. "L, I need your help to put this whole puzzle together before someone I love gets hurt."

I know the comics. I know enough about the crime scenes to get me started. I'm going to have to be *very* careful not to get caught, but if anyone can catch the Golden Arrow at his own game, it is me. This is do or die, life or death.

Lawrence regards me, then revs the engine of my little car. "Game on, bitches."

We park two blocks away from the warehouse in an alley behind a dumpster, per Lawrence's insistence. Sometimes even Han took suggestions from Leia.

"I should have been more specific about Operation Janeway's uniform requirements." I push my black wig off my forehead and glare through the curls at Lawrence, who seems to be monitoring everything while still walking down a dark alley without tripping. There is no sign of a wiggle in his walk. This is game face for Lawrence, and if I'm right, he's carrying at least one gun on his person.

"I look like a castoff from *Saturday Night Fever*," I grumble. Truth be told, I rather love the maroon leather jumpsuit I'm rocking, and the knee-high brown boots are very *Kill Bill*. Better for a little B and E than my lace dress by a mile.

"I wish. I'd kill for some bling and a good pair of bell-bottoms right now," Lawrence answers. Beside me he looks right out of *The Matrix* in his black pants, black sparkle T-shirt with a hot pink "L" on it, trench coat, and *Blade Runner* black boots. "You don't want them to instantly recognize you on surveillance, do you?"

I glance around. "Who is *them*?"

Lawrence shrugs. "The police. Your boyfriend. The drug dealers."

We're standing just outside *the* alcove. It looks less mysterious and sexy tonight and more . . . trashy, filthy, and it smells like urine. I miss Matteo's strong presence and his Kevlar vest.

"So tell me again why we're here." Lawrence glances around.

I rattle the door and find that it's locked, as I expected. "We're looking for a way inside." I pull at the window to find it's fixed shut. "The journal said the White Rabbit was going to be here at eleven, and to follow the arrows." I pull the journal out of my pocket, and hand it to him so he can read the message.

While Lawrence is overjoyed to have his journal back, he's also beyond pissed that someone scribbled in it. Not just anyone. The Golden Arrow intentionally left evidence on my person that the police are looking for. Either our hero wants to help me find the White Rabbit, or the Golden Arrow wants me off the case. I've chosen to see this as an olive branch, but standing in the dark outside a warehouse makes me realize that it very well could be hemlock.

The sound of breaking glass has me whirling around to face Lawrence. His paisley head scarf is wrapped around his hand, and he's leaning against the building with a forced expression of innocence.

"What did you just do?"

"I slipped."

I peer around him. "Did you break that window?"

"It was already broken." He turns and studies it. "But yes, when I slipped, I did happen to make the hole bigger. Big enough that half of a crime-fighting duo can get in there and go let the bigger half in through the door."

"I thought you said I was in charge."

He shrugs. "I'm helping. My guess is since this one was already broken, they've turned the alarms off. Thank God it's not safety glass, or I would have broken my hand."

"Yeah, we'll see about that." I turn and study the window. I'm grateful now for the thicker material of my jumpsuit. "Okay, help me up." I ignore my pulse pounding in my ears and how my knees are knocking together. I'm about to commit a *real* crime.

Lawrence grunts as he cradles me in a basket hold, and I work to balance myself to get my feet through the hole without catching on the broken glass. My butt poses a bit of a problem now that my feet are dangling inside the building and my upper body is supported by L. "You're going to have to essentially *throw* me through this window."

"That doesn't sound like a good idea."

"It's either that or my back drags across broken glass. I need to go straight through." And *nothing* at all could go wrong with that. Right? "Okay, on three. One, two—"

Before I get to three, Lawrence tosses me as best he can through the broken portion of the window. Jagged glass grabs at my back, the shoulders of the suit, and a section of the wig. A sting on my cheek says something scratched my face. All told, the worst part of the entire trip is the landing. I wish I could say that, like my hero counterparts in the comics, I do a neat tuck-and-roll and shoot to my feet ready for action. Instead, the heel of my left boot skids to the side, I land hard on my right foot, my ankle rolls, and I end up spread-eagle on my stomach, my face inches from a wooden pallet.

"You okay? That sounded bad!" Lawrence's voice is an exaggerated stage whisper.

I peel myself off the floor and test my weight on my turned ankle. "It's not life-threatening," I announce in a similar whisper, limping my way over to the door. This door isn't locked on the inside, and I simply push open the panic bar. Though I'm cringing, no alarm sounds.

"Let's make this quick," Lawrence says, ducking in. The door closes behind us, and we're left in semidarkness. He clicks on a flashlight, hands it to me, then clicks one on for him.

The warehouse looks exactly like it did when I was here last week with Matteo, Rideout, and Agent Sosa, minus the fifty-odd police officers who were there that day. Everything is neat and orderly. I don't see anything or anyone who would indicate the White Rabbit is here, or any arrows to follow. I limp through the stacks of boxes and pallets to the general area where I stood with Matteo before. The floor is empty of the big crates, instead filled with towering plastic-wrapped boxes. "Stuff has moved."

It doesn't help that I don't know what I'm looking for, if anything.

"But you said you saw the guys were *unloading* boxes? Boxes, not crates of drugs? If they were with the drug ring, wouldn't they be picking up the crates to sell or loading them into a boat like you said?"

"That's what Matteo said too. I don't know. I'm still trying to figure this out too." I trail off as I walk around the plastic-wrapped tower and spot something down the large row of boxes. It's a large black arrow drawn onto the side. Usually I wouldn't have paid it any mind, but it's the first arrow I've seen. "I see an arrow."

There's a second arrow farther down the row, and a third that points halfway down another plastic-wrapped tower at a smaller stack of boxes.

"Don't touch anything," Lawrence warns as I use my flashlight to pick my way across to the boxes. "Especially if the DEA uses this as a sting to catch the person who comes for these."

"I can't tell, but I think these are the same kinds of boxes I saw the guys loading out of the truck the night of the explosion." I turn and sweep my light to the left. No more arrows to be seen. "But if the trucking company wasn't picking up the drugs from the bust and was just dropping off boxes, *why* was the Golden Arrow here?" I sigh and run a hand over my head, which skews the wig. The sound of a door shutting comes from another part of the building, and I freeze, a cold sweat forming on my brow. Lawrence and I both click off our flashlights.

When the sound doesn't repeat, a sneaking suspicion dawns. I whisper frantically to L, "What if this is a setup by the Golden Arrow? What if he called the police to tell them we're here? I don't want to get caught for nothing." It could be *so* much worse than the Golden Arrow planting evidence on me in the hopes of Matteo discovering it. The Golden Arrow could be out-and-out framing me for the crimes.

Lawrence has ducked and is fiddling with the nearest box. *We don't have time for fiddling. We need to get out.* There's the sound of tape ripping away from cardboard, as loud as a gunshot in the silence.

"Are you opening boxes? I thought *you* said we shouldn't touch anything."

"This box says 'Genius Comics.'" Or I think that's what he says, given the flashlight clutched in his teeth.

"What?" I crouch beside him and take in the pile of boxes, all neatly marked with Genius Comics packing tape and form shipping labels.

"Did you know Genius uses this warehouse?" L asks.

"No. But this can't be a coincidence, right?"

This time I *definitely* hear something from within the warehouse, and we freeze again after clicking off our lights.

"Do you think someone's here?" I hate that my voice quavers. The police? Matteo? I should have thought twice about following some stupid scribble in a notebook. I rushed in full bore, per my usual, which is probably just what the Golden Arrow wanted me to do.

"Could be a night guard," Lawrence says, though I can tell he's placating me. His eyes are worried too. "We probably should leave." He looks briefly at his phone before shoving it into his pocket. "Shift probably starts at ten, and it's nine forty-nine."

I've stopped listening. I'm too busy leaning around Lawrence and peering at the box he opened. I click on the flashlight but keep my hand over the top to stop it from lighting up our area of the warehouse. "They're *Hooded Falcon* comics."

I reach in, expecting to meet the resistance of stapled spines, but they're loose pages. "What the heck? It's just the covers of the comics." Old-school tear sheets—the ones bookstores send back to prove they haven't sold the comics. Returning the whole comic is too costly, so they just send back the cover torn off for a refund. I reach down to see if the whole box is made up of the single-page covers of *The Hooded Falcon* or if there are full comics at the bottom. My fingers encounter a different type of paper, or not really paper at all. I press harder, and it gives ever so slightly. A brick? Why would you put a brick at the bottom of a comic book tear-sheet box?

"I thought I said we needed to go, MG." The stack of boxes blocks us from the main aisle, but that doesn't stop a fidgety Lawrence from peering around them repeatedly.

Each time he looks, I'm sure we'll be discovered, but I can't stop now. "In a second. Give me your phone." I'm frantically pulling the tag off the box Lawrence opened.

"Use yours."

"Mine slid down my boot, and it's at my ankle. Give me yours."

"MG—"

I'm positively frantic now, and I have weird tremors running through my legs. I'm panting like I've just run an Iron Man. "I need to take a picture. I think this is it. This is *the* thing we're going to find," I hiss at him. Finally I feel the weight of his phone in my hand. "Are we clear? No one is around?"

"Well, not that I can see, but, MG, I worked security for years. I think we need to go. Now. Before the shift for the guards starts."

I flick up the camera icon on his screen and start madly fiddling with the functions of the camera. "Okay. I need five seconds, and then we can get out of here."

"Five seconds to what?" he asks as I take pictures of everything around us in rapid succession, the flash on the phone blinding us in the process. "Oh shit, girl. Warn a queen before you do something like that and get us caught."

I blink tears from my eyes as I blindly snap one more picture. We pause as a door closes somewhere. Footsteps.

I want to pee my pants the way I did when I got stage fright in my third-grade musical. I don't deal with stressful situations well at all. "Oh my God, do you think they saw the light?"

"MG, the Martians saw the flash from that phone." His head swings frantically side to side, gauging the boxes around us.

The squawk of a radio and heavier footsteps approach. *Oh no, oh no, oh no.* I am going to jail. *We* are going to jail. And that's if this is a *cop.* If it's the White Rabbit . . . well, it's curtains for us.

I must have said that last part out loud because L answers, "Not if I can help it. Up."

"Up?"

"Up." He puts his hands under my butt and boosts me up. I scramble as quietly as possible on top of the towering stack of boxes wrapped in plastic and go still. Beside me I don't hear anything but a grunt, and suddenly L is on top of a taller stack of boxes.

Immobility is the name of the game. I'm an icicle. I'm a statue. I'm a box. I'm Trogdor's Halloween costume. I'm sitting on top of a stack of plastic, and if the guard below us looks up, what am I going to say? "Oh, uh . . . hi. Lovely day for warehouse tanning." The wig on my head is stifling, and I fight every urge in my body to scratch the itch on my nose.

Outside the warehouse, I hear a car backfire and tires screech, and a bright flash of headlights beams through the window as the car pulls a U-turn. I look over at L. We're completely exposed, lit up as bright as daylight. I can't breathe. My muscles feel weak and stiff at the same time. And the bridge of my nose itches something fierce, impossible to ignore.

Directly below the stack I'm sitting on, someone coughs. Then the radio crackles to life again. "It's just kids spinning doughnuts outside again. Maybe call patrol and have them cruise by."

I feel like I've heard that voice before. I chance a look down. The guard looks an awful lot like the cop who took Casey Junior's statement. What is his name? Officer James?

Why would Officer James be working guard duty on a building the police aren't supposed to be watching anymore?

We sit there as he walks around the boxes, scuffing his feet. My heart is in my throat, my ears rushing and ringing with my pulse. My drink from the party threatens to make a repeat appearance.

Several long minutes pass, and just as I'm getting ready to break, a phone rings below us. Officer James answers with a clipped hello, then silence.

"Yes, sir, the boxes are here. Pickup at eleven o'clock." A pause. "No, sir, nothing out of the ordinary." A third pause, and this time the voice is lower and shaky when it replies. "I took care of it, sir. Made it look like he hung himself in jail. I don't think he'll be making his plea bargain anymore. I would say his father has been adequately warned about the dangers of discussing this matter with the police."

A fresh wave of nausea crashes over me. My fingers clench in reaction, and it's everything I can do to keep still and quiet. Lawrence must read it on my face because his eyes narrow to slits, and he shakes his head as forcefully as he can while lying on a pile of teetering boxes.

"Yes, sir, wire it to my offshore. Thank you." A click.

Oh my *God*. Officer James has killed someone. Someone in custody. Someone whose father needed warning about working with the police, and someone whose plea bargain was to trade information about the White Rabbit. It must have been Huong Yee. Son of the printing press owner. The kid who was going to out a cop and testify about the White Rabbit. *Bastard.*

Footfalls slowly fade, and I begin to breathe again. Feeling comes back to my fingers and toes as my oxygen reaches normal levels. After a few moments of intense silence, I hear Lawrence slide down, then feel a hand on my leg.

I step into his palms and, like some sort of ill-trained acrobat, manage to turn my ankle again, landing with my stomach on his head, then fall halfway down his back before he can catch me and right us both.

"You are a terrible cat burglar," L says as he pulls me toward the illuminated exit sign.

"I like to think of myself as a corgi burglar. I don't like cats." Corgis aren't graceful either.

He uses his phone to look at the door, then pushes through, pulling me after him, and we spill out into the night air. It's thick with the smell of burning rubber and exhaust. Somewhere inside the building, a sound rings out of the dark. An impossibly loud beeping.

"Come on, we need to go. Now. That must have been a fire exit. We just set off an alarm."

In the distance, a police siren wails to life.

I'm already limping down the street toward the car when L spins me around, grabs my hand, and starts running the opposite way. "Never lead them directly to your car! We'll go two blocks up and then two over, and then double back."

I'm out of breath already as we dash down side streets and through alleys. I'm sure we make as much noise as two bulls in a china shop, but we don't stop.

"Is that something you learned as a security guard?" I ask.

"No, it's something I learned from breaking up with dramatic men."

Lawrence huffs and puffs too as we sprint across the main street.

Twenty minutes later, I'm drenched in sweat, I have insta-blisters all over both feet, my ankle is on fire, my wig is tucked into the top of my shirt, and we *finally* circle back around to the car. It's untouched behind the dumpster, and truth be told, I'm glad we parked several blocks from the warehouse in question. It would have taken either a stroke of genius or a large police force to have searched this well already.

I slide into the driver's seat and coax the engine to life. Sputtering, the Millennium Turd makes a less-than-spectacular exit from the alley, and soon we're on our way home.

Lawrence slumps against the passenger window, already stripped down to his sparkly black T-shirt. I can tell he's not impressed with my sleuthing skills. More than unimpressed. He seems out and out ticked. "We're in trouble. I want you to take me home."

"I know. Lawrence, that guard is a cop. I saw him at the station with Matteo. He's got access to all of Matteo's stuff. He's going to know you worked for Casey. He's going to hear your interview. I . . . I think he killed a suspect, a *kid*, Lawrence. He killed a kid to keep him from talking."

"What you found in there had better be worth it, girl. This is *bad*."

I flip his phone to him as I skid around a curve. "Here, look through what I took. There's something in the bottom of that box. Those are tear sheets. They come back to Genius when comics are unsold as proof that the books have been destroyed. They're trash. They're counted, then discarded. There shouldn't *be* anything else in those boxes."

Lawrence flicks through his phone, scanning the pictures. He stops on one, then sits back. "That's cash. That's a big brick of cash."

"In a box of comics?"

"This has to be how they're moving the drugs around. MG, they're using your comics. My guess is they pack their product in these boxes after the comics are printed, send the boxes to China, sell the drugs, then send back the tear sheets with the cash. It's brilliant, really." The Yees *are* a part of this. They bought into the printing press so they could package the drugs with the comics bound for Asia. Didn't Ryan say just the other week that the comic was selling gangbusters overseas? Maybe not quite as well as heroin.

I nod slowly. "I need a name. I need *proof*, because if I show up at the LAPD with these pictures, guaranteed you and I are dead. Officer James isn't working alone. I *need* the other journals. Casey Junior thinks that his father named his murderer in them. You told me Casey Senior was amassing evidence against someone. I need it to prove that he was going to unmask the White Rabbit. It's got to have his *name* on it."

The journals. Everything comes down to a dead man's journals that have been missing for thirty years. And given the fact that I came face-to-face with our mystery man in Casey Senior's office, the Golden Arrow is looking for the evidence too. I wasn't sure what the Golden Arrow's game plan was upon finding them, but given the fact that he or she set fire to a building, I'm not sure murder is off the table. Either way, I need those journals first.

And now . . . well, I've probably tipped my hand to the White Rabbit too. If Matteo tells his team that he thinks I have the journals, the double agent will leak the information. The White Rabbit will then be looking for the journals, and for me, to get rid of us both. I need to get ahead of this thing. "How can I beat the Golden Arrow at this game when I've been two steps behind this whole time?"

Lawrence taps his chin. "If it were me, I'd put the journals in plain sight. Somewhere someone wouldn't expect. Not in a safe, but inside a boring book or something."

Think, think, think, MG. What was in the office? What would Casey Junior miss for *thirty years*? In the comic book, stuff was hidden behind a painting, in a wall safe. We *saw* the wall safe. It's the most obvious place to look. And it was behind a painting. Something shifts in my mind, just like something *shifted inside the frame when we moved it*. At the time, I thought it was a broken frame, but now I'm wondering if Casey Senior's spirit is reaching out yet again and delivering the story line.

Matteo said many of the paintings were being shipped to the charity auction at the San Diego Comic-Con. This is the connection between the two story lines. The printing press. The comic book, the painting, the wall safe. I guarantee the Golden Arrow is going to be at that auction, and so are we. In fact, I'm going to make sure the Golden Arrow is there, and the White Rabbit too. We're going to catch them and end this thing once and for all.

"I have a plan."

Lawrence nods as if he's been expecting it. "I'll call in my crew. You're not doing this alone."

I need to find that painting and whatever Casey Senior hid inside, and lucky for me, I'm already going to compete in the Miss Her Galaxy fashion competition. Perfect alibi.

CHAPTER 24

"You're sure that they'll find us?" I'm scanning the crowd outside the convention center, barely able to keep my tired eyes open. I've been up past midnight the last few nights putting the finishing touches on the six feet of sequined glory I've created for Miss Her Galaxy. My Band-Aided fingers tell the cautionary tale of sewing tulle while narcoleptic.

The crush of zany characters takes my breath away, costumes from every corner of geekdom. In our plain clothes, we're pretty much mosquitoes among a butterfly gathering: boring and invisible to everyone else.

"Girl, you worry too much. It's like gaydar. Queens can find each other anywhere."

Once L agreed to my plan, he insisted his drag family were the perfect ones to pull this off. And look fabulous doing it. I glance to the side, where Ryan is still getting a selfie with an amazingly adapted steampunk Legend of Zelda character. We weren't in line twenty minutes before he put our fangirling to shame. For all that he argued about coming, Ryan has already filled half his phone storage with pictures.

"Like a kid in a candy shop," Lawrence confirms, looking over my shoulder. The line shuffles forward, and we dutifully follow. I'm on pins and needles for so many reasons, I kind of feel like throwing up now that I'm forced to be mostly still in line for our badges. Kinda like that time I had three butterbeers, then went on the Flight of the Hippogriff at the Wizarding World of Harry Potter. Barf city.

"What did you end up telling Ryan? You didn't tell him . . . all of it, did you?" I eye Lawrence. I also can't help but go back to my last conversation with Matteo, where he all but told me he suspected Ryan of being the Golden Arrow. I almost convinced him—and myself—that it's impossible. Yet . . . Ryan and I haven't talked about our conversation at the gala either. Ryan has basically been MIA since the gala, though I saw him at work a few times. I've also been busy: watching the news, preparing for my fashion show, brainstorming with L, and actively avoiding Matteo while I'm meddling in his investigation . . . Well, I didn't have the time to track Ryan down to talk. In fact, this is already the most I've seen of Ryan in a week.

Lawrence makes a sound of disapproval in the back of his throat. "I said I wouldn't, didn't I? I just had him tell his girlfriend that our drag family does a mean after-party show. She pulled a few strings, and now the official Homage to Todrick Hall Disney Queens will be featured at the Genius Comics After-Party. Oh! There they are!" Lawrence raises his arm and waves.

"I still can't believe they found you badges. I bought mine in March."

"It pays to be me sometimes," Lawrence answers with a sassy hip toss. Even in his dark denim jeans and Captain America tee—whom L insists is a closet queen because, *girl*, have you seen his hair?—Lawrence manages to look perfectly put together and ever-so-slightly sultry.

"Okay, so you remember our main job today is to check out the auction items and get ready for the show." I'm chewing my nails to the quick now. This all has to go *perfectly*. Everything I've set up. Everything I've gambled and guessed on. All of my hopes wrapped up in the fashion design competition that brought me here. Everything.

"Recon. Check." Lawrence gives me a salute.

The line moves forward again, and I hold out my ID to the guy at the gate. No big deal. MG Martin. Undercover vigilante-hero-apprehender and hopeful fashion maven. Lawrence and Ryan follow, and soon we're standing inside the arched glass–ceilinged lobby of the convention center.

Lawrence looks around, using his height to his advantage. "Now all we're missing is my family."

"Darling!" Lawrence is swooped up in a hug from behind by a tall black queen whom I instantly peg as Lawrence's infamous drag mother. She's tall, thinner than L, and her close-cropped curls are dyed a platinum blonde.

I catch sight of another figure behind Shwanda before turning my attention to Lawrence. I guess it's probably one of L's drag family, though I don't recognize him.

L looks positively adoring introducing his Mother. "MG, Ryan, I'd like you to meet Shwanda."

"Shwanda Knuts," she says, extending a regal hand first to Ryan then to me. Rings glitter on every finger, bracelets jangle at her wrists, and a huge gold chain rests against the neck of her black eighties jumpsuit. Shwanda may not be in full costume, makeup, or character, but there's no missing that this queen is full-time fierce. Man or woman, *always* Shwanda.

"I can't believe we haven't met yet—either of you—after hearing so much about you, Ms. Knuts," I gush, trying to take in the spectacularness that is the drag mama.

"Just Shwanda, if you please. Like Cher. And this is Vince, or Amy Blondonis." Shwanda motions to an extremely tall and angular white guy, who I'm ashamed to admit I thought was a person waiting for another group. He's got intensely pale-blue eyes and is tattooed from head to toe. He looks nothing like a queen in a white T-shirt, baggy jeans, and a hat turned backward. Unlike the bubbly Shwanda, Vince is silent. He's intense. I can see why Lawrence invited him for a crime-solving mission.

I paste a cheery smile on my face even though I've literally never been this nervous in my life. It's not just the show that might make my new career. It's Matteo and the message I left him. It's the fact that I'm banking on Rideout being a leak. It's that I've based all of this on a rattle in a frame in a dead guy's office. "Okay, so are we ready to look at the exhibition hall?"

"I was born ready, darling." Shwanda kisses my cheek before bustling off toward the doors to the trade show.

"She's really something," I say to Lawrence as we trail behind. "But what about Vince?"

"Oh, that's just Vince. He's really quiet as a man, but he has the best singing voice as a queen. He's our secret weapon for the after-party."

As much as I'd like to keep our group together, it proves considerably difficult, bordering on impossible. We're pushed and pulled apart by the crowd, and two kids dressed as minions literally run between us. Then there's the draw of the shopping. The second Lawrence sets sights on the clothing alley, he squeals, "Ooo! Vintage bustiers!" and dashes off to the left.

I turn to Ryan. "Well, so much for—" But Ryan's already wandering away toward the large game banners that hang over the middle of the exhibition space. Likewise, Shwanda and Vince have dispersed. And I'm left all alone, swept along by the churning crowd, surrounded by life-size pink Wookiees, enough *Star Trek* uniforms to fill the *Enterprise*, hobbits, gremlins, and sexy gaming characters I don't recognize by name. The sights and sounds bombard my senses, the huge banners flying overhead catnip for every sort of nerd delight. A convincing droid walks behind me, and I hear her say to her companion, "You know, next year I think I'm going to do crossover cosplay. Maybe R2-D2 Wonder Woman."

I close my eyes, hold out my hands, take a deep breath, and let it out. For everything else that's going on . . . these are my people. I feel like I've come home.

I make my way through the clothing vendors to the heart of the exhibition hall, where I can see the Genius banner among some of the largest displayed. The superhero heart of the con beats large and strong this year. I fight the urge to stop and take pictures every four steps; people have taken Genius characters and created costumes that any designer would covet. As much as I'm anxious about the case, habit takes over. Cons for me are about costumes. And fabric. I feel that familiar pull, and I decide that it's okay to give in for just a little while. The auction isn't until tomorrow.

As I approach the sprawling Genius booth itself, a Red Cardinal costume literally stops me in my tracks. The Red Cardinal has her own series, but she's best known as the on-again–off-again love interest of the Hooded Falcon. This costume is beyond gorgeous—layers of red feathers create a striking one-shoulder gown bodice and gradually give way to pinned and tucked layers of bloodred ruched silk cut through with silvery, gauzy fabric. I might be drooling, and I am definitely stopping traffic.

"I love your dress," I can't help myself saying.

I'm absolutely mesmerized by the creation she's wearing, and I'm not the only one. All around her people are taking pictures. She's essentially holding court.

"Thank you." She smiles, and I move my fangirling upward from her gorgeous dress to the intricate way her glossy black hair piles around a jeweled circlet, complete with a bejeweled cardinal. Then I see her face. I take a step back, muffling an oath. Of course it would be perfect Lelani, ex-fiancée of the guy I may or may not be falling in love with.

"Oh, MG. Good to see you. What are you up to?" Andy appears behind Lelani, dressed in dark jeans and a black T-shirt that says "Genius Comics" across the front. I need to get my head back in the game of solving a thirty-year-old murder case.

"I was just telling Lelani how wonderful her costume is." I brush my hands on my dark skinny jeans and face Andy. "I didn't know you were working the booth this year. I thought it was mostly marketing people."

"I volunteered." It's Andy's turn to turn red, accentuated by his light-colored surfer curls. "You know, to help our company since now I'm . . ." His face pinkens as he trails off. Now that he's an executive. "I wanted to be here in case Lelani had questions or can't answer a fan since I've worked at Genius forever." Andy tries to act like he hasn't been staring at her ample cleavage, but hell, who *wouldn't* stare at Lelani? She's like a Pacific Island princess in that dress.

"I should get going," I say to them both.

Lelani waves, her smile not quite reaching her eyes. "I'm looking forward to seeing your work in the Her Galaxy show. It's my favorite event. And you'll be at the charity auction tomorrow, right?"

Behind us, someone calls for Lelani from the main Genius booth. I can't see who through the piles of clothes and toys and stands of comic books spilling into the aisleway.

"If you'll excuse me," Lelani says before turning and walking back to the booth in a cloud of red silk and feathers.

"Wow," I say, marveling at the train of the dress, which has hand-stitched feathers attached.

"Yeah," Andy agrees, his tone dreamy.

I cut him a glance. "I was talking about the dress."

A pause. "Yeah. Me too."

I debate about telling Andy that Ryan and Lelani are an item, but I'm not feeling *that* friendly toward Andy yet. "Come on, let's go back to the booth. I need information about the auction." I steer him between Captain Genius T-shirts and a stack of Justice League action figure sets. I need to find out where the auction items are being kept. That is Genius inside information.

I follow Andy into the main part of the booth where there are other costumed Genius characters posing with fans. Captain Genius is particularly popular this year since a movie just released a few months ago. The line to take pictures with him stretches into the aisle. Beyond that, a few of our popular characters mingle, including the new Hooded Falcon in his garish multicolored armorlike gear. Lelani returns to her line, fans waiting to take pictures with her.

"Hey, Tej." I grab a schedule off the back table and scan it until I find the auction set at 6:00 p.m. tomorrow. It's going to be tight to get there from the fashion show in enough time. A light turns on in my head. That's the *perfect* excuse. And the truth. "I want to come to the auction tomorrow. I'm hoping to get something for my personal collection. But I have the fashion show."

Tej nods. He's the only one of four people working the Genius booth whom I recognize. I feel a pang of nostalgia. Even though I worked hard to get to the point where I can enjoy cons instead of work them, I miss the camaraderie. I do *not* miss the requisite XXL black T-shirt emblazoned with "Genius Comics" they have to wear.

"I was hoping I could see the stuff that's getting sold. In case I need to have someone bid for me."

"Oh yeah, no problem." Tej pushes his thick-rimmed glasses up his nose.

"Really?"

"Yeah, there's this really handy catalog . . ." His voice is muffled as he digs under the back table. "Ah. Here it is." He hands me a three-ring binder with pages of pictures and descriptions in it.

"Oh." I try to look pleased. "Yay. Perfect. Thanks, Tej." Inside, my stomach sinks. I really need to inspect the items themselves. I stand at the back table for a stretch thumbing through the binder. First editions, action figures, set pieces from the first TV adaptation—there really are some interesting items being sold, but I'm looking for something specific. The painting with the frame that went clunk. I hand the binder back to Tej.

"So what ballroom is it in? You know, so I can get there after my show?"

Tej points toward a far wall. "I think it's over there. Andy helped them set up yesterday. He would know. Oh hey, that kid is messing with those toys again. Little bastards." Tej bolts to the front of the booth, where someone is perilously close to toppling a stack of figurine boxes.

I glance at the schedule and note the ballroom number. Wading across the sea of people, I make my way over to the bank of doors on the other side of the hall. "One-oh-two, one-oh-three . . ." *Crap.* Standing in front of the door to ballroom 103 is a uniformed security guard. I think he's meant to look like he's casually placed there, watching the con, but I know better. And I'm going to need a way to get around him. I head to room 102 and jiggle the handle. Locked.

"And just what do you think you're doing?" a voice comes from behind me.

Busted. I whirl to find a smirking Lawrence.

I gasp, hand over my heart. "You scared the bejesus out of me."

"Well, you're not going to get anywhere looking as guilty as you do."

"Thanks for the pro tip," I mutter.

"What did you find out?"

"The auction goods aren't at the Genius booth like I hoped. They already set up the auction in ballroom 103, which has a guard. So I'm going to get into this one and try to get to 103 from inside."

"Nope. Not going to work."

"Why on earth not?"

Lawrence shifts some bags in his hands. He's been busy shopping already. "Because, like I said, you look too guilty. Best way to do this is straight on."

He digs in his bags and produces a thick pair of black lensless frames.

I try to look merely confused instead of annoyed as hell, which is how I feel. "Clark Kent glasses? I'm wearing my contacts today, and I don't see how this will get us past a guard."

He shrugs and, without asking permission, pulls out a purple pashmina and wraps it around my shoulders. "If we have to try getting in another way, it will be harder to determine you're the same person. We'll just switch your costume . . . Oh, that damn hair." He glances up at the recognizable shock of blue. Rummaging around in the bag, he produces a too-big black top hat, which he puts on my head in a pushed-back manner.

"I look ridiculous."

"It's Comic-Con. You look downright normal."

Touché. I roll my eyes at him, square my shoulders, and march up to the guard. He eyes me as I approach.

"Hello," I say in my best businesslike manner. "Andy sent me over to check one of the auction items." I reach under the pashmina and pull out my Genius lanyard displaying my picture ID.

The guard shifts on his feet. "I'm not supposed to let anyone in."

"And you're doing a fine job." *Jerk.* I smile. Time to unleash the Force. My "these aren't the droids you're looking for" tactic. "It's okay. I can come back later. Or I could go get Lelani to talk to you. Would that work? Or Edward Casey. He's the one who wants me to check to make sure one of the items wasn't damaged." I'm inventing wildly at this point and decide to add humor. "I could go get a teacher's note from him if you need."

The guard hesitates.

"It will take three seconds," I say, sensing weakness. "Andy says one of the frames might have cracked in transport. We might have to fix it before the auction tomorrow. But like I said, I can come back later if you need a note or something."

He saw my badge. He knows I work for Genius. He wavers and finally steps aside. "A few minutes?"

"Or less," I say, doing my best to keep a straight face. "I appreciate your diligence. We wouldn't want anything in here to go missing."

I slip through the door and into the dark, quiet ballroom. In here, the buzz from the hall is diminished, sounding like a faraway swarm of bees. A row of covered folding tables is set up on the stage, lined with various groups of items, each one with an official-looking placard describing the lot. I waste no time ascending the stairs, bypassing the podium, and walking quickly down the line of elements.

My fingers itch to touch everything, including early editions of *The Hooded Falcon*. Signed pen-and-ink drawings on card stock. I'm passing the first large framed piece when I hear a noise in the room. Instantly I am on alert, and I straighten.

"Find anything?"

Guard Guy pokes his head into the room and regards me uneasily. I can tell he's still not sure he should have let me in.

I make a show of pointing to the large framed piece in front of me. It's the same one that sat behind Casey Senior's desk, and the last time I saw it, it was on the floor of Casey's office. Thor's hammer, the sight of it has me buzzing with excited energy. "I think this is the one Andy told me about. I'm just going to have to inspect it for damage." I brandish my phone, turn on the flashlight function, and proceed to check over the frame front and back, hoping the guard will get the hint and leave again.

Instead, he walks up the dark aisle toward the stage. No, no, no. I cannot properly look at this frame with him in the room. I feel like crying. I'm *this close*.

It's going to be hard to fake a damaged frame if it looks perfect.

"Oh, I see what you're looking at," he says, motioning to the frame.

He does? I blink. "Oh yeah." I lean over the frame with my phone flashlight. "It's just easier to see with some light . . ." But he's right. From this angle, I notice that the black paper covering the back of the frame is torn. About the right size tear for someone to slip a journal through. My heart does a victory dance.

Not only my heart, but I execute a tiny shimmy of joy. I just cannot contain my excitement. "I, uh, just need to look inside and see if the cornice pieces are affected." I have no idea what I'm talking about, but I'm a writer. Making up stuff is my job. I make up monsters daily; surely I can fool one measly guard. "It's okay if the outer layer tears, but you don't want the protective layer to be punctured; the integrity of the structural layer holding the cornice pieces has to stay intact."

I'm positive he's going to call my bluff. He's most certainly the son of a professional painting framer. He probably knows what cornice pieces are, which I don't. I hold my breath.

"Oh *yeah*, that sounds serious."

"I'll just take a few pictures, and then I'll be on my way. We won't need to fix it if the structural layer still protects the art."

I use my pen to hold the torn piece away from the frame and snap a picture. There is *something* in there, but I don't want to pull it out in front of Guard Guy. I squint harder. The corner of a black journal is barely distinguishable inside the tear. I squint harder, thinking I make out a second black corner . . . so, possibly two journals. Not only that, I catch the flash of something manila colored. *Please, oh please, let that be Casey Senior's evidence.*

If it is, my plan will work. I texted Matteo yesterday and told him there is a journal in the memorabilia, possibly inside this picture, and that I am worried about it going to auction and will try to buy it. If he behaved as expected, he'd have told the whole team—most importantly Rideout—and the information would get to the White Rabbit. Hopefully the Golden Arrow too. All the players in this chess game would be present. All I have to do is sit back and see who's intent on bidding for the painting that only a few select people *know* contains a journal. Brilliance, if I do say so myself.

"So is it bad?" The guard's face hovers right next to mine now. I can't let him see the journal.

"Nope. No. Not at all. Just a little tear. Nothing to worry about. This piece won't need to be touched. Or fixed. By anyone. At all. I took a picture for insurance purposes, so we're all good here." I tap my phone importantly. The last thing I need is Andy coming in and fiddling with the frame. I nearly drag Guard Guy out of the room with me.

"Well?" Lawrence pounces on me the minute I wave at the guard and walk back toward the Genius booth.

"I found it." I can hardly keep my voice steady. I manage to stop shaking long enough to pull up the picture on my phone and zoom in. It's no work of art, but the picture *does* show the spines of the journals. Bazinga. "And I sure hope you're going to buy me dinner because I'm going to have to spend a year's salary to win it at auction. And now it's time to focus on the fashion show because there's nothing much more we can do until tomorrow."

"What happens if you don't win the journals?" Lawrence is frowning now.

"We have to win. That's what Operation Janeway is all about. And if we don't, well, I hope you like wearing orange."

CHAPTER 25

The wheels of the suitcase I'm dragging protest against the concrete ramp outside the Hyatt hotel, just next door to the convention center. "What did you pack in here? Bricks?" The bag in question lurches side to side as we level off near the lobby, and I drop the second bag slung over my shoulder.

"That's my makeup case, so be *careful* with it."

"L, you packed an entire suitcase of makeup? I packed one bag total." I open the door for L and hold it as he wheels in the rolling garment hanger we snagged from the valet.

"The next time you're the star of a fashion show and responsible for the future of a talented designer, you can let me know how much makeup *you* pack."

"L, we're in a competition. There isn't a 'star.'"

"So you say. I look so delicious in this thing. Everyone else is just a side dish." He eyes me over the oversize garment bag holding the wig. "But I promise to share the spotlight with you, sugar."

I chortle as we walk down the deeply padded floral carpet, following the signs to the fashion show backstage. My stomach is a mess of knots, and not just because I'll be racing to an auction after my show to apprehend a criminal. That should be enough, but I've spent months prepping for this, plus the cost of travel, and my future plans to go into business for myself hinge on today's results. I'll either leave with valuable feedback about areas I need to work on as a designer, or I could leave with the offer to help a well-known chain of stores develop a line of geek clothing for their customers. Either way, this contest is a launching point for MG version 3.0.

My fingers inch their way to my phone, and I find it in my hand, Matteo's number pulled up. For the fifth time in the same number of minutes, I stick it back in my pocket. I want to know if he's coming. I want to know if he's mad I'm here and I'm pulling strings on the case. I want to know if the information has been leaked. I need to play this cool, but it's damn hard.

"Come on, L." I stop outside the backstage door and show my badge, my ID, and my pass for the fashion show. "Let's go get you dressed."

I survey L's final touches on the drag makeup and breathe a huge sigh of relief and appreciation. Latifah Nile is a vision. Well, if Ursula the Sea Witch can be a vision instead of a nightmare.

All around us, girls are scrambling to finish costumes, stitch pieces that have come loose, touch up mascara. The nervous energy is unreal. I haven't had much time to talk to the other designers; we're all focused on helping our creations look spectacular.

"You're freaking out." It's not a question. L looks at me in the rectangular mirror that is propped on the folding table given to us by the fashion show. "Look at me. *Look at me*, Michael-Grace Martin. You've got this. *We've* got this. This is who we are, and that's all we can be today, okay? We've got *all* of this."

I let out a breath. L isn't just talking about the show. It's the auction. The case. Matteo. My job. So much at stake everywhere. "How do you know exactly what I'm thinking?"

"Because I know you." Latifah squeezes my shoulders, then turns back to the mirror to fluff her spectacularly tall wig.

"Michael-Grace Martin and . . . Latifah Nile?" The crew member reading our names stumbles over L's and gives us a double take. I don't blame her. With the wig, L is six foot five of sea-witch fashion fabulousness.

"Let's go," I mutter, straightening my own simple white pantsuit, accented with bright-blue stilettos, a chunky gold necklace, and my fire-engine-red glasses. The blue has faded in my hair, but I dabbed in some blue powder near the roots this morning for an intense ombré effect. Though I wear my makeup more toned down than Lawrence's, I've penciled in my lighter brows with a blue tint and wear blue-purple lipstick. My battle armor is on, and I'm ready to go kick some ass.

We wait for what seems like forever in a decidedly *unglamorous* back hallway while the show proceeds in the ballroom. Slowly our line inches forward, and finally it's our turn.

"Right in here. Watch your . . . hair." A girl dressed in black and carrying a clipboard holds open a side door in the hallway so L can duck slightly into the well-lit runway. The glare of the lights blocks most of my vision of the large ballroom, but it doesn't matter. I watch every strutting step Latifah takes up and down the catwalk. She *owns* it like no other model could. My Ursula the Sea Witch costume looks fantastic under the lights. The bodice is hand-dyed black-green tulle with glitter, woven and overlapped to create the effect of seaweed around the neckline. The frothy neckline gives way to a leather bustier with shell buttons up the front and laces up the back, giving Latifah an even fuller figure. The leather wraps over L's hips, giving way to a sexy, seductive mermaid-style skirt, green parachute material peeking through the darts just enough to look like seaweed underneath sheathed tentacles.

At the end of the catwalk, L executes a perfect spin, revealing the last surprise of the costume. The skirt flares out at the bottom in points, mimicking tentacles reaching out. The crowd breaks into applause, and L grins as she shimmies back toward me. I cannot fathom this costume on any other person. L embodies my vision for it perfectly.

We're the last runway model, so we don't have too long to wait until we're all called back up onstage to showcase the amazing costumes shown. The bright stage lights are glaring, and I can't really see many people past the front row. I wonder briefly if the Golden Arrow is in attendance, watching me.

We stand up front while the judges tally their votes, and I lean in to L. "So we're all set? For afterward?"

"Everyone's dressed in their appropriate costumes and ready for action."

The host, Auburn Elo—well-known geek fashion maven and my personal hero right now—approaches the mic. Her voice booms out as she thanks the audience for attending and announces that there will be two winners. The judges' pick and the audience pick.

"The judges' pick is . . ."

I hold my breath. I can imagine her saying my name. Several times over.

"Kelsey Maya, for the Black Widow!"

The crowd yells, but I deflate. I didn't win. Tears fill my eyes. Everything I've done. Everything I've worked for. But I square my shoulders, a ray of sunshine breaking through the clouds. This isn't the end. I'm still *here*. I still did this, and I'm still going to do this as a business. This exposure can only help me, even without a crown. I don't need any more proof that I should take a chance on myself. L is hugging me fiercely. I pat her arm.

"I'm sorry, L," I say.

"What are you talking about?" She picks me up and swings me around. "Aren't you listening? We just won the Audience Favorite!"

I look around in astonishment. Latifah hugs me to the glue-scented tulle neckline of her dress, and I am shocked to find I'm crying. Zero to sixty. I'm so excited and happy. Everything is a blur of disco lights, thumping music, and happy tears.

"We won!" I say, leaning against the wall backstage and closing my eyes. I don't even care that it wasn't the judges' favorite. My heart doesn't know the difference. I'm basking in the euphoria of knowing I'm *finally* on the right track scaling back on the writing and pursuing costuming. It's not what I ever planned, but it feels like the universe gives its nod of approval. In a world of mortals, I most definitely feel like Wonder Woman right now.

"I wish we had time to soak it in." L's already at the makeup station, though she's not disrobing like I thought she would be. "Vince just texted me and said that someone wearing a T-shirt with a golden arrow painted on it just walked into the auction and asked about the painting."

Right. That whole freaking fate-of-the-world thing. *Crap.* No big deal, I just won my first national fashion competition, but I still have hidden journals to buy, a masked avenger and a murderer to identify, and a man to win over.

"It's like sardines in here," L mutters as we push our way into the packed ballroom for the auction. Edward Casey Junior is already onstage, introducing the curator for the museum, who will be retaining one of the pieces and gaining the charitable funds.

My gaze sweeps the crowded room, already too warm, or maybe that's from my sprint over here. The first queen I spot is Shwanda, L's drag mama, dressed as much like a security guard as L and I could costume her on short notice. She's standing along the back wall, looking official and important, and meets my eye immediately. She motions with a nod toward one section of the room, so I pull L along with me through the crowd.

It takes a bit to get there, and by the time I locate two empty seats, Edward Casey Junior finishes his speech. I face forward and groan. He's shaking hands and posing for a photograph with the piece he's donating to the museum, and it's the large print. The one with the journals in it. Donated, *not* for auction. I apparently misread the stupid booklet Tej had given me. Dammit.

They set the painting—nay, my carefully placed criminal trap, now rendered *useless*—to the side, and the auction starts in earnest.

"This is all wrong," I say to L. I feel crushing defeat for the second time in as many hours. "That's it. This plan will never work now. I won't be able to see who bids on it because nobody gets to."

Someone slides into the chair on my left, and I whip my head to the side, ready for combat. My adrenaline and nerves are just about shot. "Ryan, you scared me stupid!"

"Sorry. Has the auction started? This place is a zoo." Ryan picks up on my nervous energy, evidenced by my fidgeting like a kindergartner on a Fruit Roll-Up high. I follow his gaze to Lelani, who's standing near Shwanda. Lelani's brows are pulled down, her face in a scowl. I'd be mad too if my huge dress kept me from being able to take a seat.

"No, it's just starting. You didn't miss anything." Except my plan to capture one or two suspects in my case going up in flames. Suddenly suffocating in my suit coat, I peel it off and toss it across the back of my chair. It leaves me in only my white silk camisole, but in this stifling room, I'd give anything to be wearing less. Or maybe it's nerves. Or both. I swallow noisily, panic rising in my throat.

L leans in, whispering so just I can hear, "Just sit tight. I'm sure we can get up there after the auction. We've got other problems. There are at least three Golden Arrows here."

"What?" My eyes scan the room, and dread fills my limbs.

There are several people here dressed like the Golden Arrow. The social superhero has been in the media long enough that people have made costumes based on it. Not that I'm even sure the Golden Arrow will be dressed like the Golden Arrow. There are Hooded Falcons in the crowd too. Considering this is a Hooded Falcon memorabilia auction, it's to be expected. And surely the White Rabbit won't be wearing a costume that says, "I'm a drug lord and murderer." I'm not sure why I thought I'd be able to pick them out.

I search for Amy Blondonis, the last queen on our private crew. I spot her by the back door, easy to pinpoint because of the copious tattoos on her person. The long half-black, half–icy blonde wig sticks straight with blunt bangs. It complements her huge fur stole and signature Cruella de Vil slinky black dress. Amy meets my eyes, and I suppress a shiver—I'm glad she's on our side; Amy is intense.

How are we ever going to identify anyone in here? There have to be a thousand people.

I turn forward and sink in my chair. An air of electricity charges in the room, and it doesn't have anything to do with the action figure that makes up the first lot at auction. "I guess we just wait and see," I say to L. "Something will work out; I feel sure of it. Hold your sweet black tauntauns. All hope isn't lost." *Or I'm wrong, and we're both in a huge pile of crap.*

A hush falls as the auctioneer steps up on the stage. Bidding starts, and I sneak looks around. No one seems particularly suspicious or familiar. Well, that I can tell anyway. One of the bidders is Groot, and I can't see even a bit of face.

"L, maybe you're right. With the costumes, I can't even tell who anyone is; this whole plan is a bust . . ." I trail off and turn to look behind me. A scuffle has broken out in the back among bidders. I'm not the only one to pause. The auctioneer slows the bidding, obviously unsure if he should continue. The scuffle increases in intensity. It's odd for a fight to break out *before* the auction has even really started. A chill snakes down my spine, and I get the inkling of an idea that this is no mere scuffle just seconds before the entire room plunges into darkness.

CHAPTER 26

Instantly, L pulls me to my feet. "Get to the door!" I can barely hear her over the screams of the patrons around me. I hear a strange whizzing as something flies by my head and an *ooof* as the item that grazes my head goes on to hit Ryan. Something sharp scrapes my face, and I feel the instant ooze of blood. Between this and the damn warehouse break-in, I am going to look like Deadpool when this is finished. I'm aware of Ryan climbing straight over the chairs in front of us, making his way to the stage. He seems pissed, which is so completely odd, I just stop and stare for a moment.

There's a brief loud ripping sound, then a crash and a thump that sounds a *lot* like someone falling off a chair onstage. *The hell?* This isn't in Operation Janeway anywhere.

L pulls my arm out of my socket, requiring me to climb over people to get out of our seats. All around me in the dark, mass hysteria reigns. Chairs clatter to the floor. I can only vaguely see L's form as we plow through the rest of the row into the aisleway. The emergency exit is the only source of light in the ballroom now.

The auctioneer tries feebly to calm people using the PA system, talking about an orderly exit, when all the lights flood back on. Pandemonium ceases; everyone freezes midflight. Chairs are everywhere, people and costume pieces scattered. The auctioneer waves a hand. "It's okay, it's okay. Someone just bumped the bank of lights. We can all settle down now and return to order."

I think I see Ryan hurtling past the hulking form of Casey Junior, sitting and moaning on the stage like he's been sucker punched in the dark.

"That was weird," I grouse, rubbing at my temple.

L is still on high alert. I can feel her vibrating next to me. "More than weird. That was a diversion. Look at the stage."

My eyes trail over the covered tables to the round one where they set the large print after the presentation. *My* print. The one with the journals and the evidence in it . . . or the remnant of what was once the beautiful piece. I gasp. *No, no, no.* The canvas sags open, a gaping slice straight through the middle. The top and bottom curl away, revealing the back of the frame. No journals. Nothing. Gone. But . . . I didn't see anyone. Not a White Rabbit. Not a Golden Arrow. Not a damn thing.

"The painting! The journals!" I spin to L. "What do we do?"

"Hang on." L looks to Shwanda's corner, then to the corner with Amy Blondonis. They exchange complicated hand gestures, and her shoulders relax a fraction. "Unless someone went through the ceiling, I don't think anyone made it through an exit. The girls gave me the all clear, which means the doors haven't been opened. The thief is still here."

And I still have a chance to slay this monster. Good thing I have my ass-kicking heels on. "I need to get to that microphone."

I make my way as fast as I can up the side of the stage and walk across to the auctioneer, who eyes me with alarm. It could be the blood oozing down my face. Or my disheveled appearance. Who knows?

"It's okay; I work for Genius. I need to make an announcement." I step up to the microphone and address the audience. "Someone call security. We need to keep the doors closed. One of the items has been destroyed, and the person responsible may have an item of interest—"

I don't even get to finish. There is a second scuffle, this time by the back door. Abandoning my announcement, I race to the edge of the stage in time to see the long blonde hair of Amy Blondonis diving into the center of a circle of costumed bystanders, her fingers grasping just shy of the shirt of a figure who bolts through the back door.

"L! We have to go! He's getting away!" I leap off the stage, only to find Latifah already racing through the crowd, her ample curves and ample height no match for the flummoxed herd of attendees. Behind me I hear several people take up the cry as they see the damaged painting, but we're already off and away, chasing after our villain.

"Which one is it? Arrow or Rabbit?"

"I don't know!" I'm yelling to be heard over the pandemonium as we careen around a group of six-foot dragons and scramble through the back door. Amy and Shwanda are in hot pursuit, just the glimpse of a figure up ahead, wearing a big black leather jacket and a black ball cap pulled low over the face.

I'm impressed at the speed Latifah manages in her five-inch stilettos. Mine are inches shorter, and I'm barely making muster. Amy Blondonis dodges costumed folks in the small hallway, yelling something I can't hear or understand.

"What do we do?" I gasp, already tiring. We're approaching the exhibition hall, and I groan inwardly. There's no way to track this person if they make it in there. We're sunk.

"In gaming terms, we are going to Leeroy Jenkins the *shit* out of this bitch," Latifah yells. "Hold my wig." She yanks the confection right off her head, exposing the wig cap as she runs, and throws it over her shoulder at me. "You find a way to navigate. I'm going to catch this mother." In an unbelievable burst of speed, L is at the heels of Amy Blondonis.

"Navigate. Navigate. I've got to *navigate*?" I'm not even sure what that means. Eyes on the ground, maybe? *Up.* I need to get up above to see the Golden Arrow. I need the Genius booth.

Not two seconds later, Shwanda screeches past, taking an alternate route. I hope L is trying to circle around to cover the other exits.

Yells and a large crash explode from within Artists' Alley, likely our villain having a hell of a time shaking Amy and Latifah. My suspicions are confirmed when a shout rises above the general murmur of the crowd and I see a booth topple not two hundred yards to my right.

I *need* to find something to climb on. My eyes alight on the huge Genius banner. It's held by a PVC frame and attached to the ceiling with cables. There is *no* way it's safe, but it's sitting on top of the booth, so I sprint for it.

"MG!" I hear my name shouted, but I can't spare time to look. I need to get eyes on the ground, and it needs to be *now*. Not even bothering to explain, I burst through the line of people waiting for pictures with characters, practically bowling over Captain Genius before I right myself and race to the back table.

Tej stands ramrod straight, his eyes round with fear. "MG, what the *hell* are you doing?"

I don't answer; I vault—well, really I slide and bounce—over the folding table into the back area and grab on to the booth frame.

"Lift me up." I pull Tej's arm.

"What? No! What the—" The last words are muffled because I've used the table to climb onto Tej's shoulders before hefting myself onto the roof of the booth. It sways underneath my feet, and I grab the PVC frame holding the banner, praying that it will hold my weight steady. It does, and I breathe a visceral sigh of relief, even with the floor swaying many feet below me.

I gather my bearings and recognize a huge Sea Witch racing down the next aisle. "Up here! L!" I frantically wave until Latifah looks up and catches sight of me.

"Which way?" Latifah searches the crowd in front of the Genius booth.

"I don't know! I . . ." I'm scanning the crowd and happen to catch sight of a dark jacket turning the corner. "Over that way! Artists' Alley, wearing a red top hat now!" The jacket looks to be the same size and shape as the one I saw in our chase.

Surely L can catch our thief. I have clear eyes on the figure, and we have hundreds of feet to the main entrance. I glance up again, pondering why the figure in the jacket doesn't seem to be going *toward* the main entrance, and freeze.

"Latifah! The fire exit! He's headed to the fire exit!" *There's no way L heard me.* I can't think of anything else to do, so I yell, "Stop that masked—er, hatted man!" I've always wanted to say that. Too bad we're in a *room* full of masked men. Chaos breaks out beneath me.

And now there's nothing left to do but shimmy down the booth, chuck my heels to the side, and sprint as fast as I can toward the fire exit.

It's not pretty. I'm tearing through booths, clothing and toys are flying everywhere, and I'm just yelling blanket apologies as I run. I careen around a corner and spot the fire door. No one has gone through yet, or the alarm would be ringing. I slide on the floor, intent on my goal. In front of me, a dark figure bursts through the back curtain of a booth and sails into the aisleway looking over his shoulder.

I glance too and see an irate Amy Blondonis hopping through the mess of a booth, her dress caught on the booth itself. Our thief in the jacket straightens, looks at the door, then bolts. I'm outdistanced and outpaced, and there's no way I can reach the figure before he's in the open.

"Stop!" I scream, nothing else at my disposal. I take a risk. "We know you're the White Rabbit! There are police outside that door. This is a setup!"

The hat turns in my direction, and the person's steps falter. It's enough to shift their focus to me, just enough time for L to save the day.

In slow motion, a monstrous Sea Witch rises from the tangled curtain of a booth. Latifah steps forward, holds her arm out the booth exit and across the narrow aisle, and clotheslines the fleeing thief. At the same time, a black stiletto heel flies in from the other direction, landing with a solid thunk against the back of our perpetrator's head. It's enough to knock the person to the ground, facedown on the carpet.

"That's right, *bitch*. You don't mess with Shwanda!"

Shwanda fishes Amy out of the crumpled booth, sans one shoe.

L is already using one of the belts from a clothing booth we demolished to truss up the victim.

The world rushes in, and I look around, realizing we've essentially stopped San Diego Comic-Con. There are at least five cell phone cameras pointed in our direction and not a small number of irate booth owners storming toward us.

"We need to call the police," I say.

"Shouldn't we look for the journals first? You know, since we're trying to use them to keep ourselves out of jail?" L's chest heaves, my gorgeous creation hanging half off her body. The costume looks like it's been hit by a tsunami.

"Right. Yes." I surge forward. I want those journals. I *need* those journals.

L grunts as she flips the squirming body on the ground over, then goes still. I pounce, searching the outside jacket pockets for the journals. For *anything* when I realize that L's not just waiting. She's . . . freaked out.

"What—" The words die on my lips the moment I see the criminal's face.

It's not Rideout. It's not Tony Munez. It's not even Officer James. *Her* face.

Agent Sosa's dark-brown eyes meet mine from the floor. "Hello, Ms. Martin," she says conversationally. As if we've just run into each other in a bar and not run through countless booths and over countless Wookiees in a chase scene that should be in some campy meta musical episode of *Supernatural*.

But it doesn't make any sense. Why would Agent Sosa be involved in this? Did we tackle an officer giving chase by mistake? I don't think so. Why would *she* want the journals? My first inclination is to let her up, but my gut churns. She's the *one* person I dismissed because she wasn't an integral part of Matteo's team. But she'd been at *every* scene with the DEA. And has access to the interviews and the *suspects. And probably Matteo's text about my suspicions of the painting at auction.* My heart flips over as I think about Song Yee. The dawning crashes like the space shuttle in *The Martian*—I want to hit my own head with my hand, but my hands are still splayed on her jacket, holding her down.

I don't have to wonder what to do for long, because from behind me a voice I recognize very, *very* well rises above the chaos.

"Don't *anyone* move. I'm Detective Kildaire of the LAPD, and as far as I'm concerned, *all* of you are under arrest."

CHAPTER 27

"Matteo!" I'm delighted and *mortified* to see him in front of me. "You came!" I note with distaste that Detective Rideout is present, along with a few other police wearing San Diego uniforms.

"Yes, I got your text . . . I also found you on a surveillance tape at a warehouse, as well as your fingerprints on some items of interest in a box of comic tear sheets. You failed to mention that when you told me about the painting."

I wince.

He spares me a quick glance, then back to Agent Sosa. His eyebrows shoot up as recognition dawns on his face.

"Kildaire, get this crazy woman off of me. We're in pursuit of a suspect; they tackled me by mistake." The police behind Matteo shuffle around, gearing up for action, instantly on alert for a person of interest.

"No, you *are* the suspect," I argue back, turning to Matteo. "Don't let her go. I promise I'm right." It makes sense. She had access to the drugs. She had access to the reports. Matteo asked her to watch Yee's interview, and she probably saw the Casey interview too. Enough to know we were on her trail. This explains her icy disdain for me at the party. How she didn't want me taking a picture of Anthony Munez. Maybe afraid I'd put two and two together and recognize the similar dark eyes, the same straight nose. Only I didn't. Not until now, when I could study her face up close. Sosa. A married name. I'd been looking for *one* White Rabbit, but she is the protégé—a family business. I remember the day James handed her a baggie at the warehouse. And when I heard Officer James admit to interfering in the case, potentially committing *murder*. And though I was wrong in assuming Rideout, I was right on all other counts.

Matteo's gaze rakes my face, taking in the blood covering my cheek. His shoulders relax momentarily when he realizes I'm not mortally wounded, but the royally pissed look doesn't take long to surface again. He helps me up, then squats down next to Sosa, placing a restraining hand on her back to keep her prone while he continues speaking. "I am going to give you thirty seconds to explain what went on here before you're all taken to the station. MG, you told me you wouldn't do anything stupid. Assaulting an officer qualifies as *really* stupid." There's no hint of a smile or smirk in his gorgeous hazel eyes.

I have to gather myself, heart hammering inside my chest. I'm surprised my ribs contain it. This is where the rubber meets the road. I need to lay it all out and hope Matteo believes me. Forgives me for doing it on my own. I take a breath and recap how I texted him to encourage the leak and lure the Golden Arrow and/or the White Rabbit to the auction.

The story tumbles from my lips. The auction, the chase.

"I was *attacked*," Sosa interjects. "I arrived just as the lights went out. Someone shoved me through that doorway. I was giving chase." She does have a lump rising on her cheek. But so do I. Shit went *down* in that room; it's not a stretch of the imagination that someone's elbow caught her face as she dove out the door.

She's pretty convincing. I have the slightest moment of self-doubt. Could I have seen this wrong? No. The story fits.

I can't read Matteo's face. He's *Detective Kildaire* all the way right now. He looks to each of us in turn. Weighing my testimony. Assessing. "And you all"—Matteo motions to Amy, Shwanda, and Latifah—"just thought that rather than waiting for security or calling the police, you'd ruin merchandise and put lives at risk by chasing a thief through a convention by yourselves?"

No one answers, but all eyes turn to me. *The captain goes down with the ship.* "It's my fault. Waiting at the auction. This whole idea. The chase just . . . happened. I'm sorry about that." But I caught one of the suspects we've been searching for. That has to count for something, right?

I can hardly bring myself to meet Matteo's eyes, but when I do, I wince. There's condemnation in his gaze, but beyond that, there's hurt. Betrayal. Maybe a semibroken heart. And definitely broken trust. I feel as badly about that as anything. It's hard to breathe, like someone is sitting on my chest. I did the right thing, but I'll have to pay the price.

Matteo's mouth is a thin line. "You're going to have to come in for questioning."

My shoulders sink slightly, but I take a deep breath. "I realize that. And I'm ready to accept my punishment."

Matteo's gaze flicks away like he can't keep looking at me. He grunts and rises to his feet. "Fine. Rideout, call Officer James. Tell him we need holding cells for questioning." He motions to two officers who step forward and lift Agent Sosa off the ground. The snap of handcuffs is audible as they tighten around her wrists.

But I can't get past the mention of Officer James. We can*not* go into custody with him around. We'll end up dead for sure. "Wait! You can't!"

The cops stop what they're doing and face me again, most wearing expressions that say they clearly think I'm off my rocker. I clear my throat and drop my voice so that only Matteo can hear me. "Um, you can't have Officer James involved. He's been working with the White Rabbit."

Matteo rocks back on his heels like I've slammed him bodily. "What?"

"Lawrence and I saw him in the warehouse."

"Officer James has been doing patrols. That does *not* mean he's dealing drugs."

My head shakes back and forth before he's finished speaking. "We heard him say that he'd helped make it look like Yee hung himself in his cell."

Matteo's eyes widen, a hint I'm breaking through the natural detective skepticism. I get the sense that not many people know the details about that, certainly not the public.

Feeling faint hope he'll believe me, I continue, "Look, all I can tell you is what I heard. I know it's my word against his, but—no, wait. I heard something else. Something you can use to check it out. He asked that money be wired to his offshore account. Matteo, that would be proof, right?"

Matteo's expression is still shuttered. He is silent for a count of five, in which I don't move or breathe. Then he turns to his partner and says, "Rideout, call the captain. Apprise her of the situation. Have Officer James put into custody pending investigation as well. We can cite two eyewitnesses until we get a look at his financials. Better yet, ask her to confiscate his phone also."

Rideout studies me, and I'm expecting some sort of remark, but he just looks . . . rattled. Ashen-faced, he turns and lifts his cell to his ear, presumably to make a call to the captain.

Sosa has apparently been able to hear some of what we said because she struggles against the officers holding her, cheeks a bright red. "Kildaire, this is ludicrous. This whole fairy tale about a White Rabbit is stupid. I'm just out here trying to chase down a guy who stole a painting. Look, let me go. I am a fellow officer, and we are letting our true perpetrator get away."

Matteo hesitates again.

It's zero hour. And she's about to talk her way out of this because I have no proof. I snap my fingers, startling everyone beside me. *Proof.*

"It's not a fairy tale, and I can prove it. Matteo, if she's who we were chasing, she hasn't had time to ditch the journals. She's got them on her somewhere. I swear." I've never been so sure of anything in my entire life. I *will* Matteo to believe me.

Matteo reaches forward and unzips her jacket. A manila envelope falls out, along with a journal.

Bazinga.

Agent Sosa screeches, face beet red now. "That's not *mine*. Someone planted those there. Why would I have some journal? That huge sea beast put it in my jacket when I fell! You're arresting the wrong person!"

She's right. We can't *prove* she took them. Another thought occurs to me as I eye her open coat. The painting. The ripped canvas. "Look for a knife," I tell Matteo as he pulls on a glove and scoops up the envelope. "Do officers carry knives? Anything sharp that could, say, slice through a canvas?"

Silence stretches as he pats her pockets and produces a small folding utility knife, black in color. It looks like military issue, and I'd be willing to believe it's Sosa's personal knife. He drops it into a baggie while Sosa glares at me.

The yelling has gathered a crowd, and though the officers are doing their best to keep people out, I see a multitude of cell-phone cameras pointed in our direction. For better or for worse, the Golden Arrow and the White Rabbit—and me and my crew—are evening news fodder. A familiar face pushing through the crowd draws my attention.

Ryan's face is white. He's sans coat and bag of freebies, and he all but launches himself to land near Matteo. "MG, what the *hell* is going on?"

I cut a glance at Latifah, cuffs placed on her beefy arms. "Minor misunderstanding. It seems we happened upon a bad guy—er—girl and got in the way of her escape. Ry, you're going to have to feed Trog for me until this is cleared up, okay?"

Ryan looks around, sees the rest of his party being handcuffed, and swings his gaze back to me. "No, I'm coming with you guys. I'll witness to . . . whatever."

"Actually, that's a great idea," Matteo cuts in. He turns to Ryan. "Were you involved in this chase too?"

Ryan raises his eyebrows. "Chase? No. I was in the auction room. Everyone was panicking, and I got stuck in the crowd. Didn't see where anyone went."

I squint my eyes. That's not exactly how I remember it.

"I want you to come give a statement. Sit for questioning anyhow." Matteo says this like a challenge.

Ryan shrugs like it's no big deal. "Sure. I'll meet you at the station." He turns to me. "And I'll call the neighbor to let Trog out."

Matteo rolls his shoulders back, rocks his head side to side, and faces Agent Sosa. "Okay. Back to you. I think this notebook is enough to hold you until we take a look at this evidence. Book her."

"Kildaire, are you sure about this?" It's Rideout. But he's not being an ass. He sounds nervous. I mean, we're accusing two people on his team—and his idol's daughter—of drug dealing, murder, and smuggling. Big stuff.

Matteo searches my face, and I nod, pointing to the journal. "Read it. Open the manila envelope. Everything you need is in there."

He nods and rips open the manila paper, which almost disintegrates. A VHS tape falls out, along with some photography prints and another journal.

The prints show a young man weighing bricks of heroin. The man's features had aged by the time of the anniversary party, but it's unmistakably Agent Sosa's father, Anthony Munez.

"So, your dad is the White Rabbit." I know she won't answer me. "Is that why you blocked this case at every turn?"

Agent Sosa won't meet my eye.

I press on. "Was Huong Yee going to out your father? Or was it you he'd seen—the *new* White Rabbit?"

She is still silent, but her chest rises and falls at a rapid rate.

I shrug and look at the group gathered around us in silence. This feels so *dramatic*. "Fine. Stay quiet. I don't know what's on this video, but I'm guessing it's going to incriminate your father. It's why your father killed Edward Casey Senior."

The crowd does an impressive imitation of a movie scene: a collective gasp, complete with an outbreak of rabid conversation.

I turn to Matteo, guilt melting all my bravado. We're back to the fact that this man is now well aware that I lied to him, withheld evidence, aided a suspect in eluding police, and set up a sting operation on my own. Quite the little superhero story line of my own. "I couldn't tell you because . . . well, I thought Rideout was the double agent. I was wrong about that." My eyes flick to Rideout and his ashen face. "Anthony Munez not only killed Casey Senior to protect his identity but claimed to have used the information Casey sent to the police department to fake a drug war, round up his competition, and put them all away. It really was brilliant. For thirty years, it worked. But Edward Casey's journal resurfaced. He got his revenge. He got his justice in the end."

"That's quite the story," Rideout says. No condemnation. Just fact.

I shrug. "It *is* just a story at this point, but I'm pretty good with stories. I bet you'll find that I'm right when you do the hard work of pulling together the evidence."

"I want a lawyer," Agent Sosa announces as she's escorted ahead of us.

"I bet you do."

I nearly crack a smile at Rideout's dry response. At least he's a jerk to everyone, and not just me.

"The only thing I *can't* figure out," I say more to myself, "is where the other journal went. Either Sosa ditched it, which could be possible, *or* . . ."

"Or what?" Rideout barks, a touch of his old bite in evidence. "Spill it, story girl."

"Or the Golden Arrow was here and tried to nab the envelope. Maybe that's what the scuffle was. If you find the journal, maybe you'll find our vigilante. They might not even know we've caught Sosa or that she had the envelope."

"Or you're the Golden Arrow and trying to draw up a ruse."

The accusation is so simple, it takes my breath away. "Why would I go to all the trouble of pointing out a loose end if I was hoping to get away with it?"

"Criminal brilliance?"

I look down, my slinky white slacks and rumpled thin cami clinging to my body. "And just where do you think I'd be keeping it?"

Rideout has the decency to look away and mutters something about a pat-down at the station.

"I'm fairly certain there's another journal missing. I took a picture when I snuck in to see the painting—sorry," I mutter as Matteo shoots me a look. "My cell phone is in my jacket pocket. But I know I have a picture showing two journals. My jacket is back in the auction room," I say, and a police officer is dispatched while we wait.

Matteo holds up his hand to Rideout and signals another cop forward. "If MG is right and Sosa doesn't have both journals on her, then maybe it's true that someone attempted to stop her, or she dropped one of them. Engage the con security team, and let's do a sweep for the item. *And* hope to God that there are two sets of prints on the journal if we find it," he adds, cutting off Rideout's retort before he can voice it. "Since MG doesn't have a journal on her person, I'm going to go with innocent until proven guilty." He turns an eye to me. "You'll have to come in for formal questioning, though, and your cell will be kept as evidence until you're cleared."

I hold out my wrists to Matteo. "I'll come willingly to the station for questioning, but you can cuff me if you'd like."

"Maybe later." He still looks *pissed*, but there's a hint of a smile tugging at the corner of his lips.

CHAPTER 28

I ring the doorbell on the exterior of the metal gate. It's an old-fashioned one that rings a real bell, nothing digital, nothing electric. I have to ring it twice before I get a response from the house. The blinds move slightly as someone looks out; then the door cracks open.

Dragons dance in my belly; I wonder if he's going to shut the door in my face. If he's going to dismiss me before I can explain. It's been two months of hell—seeing him interrogated in the hearings for the trial—and not getting to talk to him or touch him. Explain myself other than through my testimony.

"Hey, I wasn't expecting you." Matteo is in bare feet and pajama pants. He looks relaxed and scrump-diddly-umptious. That is, minus the frown lines that crease his face and the set of his shoulders. Those say that he's nervous to see me too.

"I'm officially not a suspect anymore. I just thought I'd let you know. I know a guy who says face-to-face is best for important conversations."

Matteo smirks. He studies me for a moment, then sighs and opens the door wide, allowing me into his house. "In that case, let me welcome you into my home, *normal civilian*."

His shoes sit by the door, and I take care to place my bright-purple kitten heels right next to his neat brown shoes. The living room is dark, save for the glow from a TV—he *does* have one!—tucked away on the far wall. I note the scene paused on the TV, and I laugh. "*The Princess Bride?*"

Matteo shrugs. "Kyle recommended it."

"I bet he did." This time Matteo returns my grin with a small one of his own, and the world seems a lot friendlier.

He shuffles his feet in the carpet. "So how does it feel to be 'not a person of interest'?" It's a simple question, but it carries weight.

I lift my hands out to the side and shrug. "Glad it's over. So lovely, I guess. But I'm a little sad it's over. I feel like I *was* the superhero. I got to be the Golden Arrow, or the Hooded Falcon. I did a little vigilante justice, brought a double agent to her knees." I need to get to my point, though. "But, um, I kinda hurt someone I like in the process, and I want to apologize."

Matteo's eyes flick to the ground then back up to mine. "Apologies are quite the work of art, so I hear."

Great, he isn't going to let me off easy. I give a dramatic sigh, run my hands through my hair—I've returned it to my natural white blonde for the hearings—and square my shoulders to him. "I'm sorry I didn't tell you about the journal. Or Lawrence." I tick them off on my fingers. "Or Officer James. Or call you when I found the drug money in the warehouse. Sorry about breaking into a warehouse too. Probably a bad call."

He raises his eyebrows and rolls his hand forward to indicate that I should continue.

I squint one eye. "I'm also sorry I set up a sting without your knowledge or permission and that I attempted to catch a dangerous criminal on my own, making this case messy and a logistical nightmare." I had to sit through hearing after hearing while it was sorted through. I *know* I made this a tough one for Matteo to wrap up neatly.

He still doesn't look appeased. "And?"

I rack my brain. "And . . . Matteo, I think that's everything. I swear."

He sighs and crosses his arms. He's standing with his feet shoulder width apart, and even in his pajamas, I recognize *Detective Kildaire.* "Michael-Grace Martin, you need to apologize for putting *yourself* in an inordinate amount of danger. I couldn't protect you from the bad guys. Hell, I couldn't even protect you from *you* because I was in the goddamn bloody dark." Color rises to his cheeks, and he swipes his hand over his face.

I'd like to sink into the carpet. "I know."

Detective Kildaire isn't done. "You're my partner. We're supposed to have each other's backs, be honest with each other, even when it's hard. That's what *partners* do."

I feel like my heart is coming out of my chest like in the old cartoons. He said "you *are*," not "*were*."

"I was a crappy partner."

"Damn right you were."

"But it's because of the dirty cop, Matteo. I was afraid Lawrence would end up dead or *I* would end up in jail. I didn't know who to trust, and I was worried about you too, getting in trouble because of me. I just thought it best to keep my own counsel."

"You couldn't trust me to keep you safe? You thought I was the dirty cop?" His stance hasn't changed, but I hear the hurt in his voice. Ah, this is the crux of it. He thinks I didn't trust him.

My voice comes out small, but I'm being honest. "I suspected you for about thirty seconds, and then it was obvious that you're the least crooked cop that ever existed. I tried to protect *you*. I was wrong not to trust you. I'm sorry. I'll be a better partner in the future, I promise, if you'll still have me?"

I hold my breath, terrified for having put myself out there for rejection that openly. He could stomp all over my heart now if he wants.

"You didn't just catch one double agent."

I blink. "What?"

"Two of them, as I recall from the hearing." There's a note of pride in his voice now.

"Yes, two of them." I lean forward. "So does this mean I'm forgiven?"

Matteo studies me, then rolls his eyes to the ceiling and mutters what looks like a prayer for patience. "I guess so. And I never suspected. I just showed that text to the team without thinking. Does this make us both crazy?" He reaches forward and hauls me to his chest. I breathe in the smell of toothpaste and revel in the static cling of his pajama pants against my jeans.

I speak into his chest, anxious to discuss the case, since I haven't been able to for two long months. "It's crazy to me that Agent Sosa would take over her father's business like that. The drugs, the lies, the false reports, tossing out cases, deflecting suspicion." I sat in on only two hearings with Munez and Sosa present, but now that I'm cleared of all my charges, I'd get to sit in on more. I'm now a witness for the prosecution, though the lawyers are thinking this case could take *years* to sort through in court.

His arms are still wrapped around me like a vise, and he leans his chin against my head. "She did it because she loves him. His health is bad—very bad. He won't live to see his sentencing, I don't think. Dementia is a terrible thing, even worse when you're a kingpin. From what I've heard in the hearings you missed, he had started to make business mistakes. His mind was going. She didn't want him to get caught, so she took on more and more gradually. At first just to keep him out of jail, and then . . . well, money can be a powerful motivator. Unfortunately, she was good at what she did." He pauses for a moment.

"I don't think she knew that he had killed Casey until we discovered it. Then she knew for certain he'd die in jail if the case was solved. She was just trying to protect her father. In fact, had she not been falsifying the test results from this specific case, I don't know that we'd have enough to hold her on. Officer James agreed to identify her in exchange for a plea deal, and that helps. Though he'll still get close to life for killing Yee. His only chance is to hope he drops that sentence for parole."

"All of this has been so crazy. The costumes, the crimes, the real-life superheroes. I'm ready for my life to settle down a bit."

A rumble starts in his chest, and his shoulders shake beneath my cheek. He still hasn't loosened his hold on me. "It's been pretty crazy. But I have a feeling that life with you isn't calm and boring."

I grin against his chest and slip my hands into his. "No, probably not. Actually, did you see the latest copy of *The Hooded Falcon*?" I look up to gauge his reaction.

Matteo's mouth presses into a line. "Yes, we've seen it." A month ago, an independently produced comic showed up online and in retail stores bearing the name of *The Hooded Falcon*. Instead of it being a rip-off of ours, though, it was a slim comic containing the cleaned-up sketches of the original Falcon. The sketches from the journals that had been in the frame. The Golden Arrow had presumably managed to somehow take the journals, clean them up, and publish them as close to what Casey would have done as possible.

"You'll go after the Golden Arrow now?"

Matteo eyes me. "Are you *sure* it's not you?"

I laugh. "I've been cleared by the courts of men and God."

"I mean, yes . . . but we have no leads at this point, although we're looking. We're still busting the drug rings involved with the White Rabbit. I think things will quiet down a bit with Sosa and her father behind bars." Matteo looks shell-shocked as he shakes his head in wonder at me. "Anthony was *the* purveyor of heroin in LA for thirty years, and we never knew."

I nod. The waves of this case touch every part of the LAPD. Everyone has been in for questioning, Matteo and Rideout included.

"How are Lawrence and Ryan?" Matteo's question pulls me back to the present.

I shrug, and he wraps his arms around me and rubs slowly up and down my back with one hand. "Okay. Everyone's shaken up about this. No one's acting normally. But I think we'll get there." Lawrence and Ryan had the charges of aiding and abetting dropped when their alibis panned out. Lelani had actually been a huge help in backing up Ryan's story. I guess she wasn't just good in the boardroom; she was good in the courtroom too.

I'm hesitant to share my next bit of information, but Matteo has just said that honesty is everything. "I have to admit, I kind of like the idea of our masked avenger still being out there. Instead of these journals rotting in evidence, they're seeing the light of day. I know it's not how the case should be. But it's a little bit like Robin Hood, don't you think? Rob from the rich—er, police, and give to the masses? Everyone gets to find out how the comics would have ended. Anyhow, I told you I'm *not* a suspect anymore. I don't want to talk about the case."

I want to talk about *us*. I want to talk about how my hands don't ever want to stop holding his. I want to talk about our partnership and where we're going to go from here.

Matteo pulls me to the sofa and scoots closer until our thighs are pressed together. "No work talk?"

My heart races, and I have trouble focusing on his actual words.

"No." I reach out, wrap my arm around his neck, and pull him to me. I breathe him in, so happy to find that he's real and warm and willing to forgive me. We sit like that, cozy in the couch corner, for a long moment, and I drink in his presence. I feel like I'm home, something I've never felt with anyone else. I take the time to sort through the fact that Matteo *isn't* my type. Instead, he balances me out. He doesn't have to fit into my standards for a boyfriend . . . He cares about me. He may not know enough to ask me to watch a *Doctor Who* marathon yet, but he'll watch it with me because he knows it will make me happy. I spent so much time pushing people away because they didn't fit what I was looking for, and in the end what I needed was someone to bring *me* out of *my* prejudices. Open my eyes to the world. To realize that the perfect person will support my fashion design, my wacky hair, my comics, my job, because those things are all a part of me.

Thank God for the Hooded Falcon. Yet again, he knew exactly what I needed in my life. He led me from original and unhappy MG to MG

2.0, who kicked ass at Genius but was a little lonely. Now, through this case, and through Casey Senior's presence in my life yet again, MG 3.0 is ready to be released into the world.

Here I am with a gorgeous Muggle, and the world still has magic in it. *The Princess Bride* is on TV, and there is a masked vigilante still out there in the world if things get too crazy. The universe is just about perfect.

I roll my shoulders back. "You know what I'm really in the mood for?" I give him my best bedroom eyes.

"What's that?" His thumbs are already on my rib cage, his mouth inches from mine.

"Herbal tea."

"You minx."

"All right, fine. I don't want tea. I just want to be Matteo and MG for a bit. No capes, no costumes, no crimes, just . . . us. Can we do that?" I run my hand up his arm, feeling the goose bumps rise on his skin in the wake of my touch.

He leans forward and seals my query with a kiss. "What does the hero say now? Oh yes. 'As you wish.'"

ACKNOWLEDGMENTS

First off, a huge thanks to Kristi—the "real" MG. Without you and your zany life, this book would never have existed.

This book was a lark, a "fun" project to work on while I was supposed to be revising my "real" book for submission. A huge thank-you to the team of friends who convinced me that *this* project was the one that deserved my attention. To "the Girls," for reading the first version chapter by chapter. Thanks to Erin, for listening to me talk about this project ad nauseam and cheerleading the whole journey, and Trisha, for the insane late-night plotting that you've done with me. Thanks for being my partner in crime, as you put it! A thank-you to John, for spending hours telling me what it was *really* like to be a narcotics detective, and to my sensitivity readers. To my husband, for both laughing out loud at the dream that inspired the book and for pushing me to write it because "this is probably going to be the one that sells, because it's ridiculous and awesome." He was right! (Don't tell him I said that.) For my family, who continue to be completely supportive of me and my crazy dreams, even though I'm often overtired and cranky from pursuing them at all hours of the night/day. And thanks to my son, Noah, who is absolutely a real superhero and reminds me daily why the world needs laughter, fun, and "real people" in literature.

This book wouldn't exist without my amazing professional support system. First and foremost, my agent, Joanna MacKenzie, who felt like an old friend the first time we talked. She's the (more capable) other half of my awesome nerd team, and I cannot imagine my book ending up in better hands. And, of course, my inimitable mentor, Kelly Siskind. This book took shape because she took a chance on my manuscript in Pitchwars. I never would have been able to accomplish those initial revisions on my own (plus, her writing and dedication to the craft and business of writing are second to none!), and her tireless optimism in the project kept me afloat. To my editor(s) Adrienne, Jason, and Jaym: you guys have made this debut process so enjoyable and easy.

Last but not least, a thanks to Brenda Drake and my Pitchwars community. Specifically to my critique partner and comic guru, Ian, for always being there to vent/celebrate/send corgi gifs/give guidance on pages. To the rest of my writing crew I gained from PW—Christine, Elise, Kelli, Helen, Suzie, Jen, Julie, and the whole "Raptor Pack." You all are the gift that keeps on giving, my coworkers, my inspiration, my confidants, and my peers. I can't imagine this journey without you.

ABOUT THE AUTHOR

Photo © 2018 Julie Patton Photography

Meghan Scott Molin loves all kinds of storytelling. After studying architecture and opera at college, she worked as a barn manager before becoming a professional photographer. *The Frame-Up* is her first published book. An avid lover of all the nerd things—*Star Wars*, *Star Trek*, hobbits, *Doctor Who*, and more—Meghan also enjoys cooking, dreaming of travel, coveting more corgis, and listening to audiobooks in the barn. She lives in Colorado with her husband (and fellow zookeeper), her sons, two horses, a cat, and a rambunctious corgi. For more information about Meghan, visit her website at www.MeghanScottMolin.com or follow her on Twitter (@megfuzzle).

W9-BST-261

PRAISE FOR
THE ONLY GIRL IN THE CAR

"This undercover report from the all-American girlhood of a cherished daughter is a true horror story, and an exercise in suspense at once blithe and terrifying."
—Nuala O'Faolain, author of *Are You Somebody?* and *My Dream of You*

"Evoking the stark power of Mary Karr's landmark memoirs *The Liars' Club* and *Cherry*, Dobie . . . charts her discovery of boys . . . and subsequent entanglements with them in an unapologetic voice that is surprisingly sympathetic. But just as the reader begins to understand her desire to act like one of the guys, the book savagely reminds us of the dangers of adolescent recklessness." —*Vogue*

"In the wake of publication, once again people couldn't stop talking about Kathy Dobie. It was almost scandalous—the clarity of her writing and the depths of suburban darkness she chronicled. . . . She took the words used to shame her and made meaning out of them, she took the night she was told to forget and remembered it with relentless clarity. She got away." —*Newsday*

"Kathy Dobie writes of herself as a girl out of control. That girl who looked so frantically for love has been rewarded, at last, by the woman who writes a prose so fine that she leaves the reader breathless with pleasure." —Richard Rodriguez, author of *Hunger of Memory*

"Dobie writes of her sexually precocious adolescence with a keen, unsparing eye and avoids depicting herself as a victim, a temptation few could resist." —*The Washington Post Book World*

"[Dobie's] lyrical, harrowing memoir transcends the genre; it delivers the complex satisfactions of a well-realized novel."
—*The New York Observer*

"With fresh, lively prose and a thoughtful delivery, Dobie . . . capture[s] the eagerness and childlike trust that led her into danger, and the mental toughness and fortitude that helped her recover. . . . Eloquent and sharp, *The Only Girl in the Car* is a lyrically rendered, candid book about teenage sexuality, and one girl with enough courage to strike out on her own—and keep going." —*BookPage*

"A singular story . . . an authentic picture of the emotional fog and urgent needs that sometimes lead teenagers to self-destruct."
—*Kirkus Reviews*

"Marvelously evocative." —O *Magazine*

"A lyrical writer who . . . uses delay and flashback as skillfully as Hitchcock." —*The Nashville Scene*

"This is a cautionary tale, a dizzying mixture of sunshine and shadows, lyrical and tough-minded. Her memoir explains the sexual education of Kathy D. in a way that earns the utmost respect, the very thing she lost that night in that car full of boys." —*The Hartford Courant*

THE
ONLY GIRL
IN THE CAR

A Memoir

Kathy Dobie

Delta Trade Paperbacks

THE ONLY GIRL IN THE CAR
A Delta Book

PUBLISHING HISTORY
Dial Press hardcover edition published March 2003
Delta trade paperback edition / March 2004

Published by Bantam Dell
A division of Random House, Inc.
New York, New York

All rights reserved.
Copyright © 2003 by Kathy Dobie

Book design by Virginia Norey

Library of Congress Catalog Card Number: 2002029928

No part of this book may be reproduced or transmitted in
any form or by any means, electronic or mechanical,
including photocopying, recording, or by any information
storage and retrieval system, without the written permission
of the publisher, except where permitted by law.

Delta is a registered trademark of Random House, Inc.,
and the colophon is a trademark of Random House, Inc.

ISBN 0-385-31883-9

Manufactured in the United States of America
Published simultaneously in Canada

BVG   10 9 8 7 6 5 4 3 2 1

To James, who from the moment he heard this story
said that one day I must write it down

All the names have been changed,
except for Roscoe, Craig, Linda, Leslie, Mrs. Colasanto,
Chris, and the members of the DeAngelis family and my own.

THE
ONLY GIRL
IN THE CAR

Prologue

IN THE SPRING OF MY FOURTEENTH YEAR, THE EARTH BLOSSOMED with men and boys, staggered under the weight and richness of their profusion. They were everywhere. Driving cranes alongside the highway, bagging groceries in the supermarket, mowing lawns, filling up our station wagon with gas, taking my father's money, giving him directions. They wore bandannas and their chests shone with sweat; they wore suits and their thighs were thick under the soft, hot cloth.

In the supermarket, my eye found the restless son; at the picnic grounds, the sullen brother hanging back, slouching in all that sunshine. From the backseat of my father's car, I scanned I-95. Under the signs that said "New York" and "New Haven," an endless river of men in trucks and cars. Men at the wheel. A man with his face in shadow, revealing only an arm and a slice of downy T-shirt. The arm was tanned with a strand of leather tied around the wrist. The hand beat out a tune on the van door. The cigarette was thrown sharp and hard, like a spear, down into the speeding pavement. Sparks flew. Every boy was an orphan; every man, unfulfilled.

One Saturday that following September, I put on my candy-striped halter top, bell-bottom jeans, and platform shoes, went out the front door of my parents' house, and sat myself down in the middle of the green, green lawn. I'd made a decision. I was going to lose my virginity.

Our front lawn faced the intersection of Treadwell and Clifford. There was a traffic light by then and enough cars to make things interesting. The grass looked silky, but it was sharp and sticky against my skin. Our dog was at my side, clumsy, faithful Sebastian, named after the butler in the TV show *Family Affair*. He was a miniature Shetland sheepdog with a round, friendly-looking rump and an orange and white coat, like a Creamsicle. His feathery tail swished back and forth across the grass. I stroked and knotted his fur, and waited.

Cars sped by, honking. Boys hissed, whistled, blew kisses, yelled. If they had to wait at a red light, they grew shy, though one boy wagged his tongue at me like a pendulum and then ran it, slowly, up the window.

It was a full-grown man who finally stopped. He did a U-turn, parked in front of the house, and got out. He made his way over to me, long hair swinging. He had a pockmarked face and eyes that pretended friendliness.

Brian was thirty-three. I remember that, because it impressed me that he was the same age as Jesus was when he died on the cross. It seemed right that there should be something so significant about him. It didn't matter that I wasn't attracted to him. He was what other girls would call "sleazy," a loser. He still lived with his mother; he had bad skin; he was picking up fourteen-year-olds. But to see that man's form, tight-jeaned, T-shirted, gliding through the grass, intent on me, and already mine in ways I didn't yet fully understand . . .

He smiled cagily, nodded at the house. "You live here?" And then, "Are your parents home?" He crouched down in the grass and picked at a blade. "Uh . . . so you're just hanging out with your dog?" He circled me with questions, patronizing, nervous as a thief. A jewel out in the open—was there really no one looking? No cop behind a tree, no string attached?

"So, uh, what's your dog's name?"

Slowly, carefully, he reeled me in—or so he thought. He was so sure that was the way it went, he'd missed the obvious: A minute ago he'd been sailing down Treadwell Street, as free as you please, and yet here he was, flung up on the lawn. I hadn't moved an inch.

"So . . . you want to go to the movies sometime?"

"Okay."

"Oh. Uh, good. When?"

That night, he picked me up at my parents' house.

I like to think of myself as having sprung fully formed from that green lawn, coming into the world at fourteen wearing a halter top and platform shoes, like a boy I once saw wearing a python at an outdoor fair, an everyday boy who volunteered from the audience when the man with the python asked if anyone wanted to come up and hold it. The boy jumped right up onto the stage before anyone else had even raised their hand. The snake was thicker than the boy's torso and easily twice his length, but as the man draped it carefully over him, the boy just grinned and widened his stance to take the weight, as if he had always known what to do if a python were set on his shoulders.

Immediately the snake began to wind itself around the boy's body, creeping under his arm and around his waist. When it slipped, the boy hitched it back up over his hip, and then helped it stay there by curling his arm under it. His chin was lifted high, his brown eyes blazing with glory and pride. Not once did he scan the crowd, as children will, looking for someone's approval, an echo to his joy. He seemed motherless, fatherless, a boy out of Mark Twain, a boy who joins circuses or travels west with a pistol and a dog; a boy born to wear a python. That's how I felt at fourteen.

1

A House for Children

LET ME SHOW YOU THE HOUSE OF MY CHILDHOOD. A GRAY HOUSE, oyster gray with white trim, sitting on the intersection of Treadwell and Clifford streets in Hamden, Connecticut, neither grand nor mean, just a solid-looking house with a small backyard, a one-car garage with an orange basketball hoop set above the doors, and tiger lilies languid along the driveway. In the backyard, there's a red-and-green jungle gym and swing set that my parents bought at Sears and my father put together himself, kneeling down in the grass in his shirtsleeves, the instructions spread out in front of him, holding a metal rod in each hand, sweat pouring down his face.

The front yard is moon-shaped and open to the street, giving it a wild and friendly feeling like you might get running down a hill or holding your arms out to someone else running down. On the right side of the house, there's a sunporch with a red-and-green striped awning, which faces Clifford, a fence and a privet hedge. Between the fence and the hedge, a dirt path has been worn through by my brothers, sisters, and me, a shortcut, a children's way to go from front yard to back. The adults must go up the driveway that runs along the other side of the house. There, our blue station wagon is parked under the basketball net.

A white picket fence runs between our house and the house of the family next door, the Wrights, who have a girl named Terry who is my age—eight on the day I'm picturing—and a tomboy. Terry takes trumpet lessons and so does my older brother Bill, and sometimes they take their trumpets and play out of the attic windows to each other, leaning out over the driveway below.

Terry also takes dance classes with me at Miss Marie's Dance Studio on Whitney Avenue. I like ballet, she hates it. Only tap is rough and noisy enough for her. Tap, tap, tap, jump and bang away on the wood floor. Once in ballet class, we had our legs up on the bar and Terry fell over backward. She stayed in the same pose, flat on her back but with one leg up and her toes pointed prettily in the air, did it because she thought it was funny to see Miss Marie and Miss Vera—who didn't give a damn about her—fuss and fuss because they thought she might be hurt, a hopeless dancer but still a tuition-paying daughter of somebody. When I want to play with Terry, I don't ring the doorbell, I stand at the back fence and yell, "Ohhhhh, Terr-eeeeee!" And sometimes to make her laugh I say, "When you're wright, you're wright."

Here's the attic of our house with its slanted, wood-paneled ceilings and the windows tucked under them. There are two bedrooms up here, my sister Cindy's and mine, and our older brothers' room, Michael and Bill's.

In my brothers' room, two of the three windows look out over the intersection of Treadwell and Clifford. It's not much of a view, I suppose, gray and white houses going up along the block, smallish yards, telephone wires looping above the trees like a pencil sketching, a solitary traffic light bobbing above the intersection like a boat on a breeze; but to a child of the suburbs, the view from an attic window is like the view from a castle or a hilltop. Only three floors up but you're as high as almost any high suburban thing, up there with the treetops, the gray roofs and chimneys, the crows, the sparrows, the rain when it's coming down fast before it hits anything.

Michael and Bill have a nubby red carpet in their room, red-and-tan bedspreads, and twin beds that are always made up—we can't go downstairs in the morning without first making our beds. Their desks are already boys' desks, the ink blotters covered with graffiti, the shelves above lined with basketball trophies and not much more, none of the pretty little knickknacks that my sister Cindy and I have collected. Michael's the oldest in the family, a redhead like me, wiry and energetic, and that's his bed by the two windows overlooking the intersection, and his desk next to the third window in the room, the one that looks down onto the backyard with its swing set and jungle gym. Michael's ten and already confident of his place in the world. Or so it seems to me.

After we come home from church on Sunday, Michael makes the rest of us kids play Mass in the dining room—he is the priest and we are the parishioners, standing and kneeling and standing and sitting and kneeling all over again. We call him Captain Catfish because he's the firstborn and because we have a catfish in the tank downstairs that is the same coloring as Michael, an orangy red, like a flame.

Michael gets the window views but Bill, one year younger, blond and blue-eyed, the family wit, if you can be a wit at nine, gets the bigger desk and dresser. My parents try hard to keep things balanced between us.

"I love all of my children equally!" my mother says, so fervently and so often that I feel it should be inscribed in the house somewhere, above the kitchen doorway perhaps.

Here's the bedroom I share with my sister Cindy, who's one year younger than I—our twin beds with their white blankets, our blue-painted desks, hers covered with statues and pictures of owls and mine with bells and dolls. We have only two little windows, and they look out over the driveway and into the attic of Terry Wright's house, so close it seems like the houses might be secretly talking to each other.

A real live hamster lives in a cage on the shelf above Cindy's desk. His name is Mr. H., and when he's not hurrying and snuffling along the sawdust on the cage floor, he's running on the wheel, running and running and running, his long claws clicking on the wheel and the wheel making a rattling, whirring sound. Between his running and the fact that he ate his mate after she ate all her babies, Cindy and I don't like him much, but what can we do? We have to live with this murderer, this monster, feed him pellets and water in the morning, clean his cage on Saturdays, and watch him exercise all day.

The four of us older kids are only one year apart from each other—ten, nine, eight, and seven. We make up a little tribe of our own, a merry band, the Four Musketeers, and the attic is our domain and hideaway.

Up until this year, we all slept together in the boys' bedroom, but then my father and my great-uncle Lance built another room and we were divided, the boys and the girls, a division I think of as not unlike one of God's acts of creation in Genesis, which seem to me to be about making distinctions, separating the day from the night, the land from the sea, sending birds up, fish down.

We're very close, the four of us, and we manage that without really knowing one another. We don't talk about our feelings. We don't know the exact shape of each other's fears and joys, but we know the scent of each other when we sleep, the sharp, sweet smell and rushing sound of one of us peeing in the toilet bowl in the morning, the feel of Michael's stiff curly hair, springy on the palm of my hand, the shape of the whitish scar on Billy's knee where a long sliver of wood pierced it when he went sliding across a wooden floor one day, the sound of Cindy's dreams at night, the murmurs and quickened breath and sudden shouts of "Help! He's getting away! The frog's on the bridge!"

Our closeness is mute and sensual. We're like a pack of wild animals, eating, drinking, running, always running together until we rest together, running up and down the stairs, through all the rooms of the house, out the back door and over the green, green lawn like lions or birds or floods.

In the weeks after our parents separated us, the girls in one room, the boys in the other, we slept with our doors open, not wanting to shut one another out. Michael and Bill sang Cindy and me to sleep at night, or tried to. Mostly they sang church songs, rousing and mournful and not in any particular order, so their dirgelike rendition of

"Swing Low, Sweet Chariot" might be followed with their shouting out, "When the Saints Go Marching In." Cindy and I were so appreciative, and so worried that they wouldn't know how appreciative, that we felt obliged to applaud after each song and call out, "Encore! Encore!" It became what you call a vicious cycle—we couldn't sleep and they couldn't stop singing, and so after a while they gave it up. One night, the bedroom doors seemed to close of their own accord.

Down the stairs we go, to the second floor, where my parents sleep, and little Beth, and where the baby will sleep, too, when he arrives. Beth Ann has a tribe of stuffed animals in her bedroom. She needs a tribe of them, I think, for she is a few years apart from the rest of us and so just a little outside of our merry band. I don't know if she's lonely. I know she's solitary, telling her secrets to her animals and her Mrs. Beasley doll. It makes me feel odd that she has an old lady for a doll, a blue-and-white polka-dotted lady, but old nonetheless with an apron and granny spectacles. Who is taking care of who here?

She's four and she will become Mommy's helper once I stop—the oldest girl and then the youngest, each stepping up in her own time to pound the cutlets, peel the carrots, measure the flour, run down to the basement and put the laundry in the dryer.

Beth Ann's real name is Elizabeth Ann. Our parents named her after the newest saint to be canonized, Elizabeth Ann Seton, but from the start they simply called her Beth Ann.

Beth Ann has long blond hair, which my mother or I brush back into a ponytail. The tail makes a corkscrew and bounces up and down just like a spring when she walks. She has tiny features, pink cheeks, blue eyes. This fifth child was born with arthritis in one leg, and before she even turned two, they made her wear a cast and then a brace for a year. So Beth Ann didn't stand and then walk the way other toddlers do. She got as far as standing, and then they put her in a brace and she had to go back down on the ground, pulling herself along with her arms. My father called her a "trouper." When she looked up at me from the floor, all wide blue eyes and pink cheeks, her little lips in a Cupid sort of bow, she looked like a cheerful storybook caterpillar.

Stephen isn't born yet. He's in my mother's belly. It's fall and he won't arrive until the middle of winter.

Let's take a morning, any morning, a school morning in the fall of that year. The second-floor hallway smells of Irish Spring soap and shaving cream. The bathroom door is open and the steam from my father's shower is still tunneling out and filling the cold autumn hallway with moist heat and prickly scent, like the tracks a big animal might leave, for my father has just finished his shower and left to begin dressing. From my parents' bedroom, I can hear bureau drawers being pulled out and slammed shut, their brass pulls clanking with each motion, closet doors opening and closing, the sharp, swift sounds of my father getting ready to go to work, his feet, in shoes now, tapping briskly across the wood floor, a readiness and an energy that puts my sleepiness to shame and thrusts me down the stairs—late, late, I can't be late! I'm always late, it seems, always one step behind where I'm supposed to be.

The hallway stairs lead into the living room, and both are covered in a blue and green shag carpet, an ocean of a carpet, all waving tendrils, lovely on the feet and the source of many games for us children, games I'm beginning to grow out of, like "shark," in which we must hop from one piece of the furniture to the other, never letting our feet touch the sharky sea of the carpet, lest we be eaten alive.

In the kitchen, the light is fluorescent bright on the white linoleum floor and the gray Formica table, and my brothers and sisters are already seated and bent into their cereal bowls, tucked in behind boxes of Cheerios and Kix and Lucky Charms, Michael and Bill and Cindy reading the backs of theirs while they eat, Beth Ann pretending to.

"Hi, honey," my mother says. "Did you have a good sleep?"

She is in her lacy pink nightgown, her green furry robe, her satiny slippers and white athletic socks, and still she shivers. The end of her nose is pink. She has hazel eyes, and her short hair, a brownish blond, is tousled. Her face is young, though varicose veins wind themselves around her slender legs, pushing out knots here and there as if a beautiful blue vine were putting out hard buds.

My mother spends her days in the kingdom of children. There, she is our queen, and also our most lowly servant. She was only nineteen when she married my father, dropping out of college against her mother's wishes, twenty when Michael was born, twenty-one when Bill came along, twenty-three and -four for me and Cindy. Her childhood was the exact opposite of ours; it's as if she was born in another country altogether. She was an only child, and fatherless, too, for her parents separated when she was two years old. Her mother had left her husband and driven halfway across the country from Oklahoma to Connecticut, where her sister Bert was living, and my mother never saw her father again. When she was a girl, she prayed to God for a brother or a sister just so she would have some company. Now, with five of us and another one snuggled inside, she's never alone, but she's shy around other adults, and when we are out among strangers I feel that we, her children, serve to cloak and protect her.

She's allergic to something in the morning air, and while she fixes our lunches and tells us to take our elbows off the table or get our pajama sleeves out of the milk, she furiously rubs the end of her nose and sneezes, always in groups of three, achoo achoo achoo. From behind his cereal box, my brother Bill says, "God bless, God bless, God bless you." And no matter how many times he has said that, and this must be the seven hundredth, my siblings and I marvel at his wit.

We're a grim lot most weekday mornings, though; silent, bleary-eyed, hanging over our cereal bowls like dogs, milk dripping from our mouths. We grip our spoons in our fists like laborers with shovels, digging our way into the day ahead.

For long moments there's no talk, just the sound of the sugar bowl skating back and forth between us like a busy waiter. Michael's knee keeps up a steady beat against the underside of the table. He never stops moving; he's not even aware of it. The table shakes slightly, continuously, jiggling the milk in my bowl until my mother pulls him into consciousness, saying only, "Michael!" For a minute, the table is still and I can hear all their spoons clicking like clocks.

The refrigerator door opening and closing, Michael's knee moving faster and faster, the slurping of milk and ticking of spoons, the faces of my brothers and sisters growing more animated, sharper and brighter as the day outside the window takes its shape—these are the conveyor belts pulling me toward yet another school day.

Is there any way I can stop it? Slow the morning down enough to jump off and stay here at home with *her*? A stomachache, a sore throat, something that I can use like a brake on the hour that is moving me swiftly and surely away from her?

And then in the middle of my anxious deliberations, my father comes shooting into the kitchen in his sharp dark suit, his high forehead lit like a lantern, jaw freshly shaved, calling for his glasses, every day the same question: "Kay! Did you see my glasses?"

In his breast pocket is a monogrammed white handkerchief that Cindy or I would have ironed. He bears the spicy, cold scent of cologne but he's warm, his lips are a schoolboy red, slightly wet when he leans over and kisses me on the top of my forehead. Auburn hair, blue eyes, freckles. He kisses my mother on the mouth and calls out to us, "You guys have a good day at school!" and sails out the back door with a smoking mug of coffee in one hand, an attaché case in the other. The station wagon gives a kick, and then we watch the plume of exhaust smoke sail by the kitchen window, backward down the drive.

It's only a fifteen-minute drive to New Haven and his job at Yale, where he runs the dining halls and food service; he'll get there in ten. He likes to drive fast.

How does he do it? Leave us every day so easily, so, you have to say, triumphantly. It is unimaginable to me that I will ever feel the way he does, so cold, so sure, so hot, so ready.

His leaving is a signal to us kids—now or never. If one of us is going to fake being sick and try to stay home, this is the time to tell my mother about the sore throat or upset stomach. If not, it's time to run upstairs and shower and dress.

I push my cereal bowl away and hold my stomach, but like a waitress who has been given too many tables to serve, my mother cleverly avoids making eye contact. She begins to pack up the cereal boxes, says to the air, "Kids, you're going to be late."

In our attic bedroom, Cindy and I pull on our St. Rita's school uniforms—white blouses and red-and-green plaid jumpers, green knee socks, red ties, and fat, rubber-soled shoes that look like closemouthed bugs when you lace them up.

Cindy's blond hair is cut short, pixie-style, and because of her widow's peak she has half a bang hanging out over her forehead like the brim of a rakishly set hat. Cindy's a tomboy. Almost every girl I know at this point of my life is, though I am not.

My parents and teachers say that I'm a dreamer, a girl with her head in the clouds. "Earth to Kathy! Come in, please!" my father often calls out to me, because I'm a girl who loses hats and mittens and forgets to turn off lights and gets so lost in her imagination that once she even forgot she had the bathwater running until it overflowed. "You'd forget your head altogether if it wasn't attached to your body by its neck," he'll say to me, joking in that fierce way he has sometimes, his blue eyes lit and boring into me. Even my brothers join in the fun. They call me the Absentminded Professor, making me sorry that we went to see that movie, though I liked it when we did.

On the shelf above Cindy's desk, Mr. H. begins his morning run on the wheel, around and around, the whole cage rattling. Cindy and I move in a rush that is by turns nervous and eager, but even with the clock ticking and the hamster racing, we stop for a moment to play a private game of ours, not a game so much as the setting up of a tableau. We call it the Mad Family Band and arrange ourselves side by side in front of the bedroom door, scowling and strumming air guitars and tapping our feet angrily. We twist our heads from side to side, Cindy's bangs flying out each time, and we hum a dark music louder and louder, as we imagine The Family waiting for us downstairs, mad as hell because we're late. "Late, late! For a very important date!" we shriek, and tumble out the door.

Perhaps every child born to a big family feels the same—that the family itself has a personality. To me, The Family was an entity, a being with needs and desires, an appetite all its own. Often those needs and desires were quite different from mine. The Family had to have clean rooms, for instance, and order at the dinner table. It needed our children's prayers at night and our cooperation all day. It had a great appetite for activity, for cheerfulness and busyness, and it would never let me sleep late in the morning or disappear into an afternoon nap. The Family got up early and went off to school and work; it had dinner at six sharp. It did its chores on Saturday, and on Sunday after church it went into action when the call went out—"Saddle up! Grab your towels and sunglasses! We're off to the lake! Last one in the car is a rotten egg!"

"Your family's like the Army!" my best friend in high school, Sylvia, would exclaim. She was impressed by the order, the prescribed chores, the routines that seemed to be written in stone, but she missed the act of devotion involved. For whenever I picked up a dust cloth, or Cindy and I trundled the vacuum cleaner upstairs, singing, "Whistle while you work," I knew I was in service to something much bigger than myself.

And when I would hear someone say our name aloud back then, or even see it printed on an envelope, *The Dobie Family*, a strange and fevered jumble of things would come to my mind—the red and green jungle gym in the backyard and my mother's tiger lilies; my grandfather's gray hat and his nickname for me, Old Bricktop; the mean old man neighbor with his rake; the red stop sign on our corner; the squeaking birds in the trees; the bloodworms in the ground and my brothers dragging them out. In short, everything. It seemed we had only to look at a thing and it became a part of us, a part of who we were. My family astonished me.

2

Chain of Desire

THEY CAME IN THROUGH THE FRONT DOOR TOGETHER, ALL THREE OF them, on a sunny winter's day, my father's large face beaming over my mother's shoulder, my mother returned to us from the hospital, not only alive but wearing a glamorous cherry-colored car coat with bright lipstick to match, and expertly, tenderly cradling a brand-new baby in a blue blanket, the tiniest human being I'd ever seen. A gust of snow swirled up from the steps, showering my mother's stockinged ankles and glittering in the brief seconds before the door was closed. My brothers and sisters were up on their toes trying to get a better look.

"You can all take turns holding him," my mother told us, a smile in her voice. I waited for mine and then I sat down in the living room rocking chair, my brothers and sisters crowded around, as she carefully handed our new little brother to me. I looked down at his sleeping face—his eyelids were purplish and paper-thin, his nose barely more than nostrils, his lips, poked into the air, smaller than a creamer spout. He squirmed once, scrunched his face into a red ball—was he going to cry? what should I do?—and then his face relaxed and he fell back into sleep, his breath not even a whisper. I leaned down and sniffed the top of his head; he smelled like milk and sugar. His hair was so fine and soft it looked like a puff of wind might blow it away, but his fingers were long and skinny and red, a monkey's wrinkled fingers. . . .

"Look at his fingernails!" I cried, and my brothers and sisters leaned in close while my parents smiled.

"You were all that small once," my mother said. Impossible.

When the Baby Stephen was born, the *Hamden Chronicle* reported, "The Dobie household is bursting at the seams with the arrival of . . ." Grandma Dobie, my father's mother, had called the item in. I was nine and I thought I detected a sneer at our fecundity.

I commemorated his birth with a poem, my first: "Now that we have Stephen / The boys and girls are even." When I recited it to my brothers and sisters, Billy looked halfway astonished and then he rubbed my hair, saying roughly, "You're a poet and don't even know it." He was only ten, but the look on his face was that of a proud father.

I was so delighted with that poem, and the fact that my brothers and sisters went around the house loudly repeating it, that I sat down and wrote a letter to God, promising Him I would be a writer when I grew up. I signed it *Your Most Loving and Adoring Servant* and then hid it in the bottom drawer of my dresser with the seashells and plastic saints. This was my secret chapel, a rendezvous point for me and God. At night, I prayed with my head bowed into my chapel drawer.

You would have thought that when the new baby was born I'd feel crowded and pushed aside. Instead, I fell in love.

The day he arrived we would all compete to hold him, but in the weeks and months to come, as his novelty wore off for the others, my own enthusiasm for the Baby Stephen never lessened. Every afternoon, I would rush home from school to be with him and he would crow like a rooster when I came in the door. Sometimes Stephen sucked my thumb instead of his own; sometimes, when I held him on my hip, he hid his soft face inside my hair. *I will be your nest*, I thought. *I'll be your hideaway.* He made me regret every bony part of my little girl's body.

What a relief it was to love physically and with abandon. To touch someone I cared for. To sing him to sleep while rubbing his back and patting his diapered behind. To feel his arms wrapped tightly around my neck and his low giggle in my ear. Extravagant feelings need to be expressed physically, but I hadn't found a way to love like that until Stephen. Just to hold him was a revelation.

"There is no love without exaggeration," Oscar Wilde wrote. I loved my youngest brother without any carefulness. I loved him the way I was taught to love God—with all my heart and soul. And I loved him with my body, too.

I would have liked to pet my mother's face, I think, as I've watched my sister Cindy's children touch and pet and trace hers. But we didn't have that kind of physical intimacy. I never "owned" my mother the way I've seen Cindy's little girls own her, examining her teeth and pulling at her nose like curious monkeys, burrowing their heads into her belly, climbing her legs as if they were a steep hill, the youngest one making Cindy's hand into her "baby," cradling it and singing to it. My sister bathes with her daughters, something we never would've done with our mother. Once when I was a child, I walked into my parents' bedroom when my mother was changing and she turned away abruptly, blushing, covering her bare breasts with her arms. "Kathy, you're supposed to knock!" she said in a voice both angry and embarrassed, and I felt confused; it was as if someone had thrown a veil over my eyes, for the room went dark and hazy; her breasts, in that one glimpse, had looked blue.

Sometimes it seemed that the women in my family wore signs that read, "Approach with Caution. Handle with Care." There was something electric and bristling inside each one, and I didn't know when I would set it off. I had to be careful with my mother. That's the way I felt as a child. My love for her felt too aggressive, too bold and clumsy, like a big enthusiastic dog chasing a butterfly. She was delicate, tricky; a puzzle to me. Sometimes she disappeared inside of herself, into a place I didn't know, but thinking she was sad or lonely, I stuck close by her.

At those moments my presence, what I thought of as my affection but was actually my need, was an intrusion—I could feel her tense up, though I didn't know why. It never occurred to me that she needed a break from us children.

And so I became cautious, clever, even devious in my loving of her. Early in the morning, I would take the valentines I'd made for her and hide them in the laundry basket, the frying pan, the broom closet, for her to find after I'd left for school. My love, a kind of haunting. I thought of myself as a giving child, not a hungry one. My mother and I were very much alike. I don't think she liked to see that part of herself in me.

Once, when I was around seven or eight, I remember waking from a nap at the home of my great-aunt Bert and walking down the hall from her bedroom to the kitchen, drawn by the sound of women's voices. I paused in the doorway. There she was, my mother, up on a footstool wearing a sleeveless black-and-white polka-dotted dress my grandmother had bought for her, turning slowly, like a ballerina in a music box, while Bert, who was a professional seamstress, knelt in front of her, sticking pins into the hem. Bert tapped and my mother turned. A pin went in. A tap. A turn.

"What do you think, Elsie?" Bert asked her sister, my grandma Callahan, who lived upstairs in the duplex they'd recently bought together. "A half-inch shorter?"

And Grandma warned, "You don't want it too short or it won't hang right!" Tap, turn. This is how they loved my mother, these two women who together had raised this fatherless child—not with embraces, words, a rush of affection, but with clothes shopping, tapping and turning, making sure she looked just right.

"Hi, honey! Did you sleep?" Mommy asked when she noticed me standing at the door. (The girl on the footstool, the daughter in the new spring dress holding her breath to make her stomach flat, was also my mother; the combined effect was mesmerizing.)

I thought I knew exactly what my mother was feeling up there on the kitchen stool, Grandma watching her as she smoked her Pall Malls, Bert's fingers tapping at her calf and then stroking my mother's thighs as she smoothed down the dress—*What do you think, Elsie?*

How mute and still my mother was as she soaked up their attention, taking in their love secretly, slyly, almost like a thief who was stealing it. She didn't want to ruin the moment.

From a young age, I had learned the unpredictable and sensual joys of passivity. When my mother combed my hair, I sat very still, my scalp rippling with pleasure, warmth moving down my body. The sensation reached a peak when my mother combed my hair absentmindedly, perhaps while answering one of my sisters' questions about her homework or explaining a Cub Scout merit badge to Michael or Bill.

When I was touched without really being noticed, I swooned with pleasure. Sixteen-year-old boys were my destiny.

But in the meantime, I had only these women, my mother's preoccupied attention to my hair or unbuttoned coat, the inadvertent touch of Bert and Grandma fixing my collar, yanking down the hem of my skirt, the secret thrill of being treated like an object, tugged and yanked at and talked about as if I weren't there. "It fits her well around the hips," Bert would say to Grandma as they eyed me in one of the outfits they had bought for me. "What about the shoulders?" Grandma would ask. "It seems a little tight across there." And then they would tell me to lift my arms while they plucked at the dress.

I wouldn't have dreamed of cuddling up to them. Grandma actually squirmed if I hugged her too close or for a few seconds too long. She was not a physical woman and she knew it. Many times she told me that she didn't think she was a very good mother to mine.

"I think your mother needed someone who was more physically affectionate," she would say. And then her watery blue eyes would go bright, her flat, emphatic voice suddenly arch upward. "Do you know my mother never kissed me, Kathy? Not a once!"

She wasn't feeling sorry for herself, not Elsie Callahan. She was an adult in the gratifying grip of a revelation.

"So you could say I *just didn't have the practice*!" she said, rapping the words out in her excitement. "I just didn't know how to be that way with your mother! I never had the knack."

I never got to really touch my grandmother until many years later when she was in her eighties and very sick. Then, one day in the hospital, I massaged her feet and hands with cream and carefully combed her baby-soft hair. She closed her eyes and sighed—never kissed by her mother!—and then, like a small child, drifted off to sleep.

I think when I was a child I felt ashamed of my extravagant feelings and ashamed of my physical nature—can a body have inclinations?—my desire not for sports or climbing trees or wrestling about on the carpet with my brothers and sisters but for acts of devotion and tenderness. Even now, when I love a man, I want to wash his feet.

After we buried my grandmother, the mourners came over to my parents' house for food. There was the usual air of unreality, the half-light, the full plates, the conversation drifting on to other things . . . a family unmoored. By nine o'clock everyone had left but my sisters and me. We had all moved away by then but had come back for the funeral.

My mother and I were alone, cleaning up in the kitchen, when she stopped, a dish towel in her hand, her back against the refrigerator, and asked, "Did she love me?"

She started to cry, her face screwed up, and tears smearing her mascara. All the while she was appealing to me with her eyes. She looked like someone had nailed her to the refrigerator door.

"I feel like I never measured up," she sobbed. Grandma had wanted her to be a college-educated career woman; Grandma had wanted her to lose weight. "I feel like I always disappointed her."

There she was again, the thin-skinned, beseeching little girl my mother could never shake. She was as visible to me when I was a child as the woman who taught me how to read and tucked me into bed each night.

When I was very young, I thought I could make my mother strong and secure. I wanted her happiness, of course, but being a child what I wanted most of all was her loving approval, just as she wanted her mother's. We seemed to make up a chain of desire, my mother, grandmother, and I, tied to one another quite hopelessly.

I didn't strive for freedom as a small child—that only came later. While other children were testing their independence, I was binding myself more tightly to my mother, as if I didn't trust her hold on me. "Kathy," she said to me once in a moment of exasperation at my clinginess, "you're too tied to my apron strings!" I was, and no less tightly for having tied the knots myself.

3

A Girl So Good

I WOULD BE KIND; I WOULD BE GOOD. WHEN MY MOTHER TOLD ME TO walk to school with the fat girl in my class, I jumped at the assignment. And I wouldn't step on a single line or crack in the sidewalk on the way. I wouldn't even *think* the words of that horrible rhyme. I would help old ladies cross the street and smile at the mentally retarded boy if I ever saw him again. (*Oh please, God, let me see him again!*) I would befriend all the lonely children, find the strays, feed the hungry, clothe the naked if the hungry and the naked ever crossed my path—they were hard to come by in Hamden.

No doubt these lessons about kindness and goodness were important to my mother, but she could hardly have imagined how feverishly I took them in. I wanted to be special, but that was a sin. You might call that my Original Dilemma, the first really difficult problem I had to solve for myself, for I was the oldest girl in a Catholic family and I was supposed to be generous and self-effacing—to give and give way, step aside and let the younger ones go first. But I could hardly just step aside and let my brothers and sisters take center stage. In a family of six small children, all clamoring for our mother's attention, I would have risked disappearing altogether.

Well, I thought I had found a solution to my dilemma. I would become special through selflessness, but a complete and astonishing selflessness. In short, I would become a saint.

There was no Saint Kathleen. I had found that out when I went looking through a book of saints to pick my confirmation name. I was disappointed at first, surprised, even shocked, that my parents, my churchgoing Catholic parents, hadn't thought to name me after a saint. But in the middle of my disappointment, I suddenly had a glimpse of God. He didn't say anything—I could hardly let Him open His mouth, His coming to me was already far too grand. He merely looked sideways at me, all-knowing and even a bit bug-eyed, like he was trying to point out something to me with his eyeballs alone. Didn't I see? No Saint Kathleen; a blank space where a saint could be.

Eagerly, I began throwing myself into the middle of my brothers' and sisters' fights, holding my arms out in a gesture of peace. "The little martyr," Bill sneered, but instead of feeling crushed I swelled with pride.

They gave me a nickname. "Peacemaker, peacemaker," they chanted. I wore a sorrowful look on my face. I was tied to the stake, in the middle of the screaming mob, craning my neck, looking to see if *she* was watching.

I vacuumed excessively, I dusted the venetian blinds, I sang religious songs as I worked: "Holy, holy, holy, Lord God Almighty!" I let Cindy and Beth Ann go first and second and third. "Forget me, I'm okay, you go ahead!" I called out softly while Cindy snorted and rolled her eyes. My devotion—and ambition—knew no bounds. It was all very Catholic. I was racing fast to be last, meekly trying to inherit the earth.

When Advent arrived that year, it was as if someone had taken a whip to an already galloping horse, for this was a holy season and I was a saint-in-the-making. Every afternoon I could be found kneeling and praying in front of the Nativity scene we had set up on an end table in the dining room. My brothers and sisters and I had covered the table with fake snow, placed the stable on top of that snowy field, and then, lovingly, arranged the figures of Mary and Joseph, the shepherds and the farm animals, around the empty manger where the baby Jesus would lie on Christmas morning. It was like a dollhouse, only much more beautiful and serious, for the figures were painted in the rich and faded colors you find in museums.

My mother told us that for every good deed we performed, we could put a straw in the manger—the better we were, the softer the baby's bed would be when He arrived.

These were private good deeds. We weren't supposed to tell our mother or brag about them. The only one who would know was God and, I supposed, any angels who happened to be watching. But one day I felt I'd been spectacularly good—a very busy, ten-straw kind of day!—and I waited until early evening to put my straws in the manger. By then, my mother was at the stove cooking dinner, and from there she had a perfect view of me through the kitchen doors. I knelt down in front of the stable, made the sign of the cross, bowed my head and prayed as if I were at the altar in St. Rita's church. Then I put my straws on the little wooden manger one at a time, a straw for smiling at an old lady I'd seen on the way home from school, another one for doing a load of laundry, a third for forgiving Beth Ann when she broke the leg off my Barbie doll. . . . Between each straw, I peeked up at my mother as she worked, hoping she would note how long I was kneeling at the stable.

In my mind's eye, I could see her turning to my father at the end of the day, when we were all in bed, and telling him how incredibly selfless I was. He would shake his head in admiration. "Our daughter sure is something," he would say.

It was in my search for goodness, guiltlessness, my mother's approval—and a desire to impress God, too—that I arrived home one afternoon without my blue coat.

I'd walked the mile and a half from St. Rita's alone, because Cindy was out sick that day and Michael and Bill had gone ahead, racing or

fighting each other as they often did. There was snow on the ground
and patches of ice that we used as mini–skating rinks most days, zip-
ping across them on our rubber-soled shoes, twirling on one foot like
fancy skaters.

A soft silence came off the lakes, frozen solid almost clear across,
reflecting nothing but a watery, wintery light. I imagined the cold
water on the bottoms of floating birds, the cold ice on their webbed
feet, and shivered for them, though there were no birds in sight.

When I walked into the brightly lit kitchen, I was wearing only my
plaid jumper, a sweater, knee socks, and shoes. My knuckles, nose, and
knees were a scarlet red.

"Kathy, where is your coat?" my mother exclaimed.

I looked down at my body, shocked into silence, not because my
coat was missing but because of her alarm. "I don't know," I said.

"You don't know? What do you mean? What did you do with it?"

No matter what she asked—did I leave school with it on, did I
stop anywhere on the way home?—I couldn't bring myself to tell her.
I knew I'd gone too far this time. The nuns were called, the classroom
and coatroom searched, the janitor even looked in the school yard,
but it was never found. Losing that coat cemented my reputation as a
dreamer, as the girl who would forget her head if it weren't attached
to her body.

It was a brand-new blue coat, I remember it still, with large, glassy
buttons. Grandma Callahan had given it to me that Christmas.
Halfway home from school, at the abandoned parking lot next to the
Servoss Street woods, I'd taken it off and laid it on a rock for some
poor, coatless child. I felt like I was opening up a conversation with
God, He who saw all things. What would be His reply?

I had visions of birds swooping down from the sky in a bolt of light
to carry away my coat in their beaks and drop it at the feet of a shivering street urchin. What joy then! I felt like the giver *and* the receiver, so vividly did I imagine the scene.

And wouldn't I arrive home as both? Giver of coats and coatless?
Generous and pathetic? I'd been so taken by the beauty of my plan,

the perfection of metaphor, that I hadn't exactly thought out what I'd say to my mother.

But when I stepped into the bright kitchen and her shocked question, I froze. It seemed like the worst idea I'd ever had, and impossible now to explain. I looked down at my coatless body, dumbfounded by my own self.

4

A Boy So Bad

ST. RITA'S GRAMMAR SCHOOL, WHERE ALL THE DOBIE CHILDREN WERE sent, each in his or her own turn, stood on top of a hill, a steep green hill rising up from Whitney Avenue toward heaven. A silver cross hung on the pinkish-red bricks, calling all Catholic boys and girls inside.

It took me three years to get used to going to that school. I couldn't understand the scratchy uniforms we all had to wear, the way my knees were always cold (why were the adults letting us go bare-legged in winter?), the black-winged nuns, the desks lined up like soldiers, the closed door of the classroom, which became a cell imprisoning me with a group of strange children. Where were my brothers? Why were they kept in separate classrooms, away from me and from each other? And where, above all, was Cindy, whom I slept with every night and woke with every morning, so in tune with each other that we never had to discuss whether we were waking up as rabbits or horses, nuzzling each other with our cold rabbit noses or galloping around the bedroom unable to get out because, as everyone knows, horses can't turn door handles?

One morning during that first year at St. Rita's, I was standing alone at the end of the long corridor, looking down at the ice-cold moss-green linoleum and then up as a nun started making her way toward me from the other end. I watched as her black dress sailed out wider and wider, her white face grew larger and larger, until I could see the gold crucifix swinging and banging on her chest like a bell clapper. Now, I thought, as I waited there for her, she was going to explain it all to me, meaning would be revealed, the pieces would fall into place.

"The cheese stands alone," she said briskly, almost merrily, as she stared down at me. "Has Little Bo Peep lost her sheep?"

And that's the way it went, for three long years, strangeness heaped upon strangeness, absurdity on absurdity.

The nuns clacked their handheld clickers—they looked like giant clothespins—and called us "wild Indians" or "children of God"; they hit the big blackboards with their long wooden pointers; and they spanked the boys when they were bad. When Bill was in first grade, Sister Joseph Mary spanked him, taking him completely by surprise. Down went Billy's pants in front of the classroom. Smack went her hand on his bottom. The same nun gave me a gold star for my reading test—it twinkled on the top of the page.

When boys were bad, they were badder than girls—that's what we were being taught at St. Rita's. And boys were sturdier, they could take more punishment, though Bill, six-year-old Billy, standing there in his underwear, was crushed.

The year I entered fourth grade, I became obsessed with Frank Lee—no one called him simply Frank—a boy so bad and crazy that the rest of us kids were dull, stupefied angels next to him. Frank Lee was in my class.

Perhaps his father had given him that crew cut, so close to the head he looked bald until he was right up in front of you. He had a big head, ash-blond hair. His glasses were broken and heavily taped, but he wore them like they were something dangerous. He had tattooed his arms with Nazi crosses, cutting the skin with a razor first and, once the skin had scarred over, drawing the lines in with a blue pen. He wore steel-toed boots and a trench coat over his school uniform.

Some evenings when the four of us kids were up in the attic playing and goofing around before bedtime, I would make a show of hugging and kissing my pillow and crooning, "Frank Lee, honey, baby!"

"Ecchhhh, cut it out!"

"Shut up!"

"Kathy, you're disgusting!" I enjoyed making my brothers and sister squirm, it's true, but there was also something about Frank Lee that touched me. He was the first person I ever met who was "beyond the pale," a phrase the adults sometimes used that made me think confusedly of someone so white as to be almost ghostlike. All of the kids in St. Rita's hated Frank Lee, not just the kids in my class. He had not a single friend in the world and no clue, it seemed, as to how to go about getting one. Walking behind him after school I'd heard him sigh heavily to himself—little Nazi prince clumping home alone.

One day when Henry Brastberger was taking his seat in class, Frank Lee put a pencil under him, pointed side up. Henry was a big kid with womanly skin and a talent for science and math. Henry shrieked. The pencil had pierced the skin. He was rushed to the hospital with lead poisoning. It went straight to his spine. He almost died, they said. He was gone from school for weeks.

As for Frank Lee, he was never seen again. I couldn't get him out of my mind. Couldn't get over the fact that the first great sinner I ever met, in the flesh, not in the books, not Lucifer or Judas but someone alive and wearing glasses, was a boy my age.

I saw Frank Lee do it. I was seated next to him and watched him lean over his desk with his pencil and hold it, waiting for Henry to sit down, a look of great anticipation on his face. I knew he wasn't thinking: lead poisoning, hospital, near death. I wondered how the adults could miss this, or worse, know and not care.

I should've learned from Frank Lee that you could be too lonely and too hungry. You might try too hard to connect. You might do something horrific and then be condemned to your solitude forever.

5

Spinster

EVEN WHEN I WAS A CHILD, GREAT-AUNT EMMA, PROPER AND STIFF-backed, wearing dresses made of a material as densely woven as upholstery, seemed to have come out of a storybook. Maybe not a very pleasant book, but something shivery that children would like.

Tall as a man and regal in bearing, Emma towered over us. Her wrists and fingers were thin and elegant and looked quite brittle. She kept a handkerchief tucked into the cuff of her sweater. Her head was smallish. Her metal-rimmed glasses and her hair were the same glinting gray. She lived with Grandma and Grandpa Dobie, as unmarried sisters were supposed to do at one time. That time had come and gone, but not for proper Emma, and so not for her sister, Betty, and her brother-in-law, Albert, either.

Every other Sunday we had dinner at Grandpa and Grandma Dobie's house, only three blocks from ours. And every time we arrived you would have thought they hadn't seen us in years. "Well, look who's here!" Aunt Barbara, my father's sister, would cry out, as if our presence was a complete surprise. Blue-eyed and auburn-haired, just like my father, she had a voice that was warm and rushing and sugary. "And in all of your springtime finery!" Then she'd look at my parents with a gleam in her eyes. "Hello, Mom and Dad," she'd say, and that gleam, the suddenly wry tone of her voice, were like secret codes. Adults were infinitely subtle. With one raised eyebrow they could call up years of shared experience, and that experience seemed to have led them to believe that life, at its heart, was comic.

We always got there at four in the afternoon, and by then the house was already filled with the rich smells of pork loin and boiled potatoes, canned green beans set to boiling on the stove until they were as dark and limp as something you might pull from the sea, Mott's applesauce, taken out of its jar and served ice-cold in a china bowl with a silver spoon. Grandma Dobie bustled in from the kitchen, her cheeks as pink as if she'd painted them, announcing with pride, "My family's arrived!" Grandpa came down the stairs, jiggling the change in his pocket and whistling five notes, always the same five, the beautiful beginning of an unnamed melody. First his big black shoes materialized, then his long legs in their gray pants, then his white shirt, the buttons dropping into view—my grandfather seemed to go on forever—and finally his long-jawed, high-browed face with the kind gray-blue eyes and the sparse gray hair swept back so his head seemed even larger, more horselike. When all of him had come into view, I'd feel his hand land on the top of my head, covering it like an overlarge hat: "Hello, ole bricktop, ole carrottop!" Great-aunt Emma hovered in the background, and after everyone else had greeted us, my brothers and sisters and I steeled ourselves for her touch. Her lips were liver-colored and very thin. She had to crank herself down low to kiss us; a quick, bony peck.

When it was time for the adults to have their cocktails, Emma was always very particular about hers: "Remember, don't make it too strong now, Barbara!" she would say. Then I could hear Aunt Barbara singing out the order in the kitchen—"And a not-too-strong whiskey sour for Miss Emma!"—and I knew the adults were signaling to each other again. Barbara always brought the cocktail into the living room with a towel thrown over her arm like a waiter, making a great flourish of bowing down and serving Emma, who was perched imperiously on the couch. "Queen Emma," Aunt Barbara called her.

Emma was big-breasted, and sometimes at dinner a crumb would fall and land on that broad expanse. As I watched, she would pick up her napkin and, pinching it between those bony, elegant fingers, use it to whisk the offending crumb away. Her hand never touched her breast; her lips were sucked in as if this close brush with her own body filled her with distaste.

There was no tenderness or sympathy to inform my picture of her, which is why so many childhood memories are so appalling. Emma reminded me of the dinosaur skeleton in the Peabody Museum in New Haven, the overlarge one in the central room with its tiny legs—how does it stay upright?

Though Emma was really only a guest in Grandpa and Grandma's house (a permanent guest, but still . . .), she insisted that the milk go into a pitcher before it was put on the big dining room table, the butter in a butter dish. If Grandma forgot the butter knife, Emma would remind her and Grandma would snort angrily and trot back into the kitchen to retrieve it.

When the meat platter was passed around, Emma carefully levered the serving fork under a slice, her pinky and index fingers pointed in the air like antennae. Around the table, eyes rolled and the next Dobie served would *stab* the meat. "Breast or thigh, Emma, what will it be?" Aunt Barbara would ask roughly, gaily, and Emma would suck in her lips and say, "White meat, please." I don't know when I realized that Emma was caught inside her spinsterhood, that when given a chance she was, in fact, curious and kind. It probably wasn't until my late twenties. I wasn't a kind, warmhearted child—I was highly sensitive, which isn't the same thing at all.

When I sat down next to her on the couch, Aunt Emma always asked the same question, "So how is school?" I didn't know what to say besides "Good," to which she would reply, "That's good," and then there was only silence tightening in the air between us like a screw. She had a smile on her face, a thin, close-lipped smile as she looked at me. Was she waiting for me, a child of eight or nine or ten, to pick up the conversation? First chance I got, I slid away—off to the sun parlor where my brothers and sisters were playing Mouse Trap or to the cheerful din of the kitchen where Aunt Barbara and Dad were teasing each other or arguing with Grandpa about his beloved Red Sox. If I looked back into the empty living room, there was Great-aunt Emma sitting stiffly on the couch, hands pinned to her lap, a smile frozen on her mouth.

Emma's bedroom was directly next to Grandma and Grandpa's, the door always open, as if the room were saying to unexpected company, "This is a bedroom, but everything is aboveboard!"

An armchair sat rigidly under the tasseled shade of a reading lamp. At the desk where she wrote letters and paid bills, the cubbyholes were neatly filled. There were letters from distant relatives in Germany whom none of us ever knew or cared to; stamps and stationery; rubber bands and paper clips kept in little boxes; figurines, music boxes, a Currier & Ives print of ice-skaters, and, everywhere, those pillows she embroidered with black-eyed daisies and purple clover, busy enough to attract bees.

The bed of a spinster aunt must, of course, be a modest-size bed, just big enough to sleep in. No spreading out for the spinster aunt, no hint of what beds are sometimes used for. Married people had big beds, as boastful and secure as ocean liners. The pillows were plumper, the bedspread seemed to go on forever before falling in luxurious folds to the floor. That big expanse of white seemed to be smiling mysteriously, testifying to the power of the married couple.

I couldn't stop myself from imagining Emma's chaste life in that bedroom. Thinking about no sex was not exactly like thinking about sex, but in its own way it was just as thrilling, and so I thought about it obsessively—Emma undressing for bed at night; Emma avoiding the sight of her body in the dresser mirror; Emma in her bed alone, long-legged, big-breasted Emma never making babies. Sometimes I would hold the figure of Great-aunt Emma and the figure of Frank Lee in my head at the same time until my skin prickled and my head swam.

Of course, it didn't occur to me then that Emma and Frank Lee had become objects of my obsession because they were both outsiders, each in their different ways. The tattooed misfit of a boy, the prim spinster aunt—both of them evidence that love had its limits, something I really didn't want to consider as a child. Frank Lee was too bad for the good nuns to keep around, too bad to be forgiven. And Great-aunt Emma was often only tolerated by the adults in our family, though she seemed impervious to their rolling eyes and quick retorts. No matter how many times she was teased, she went on tying plastic bags over her shoes whenever she went out in the rain. One afternoon, a few years after Grandpa had died, leaving the two sisters to live alone with each other, I watched Grandma chase Emma around the house, sweet little Grandma, brandishing Emma's umbrella and saying sarcastically, "Don't forget your umbrella, Emma, it might rain! Don't forget your galoshes!" There was nary a cloud in the sky.

Emma's carefulness around rain and children and food, that stiff posture and well-upholstered body, were anti-Dobie, for Dobies didn't fuss. They got down on the carpet and *played* with their children. They were quick with a joke, no-nonsense and plucky. When it rained on a picnic, they just laughed and said, "Typical Dobie weather." And you knew you had won their hearts if they called you "a real trouper."

When Great-aunt Emma fainted one night after just one predinner cocktail, Aunt Barbara said, "Out like a light!" and Dad added, "Down for the count!" They laid her out on the couch, and having reached the consensus that Emma's girdle was probably too tight, everyone fled to the warm, noisy kitchen to have another drink, while Aunt Barbara, who was a nurse, was left to tend to her, and I stayed behind in the suddenly shadowy living room to watch.

There had been something deeply embarrassing about straight-backed Emma holding her cocktail glass with one bony finger pointed out and away and then saying with an apologetic chuckle, "I feel a little woozy." Something awful about watching Emma laid out in the dim light, proper Emma undone—all those straps and hooks!—undone roughly, while pots clattered and voices rang heartily in the other room. Emma's head was directly underneath a table lamp, and so it seemed she was about to be scientifically examined. Her cheeks were colorless and slack; her hair, a tinsely gray, though still black at the roots, sparkled in the light. Barbara unbuttoned her dress swiftly, as if she'd been called upon to do this many times before, and then began unsnapping her girdle, each snap going pop!, one small explosion of impatience after another.

"Well, at least you can breathe now, Emma," she said, though Emma couldn't hear her, and then she joined the others in the kitchen. "The patient's resting peacefully," I heard her announce. I stayed there in the dim living room, transfixed by Emma's solitude, her undone state. From the kitchen, I could hear Emma being discussed—my mother wondering softly if my father had made her drink too strong, my father protesting, and Barbara and Grandpa coming in fast and sure to say it wasn't the drink but the drinker. A screen door slammed and I heard Barbara greeting one of my brothers or sisters: "The sailor's home from the sea!" Grandma asked who was going to carve the roast, and everyone insisted that it must be my father—he was in food service, after all—and with that the conversation moved on to other things.

The kitchen doorway blazed with a sunny light, the roast was spilling its juice as my father carved, the sounds of laughter rang out. And yet I couldn't go in there. I was afraid. I imagined my mother trying to pretend she was as robust and stouthearted as her husband and in-laws. Suddenly it seemed that she and I had fallen in with a pretty rough crowd.

6

Julie the Slut

IN SIXTH GRADE, MY GIRLFRIENDS MAUREEN AND MARISA AND I, throwing caution to the winds, began writing dirty letters to the most popular boy in our class and signing them "Julie." That was the year that some of the girls began wearing bras and the boys started snickering, a brand-new sound from them. At recess, the boys did fly-by attacks, running up behind the girls and trying to unhook their bras, or at least yank them and make them snap like elastic bands. They began to "moo" at us, too, and at lunch they drank from their milk cartons with a sucking sound and a leer.

Suddenly, we girls were divided into two groups, the girls with bras and the girls without, the big-breasted and the no-breasted—because that is how all of us small-breasted girls felt. We would be freer than those girls with bras, not pushed around as much, but also irrelevant.

Under their desks, the boys' shoes looked bigger and sharper, more like our fathers' shoes. Their schoolboy uniforms began to resemble men's business suits—weren't they wearing belts, button-down shirts, and ties? Someday they would have to shave. They became more manly and much sillier that year. I could tell we weren't going to be friends anymore. Liking was no longer the currency. They were more like big brothers teasing and bullying us, only with more excitement all around.

We girls no longer wore our plaid jumpers to school. From sixth grade on, we had to wear skirts, and though no adult ever explained why, I was sure that it was because the front panels of the jumpers would accent our growing breasts. My imagination pictured those panels straining to contain two giant breasts, buoyant as balloons.

The adults tried to act like nothing was going on. When one of the boys asked a young, pretty nun to explain the story of "the burning bush," she must have known exactly what he was saying because she blushed tomato red, but then she just went on with the lesson, plunging into it with a nervous, reckless air. We understood. When it came to sex, we were on our own. The adults had left the scene, tiptoeing away, hoping, no doubt, that we would follow. Not a chance.

They had gone blind, but we could finally see—with our own eyes now, and not only what we were supposed to see. They went silent but we could talk, and we didn't bother to sound pleasing or nice, or even very sensible. Why should we? We understood each other perfectly—what was indecipherable about a "moo"?

At recess, Maureen, Marisa, and I huddled on the cement steps at the back of St. Rita's, keeping one eye out for the nun patrolling the school yard. I used my heavy geography book as a writing table.

Dear Danny, Hi, handsome! I wrote in that first letter.

"You don't know me but I know you," Marisa dictated, looking eagerly over my shoulder while I wrote it down. Marisa was a very freckled, light-skinned redhead; pale and bright, orange and white. She had a round face, a snub nose, a sturdy, farm girl's body.

I think about you all the time . . . I continued. *Especially when I'm in my bed at night.*

Maureen and Marisa giggled.

"I'm dying for you," Maureen added, her face suddenly serious. She reminded me of a beautiful monkey, all long limbs, sharp bones, and short, fluffy brown hair. Maureen was the first girlfriend I fell in love with. I thought the yoke of her collarbone and her jutting, deeply dimpled knees were like perfect pieces of architecture.

I want you to touch my titties, I wrote.

Danny Moore was good-natured and good-looking, with black

hair, dark, friendly eyes, and pink cheeks (though not too pink). His head was a little large for his body, so that part of him seemed to be a grown man. We could imagine Danny married; Danny in an office, sitting at a big desk on the phone; Danny fathering children. There was nothing sexier back then.

He blushed easily but he never tried to cover it up with bluster. He had a kind of grace to him, born simply of being good-hearted. We all loved Danny Moore, truant boys and nuns alike.

Danny had a girlfriend named Angela, the first girl in our grade to grow breasts, and it says something, says everything, that she was the only girl never to get into trouble for it. No boy ever mooed when she walked by. Or asked for some milk. No boy grabbed a squeeze, as Marty Egan did to me, walking behind my chair one day and quickly reaching over my shoulder and grabbing my right breast. He pumped it twice like it was a turkey baster. As soon as he squeezed, it seemed smaller.

When he lifted his hand, my chest felt blank, as though he'd taken the breast away and now it was lying there in his hand, warm and plump. It went with him when he went back to his seat, smirking. I was sorry it was so small; the word *titmouse* flew into my head, and *this little piggy*, and then *a bird in the hand is worth two* . . . Humiliation and titillation combined, and for the next few days whenever I was alone, I poked and prodded the moment mentally, like a boy with a stick.

But Danny and Angela were above all of this. He was our gentle prince and she was our little mother, our head cheerleader, the lilac-crowned May Queen that year. She had a woman's breasts, an improbable streak of gray in her black hair, and she was a foot taller than Danny. We would hand him a footstool so he could climb up on it and kiss her while we watched and cheered. They were our perfect bride and groom, mother and father shrunk down to size, and we were seriously invested in their romance.

Still, Maureen and Marisa and I wrote, *Baby, I'm here all alone. I wish you would sneak into my bedroom one night and squeeze my big titties.*

We closed with *Yours Forever,* tacked on some kisses and hugs. And then, after a quick discussion, signed the name "Julie," a pretty name and the name of no one we knew. Julie was free to become whatever we wanted her to become.

That afternoon, I handed Danny the letter, explaining that this girl named Julie had given it to me after school the day before. "She asked me to deliver it to you," I said solemnly, excitement twitching my toes.

When he read it, Danny blushed. The color streaked straight up his cheeks, red mercury rising. We told him that Julie was a girl we had met outside school and we didn't know how she knew him. "I guess she has a crush on you," Maureen said with remarkable nonchalance, revealing herself to be a pretty smooth liar and filling me with admiration.

Danny asked where this Julie lived, but we said we didn't know if she even *had* a home. "She just kind of hangs out in back of the school yard. That's where we met her."

Two days later—we could barely wait *that* long—we gave Danny another letter and he blushed again, but this time he asked us what she looked like.

"She's kind of fat," I said.

"Really?" His expression was impossible to pin down—pained, yes, but with what? Disappointment, pity, increased longing?

I went for broke. "Yeah, she's really fat. She doesn't have any friends, either, except us. . . ."

"Kind of us," Maureen said. "But we're not really her friends, we just see her sometimes."

He didn't ask why Julie was friendless; he wanted to know her last name. And the color of her hair, her eyes; did we find out where she lived yet? He began to sidle over to me at the beginning of each school day and ask if I had a letter from her. He was shy about it, but helplessly driven. We wrote him constantly.

I was becoming a different creature outside my family, outside of the gaze of adults; bolder, freer, a leader in many a strange expedition, more of a Dobie away from the Dobies, you might say. (Or away from my mother, at least, and my obsession with her every glance.) But the boldness of a dreamer is quite a different thing from the boldness of a tomboy; it can easily end in humiliation. An idea forms in your head, a marvelous idea—a blue coat sacrificed on a rock, perhaps—but act out that idea, let it take on flesh for all the world to see, and the idea is suddenly ridiculous.

But Julie wasn't my dream alone. Three of us had brought her into being, and as the weeks went by, she grew more and more real. She was fat. She was lonely. She was shameless.

My girlfriends and I never had to explain ourselves to one another; we seemed to share the same imagination, the way some friends share the same taste in movies or clothes. When we had sleep-overs at one another's houses, we conducted séances, circling around a flickering candle and calling Lizzie Borden back from the dead, terrifying ourselves. We rehearsed sultry voices and then made obscene calls to people picked randomly from the phone book, dialing the number for a John Anderson and asking the woman who answered the phone, "Is John home? He was supposed to meet me this afternoon." Maureen and I wrote love letters to each other under the names of Christopher Columbus and Queen Isabella; *My Nina, My Pinta, My Santa Maria!*

We were becoming enthralled with our Julie. We no longer giggled and snickered when writing her letters. I was so carried away by our project that I had begun writing some of them by myself in my room at night. She was as much a reply to my day at school as some other girl's diary might have been. Julie took everything the boys were throwing at us, the leering and mooing and grabbing at our breasts, and made it her own. If the boys made sucking sounds while drinking their milk, Julie listened and then wrote Danny, straight out, *I really want you to suck my tits.*

Even as I wrote the letters, I wondered what was going to come out of her mouth next. Sometimes she shocked me. I'd begun to like her, but I didn't think Julie had much use for girlfriends. It was too late for that. We may have created her, but now she was alive! Alive and dead-set on Danny Moore. I knew other girls couldn't cure her of her loneliness.

She had gotten under Danny's skin, too. Her isolation was the clincher. Who would've thought? The most popular boy in school, friend to all, enemy of none, and yet I could feel he had something private going with Julie, a mental pipeline that went direct to her, sitting alone in a room, waiting for him. And who would he be when he was with her, this straight-B student, this mother's son, this pride of nuns?

"She's got long brown hair, really long," I told him, pointing below my hips. He liked that. Julie wrote that she would come to him wearing only her hair, like Lady Godiva. Danny asked me who Lady Godiva was. "You know, on the candy boxes, the naked lady on the horse."

He seemed to trust me more than Maureen or Marisa, and he would wait till they weren't around and then ask me questions about Julie. It was as if he knew that I felt strongly about her, too.

Julie wrote that she wanted him to rest his head on her tits; they were as soft as pillows. She got fatter, and I had to tell Danny that people made fun of her. That hurt him. I said she had hazel eyes.

"Really beautiful eyes," I added casually, like a fact you couldn't argue with. Back and forth I went, making her grotesque in some small way (wasn't sex grotesque?) and then giving her something pretty (and tantalizing, too?), giving it to the both of them because I'd begun to want their relationship to work out.

On the day I told him that Julie was as big as a horse, he got a letter from her saying he could ride her bareback if he wanted. I picked that up from a boy in our class named Jerry.

Jerry had shiny blond hair, a suave demeanor. For an eleven-year-old, he was sleek and prosperous-looking, the only rich boy in our class and the only one whose parents had divorced. We didn't feel sorry for Jerry—he didn't appear the least bit crushed by his parents' separation. It only made him seem more sophisticated, especially when we learned that he got to read his father's *Playboy*s and call his mother by her first name. He was always one step ahead of us. Marty Egan may have grabbed my breast but it was Jerry who one day decided that *bike* meant vagina. He went up to each girl and asked what color her bike was. And from innocent answers like "Blue," he reaped pleasure, or reaped it for the other boys. There was a certain joylessness to Jerry's corruption of us. It was as if he'd already seen and done everything, and he was only interested in giving the other boys a thrill.

I figured out what *bike* was, but then Jerry asked, "Do you have a fat bike or a skinny one?" There was so much to consider now.

Jerry changed euphemisms so fast that you always got caught saying something dirty. Once he got the boys thinking about cup size, you couldn't even get a grade on your test without feeling sticky and strange. When the nun read the grades aloud, you found yourself hoping you didn't get an A.

One morning when I walked into school, Jerry asked me if I had a pussycat—"Is she furry?" I'd just come from the breakfast table, from Sugar Pops and orange juice, my mother's and father's kisses goodbye. I blushed wildly and couldn't think of anything to say, but that night Julie sat down and wrote a letter. She signed it, *Love from YOUR PUSSYCAT.* Danny began to look haggard.

"How can I see her?" he asked again and again.

Finally, we arranged for them to meet at the ballpark after school.

When Danny arrived, Maureen and Marisa and I were standing at the edge of the baseball diamond, scraggly black woods and yellow brush behind us. We told Danny she was back there in the high brush and waiting for our signal.

We started singing, "Julie, Julie, Julie, do you love me? Julie, Julie, Julie, do you care?" We were corny girls, young for our age; we were wildly excited. "Julie, Julie, will you still be there!" And then we counted to ten and yelled like Ed McMahon, "Heeeeeere's *Julie!*"

We turned, arms spread, and I held my breath. For a split second I half-expected her to come striding out of those woods, huge, naked, hair tumbling, a bear of a girl, a girl beyond my imagination. I watched the brush, the high reeds, and waited for the rustle—anything could happen in God's world, so why not Julie? I had a powerful desire to see her in the flesh, to see what she'd do next. But the woods revealed nothing.

We ran through the drumroll again but this time, after shouting, "Here's Julie!" we pointed at one another.

It took ten stop-and-go seconds for the meaning to reach Danny, and then he blushed.

"No. You? You're . . . ? No. You wrote . . . ?"

We confessed, doubled over with laughter, hiding our own reddening cheeks—what had we done? It never occurred to us until that moment that we'd be revealing ourselves. We were filled with confusion and embarrassment—*pussycat, big titties, please pet me, please, we* wrote that!—but Danny began laughing and shaking his head at our boldness. He was a good-natured boy, a heart like the sun.

When we left the park, we were quiet. Occasionally one of us giggled, and Danny would give a halfhearted shove to shove the giggler and we would all laugh loudly, but we were feeling kind of low.

"So, she doesn't . . . She's not real at all?" Danny asked one more time, embarrassed to bring her up again, but he had to. Maureen or Marisa started humming "Taps" and we all joined in.

I found myself missing Julie in the days and weeks ahead. Though I know that Danny and Maureen and Marisa felt the same way, none of us ever mentioned her again. Julie should have existed. That girl we created, lonely and bold, the composite of all the loathing and desire we had begun to feel in the air around us, that girl continued to take up space in my head. It was like a real person had died.

Mirror in the Window

"IN THE NEXT LIFE I'M COMING BACK AS LOUIS ARMSTRONG," MY FATHER always said, but in the meantime his horn, a saxophone, collected dust in the basement. Still, the wonderful world was on him; he brought it home the way other men bring home the bacon. When he walked in the door after work, sometimes he'd put a record on the turntable, loosen his tie, and dance across the living room in his black suit, fingers snapping, hips wagging, beckoning my mother to him while she stood watching in the kitchen doorway. He danced funky, then goofy, danced with his attaché case, danced with his tie, held his hand out to her. In her apron, she hesitated.

Ah, the leap to joy! Could she make it? Would she try? Each time I held my breath. It all depended. Dark day? Happy day? Longing flew out of her—to be that lovely in his eyes!—but her heels dug deeper into the linoleum. Where was her self? In that room, laughing, twirling, or in the long day behind her, housebound, nothing changing but the diapers? It was almost a moral battle. Could she, should she, would she snap out of her day, leave dishes, diapers, doubt, weariness behind, just because he was home, because he was happy? He withdrew his hand; my heart sank. But then he took his tie and roped her, pulling her from the doorway, from gloom to living room, to light, to him.

"Al!" She laughed, her white teeth flashing against the red, red lipstick. They danced.

And Louie went, *"Boo-bah-dah-dah."*

At night, under the bedcovers, I rode my barrette out to the high plains. Tall in the saddle, riding riding riding . . . I was Roy Rogers! Then Dale Evans! Sometimes both of them at once, astride my barrette, breaking into a gallop . . . Oh, married cowboy love!

My father had the swift gait and commanding, vigorous air of a man on a mission, but he also had Tom Sawyer freckles and dancing blue eyes. His lips would curl at the corners when he was up to some mischief—which was often. It was a very expressive face.

"It always gives me away," he would say to us kids, wagging his large head dolefully as if he were really upset, his eyes twinkling all the while, his lips tightening against the grin he could never quite repress. He loved to tell us stories, sometimes make-believe stories with ridiculously named characters like McGruff, McDuff, McWhosit, and McGillacutty, and sometimes real ones, but real or imaginary he always told them like they were stories written down in a book. Before he began, he would take a deep breath and then, following the rhythm of once-upon-a-time, he would say, "When I was just a boy . . ."

At St. Boniface in New Haven, where he went to grammar school, the nuns were not only strict, he told us, but vicious. "They would've been street thugs if they'd been born men." One winter afternoon at recess, young Albert and his friends had a snowball fight, and when they returned to class, the nun asked the boys who'd been playing in the snow to give themselves up. No one spoke, no one moved. But once again Albert's eyes gave him away. The nun ordered him out of his seat and handed him a bucket, telling him to go fill it with snow.

When he returned, she made him sink his hands in the snow and sit there like that for the rest of the hour. When the class was over, and his hands were swollen and red, she took a ruler and, using the sharp edge, struck the backs of his hands. At each strike, the frozen skin split.

When my father told us this story, he told it as an adventure, not a tale of woe. It was like a fairy tale, really, with hatchet-faced nuns who were wonderfully wicked and shrouded in black. They cackled as they stirred the cauldron and waited for little boys to come by so they could *eat*! But this boy was clever and brave; he would make it out of the woods alive.

And so I was given two opposing narratives as a child: My father's depicted life as filled with tests, danger, hard tasks, and adventure. Not only were these things interesting in and of themselves, but they made a rousing good story later. My mother, an only child whose memories were of a lonely childhood with no one but her mother, aunt, and uncle for company, spoke very rarely about her past, and when she did it wasn't a story so much as a keening complaint. Her narrative was mostly interior, about hurt feelings and unhappiness. There were never any happy endings, never any resolutions at all, really. My mother seemed to be struggling mightily against her past, even, you might say, against her own personality.

Nonetheless, for most of my childhood my mother's narrative was the one I identified and allied myself with. But as adolescence approached, my lovestruck gaze moved from my mother to my father. It felt like a betrayal, but of course I couldn't become myself while I was tied to her. One time she protested, "You all admire your father so much!" And how could we not? He came home each night with his chin up, forehead glowing, black shoes snapping on the linoleum, so at home in the world, so happy and energized there, it was as if he had a mistress. Sometimes he brought my mother red roses, and we would watch as her face softened and lit up. Often he delighted us by telling the story of meeting her. "As soon as I saw her standing on top of the stairs in that yellow dress, I was a goner," he would say, clutching his heart and slowly shaking his big, handsome head, a goner for all to see.

* * *

When my father came up the walk at the end of the day, we flew into his legs, his hips, his sharp dark suit, sniffing him like dogs. There, in the dense weave, was the faint smell of the rivers and continents he'd crossed.

After hugging and kissing us, he went into the kitchen and closed the folding doors. Then we heard the tinkle of ice in glasses and the murmur of voices. This was strictly grown-up time, treacherous and seductive. We gathered by the doors, like souls crowding the heavenly gates, listened hard but heard only tones—his spirited, hers murmuring. Trumpet and violin. And then their voices would almost disappear until finally the doors were flung open and we'd hear my father's shout, "Fee fie foe fum, I smell the blood of an Englishmun!" The giant emerged and we fled!

The best game was when Daddy was a bull, down on the living room floor, snorting and pawing the ground and wheeling angrily around as we attacked him in force, all four or five or six of us charging him and trying to knock him down, as we dodged his sharp horns and flaming eyes. Sometimes he fell with a groan and lay there, whimpering, and our hearts broke.

"Oh, don't hurt him!" we cried.

We petted his stiff auburn hair, cooing, "Poor little bull." Always a mistake, because he'd roar back to life, take a swipe, and then I'd be under him while he tickled my ribs ferociously.

"Help me! Save me!" I yelled. His belt buckle dug into my chest as he flailed about, grabbing at my brothers and sisters, who were now dashing in to try to pull me out from under him.

"Big ugly bull!" I grunted, trying to push him off of me.

He caught Cindy by the leg and pulled her down, her head clunking into mine, and she, too, started screaming: "Help! Save us!"

We always had to save one another, even if you really really didn't want to get caught by those octopus arms and tickled until it hurt and you had no breath left. The call of our siblings went straight to the heart. One cry for help and we had to throw ourselves into the battle. We were duty-bound, we were inflamed; we were positively patriotic about one another.

Sometimes the whole weight of his body would be pinning me down so that I could hardly breathe, or maybe I was wearing a dress and I knew my underwear was showing—and then I would cry, and my mother would come to my rescue, calling for him to stop. "Al, you're hurting her. You're playing too rough!" His face would look shocked and innocent. "I am not!" he'd protest. But if I kept wailing, he'd pull himself off the floor and with a long, sad face trudge out of the room and up the stairs, like an old bull or that dragon by the sea who knew Jack would come no more.

Up the stairs he went, one sad shoe at a time. And then even his shoes disappeared from view. No more play—would we ever play again?

When he returned, the fun would begin anew, though it would be muted at first, for he was like a chastised boy. But soon he would be sitting with us at the piano (though he didn't know how to play), banging out notes, saying this was a composition he had written specially for us, entitled "Reflections on a Garbage Dump in May." If we started giggling, he'd look astonished and cry, "This is a very serious composition!"

The playing father, the one who would wrestle with us, or make up songs at the piano, or suddenly start singing instead of speaking, so our dinner table sounded like an amateur opera with each of us joining in the fun and trilling, "Please pass the peas," that father was a continual delight to all his children—he was wilder than we were! But for me, that father wasn't as potent, as desirable, as the father in the suit. Almost every night at dinner, that man held court. Amid the clatter of silverware, my father would launch into a story about his day at Yale. (What stories did my mother have to tell? We knew her day. She'd spent it with us.) My father was like one of the four winds returning to the firelit cave in Hans Christian Andersen's fairy tale—the South Wind, perhaps, who had chased ostriches in Africa all day—reporting to his mother and brothers what he'd seen on his travels.

*   *   *

In the spring of my eleventh year, the Black Panthers came to New Haven. My older relatives sounded scared, and I'd never heard them sound scared about anything before. So at first I thought they were talking about an invasion of animals. I imagined scores of them, sleek and shadowy, as they leaped over the hills and trotted across the New Haven Green. Looking for shoppers.

It was my father who set me straight—men not beasts, he explained. Bobby Seale was being tried in the New Haven courthouse for the murder of Alex Rackley, another Black Panther. Seventy-five thousand people were expected to arrive for a weekend of protests. Yale had decided to feed and house as many of them as they could; my father was on the planning committee.

As we dug into our meat loaf and mashed potatoes, he told us that Nixon had sent paratroopers to Rhode Island, a seventeen-minute helicopter ride away from New Haven, and that the National Guard had troops stationed a few miles from the New Haven Green, "in full riot gear with bayonets fixed to their rifles"—a firsthand description he was able to offer us because he had driven out to the armory to see them.

Yale students and faculty left town in droves as the weekend approached. Downtown stores and restaurants closed. Signs in their windows read, "Our insurance company has canceled our coverage for the weekend—please don't break our windows."

"All of the administrators went out and bought dungarees and flannel shirts and loafers," he told us, laughing. "So there they are, and they've got the spanking-new blue jeans, the pressed flannel shirt, the polished loafers, trying to blend in with the crowd." But not my father. "There's no way I'm gonna hide," he said. "I'm an administrator. I've got a job to do. I'm gonna wear my suit."

He had a job to do, but he also had a whole newsworthy world unfolding in front of him. He went everywhere, checked out everything, and brought the stories back to us.

That Friday night, to kick off the weekend of protests, a big rally was held at Ingalls Rink. Huey Newton and William Kunstler would speak. When my father got there, the auditorium was packed. Speaker after speaker took to the microphone on a stage ringed by armed Black Panthers, Huey Newton's bodyguards.

With each speaker the crowd grew louder and angrier. "They were trying to inflame people, to get them into a riot mode," my father said. "Of course, all cops were pigs, anybody who wore a uniform was a pig, and any white male was a motherfucker."

"Al!" my mother warned, but he overrode her with a flashing glance, impatient, almost scornful; he was in full storytelling swing. When a student tried to walk onstage, Huey Newton's bodyguards grabbed him, threw him to the ground, and started kicking him. The other students yelled, "Stop it! Let him talk! Let him talk!" The guards stepped back. The student went up to the podium.

"And then he just stood there. He didn't say a word," my father told us. "The crowd went absolutely dead silent. One minute they were roaring, the next you could've heard a pin drop."

At the dinner table, we too were struck into silence. The student wavered at the microphone. Our forks were suspended midair. Six Dobie children watched and waited, just as hundreds of Yale students had done.

My father's stories mesmerized me; they were as colorful as any fiction I was reading in books. But I always dreaded the moment when the storytelling ended, because that was when the discussion of current events began.

My father would bring up a topic—the death penalty, women's lib, "youth-in-Asia," something the President had done that day—and then we each had to take a turn at giving our "opinion." I didn't have any. I scoured my brain but I could never find even one small opinion lying around in there. I didn't even like the word, it was colorless and it cramped itself up at the end: *oh-pinyon*.

Topic and *current events* were also dull and frightening words; they reminded me of scissors slicing into construction paper. I preferred *moonlight* and *sonata*, *swan lake*, *snow queen*. But they weren't opinions—they weren't even thoughts! I didn't "think things out." I daydreamed, I drifted out to sea in a beautiful pea-green boat with the owl, the pussycat, and a five-pound note. . . .

Although I would do my best to make up an opinion, if my father didn't agree, he'd pounce, arguing with us as if we were twenty, not nine or ten or eleven. Sometimes I'd break down and cry. Once or twice, even my mother ran weeping from the room. Each time he would look astonished, and then both angry and ashamed. He'd forgotten we were children; forgotten how sensitive my mother was. He was just looking for a good sparring partner, but suddenly he'd become a bully.

"I bet you don't even know who the President of the United States is," he said to me at the table one night, fixing me with his hot blue eyes. "Do you even know what *year* it is?"

My father could be hard on me, it's true. I believe that there was something about my nature, my dreaminess and forgetfulness, that alarmed him. Perhaps it was his Germanic background, a trained distaste for both disorder and vulnerability. When I forgot to turn off lights or the bathwater, broke and spilled things, left my clothes lying around, he would leap on my mistake—"*Where* is your brain?"—and then, to make matters worse, I would only stare at him, dumbstruck. I was defenseless at those moments; a sleeper shaken awake. That vulnerability set off something inside of him, and I feared his temper then. And yet he greatly inspired me. He wanted us to read the newspapers, be informed, have opinions, *live in the world* and not inside our heads.

Well, I wanted to live there, too, even more than he wanted it for me. That was where all the action was taking place, not here inside our house; strikes, rebellions, noble battles. The world according to my father was a very democratic place. His stories were peopled with dishwashers and chefs, plumbers, professors, college deans, the police chief and the mayor, every class and color of people.

Listening, I felt that life itself was democratic. Everyone had a part to play, the lowly cop in trouble, the princelike president of Yale. Life liked life, plain and simple, and as long as you were willing to live it fully, it wouldn't abandon you. It would pick you up, throw you into the fray, again and again, give you trouble and joy; ravish you. The entire world outside our family seemed to be in agitation. Everyone else was blossoming and becoming themselves. I wanted to join them, to enter that world. But how to get there?

On that question, I was completely in the dark.

When I think about those final years of my childhood, I remember a story my father once told me, one that now appears to me to be about an inheritance, a gift passed from my grandfather to my father and then to me. In the story, my father was a young boy, stranded in bed with a broken ankle, restless and bored. Every afternoon, Grandpa would come home from the Winchester gun factory on his lunch hour to take his meal by his son's bed. One day, he rigged up a mirror by the window, slanting it so Albert could see the world outside.

I like to imagine that boy propped on his pillows, watching that flickering mirror hour upon hour . . . sky and sky, an occasional cloud plowing the blue sea, a gusty branch, wind-riding birds. The boy growing impatient, seeing in that framed rectangle, that living picture, how gorgeous the world was, how tempting, how perfect.

What my grandfather gave to my father, my father gave to me—a vision of the world's richness. He was my mirror in the window. I watched him as he left us every morning to go to work, to more adventures, as fully charged as a racehorse, and I was filled with wonder. What if I could live like my father lived, like I thought all men lived, a large life filled with drama?

"Someday . . ." I began to tell myself, my eyes following the flag of car exhaust sailing by the kitchen window as he backed quickly out of the driveway, going as fast backward as he did forward. But *someday* must be a long way off, I thought. It was hard to imagine that I could ever leave us that easily.

As it turned out, it wasn't me after all but Bill who broke away first. That it was bloody and hard is only a testament to the power and glory of The Family.

8

An A for Creativity

THE FIRST TIME THAT BILL RAN AWAY FROM HOME, WE WERE ON A family picnic at the lake at Chatfield Hollow. There were only six of us that spring Saturday, my mother and father, Cindy, Beth, little Stephen, and me. I was thirteen and about to graduate from St. Rita's, which only went to eighth grade. Bill was a freshman at Notre Dame High School; he'd just turned fifteen.

My parents had driven our new sky-blue Pinto, the one Grandma Callahan and Great-aunt Bert had helped them buy, and they'd left the big station wagon at home that day for Michael to use. As the oldest, with places to go and important, college-bound things to do, Michael was sometimes allowed to skip out on family outings. Bill didn't have any plans we knew of. He just didn't want to come with us, and my parents, surprising me, had let him have his way. He was supposed to stay at home.

When we pulled into the driveway after our day at the lake, Michael appeared at the front door, looking flushed and even a little wild-eyed. In his hand, he had one of the pieces of scrap paper my mother cut up and made her grocery lists on. Such a small scrap of paper and on it nothing but *I'm leaving. I'm sorry. Don't worry about me. Bill.*

For a second, everything took on the bright, flat colors and simple lines of a children's drawing—Michael's orange hair and white face, the rectangular doorway behind him, the green grass where we stood, the blue sky and round yellow sun high over the pointed roof of the house.

Michael had found the note on the kitchen table when he got home that afternoon, he told us. Immediately he'd jumped into the car and gone to look for Bill until he spotted him walking down a nearby street. "When he saw me, he waved me away and then he started running. I tried to catch him but he cut through the woods."

Later, Bill would give his own version—Michael was chasing him with the *car* and so intent on bringing him home that he almost ran him over. "I was running for my life," Bill said. It was the usual Bill version, funnier, darker, the complaint hidden in humor—Michael's blind ambition, his big-brother panic, the station wagon bearing down; Michael, the good son, almost killing him.

My sisters' faces were blank, astonished mirrors of my own. He ran away? Wrote a good-bye note and . . . went? Where'd he ever think of that? There was only The Family in our family. There was the big blue station wagon and the big blue tent, the dinners every night at six, chores on Saturdays and Mass on Sundays, spring picnics, summer campfires, sing-alongs in the car, Aunt Barbara, the great-aunts and uncles and grandparents, the lavish, sparkling Christmases. Bill's picking up and leaving all of that behind was a daringly original act, the most creative act performed by any of us, in fact, since my father-less mother, that only child, dreamed up a big, happy family back when she was nineteen.

After my parents raced out the door to go look for him, Cindy and I put one of our forty-fives on the record player in the living room. We sat in the two armchairs, rocking and listening to "Which Way You Goin', Billy?" sometimes looking down into our laps and sometimes staring at each other as solemnly as owls. Every time the record ended, one of us would get up and put it on again.

Where did the trouble begin? I thought we all knew that it was there, but then why were my parents so bewildered? Cindy and I knew, knew in the same deep, wordless way that we knew each other's skin and scars and faces when asleep. It was just there, the trouble; we could smell it.

Bill had always been hungry, hungrier than the rest of us. He had my father's romantic nature, and a reckless heart that was ever ready to fling itself open. Even his temper tantrums as a two-year-old were extravagant: Bill would hold his breath until he turned red, then blue, and then finally, horribly, mercifully pass out, crumpling to the carpet and lying there in a heap.

But he was as tenderhearted as he was reckless—a combination that could only lead to trouble, far more trouble for him than for anybody else. When Bill did something wrong, even the most minor of infractions, he was tormented with guilt and would obsess over his disobedience until he was driven to confess. His sneaky siblings couldn't understand him—tell on yourself? No way, José!

When he was sad or hurt, Bill looked sadder and more hurt than anyone I knew. When my parents yelled at him, his mouth would drop open like a trapdoor and then hang there, the hurt and humiliation naked on his face. As he got older, he began to work on his defenses. A big shrug of his shoulders, a quick retort. But he wasn't fooling anyone—or at least not Cindy and me.

When we were little, my mother was always having to tell Bill to leave the two of us alone. He teased us with knuckle punches to our shoulders, elastics sent zinging toward our heads, wet dish towels twisted into ropes and snapped at our bare legs. Cindy and I ran like hell. We hated him and adored him without end. He was quick and sarcastic, handsome and cool. And even then, running from flying elastic bands, we knew.

He had dirty-blond hair, floppy bangs, a closemouthed smile that tilted to the left, dark blue eyes, and my mother's coloring—cream with a bit of coffee—so he tanned easily. All of my girlfriends, and Cindy's, too, fell in love with him.

Once, when he was eight or nine, he stood at the top of the attic stairs wearing only a bath towel, performing for Cindy and me. We watched from below as Bill sang to us, using his fist as a microphone.

"Come on, baby, light my fire . . ." He slid the towel open quarter inch by quarter inch. Cindy and I were wide-eyed, giggling, beside ourselves with terror and glee, ready to run at any moment. He sang the words as suggestively as he could. "Fire" became "fie-ahhh." His bangs were still wet; his chest, smooth and shiny as a seal. The towel crept open, like a stage curtain . . . his hipbone, his thigh . . .

Cindy and I shrieked! We turned to run. We didn't go anywhere. The towel hung between his legs; he stopped there. He was a great big tease. He entertained *and* tortured us at the same time; he combined the two beautifully.

Another day, he shut me in the kitchen broom closet. Pushed me in there with the mops and brooms and rags and slammed the door. I tried to shove my way back out, pushing as hard as I could on the door; it didn't give an inch.

"Billy, let me out!" I yelled, this time throwing my whole body against the door. I got a shuddering inch of kitchen light and air before the door banged shut again, closing me inside. I had to get out! I threw myself into the door again and again. I knew if I started screaming, I would never stop. I covered my mouth with my hand.

Then, as if someone had waved a wand over me, I melted into the floor, down amid the mop heads and rags, and went quiet. It smelled of Endust and lemon furniture polish.

A minute went by, and the door cracked open. A sliver, then a wedge, of kitchen table and cool linoleum, the dining room doorway beyond. . . . I made a dive, but it closed too fast. I could hear him whistling.

I'd been on the other side of this door when he threw Cindy inside the week before, so I knew he was examining his fingernails while he whistled, then polishing them on his shirt. He might even bend over and retie his sneakers, holding the door closed with his buttocks. We knew one another's little tricks and gestures better than we knew our own.

It wasn't until my mother came into the kitchen and Cindy told her that he'd trapped me in the closet that I was released.

* * *

What Bill remembers is my coming out of that closet like a beaten dog, shoulders slumped, face paper white, and going straight to my chair at the kitchen table without making a sound.

What I remember is the look of dumb surprise on his face when he saw me, followed by pain, and then by guilt. As my mother scolded him, he looked so hurt that I was instantly set against my own best interests—*Poor Billy*, I thought, and I even felt bad for being so terrified in the closet.

But as the scolding continued, he stuck out his chin, held up his empty hands, and shot back, "I didn't even touch her." And then I didn't feel sorry for him anymore.

He was the second-oldest brother, and he walked in Michael's footsteps every day of his childhood. Michael went first, Bill one year later—to Cub Scouts, Boy Scouts, piano lessons with Mrs. L. down the block, St. Rita's basketball team, Little League, first, second, third, fourth, fifth, sixth grades . . .

In a family, everyone has a role to play: If Michael was the brainy son, the successful son, what was Bill to be? Second best at everything that Michael did? He was the second-oldest son with nothing to call his own. And so he carved out another role for himself—the rebel. He had the courage for it, the buried anger, the creativity, but he didn't really have the heart. He disguised that fact with bravado whenever he could.

From first through sixth grades, he and Michael fought in the school yard at recess at least once a week, fistfights in front of an audience of cheering boys that always ended with a nun sailing into their midst to grab one of them by the ear. One good yank and both of them howled and went soft, like puppies.

In seventh grade, my parents let Bill leave St. Rita's and attend Blessed Sacrament Junior High. Now he had a school of his own. He joined their basketball team, got straight A's. My sisters and I weren't surprised—we always knew he was smart. Basketball trophies began to fill the shelves over his desk. He joined the school band. When Bill and my girlfriend Terry Wright played their trumpets to each other out their attic windows, they sounded like they were announcing themselves to the world in triumphant blasts: *Here I am!* I think of that moment, that happy, brassy blowing, as the end of an era.

The following year, the battle of the blue jeans began. Bill wanted them; you'd almost have to say he *needed* them. He might have been the only boy his age in Hamden who didn't have a pair. My grandmother offered to buy them for him but my mother refused. She feared losing us to the world. If we went skipping into it in our bell-bottoms and blue jeans, not only would we disappear, but she wouldn't be able to follow. I believe she must have sensed that the very world that would welcome us with open arms would hold her in contempt.

A few years earlier, posters showing a gray fist had begun to appear on telephone poles all around New Haven, advertising a nationwide women's strike—a strike for day care and equal wages in the workplace. Now militant-sounding women were everywhere on the news. At the dinner table, my Catholic father asked us what was the difference between euthanasia and abortion, and under his hot bright gaze we could find none. Another night at the dinner table when my father was working late, my mother turned to the six of us and insisted that she was *not* a housewife.

"I'm not married to this house!" she proclaimed, at once bold and beseeching. "I'm married to your father," she added. "I'm a wife and a mother of six and I think what I do is important!" I'm sure it was Beth who spoke then, who said something encouraging. Stephen wouldn't have understood her agitation, and the rest of us had begun to harden our hearts against her. We had to, for she had set all her hopes and dreams, her sense of worth, on the idea of a big happy loving family. And we were going to crush her dream. It was unbearable to think about, so we did our best not to.

Our parents never considered anything but a Catholic education for their children. Bill's school, Blessed Sacrament, went from seventh to ninth grades, after which all of his friends were going to Hamden High, the big public high school. Whenever we drove past Hamden High, which stood right on Dixwell Avenue next to the mall, we'd see the lawn filled with students, some lounging on the grass and smoking cigarettes, others making out against the brick wall, hundreds of kids, each dressed differently, in halter tops and hip-hugger jeans, Farrah Fawcett hair, khakis, tennis shirts, funkadelic afros that shimmered like halos, painter's overalls, huge bell-bottoms rippling like flags in a breeze—a chaos of color and expression. To parents like ours it must've looked like a mutinous place. Your child might end up being a stranger, speaking a different language altogether. He might end up feeling scorn for you—a businessman in a suit, a housewife in an apron. So Bill was forced to leave Blessed Sacrament after eighth grade, a year before his classmates, and go to Notre Dame, once again following in Michael's footsteps, even though he begged to stay.

My mother and grandmother fought about it. Their fight was short and swift—and fierce. It left them cagey around each other for years. Grandma took Bill's side, telling my mother that he needed something of his own. The rest of us kept our mouths shut. Standing up to our parents just wasn't possible.

The year Bill started at Notre Dame was the year he began to rebel. He played the coarse, stupid boy. Played it angrily. He'd drink straight from the milk carton, burp loudly, mumble all his words, say "ain't" and "duh" and "it don't matter to me," making my mother flinch.

Then he ran.

Cindy and I wondered if he was camped out in the woods across the street. What would he do without a sleeping bag?

Beth Ann kept her worries to herself, asking only if we knew how much money Bill might have with him, revealing, at nine years old, a deeply practical side. How far could Bill stretch twenty dollars? Her blue eyes were blank and as round as nickels, but I could almost hear her brain clicking as she added up the price of bologna and cheese and milk. In the last few years she and the dog, Sebastian, had become exceedingly close. "Hey, little buddy," she said to him that afternoon, and together they went upstairs to her room, closing the door behind them and staying there until dinner.

Our parents came home empty-handed that night.

The next thing we knew there was a police officer in our living room. He stood there taking notes, judging us, it seemed, and I knew my mother wanted to tell him about the picnics, the camping trips, the six of us wrestling with Dad on the living room floor when he came home from work, the dinners she made for us every night that always included two vegetables, one yellow, one green.

My father and mother began to put together a list of Bill's friends, none of them from Notre Dame. They called and spoke to the boys, to their mothers. Bill was nowhere to be found.

That night it rained. A cold spring rain.

"Dear God, please keep Billy warm and dry and make him want to come back home," I prayed. In my mind, God was the perfect Dobie cop; God would fetch him and bring him back, not by his collar but his heart.

Bill passed the night on a wet park bench at the same ball field where we had taken Danny Moore to meet Julie. The next day he came back. And that, we thought, was that.

When Bill left the second time, a few weeks later, summer had begun. As a week passed without a word, my parents' shock gave way to shame. They had failed, their beautiful family wasn't perfect after all. So my sisters and I began to tiptoe around the subject, tiptoeing even in our thoughts, as all good Catholic children learn to do.

Then suddenly one night he was back. Home again! But not to stay, only to get his clothes.

A dark-windowed van idled out front.

Bill had slipped upstairs without anyone noticing and thrown some clothes into a grocery bag. He was heading out the front door when my father spotted him from the kitchen. He ran into the living room, hard on Bill's heels.

"Where do you think you're going?" he yelled. Bill quickened his step, shoved open the front screen door.

"You're not leaving here again!" my father shouted, following him outside. "Get back in the house!"

Bill wouldn't stop. My father shoved his shoulder and Bill whirled around. My father's large freckled fists were clenched. His face was so close, Bill must've felt his heated breath. When my father was angry, the trees bent down.

The passenger door of the van swung open and I saw Bill's friend Joey at the wheel with his veil of black hair, taking it all in. There was an audience now; a silent, judging witness. Bill had an ally, someone besides us.

He looked straight at my father and put his arms up, still holding the grocery bag in one hand.

"I won't hit my own father," he said. Who was this brother? He'd become someone outside of us, our care, our games, our knowledge of each other. He sounded completely sure of himself, of what was right and what was wrong. He'd obviously kept his own counsel, come to his own conclusions. He had a moral code, spoken aloud now, same as my father.

With his hands still raised, Bill took a step backward toward the van. Then the most shocking thing happened in a night of shocking things—my father-in-the-suit fell to his knees on the lawn.

"Just tell me what's wrong!" my father howled. Bill looked like he'd been hit. He covered his eyes for a second, then turned and went stumbling toward the van.

When he leapt inside, I saw a third boy in back, another slice of deadpan cheekbone and lank hair. The door slammed and they took off, wheels screeching. I could imagine the three of them in that van, quickly lighting a joint, cranking the music up, listening to something raw and angry enough to beat grief down.

Five times Bill ran. Five times came back. Here again, gone again, all through that spring and summer and into the fall.

I was enthralled by the drama but found it overwhelming, the weeping and breast-beating, the shouts and teary professions of love and bewilderment. It provoked my own emotions, heartbreak and confusion and awe, but left no room for them.

My mother seemed to have become someone else, some wan and pining lover out of a book. Late one night, I saw her flitting noiselessly into the bathroom. Or, to be more precise, I caught a glimpse of the corner of her pink nightgown before the door closed, and then I heard her crying. She had been so determined to be a better mother than hers was—had she failed?

"If Bill doesn't quit this business, she's going to have a nervous breakdown!" I overheard Grandma whispering fiercely to Bert not long afterward, and I wondered what that was and if my mother had already had one. I kept picturing her pink nightgown slipping through the doorway; it was so ghostlike. And in a way she had become a ghost—vanishing behind closed doors so she could cry where no one would see or hear her. My father fought on, redoubling his efforts—he wanted his son back, he wanted his wife back. Though my mother was afraid his temper might drive Bill away even further, I preferred it to her sorrow.

I remember another day, when Bill and my father were upstairs in Bill's room fighting while my sisters and I sat huddled together on the living room floor.

"You're destroying this family!" my father yelled. Cindy, Beth, and I stared at one another's faces, as raptly as if we were watching the scene unfold there.

"You're killing your mother! Do you ever think of anyone but yourself?" And then the clatter of footsteps, the sound of a body falling into the accordion fold of the closet door. Cindy dug her chin into her chest, squeezing her eyes shut.

It was easy for us to imagine Bill caught in the door, hands at his side, saying nothing, accusing Dad with his innocence, and to imagine our father looming over him, white-faced with shame. They were like two giants roaring and stumbling about, breaking their own hearts.

With her chin still buried in her chest, Cindy opened her eyes and looked at me, her face long and strained. The three of us moved closer and then reached for one another with our feet, pressing them together in the center of the circle.

One night that fall, when Bill had gone missing again, my father jumped up from his chair in the living room, returned the papers he'd been reading to his black attaché case, and snapped the lid shut.

"I'm going to go find him and bring him home," he announced to my mother with sudden decisiveness. All in a moment, he'd thrown off melodrama, befuddlement, impotence. Years later, when I heard the phrase "the nervous system is meant to act," I would remember my father's face that night. He was thirty-nine.

Within hours he was back. He had one arm hooked under Bill's shoulder and with the other he was trying to open the door.

"Watch the step here," my father said gently, and Bill's feet slid up and over the doorstep like snakes.

As they came into the living room, Bill grinned straight at me, and I started to smile back. But then I realized he was grinning at everything. When my father maneuvered him to the foot of the living room stairs, he called out to my mother and she appeared wearing her nightgown.

Bill smiled up at her, an astonishing smile, then stumbled and grabbed the rail. He made it up one stair, two, slipped, straightened, held on tighter, never taking his eyes from my mother's face, never dimming his blazing smile. Another stair, and another; gamely he held on. Nothing would stop him from reaching her. When he finally made it to the top, she folded him in her arms.

They put him in a shower to "straighten him out" and asked me to make a pot of coffee.

I was in a dark mood in the kitchen. My parents thought he was drunk; I knew he was as high as a kite. I felt bad for them and bad for him, and it was as if the two feelings, warring inside of me for so long, canceled each other out. A bewildering coldness filled me. It was clear that my days as a witness, as "handmaiden with the coffeepot," as I called myself that night, were coming to an end.

9

Scorpios and the Sacred Heart

AS I TRUDGED UP THE HILL ON MY FIRST DAY AT MY NEW SCHOOL, THE white blouse I'd put on that morning for the first time was so stiff I could hear it crinkle when I moved my arms. The blouse was tucked into a regulation brown-and-white checked skirt, the brown knee-socks I wore were pulled up tight, and the laces on my soft-soled shoes were tied into a bow and then a double knot. I felt plain and serviceable, and not much else. It was as if my insides had been washed clean, and now on this bright September day I was ready to be filled, transformed, made into something better than this plain, pale self.

At the tree-covered top of the hill, Jesus stood on a pedestal and opened his chest, displaying his thorn-pierced heart next to a small sign reading, "Sacred Heart Academy"; the school itself was invisible from the road.

The long driveway in was a perfectly smooth, velvety black—did good Catholic men repave it for the nuns every night? On either side was a cropped green lawn, thicker and plusher than any front yard I'd ever seen, its manicured expanse shaded by big oak trees with rustling leaves and tall pines pointing their spindly fingers toward heaven. Walking up the drive in my dull uniform, I felt as if I were approaching a rich man's house—not as a guest, but as someone newly hired for some menial position. The religious statues that lined the road, chalky-white faces staring blankly over my head, were like doormen who had to keep their opinions to themselves.

At the end of the driveway, the paved surface opened into a big circle, the trees dropped away, and the school came into view, white-bricked, two-storied, shaped like an L. The parking lot was filled with girls, scrubbed and shiny, God's girls, all dressed alike because that's the way He loved us, evenly. Books were clutched against breasts, hair tucked behind ears, socks pulled high, only the knees showing and a few inches of thigh, and God notwithstanding, there were pretty knees, ugly knees, knobby ones like skulls, fat and freckled ones, and some so beautifully shaped they could take your breath away.

On my way in, I saw two of my St. Rita's friends, Marisa and a black-eyed girl named Lisa Guardino, but I knew I wouldn't be seeing any of the boys from St. Rita's. Sacred Heart was an all-girls school, no boys to distract us, to make us silly and stupid, vain or jealous—that was the theory, anyway, though we were perfectly capable of being all these things without boys around. Still, the hope was that without boys or pretty clothes, makeup or jewelry, we could pay attention to what mattered: our souls, college. It made me feel important and serious, like I was off to my first day of work.

In homeroom that morning, there was nobody I knew. At the desk in front of me, however, was someone who immediately caught my interest. She sat straight in her chair and her raven-black hair, which fell to her shoulders, was brushed to such a high sheen it was almost blue. Her hands, which she kept flat on the desk, were small, olive-skinned, the nails filed into perfect moons; she wore one gold ring. She was paying strict attention to our homeroom nun. She didn't fidget once. In fact, she hardly seemed to be breathing.

The nun was welcoming us to Sacred Heart. "Young Christian women" she called us, and it was the first time I'd ever heard myself described as a woman, not a girl. I was thirteen.

When the bell rang and we packed up our books to leave for our first class, the girl in front of me turned around. She had sable-colored eyes, black eyebrows, and thin, curved lips. She was small-boned, so the uniform was almost cute on her. "Like lemmings," she said, as we began filing out. Her eyes were worried, but there was a snicker in her voice. We exchanged names.

"Sylvia," she said, sounding out each syllable, so the S was a whisper and the *a* tilted up, and I knew that was how her mother said her name, and that her mother loved her.

She repeated my name in the same precise, silky way—"Kathee"—and we became friends.

I only have three photographs of Sylvia DeAngelis now. It's hard to believe that I don't have more. She was my closest friend through all four years of high school, and for a while it seemed we shared everything, even birthdays (almost). We were excited when we found out our birthdays were just one day apart, and both of us were Scorpios. It was Sylvia who told me what that meant—we were powerful, we were difficult. She never mentioned that we were supposed to be intensely sexual, too. That didn't interest her as much as our hot temper and talent for revenge. Sylvia had only two books in her house when I first knew her: the Bible and *Linda Goodman's Sun Signs*.

"Don't cross a Scorpio," she said, cocking one inky eyebrow so she looked knowing and dangerous—like someone in one of those old movies she liked to watch. She had a wiseass attitude but a wide-open heart. Sometimes when she looked at me, her eyes would literally shine with love.

In two of the photos I have, she sits at the piano that was tucked in a corner of her family's living room. In the first, she's curled on the bench, elbow on one knee, face resting on her hand. Her bangs swoop over one half of a neatly plucked eyebrow as she stares moodily off into space. In the second, she's banging away on the piano, an unlit cigarette hanging from one corner of her mouth. Her lips are slightly parted as if she's about to say something to me—the photographer. I can almost hear her: "Of all the gin joints . . ." She just couldn't hold the deep angst pose for long.

In the third photograph, taken in the fall of our fifteenth year, she and I are standing in front of a brick wall in winter jackets, unsmiling, our fists raised in the Black Power salute. Both of us wear our hair parted in the middle, and it hangs flat on our heads. We look as limp, as slatternly, as laundry in the rain.

But I'm getting ahead of myself here. At thirteen, Sylvia and I weren't posing for the world. She wasn't trying to subvert her impishness and become someone *serious*. I hadn't yet brought Ayn Rand and *The Virtue of Selfishness* into our lives. I had no need for Rand's elitism or Black Power salutes or any fuck-you gesture to the world. Not yet. Not then.

The first time Sylvia came over to my house for dinner, shortly after we met that fall, she was shocked to see us all sit down at the kitchen table together and wait for my father to lead us in prayer.

"In the name of the Father, the Son, and the Holy Ghost . . ." Sylvia made the sign of the cross and bowed her head with the rest of us, but she made bug eyes at me from across the table, nervous and admiring. I was delighted. In fact, I was bursting with pride—in her, in my family. I couldn't wait to discuss them with her later.

After everyone had been served, we began to make up limericks, with each person at the table contributing a line. Sylvia couldn't believe that she was expected to join in, but of course she was; even little Stephen played.

"There once was a man named Jack."

"He liked to eat on his back."

"He put soup up his nose."

"It smelled like a rose."

"Stephen! Your turn!" we called out in unison, every voice artificially sweetened for our little boy child.

"And it smelled good," he said triumphantly, brandishing his spoon. Sylvia laughed aloud, her laugh ending in a purr.

"He's so cute!" she kept exclaiming. She was the youngest in her family, so Stephen and Beth Ann were amazingly adorable to her.

Sylvia thought my family was perfect. Somehow she seemed to have missed all of the storms raging around Bill. She noted the prayers and games at dinner, the way everyone, even the boys, helped clean up afterward, and then how we each set about our chores—one of us making our sandwiches for school the next day, one mixing the pitchers of powdered milk, another mixing the frozen orange juice in the blender for breakfast. Sometimes Sylvia said we were like the Brady Bunch, sometimes like a well-run army.

"Your parents are so young!" she used to exclaim. "Everyone's so smart!" She was amazed at the bookshelves that were everywhere—in the living room, the dining room, and each of our bedrooms. She saw our dinner table games as deeply competitive and highly educational. She had a working-class view of us—she thought we were always sharpening our wits on one another, always having to perform. She figured we'd each go far.

If Sylvia saw my family as a shining army, I saw hers as a renegade division hiding out in the woods, quarreling, snickering, deeply loyal to one another, suspicious of outsiders, and weary, weary to the bone. They ran a little grocery store in New Haven and worked six and a half days a week; later Sylvia would call herself "the original latchkey kid."

Night came early at Sylvia's house—there was no effort to hold it off as the daylight hours grew shorter with the advance of fall. After dinner, Mr. DeAngelis went through all the rooms of the house, checking the lights and doors and windows like a sentry on patrol. He was a short man with wide, plaintive eyes and furry eyebrows. Before he closed the curtains, he peered out each window. He opened and closed the front door, relocking it. He bent over each lamp and clicked it on, then off.

Behind his back, Sylvia saluted him. "Reporting for duty, *sir*!" she said, but Mr. DeAngelis was almost deaf so he didn't hear her. She marched stiffly behind him, hands clasped at her back, bowing from the waist into the lamps and then cocking her head as though to listen as she switched them on and off, on and off. Mr. DeAngelis noticed nothing. He was lifting the phone from its cradle, checking for a dial tone. Sylvia saluted a standing lamp. "All quiet on the Western Front," she announced.

Our families seemed like perfect opposites, so we were deeply drawn to each other's. In my house, night and day were cleanly divided. At bedtime, doors were shut and lights went out; quiet reigned in every room, on every floor, the house a no-man's-land until dawn. Morning was sunlight and raucous cheer, little Stephen throwing himself on top of me in my bed, crowing like a rooster to wake me, and then all of us racing about to open the venetian blinds and curtains and chase away the gloom.

In Sylvia's house, drapes kept the living room shrouded from every sunny day. At night, the room was locked in permanent twilight. The watery gaze of the TV flickered over the walls, the chairs, the flowered couch, the figures of her parents and of Albie, the older of her two brothers. Albie couldn't have been more than twenty-five then, but his receding hairline and heavy jowls gave him the bare, humble look of a much older man. Stretched out in the gray flickering light, mouth wide open, he seemed like a figure in someone's dream, or in a painting. *Drowning Man* you might have called it, or simply, *The Grocer's Oldest Son*.

Mr. DeAngelis would sit tilted sideways against the arm of the couch, his hands folded meekly between his legs, while Mrs. D. nodded off at the other end. Notch by notch, her head would fall toward her chest until suddenly with a snort, she'd crank it back up again.

"It looks like a mortuary in here," Sylvia would say in her Boris Karloff voice.

Then she'd shake her father's shoulder. "Dad! Dad! Go to bed! Go up to bed now!" I could imagine many a strange thing, but a girl ordering her father to bed was not one of them.

Albie lived at home and helped out at the grocery store whenever he didn't have an outside job. I liked him a lot. He was very sweet and very paranoid. He thought someone was snooping in their mail and bugging their phone.

"The FBI?" Norman, the younger brother, often teased him. "Think the FBI wants you? Or maybe the CIA? I think it's the nut farm that wants you."

Both of Sylvia's brothers had gone to boot camp at Parris Island, but Albie had had to be shipped home.

"They broke him," Sylvia told me, initiating me into some of the DeAngelis family mythology, for that was the explanation they used to account for Albie's paranoia.

Norman survived training and became a marine. The first time I saw him, one afternoon that fall when Sylvia and I had just started to become friends, he was bent over a bowl of pasta, hair in his eyes, as he sucked strands of spaghetti into his mouth. I'd come in the front door, looking for Sylvia, and there he was in a white tank top, sitting at the kitchen table, facing me but looking into his pasta bowl. Only the living room was between us. His lips were shiny with oil. His cheekbones looked like Indian arrowheads. I was glued to the carpet. Sylvia hadn't told me she had this kind of a brother. He had muddy eyes and a marine's blue tattoo on his arm. He rode a Harley. Even his name seemed significant to me—Nor*man*. He was my first, astonishing experience of love at first sight. The feeling was like a black-and-white film suddenly going full color. Or the other way around.

When he finally looked up and noticed me standing there, he said nothing, just stared at me in silence for a long moment, then went back to his pasta. He was hungry, I could tell. Very hungry.

A strand of leather was tied around his left wrist. He had long fingers, a man's large knuckles, the skin darker there—oh, I noted it all.

Norman could tame a wasp with those fingers. I saw him do it on a warm autumn day a few weeks later. He was working on his bike in their driveway. The wasp had flown into a narrow piece of pipe where it was turning itself in circles, lifting its long legs and making a furious buzzing sound. Norman slipped his finger inside slowly, slowly, and then he was petting the wasp, its soft back end, and when he withdrew his finger, the wasp followed, hanging on almost wistfully.

"See?" he said. "He likes it."

I felt sure I would kiss him someday—it came to me in a flash.

Then I put the idea away. Impossible. I was just his little sister's girl-friend. He hardly noticed me.

"So the CIA's after you?" Norman asked. It was early October, a Sunday, the only day the store was closed, and we were eating in the dining room at the big table where an oilcloth had been set over the white lace tablecloth to keep it looking nice. We helped ourselves to the bowl of ziti and sauce, the plate of fried eggplant, the tomato and bread salad soaked in olive oil and salt. There was a bottle of soda on the table, forbidden in my house because the sugar would ruin your teeth.

Albie giggled, and then went owly serious. "They might be." Norman looked at him hard. "You know what? You're screwy. You're messed up in the head."

Albie laughed. "I got a screw loose," he said. He looked appealingly at me, then at Norman. "Right? A screw loose in my head."

Norman relaxed. "One screw? You got a whole toolbox rattling around in there." Even Mrs. D. laughed.

"A whole toolbox in here," Albie said happily, childishly, pointing to his head.

"What do you think, Kathy?" Norman asked, jerking his chin at me, his eyes clear as rain. "Time to commit?"

They were constantly asking my opinion, as if glad to finally have a witness to all their crazy goings-on. I loved it. I felt like they needed me.

"Pa!" Norman shouted. "Pa! They're coming to take Albie away! They're taking your son to the funny farm, Pa!"

Mr. D. looked at me, raised his eyebrows, and tapped the side of his head.

"You don't care, Pa? I'm talking about your son. You know what they say—the fruit don't fall far from the tree." Suddenly, Norman smiled. The smile lengthened and narrowed his jaw. White teeth flashed; a lickable wolf.

"Don't you talk to your father that way!" Mrs. D. said, and then, just like that, she was mad. She went lipless, hawklike, black eyebrows arching up into a furious V.

"He works fourteen hours a day, a slave to that store, all he does is work and sleep so you can sit there with your smart mouth and—"

"Who asked him to?" Norman said, shoving his plate away, then his chair. "I'm leavin'."

Outside in the driveway, the Harley exploded into life. Then came the earsplitting chocka-chocka-chocka as he rolled past the dining room windows where we sat. He hit the shady street, ploughing it with noise. The roar faded, but so slowly that after a while I wasn't sure if I was hearing the last sounds of the bike crossing the New Haven line or just a stunned echo in my ears.

For a few minutes I couldn't see anything clearly. There was the sound of silverware on plates, of Albie saying . . . what? What did he just say?

The late-afternoon sunlight lay weakly on the table, across half-empty plates, oil smears, a wadded-up napkin. How dull it all was.

The only signs that Norman had been there among us were a crumpled Marlboro pack and the scent of Aramis on the phone receiver, which I noticed when I called home later that evening to ask my mother's permission to stay over. I closed my eyes and held the receiver against my lips. My breath slowed, and there was a sensation of warm water running down the nape of my neck and my spine. I had no idea when I'd see Norman again. Sylvia had already told me about a time he'd gotten so mad that he took off and drove his Harley straight across the country to California.

But there were wonderful nights when Norman made it through a whole dinner, lazily snapping at Albie, Albie happily egging him on, Mrs. D. laughing and Mr. D. asking what I thought of it all. Then Sylvia and I would clear the dishes and Norman would light a cigarette, and I'd pray he would stay around.

One night when he did, I watched him as he sat there in his white tank top, his jeans and motorcycle boots, playing with their dog. She was an Alaskan malamute, a silvery, blue-eyed creature he'd named Queenie. Norman buried his face in her fur, roughing it up with his hands.

"Who's my girl, huh? Who's my girl?" he said, his voice suddenly high and sweet. Queenie barked, jumped up on him, ran her wet snout through his long hair.

"She likes to smoke," Norman told me, lighting a Marlboro. "Watch this, Kathy." (My name in his mouth!)

"Sit, Queenie, sit!" he said, and she immediately went down on her haunches, watching his face for her signal.

As soon as he took a long drag off the Marlboro, her tail started sweeping the floor. He held the smoke in, looked hard at her, and then jerked his chin up. Queenie jumped on him again, her mouth open, and he blew the smoke in. She slurped and bit the air. And then she licked his lips with her long red tongue. Barked for more.

10

Little Woman

MY BROTHER BILL'S FIRST GIRLFRIEND REMINDED ME OF A CUPCAKE. Becky was dark-haired, dark-eyed, round-breasted, and so sweet and softly feminine at thirteen that I could see why Bill was always pulling her onto his lap. Whenever my parents went out, Becky baked cakes in our kitchen, chocolate with pink icing, letting the rest of us lick the batter off the spoon. Every cake she baked was in the shape of a heart. The day I'm remembering she and Bill were wound tightly around each other on the living room couch, snuggled in the corner, kissing. She was wearing a white blouse with little ruffles along the neckline, and she seemed to fit perfectly into Bill's arms. While Cindy and I watched unnoticed from the stairway, enchanted and jealous—but of which one?—Bill worked his hand into her blouse, then her white bra, rubbing her breast while she made mewing sounds like a kitten. The nipple was tawny-colored, like a doe's eye. I didn't have any breasts to speak of yet. Once again Bill was our scout, leading the way into strange new lands.

I was on my own scouting expedition one day not long after that, snooping around my parents' bedroom, when I made a strange discovery. It was late afternoon, the light liquid in the big mirror over their dresser, no one in the house but me. On the dresser top was a mirrored, gold-framed tray and on it, my mother's lipsticks, all deep shades of red. Except for the occasional dab of powder on her nose, that was the only makeup she wore.

One by one, I opened the lipsticks, sniffing them, examining the subtle differences between Rose Red and Geranium. I rummaged through her jewelry box, picked out a pair of jet-black earrings and held them up to my ears, checking myself out in the mirror—pretty. In one of her dresser drawers, I found her pastel-colored nightgowns and her panty hose. Thick white cotton socks were piled next to lacy bikini underwear, and on some of those the elastic bands were frayed. Since I preferred a completely romantic vision of my mother's femininity, I closed the drawer and moved on to her closet. Her dresses hung neatly there and I ran one hand over them, like I was stroking a harp, and they released her scent. They smelled of Dove and Secret and Alberto VO5 and, underneath, some essence that brought me back to childhood when my mother seemed like some large, warm animal with tiger-colored eyes and miles of downy skin.

Then I noticed two books on the overhead shelf, peeking out from behind some shoe boxes. We never hid books in our house, so of course I had to look. *The Godfather* and *Valley of the Dolls*. I glanced through them quickly—I didn't know when my mother might come home—and put them back.

Over the next few weeks, I returned to her closet again and again until I'd read both books from beginning to end, and then one more time to reread page ninety-seven of *The Godfather*. Sonny and the bridesmaid. He lifts her up onto the sink. A hard thrusting, and all the while the bride and groom smile and dance for the guests downstairs. "Insides like pasta," the wives cackle. I stumbled around the house in a daze.

My parents said I lived too much in my imagination. My head was in the clouds. Or in a book. To them, it must've seemed as if I'd tucked myself into a dream, far, far from reality. But books weren't a hideaway, they were an invitation. Even their titles seemed to me like inscriptions on stone archways, doorways to . . . well, something more real than the world around me. *The Power and the Glory, Long Day's Journey into Night, The Heart of the Matter*. Those were my mother's books, the ones she left lying out on the coffee table or arranged neatly on shelves, co-conspirators in plain sight.

On the bathroom radiator was my father's copy of *Pale Fire*. It sat there for a year, picking up the smells of Fantastik and Ajax. I thought it was a key to my father's mind, and when I couldn't make heads or tails of it, I was deeply impressed.

I read erratically, racing through some books cover to cover, abandoning others after a paragraph or two. When I cracked open *The Heart of the Matter*, I was intrigued by its first lines: "The police van took its place in the long line of army lorries waiting for the ferry. Their headlamps were like a little village in the night. . . ." But then I came to the phrase "red laterite slope," which I didn't understand and didn't like the sound of anyway, and I closed the book, put Graham Greene aside.

Reading this way was like seeing the countryside through the windows of a fast-moving train. Drunken priests, knife fights, donkeys on a trail, a thief in the house—the variety, the possibilities out there were staggering. I found *The Outsiders* on my own, and soon I was filled with visions of boys in gangs, boys living dangerously, romantically, on the streets.

That spring, I began to notice the shaggy-haired boys in their Army coats and dungaree jackets hanging outside the old firehouse on Putnam Avenue, only three and a half blocks from our house. I'd heard the adults debate whether they were juvenile delinquents or just bored kids. I hoped they were delinquents. The town of Hamden had refurbished the firehouse, put in pool tables, a soda machine, and a youth counselor, and officially named it the Teen Center. Every time we drove by in the station wagon, I'd sneak a look at them, those wild, beautiful boys, and I began to wonder what it would feel like if they were trying as hard to sneak a look at me.

Almost every book I read, except for *The Outsiders* (and *Little Women* and *Christy*, of course), was written by a man. I assumed the role of the protagonist in each, and if most of them were men, so what? It made no difference to me. I, too, would swoon at the sight of a beautiful woman, bare-shouldered, in a silver dress. Who wouldn't?

The women in the stories I read incited lust, memory, hope, despair. That was fine, but it wasn't a life. Being the one who *felt* those feelings, that's what mattered.

Secretly, I had begun to think that my father and I were alike, if for no other reason than the fact that I didn't want to be stuck in the house like my mother. My father wouldn't have thought that he and I were alike; he couldn't think that way, couldn't because he was a man and I was a girl. But I could slip my skin at will.

I was fourteen and the world was whispering, whispering. I thought it was talking to me in particular.

One day when my father was driving us home from church, all of us in our Sunday clothes in the blue station wagon, we passed a girl wearing dungaree cutoffs walking up Clifford Street. She had long, tanned legs and long blond hair that brushed her hips as she walked. From the backseat I saw my father's head swivel, my mother's shoulders tighten. My father didn't even notice that he had turned to look. He went on talking like nothing had happened.

She was a part of spring's beauty, that girl, same as the forsythia blooming. I, too, wanted to drink her in with my eyes. Study her until I'd had enough. And I wanted to be her, too, collecting stares as I walked down the street, pulling fathers from their suitlike selves. I was confused, but in a completely interesting way.

There was a sort of destiny in this moment. Watching that girl through my father's eyes, I sensed the future, the day when I, too, would saunter down the street in cutoffs. But unlike that girl, when my time came, I would be conscious of my effect. Fourteen, and it was getting harder and harder to wait.

11

Jailbait

"I WANT TO EAT YOUR PUSSY." AS HE DROVE THE TRUCKER HELD THE SIGN up to his window for me to see. He'd printed it out in large capital letters, and must have carried it with him to relieve the loneliness and boredom of the road. To me, it read like an SOS in a world of strangers.

There we were, rolling across the country that summer of my fourteenth year on a six-week vacation in a motor home, my father at the wheel of the lumbering beast, sitting up high over the road, my mother and Michael his copilots, Henry Mancini thundering from the stereo speakers. My father liked his music loud.

We still had a long road ahead of us. First we'd gone north to Niagara Falls, now we were heading west across Canada, all the way to Vancouver, where my father wanted to tour the university. After that, our destination was the university at Long Beach, California, where my father would be attending the National Association of College and University Food Service conference.

There was a kitchen table in the middle of the motor home, which folded into a bed for Cindy and me. During the day, Cindy and Beth spent a lot of time at that table, working on their vacation scrapbooks or playing Mad Libs, while Stephen sat next to them coloring. Above the driver's seat was a big, glossy-looking cabinet that opened into a bunk bed for my parents. At night, we could hear my father snoring.

A skinny corridor led to the back of the motor home, where overhead cabinets opened into beds for Bill and Michael. Beth Ann and Stephen slept on the couches underneath. "Six weeks in a tin can with all you boneheads" was how Bill described our trip.

When Henry Mancini filled the motor home, Bill directed the orchestra mockingly—if he was in a good mood. But mainly he wasn't. He didn't want to be with us. He spent most of his time stretched full-length on one of the foldout couches in the back, his eyes closed, perhaps asleep, perhaps just wishing he could be asleep, asleep like Rip Van Winkle, waking in six weeks when our vacation was over.

I spent a lot of time in the back, too. Sitting there at the wide window, I could make contact with the men driving behind us, and my parents couldn't see what was going on. Truckers saluted me with their horns. Men followed in their cars. I carried on conversations with them, first mouthing the words, then writing them notes. They rode our bumper so they could read what I'd written.

When the trucker showed me his "I Want to Eat Your Pussy" sign, I thought quickly, and wrote out a reply: "Meow." His eyes went wide and then he blasted his airhorn.

In the middle of one of these conversations, two dark-haired men in a red car held up a piece of paper reading, "Jailbait." I bent over my pad of construction paper, and carefully printed my response: "Want to Go Fishing?"

For a couple of seconds their faces went blank; then they laughed in astonishment. I could see them talking animatedly to each other. The driver had a mustache and a wide white smile, the passenger's hair was tied back into a ponytail. They followed us for miles down that sunlit highway, through the late afternoon. Henry Mancini gave way to Billie Holiday, Billie to Neil Young, he and the Beatles my parents' only concession to us kids, and still they were there. So there I was, stuck in the back window like a mannequin.

I was stunned by my effect—grown men, good-looking men!—deeply flattered, but no longer happy. Didn't they have somewhere else to go? We had just met and suddenly we were going steady, me and these two men in their red car. As the sun lowered, I squirmed in my skin, more worm than hook now. There at the back window, I'd run out of postures, run clean out of things to say to them. As Jailbait, my conversational topics were limited.

When we exited the highway, they did, too. When we turned in at the KOA campground, they were right behind us. By the time they'd paid the campground fee, I was beside myself with agitation. They were too close, too close . . . right there with me and my family. Cinderella and Lolita were not compatible roles.

They parked in the campsite next to us, and when my father went out to hook up the electricity and water, they started chatting with him. "How many miles per gallon do you get in this thing?" My father noticed nothing, not even the fact that these men were tentless, trailerless, extraordinarily idle.

For a long time, I was too nervous to leave the motor home, and when I did, I grabbed my baby brother's hand and dragged him with me like a prop. As soon as we came to the door, the men's faces flared up, but I bent down to Stephen and whispered in his ear. I took him and his trucks to the picnic table set up at the edge of the parking lot. While he played, I caressed his hair.

When I felt their impatience growing, I put my feet up on the bench and rebuckled my sandals, brushing invisible dirt from my leg. Once or twice I dared a glance, a look that I hoped was like a rope, saying, "Hold on." I hoped some form of action would occur to me. Perhaps, by nighttime, when my family had fallen asleep . . .

They left the campground in an angry scud of pebbles and exhaust. In one hour's time, I'd gone from being the most desirable bit of jailbait in the world to a stupid cocktease.

For most of our trip that summer I wore hip-hugger jeans, halter tops, big hoop earrings, and an Army cap Sylvia had given me as a going-away present. I had two halter tops, one candy-striped, the other a yellow mesh that clung softly to my breasts and allowed glimpses of skin to show through the little holes, quick peeks of snow white and shell pink. I didn't wear a bra; my mother said there wasn't anything there to support yet, and, technically speaking, she was quite right.

As soon as we'd left Connecticut, she and I had started arguing about the halter tops. She forbade me to wear them in Vancouver or at my father's conference in California.

"I'm ashamed to be seen with you," she said. "Do you have any idea what you look like in those?" Before I could think of a reply, she went on. "You look awful. You look like—"

"To *you* I do," I broke in quickly. "I don't care what you think. I'm not dressing this way for you."

"Who *are* you dressing that way for, then?"

"Myself," I said haughtily. "You dress the way you want to dress, I dress the way I want to dress. I don't make fun of your clothes."

"Kathy, I'm not making fun of your clothes, and besides, I'm a grown woman and you're—"

"And so? I'm a woman, too."

"Kathy, you are not! You're a fourteen-year-old girl."

Almost a decade after the fact, my mother had suddenly begun to regret allowing me to skip kindergarten. "That's where the trouble began," she explained to me. She shouldn't have listened to the nursery-school teacher who had told her I was ready for real schoolwork, she said, because "emotionally, you were too immature."

Never mind, I told myself, tying my halter top at my back; even if what she said was true, and part of me thought it was, I was not going to live in her vision of me. That summer I'd discovered another gaze, the gaze of boys and men, and in that shining light I felt myself blooming. No longer Kathy, oldest daughter, big sister, mother's helper, I was feeling the first whiff of real freedom in my life: Who might I become?

"Beaver." The day after I'd disappointed the men in the campground, two men at a truck stop spoke the word when I walked by on my way to the ladies' room. Their faces were brown and red from the sun. They were smiling at me but talking to each other. Beaver? To be honest, I didn't know what these men were saying half the time. When I took a stab at the meaning of "cleaver beaver," I pulled back almost immediately. *No, can't be*, I thought. But maybe it was. There seemed to be a continent of men out there who had made up a language that was as dirty, as strange, as the thing itself. Makin' bacon. Jelly roll. Busting cherry. They said it aloud. They said it to me. They figured I knew.

And I could fake it pretty easily. I just stuck with the metaphor of the moment and riffed.

I know we stopped at all kinds of state parks with mountains and glaciers as we headed west, but I don't remember any of them. Canada was nothing but truck drivers to me; harbingers of the world to come. Prosaic by day—red duckbill caps, *Playboy* Bunny stickers, sweat stains, sunburn—they changed into pure spirits at night as I lay awake in the motor home, listening as they rolled down the highway, riding high, headlights bent into the dark country ahead. When the sun rose, they would take on human shape again, call the waitress "doll," ask for a cup of "diesel fuel."

My mother argued with me over my halter tops, with Bill over his grammar. "It don't make no difference to me," Bill would say and burp loudly.

"It *doesn't* make *any* difference," she'd correct him, looking pained.

"That's what I said. It don't matter neither way."

My mother knew her English, knew what a dangling participle was, a split infinitive, how to diagram a sentence and write a term paper. For a long time, we had been in awe of that and her piano-playing and her ability to pronounce the French words on a menu, but in the last year, her older children had begun to tease and harass her. The harder she tried to maintain her dignity, the more we went after her. She must have felt like she was trying to run from wasps.

One night when we were all camping out in the big blue tent, my mother spoke in her sleep, clear as a bell. "Bah bah, black sheep." We stifled our giggles, called out, "What's that, Mom?" We wanted to lead her deeper into it, but she got cagey, even in her sleep, and said stiffly, "Never mind. You wouldn't understand."

That had us rolling inside our sleeping bags. We couldn't wait until the morning to give her a hard time.

She was my mother, but that year, after an entire childhood of being close to obsessed with her, trying to read her every thought and feeling, admiring her to the point of adoration, she ceased to be anything more for me: not the Catholic schoolgirl feverishly writing her high school essay on blacklisted Graham Greene, not the eighteen-year-old my father met who, on their first date, rolled the car window all the way down and let the wind play havoc with her hair. Or for that matter, the nineteen-year-old who dropped out of college and married my father against her mother's wishes, then had six kids, one after the other, while Grandma Callahan cried, "It's just too many!"

Her act of rebellion had spawned us, a big happy family, and now the rebellious girl was a mother, shepherding, correcting, corralling her teenage children. Even now I sometimes wonder why my parents were so surprised by the mass mutiny of our adolescent years—an act of rebellion was our very genesis.

In San Francisco, we escaped the motor home for a couple of days and checked into an old hotel. Bill and I found ourselves alone in a room on the third floor one afternoon. All across Canada, Bill's restlessness had plagued me. I had tried to be interesting to him, to fill in for his long-haired friends with their hash oil and their windowless vans. When he talked about running away back to Hamden, I volunteered to go with him. He wanted to be with his friends, and I wanted to be with him.

I sat on the windowsill that day, watching him as he pulled out a cigarette. A dirty neon sign blinked and buzzed outside. A breeze stirred the velvet curtains, moth-bitten and maroon. The sill was covered in soot. I straddled it, one leg suspended above the jangling street below, one in the dimly lit room.

"I smoke, too," I told him.

"You do not," he said absently. He paced the floor, frowning.

"I do, too! How would you know?"

"Okay," he said, coming over to me and holding out the cigarette. "Go ahead, take a drag."

"Drag" was a clue, but I couldn't read it. At the first puff, the smoke leaked out of my mouth. He laughed. "You smoke like a girl," he said, "and you walk like a boy." I decided I would learn to smoke like a boy and walk like a girl.

It was tricky figuring out the best way to be a girl. Love and loathing were aimed at her in equal strengths. Wearing a halter top was teaching me that. But at fourteen, I thought I could reap the desire and dodge the loathing.

The morning we arrived at Long Beach for my father's conference, there were several other families pulling into the parking lot at the same time. The fathers were shaking hands, the mothers standing by with their smiles, and then I saw him—a teenage son, long and lean with big, lazy eyes. He looked as silky and clean as a cat. He stood behind his mother and father, taller than either of them, his face blank, like he was taking a break behind it. But then those big, lazy eyes landed on me. He blinked.

When I went into the dormitory where we'd all be sleeping, the boy followed me.

"My name is Greg," he whispered, lips close to my ear. "What's yours?" All over my body, little hairs stood at attention. Our families were coming down the corridor, carrying suitcases and piles of clothes.

"We'll be together for three days now," he said, like we'd met long ago and had been waiting for just this chance. As soon as I slipped inside one of the rooms assigned to my family, I fell down on the bed. I lay very still; my body chattered excitedly.

Of all the feminine role models I had in my head, the woman in the whipped cream dress on the cover of my father's Tijuana Brass album was my favorite. Dark-haired and large-breasted; long-lashed and coy.

There was a bit of cream in her hair, and more she was licking from her finger. She was like a window into men's brains. When we were seven and eight, Cindy and I used to put on our white go-go boots (a present from Grandma and Great-aunt Bert) and dance in the living room, sliding over the shag carpet and twisting our hips to the *sexeeee!* lady in the whipped-cream dress, to nakedness and dessert.

In the dorm room shower that night, I arranged the shampoo lather over my breasts and posed in front of the mirror. My breasts seemed bigger, one pink nipple peeked out of the cream. Something so beautiful and it would never be seen. Something so powerful and it would always be hidden. Why? It seemed almost sad to me that I had become this creature—beautiful, sexy—and no one would see me as I was in this bathroom, naked and covered with cream.

I had always looked at girls with a boy's admiration, a very young, very inspired boy. I admired girls' angora sweaters, their painted nails and puzzle rings, the patchouli oil and silver bangles, their sharp little bones and hilly breasts. I looked at my girlfriends' teddy bears with their button eyes and stitched-on smiles, fuzzy bedtime companions waiting to be tucked in, and thought them the very picture of dumb luck. I watched a silver crucifix slipping into shadow and felt I'd never seen anything more beautiful. *Boys must go crazy for this girl*, I'd think.

I could put on hoop earrings and a flowery blouse, but being female still felt like a bit of an act to me, an act my mother discouraged and my grandmother encouraged. My mother didn't want me to care what I looked like, didn't want her fourteen-year-old to look sexy or even know that she could. My grandmother simply wanted me dressed in the latest styles. She liked accessories—bone bracelets, wooden beads, smart-looking belts, clever little pocketbooks. I didn't want my clothes to be that thoughtful. A halter top went straight to the point; it started its own conversations. Wearing one was as good as having a personality.

I don't know where the haunted house was, but we were all in it the next day, all the mothers and kids on a day trip, following a tour guide down a hallway, when Greg's hand folded itself around mine. How long his fingers were! No one looked down; nobody saw.

Then we were in a high-ceilinged room and they shut off the lights—everyone gasped—and he bent down and kissed me on the lips. Petal soft, his lips; petal soft, his hair swinging against my face.

When the lights came back on, we looked straight ahead, unseeing. Greg was still holding my hand.

Back at the dorm, Greg asked me if I wanted to meet him that night. I nodded yes. I felt as cool and shivery as a bowl of jello.

"You know the field past the parking lot?"

I nodded again.

"Meet me there at ten o'clock."

I was absolutely certain I was going to meet him and then, when the time drew near, absolutely certain I wasn't. I was terrified. I didn't know how I was supposed to act, how to tongue kiss, where my hands were supposed to go, which clothes would come off and when. I didn't even wear a bra! I was an impostor, not a girl at all, and Greg would know.

From inside the motor home, behind the big window, I could leer and beckon, but out on that field, there would be nothing between him and me. This boy was sweet and normal-acting—he would expect me to do or say *something*. But if the lady in the whipped cream dress opened her mouth, what would she say? "Meow"? My imagination stopped there.

It didn't matter, though. I *couldn't* go to him, no matter how much I wanted to, because . . . why? Because my mother and father had locked me in the room. Then I locked the door myself so my lie would become the truth. And then I paced, door to window, window to door, cursing my parents for locking me in. Nine-forty-five, nine-fifty . . .

By ten, my body was electric. I pictured Greg arriving and standing alone in the field, looking for me. I sat down on the bed. By tenfifteen, I was wishing for a cigarette. By ten-thirty, I wished I were another girl altogether. I wished Greg would burst in through the window, and that he had never existed at all. When the clock struck eleven, I jimmied the window screen open and slipped outside.

I crouched low until I'd passed the lighted windows, then I ran. The field was empty. I sat in the grass for a while, torturing myself with his absence. But the grief I felt disappeared every time I heard a twig snap—oh no, he's coming back! As soon as the silence returned, I let myself feel lonely again.

Finally I left the field, slid back in through the window, and went to bed. As I lay there thinking about the evening, I was relieved to be done with it. And frustrated, disgusted. To rob from yourself! Is there anything more bitter than that?

The next morning, we dragged our suitcases out to the parking lot. The conference had ended. Greg and his family were packing up their car. Every time he bent to pick up a suitcase, his hair fell across his eyes. He wouldn't look at me. Finally, I found a moment to approach him.

"What happened to you last night?" he said accusingly.

"My parents locked me in the room," I whispered. "I couldn't get out! When they fell asleep, I snuck out the window but you were already gone."

"I waited for you for an hour," he said sorrowfully, as though he hadn't even heard me. He was looking off into the distance, at the image of himself perhaps, shining and then hangdog in the grass. Just then his mother called him and he walked toward their car.

"Okay, guys, time to saddle up!" my father announced. Our families pulled out on the road at the same time, with everyone hanging out the windows, waving and yelling good-bye—everyone except for Greg. He had settled himself in the backseat and was busy looking in the other direction. As we headed down the highway that day, the tires flapped on the pavement: *last chance, last chance*, they said, *blew it, blew it, blew it*.

There was a phrase the adults sometimes used if you missed a game or a day of fun, reading perhaps, or hiding under the dining room table listening to the little people you were sure lived inside the wood. "The parade's passing you by!" they would call out cheerily, cheerily, in singsong voices, a darker note underneath—warning? disapproval? It always broke my heart.

* * *

One evening after we returned to Hamden at the end of August, my father showed our vacation photos to a man he worked with at Yale. They were sitting on the living room couch while I watched from the piano bench across the room. My father came to a photo of me, posed on a rock in a black bathing suit, my hair long, almost gold after a summer of sun, my skin still shockingly white. "Chickenskin" was the Dobie word for a pale complexion.

"Cheesecake," the man said. And the word hung there, absurd and tantalizing, over the coffee table, the blue-green shag carpet, the upright piano. My father cleared his throat, avoiding my eyes. He looked startled, embarrassed. Quickly he went on to the next photo.

Cheesecake was a door opening, but I had to walk through it alone.

12

Initiation

THERE WAS A MOMENT OF ABSOLUTE CLARITY BEFORE THE STORM OF boys, fingers, tongues, dirty words whispered hotly in my ear, then shouted at my face—the day I decided to lose my virginity.

A warm September day, a summer day almost, the green grass sharp and sticky against my fingers. Sebastian was at my side, an alert little presence, his sturdy white chest and thumping tail; the sheer friendliness of him! And in front of me, as far as the eye could see, rolled the black rivers of Treadwell and Clifford. The traffic, the boys, the men! If my mother was watching from the window, I was finally (triumphantly) indifferent to her gaze, free of worrying about what she thought of me. Sitting there on the lawn that day in my candy-striped halter top and hip-hugger jeans, I was the picture of optimism, the very definition of goodwill toward men.

That evening, when the sly, long-haired stranger I had fished from the street came to pick me up, my parents were waiting in the living room. I'd told them I was going to go to the movies with someone I'd met while running an errand at the grocery store. As soon as Brian walked in the front door, he seemed to speed into fast motion, jerking forward, thrusting out his hand to my father, "Hi-uh-how-you-doing. Glad-to-uh-nice-house." He acted overjoyed to meet them, and kept tucking his long hair behind his ears.

He mentioned his mother, telling them she lived nearby, that we'd be home as soon as the movie was over. My parents' faces were bright with discomfort or confusion, it was hard to tell which. I'd caught them unprepared. Cleverly I'd never used the word *date*; it was just me and a neighborhood guy catching a movie. Brian had almost ruined it with his nervousness and his formality, but he hadn't the time. We were there in the living room for less than three minutes, and then we were gone.

I don't remember how I dressed for the occasion. I know that I had no idea what sex might be like, though I had some of the vocabulary down. The books talked of sucking, biting, plunging, riding, thrashing, so I figured we'd both be pretty active. But it happened much faster than I expected.

We went to the drive-in where *The Godfather* was playing. Another sign! The wedding had just begun when Brian leaned over to kiss me. I was surprised by how slippery it was. He didn't so much kiss as lick me and roll his wet lips over the lower half of my face. I didn't know what to do in return except let him. I couldn't believe I'd been so in the dark—I thought tongues went *inside* mouths!

Before the wedding scene was even over, we left the movie and drove to a small parking lot behind a brick building. When Brian discovered I was having my period, he said, "Wait here," and left the car.

I'd never seen this parking lot, though it was only blocks from my house. A locked metal doorway was labeled "Deliveries" and next to it on the reddish brick, a black scrawl read, "Suck This." Somewhere in the tall wild grass behind the car, a cat cried. I felt like I'd been transported to a different town, a town of back alleys and stray cats and stranded cars. A new map of Hamden was drawing itself in my head—sketched in black and silvery gray.

I couldn't imagine where Brian had gone, but when he came back, he had a towel in his hand.

"Where'd you go?" I asked.

"My mother's house, over there," he said, pointing absently across the parking lot and the street to nothing I could see.

The mother and the towel made things fussier than I thought they'd be. I had to tuck it under me like a coaster. He had trouble getting himself inside and asked, "Are you a virgin?"

"No, of course not."

And then, "Are you *sure* you aren't a virgin?"

"I've had lots of boys," I told him. I wasn't just lying, I was bragging. He told me to stay still.

When I got home, I took a bath because it seemed more reflective than a shower. So I lay there in the bubbles and reflected. I didn't feel any different. I'd thought that sex was something you'd like no matter what. Still, I wasn't disappointed. I had posed and passed my own initiation rite into the world—losing my virginity. I figured now I was ready for my life, the real one, to begin.

The next afternoon, I walked down Treadwell Street swinging my hips and licking my lips. I wanted the boys to know I'd had sex. I was experienced. They didn't have to be careful with me anymore. I'd picked the most surprising sensation from the night before—Brian's mouth gliding wetly over my lips, cheeks, chin—and decided to wear it. I thought wet lips were a universally understood signal, which I alone had failed to recognize. If I could have worn a sign that said, "We're Open. Come On In," I would have. I licked my lips; I swung my hips from side to side.

"The way you used to walk!" my mother told me years later. "I wondered what message you thought you were trying to send." My mother saw me as a bumbler, a girl so solitary and odd that she only *thought* she was trying to send a message. But men heard my message loud and clear; they understood it perfectly.

One day that week, I missed the school bus and walked to Sacred Heart, late for classes and happy about it. I sauntered up Treadwell feeling like a hole had been cut into the day and I'd wriggled through it. My checked school skirt was rolled up high above my knees and my knee socks pushed down at my ankles. I used the heavy school pin to pull my blouse open, though I still wore an undershirt.

After three blocks, the houses and their yards and flowering bushes disappeared and Treadwell began to curve and climb, thick woods on the left, an abandoned factory on the right set below the road. The parking lot was empty; the black tar was cracked and buckled and shimmering with broken glass.

A car stopped and a man leaned over the passenger seat to say hi out the window and ask if I needed a ride. He was in his forties and dressed for golf. Checked pants, an alligator on his white shirt. His clothes were corny to me, even creepy, but his confidence was laid on thick. His eyes were bold and amused. I became aware of my undershirt, a placard on my chest that said, LITTLE GIRL. I hated it.

I leaned into the car and ran my eyes over the upholstery because I couldn't think of anything else to do at the moment. He talked; I gave him a glittering smile. Whatever Brian was, skittish, long-haired, thirty-three-year-old Brian who still lived with his mom, he wasn't a grown-up the way this man was, and losing my virginity to him gave me no clue as to how to behave now. I was a novice all over again.

The day was hot; the light strong and bland. From the trees, birds squeaked monotonously. Occasionally, a car drove by, a woman at the wheel, a child strapped in next to her. A perfectly pleasant and boring sort of day until this man slipped into it.

He was explaining how much sense it made for him to drive me to Sacred Heart—he had time on his hands, I needed to get there—but his eyes, blue as cornflowers, were saying something else. He acted like he knew me, like we were playing a game by rules we both understood. I didn't, but I was mesmerized. I'd never been at the other end of a man's cynicism. It transformed me; suddenly I was worldly-wise. Knobby knees, tiny breasts? Homework? Tricks I pulled to fool stupid little boys. He drove me to school and came back that afternoon to pick me up, suggesting we go to Knudsen's Dairy for ice cream cones.

His name was Victor. He wore a belt, drove a car, had a thick wallet—how can I capture what a grown man feels like to a girl? His flesh is pale and heavy, disgusting and exciting.

He ordered our cones, paid for them; his wrist was tanned and strapped with a heavy gold watch. He was incredibly casual about his maleness. Even when he wasn't looking at me, even when he was busy ordering and paying, I felt his awareness of me, his plans for me on my skin. It was more thrilling than being touched.

We ate our cones sitting at one of the picnic benches outside so we wouldn't mess up his new car. That's what I think we talked about that day, his car and my preference for chocolate ice cream. When we had finished our cones, he said he'd come pick me up at Sacred Heart again tomorrow.

That day I brought a dress to school and changed into it before meeting Victor in the parking lot. It was a backless black wraparound sundress my grandmother had bought for me, a dress for double takes and wolf whistles, and I was sure Victor would be bowled over. I laced my wedged-heel shoes up my ankles. My hair hung loose, covering half of my bare back. I wanted to appear grown-up to Victor. In that dress, I imagined myself as a beautiful, sexually confident woman, the perfect match for a forty-two-year-old man, never realizing, of course, that my schoolgirl uniform was exactly what a man like Victor would prefer.

That afternoon he took me straight to his condo. Victor didn't work. He lived on a trust fund, he said—not that I knew what that meant. He played golf. The rooms of his apartment were pin neat; no dust, no music, not one window cracked open to the outside. The things he talked about left me tongue-tied—golfing tournaments, tennis, money. Except for the huge mystery of what would happen next, an event completely in his hands, I would have been bored, bored in the excruciating way only children can be. But I was too nervous to be bored; my whole body was humming. What did he want from me? When would I know?

Finally, he suggested a massage and told me to take my shoes off and lie facedown on the couch. It was as if he were mocking me. Up until that moment, I hardly recognized myself. I was performing without a script and doing a pretty good job of it, I thought. But once I unlaced my shoes and lay down, I felt drab and ordinary, nothing more than a slow-witted child. "Aren't you going to take your panty hose off?" he asked sarcastically.

He said it like I was being a prude, like "Come on, girl, you know the game," said it and my panty hose became Great-aunt Emma's girdle, and I had to take them off. Then he helped me unwrap my dress and that seemed to be enough for him, to massage me as I lay there in my girl's white underwear. If he had wanted more, I would've gone along, his attention and his scorn my guides.

When I got home late that afternoon, I hardly knew what to feel about Victor. *Thinking* about him was out of the question; there was no analyzing and coming to conclusions, as an adult might do. Every time he appeared in my head—blond, large-thighed, with thick, manicured hands—a dark wave rolled down my body, but I couldn't tell if I felt excited or repelled. If he asked, I knew I'd have to see him again, but I hoped he wouldn't.

Brian didn't have Victor's terrible weight and so when he called and asked me to meet him, I said I couldn't. I didn't understand why *he* wanted to. He'd made sex seem difficult, irksome, like he was trying to do a job with the wrong tools. When he came, he gave one short grunt and right away warned me to stay on the towel until I'd wiped myself off.

On the phone, he sounded surprised that I wouldn't see him, and a little peeved. "Why not?" he asked. I answered truthfully for a change: "I don't know. I just can't."

13

A Democracy of Boys

MEN USHERED ME INTO MY SEXUALITY, BUT I WANTED BOYS, BOYS with light in their eyes, hoarse voices, hard arms, silky chests, bodies that were my size. And the boys I wanted were the bad ones—the confident, aggressive, dirty-minded ones. They put me at ease, the willfulness of their desire excited me. Timidity, awkwardness, efforts to converse, the nicely dressed boy at the door made me feel clumsy, like I was an unwieldy package they would have to get their arms around.

The bad boy was sneaky, clever, always thinking one step ahead. He was kissing me, whispering, "Baby, baby," while he raised his hips to unzip his pants and then fiddled with the snap on my jeans, all the time acting as if I might be so preoccupied with his tongue and his voice that I wouldn't notice what was going on below. I didn't even mind that they assumed they were tricking and pushing me into sex. I was dangerously careless of their opinion of me.

In my impatience for boys, I decided to run away from home. I wrote my good-bye letter, but unlike Bill's terse, heartbreaking notes, mine was an epistle. It went on for pages, though I have no idea what I wrote there. Complaint? Manifesto? A five-year plan? I only re-member going into Bill's bedroom, waking him up, and handing him a sheaf of papers to give to our parents in the morning.

He told me he didn't think Mom could handle it.

"Are you sure you have to go?" he asked, clearing his throat and pushing himself up against the pillows. His hair was smashed against his head, his eyes, clearly visible in the streetlight shining through the window, were cloudy vials of blue. He looked unhappy to be the message bearer, but who else could I ask? I thought he would understand.

"It's gonna kill Mom," he said. "I don't think she can take any more."

I thought it was unfair that he had used up all of her resources and now I wasn't supposed to get my chance. Couldn't he have run away four times instead of five? He didn't ask where I was going or how I was going to survive. He was so guilt-stricken all he could think about was how Mom and Dad would handle this—a second Dobie child running away!

"I've got to get out of here," I told him roughly, for this wasn't what I'd expected at all. He was supposed to see me as his ally, and then ask if I was wearing warm enough clothes, give me money, tell me to meet him later in the week on some street corner.

He took the letter with a sigh, slid it under his pillow, and lay back down.

"Okay, good luck," he said, a little rip cord of pain strung between his eyebrows. I went downstairs, sliding through the silent house, lonelier than I'd expected to be. But as soon as I stepped out the back door, any doubt or guilt I'd felt vanished in the cold night air, the rush to get out of sight. Halfway down Clifford, my heart unknotted and let loose all ties to the sleeping house behind me. I made straight for the Hamden Teen Center, straight and unthinking, as if it had been written down in a book beforehand.

I passed Tom's Market, which stood across from the one-room town library, and then Putnam Avenue Grammar School, hurrying every step of the way until I crossed the street to the empty parking lot that stood directly opposite the center. I sat down on the curb, crouched there, my eyes glued to the door. I had complete faith . . . but in what? I suppose only in that something would happen to me.

While I waited on the curb, one block away Grandpa, Grandma, and Great-aunt Emma would've been tuning in to the evening news while Emma sat in the stiffest chair in the living room, sitting up so straight you thought one day she'd break her own back, sitting as she had sat for forty-five years, smack in the middle of Grandpa and Grandma's marriage.

Two blocks to my left, Great-aunt Bert and Great-uncle Jim would also be watching the news, silently and in their robes. Upstairs, Grandma Callahan would be playing solitaire in front of her TV, an icy glass of Coke on the table next to her, the percolator in the kitchen filled and ready for the following morning when she would rise at dawn to drink her coffee and read the *New Haven Register*, happy to be alone.

But did I think about any of them as I sat on the curb, waiting? Not for a minute. My whole being was craned toward the Teen Center door.

I hadn't taken anything with me that night, no money, no food, no extra clothes. I wore no makeup, nothing sexy—just a T-shirt, jeans, and my fake leather jacket with its fake fur collar, for the September nights had gone cold. I'd thrown off every inessential thing. I walked like a girl but I was running away like a boy. I sat there thinking (without thinking): *Here is where it all begins.*

The Teen Center door opened. Four or five boys and girls came out, then a larger crowd behind. Right away, they caught sight of me. Of course, I was hard to miss. The whole street was empty, no cars, no one walking, just one girl, crouched on the curb across from them, watching.

They turned away and started talking to one another. In the clear autumn night, their voices had a harsh edge. Some of the girls sat on the low cement divider that ran between the firehouse driveway and the little sidewalk leading to the door. The boys stood there talking to them, but they were casting sideways looks at me, sly and curious.

The girls huddled close together, sometimes hugging each other and shivering violently. They couldn't have forgotten I was there, but they acted like they had. Then three boys broke off from the rest, lit cigarettes, and, glancing over at me, drew into a huddle. One of the boys had a baby face and white-blond hair, short and straight and fine and almost colorless in the streetlight. He was wearing a dungaree jacket; the other two had on Army coats. They laughed and smacked their arms against the cold. They acted like all boys seemed to act, as if no one ever watched them. *They* were the watchers, all unaware. They threw down their cigarettes and without any further consultation, crossed over to me.

"Want one?" The blond boy was smiling and holding out his pack of Marlboros. He said his name was Timmy. He kept pushing the bangs off his face only to have them fall back down again. "A sheepdog," my grandfather would've called him.

When they asked if I was from around here, I told them I was running away. Offered it up as tribute and membership dues.

"Where you going?"

"California or New Jersey."

They took that in silently. Smoked. The boy Timmy lifted his chin and blew a perfect smoke ring into the sky.

A man came out of the center, locked the door, and walked away. The others were beginning to drift off, but the boys didn't seem in any hurry to go and I was glad.

"When are you leaving?" Timmy asked.

"Sometime tonight," I told him, wanting to keep things open.

"How you gonna get there?"

"Hitching." I shrugged.

He squatted down next to me. "You can come over there with us if you want," he said, tilting his head toward the group across the street. The other two boys stood there, suddenly looking uncomfortable, like his crouching down next to me had left them unsure of the act of standing. When I stood up to join them, they seemed relieved.

But almost as soon as we walked up to the small group left in front of the firehouse, a girl said, "Timmy, we got to go home now." She was as white blond as he, with the same sunless skin, like they'd been raised under the earth, picnicked in the moonlight on milk and mushrooms.

"My sister," Timmy said gruffly. He had to go.

The other boys said they had to shove off, too. It hadn't occurred to me that my outlaws would have curfews. They told me that if I ever came back, I could find them at the center.

"You want some butts for the road?" Timmy asked. And then I was alone.

What now?

Every lie I told I had to live out. It was a kind of Catholic curse. I hadn't really planned to run away to California or New Jersey, but now I would have to. *I'll go and come right back*, I thought, and then I could hang out with them at the Teen Center.

But I had no idea which highways went to California or New Jersey. I didn't even know how to get to the highway. I thought, *I'll stay at Sylvia's tonight, sleep in her garage or something, and hitch a ride away in the morning.* Maybe she would know where the highway was.

The route to Sylvia's house cut through the reservoir on a small cement bridge that shone white in the streetlight. Then the sidewalk disappeared and the road swooped up, went by shady streets where rich people lived and wrapped itself around one corner of East Rock Park. I was climbing that hill, the park rustling darkly on my right, when a police car pulled in front of me. An arm beckoned from the driver's window. The man inside was middle-aged with gray hair and a wide, worn face, freshly shaved. He was the enemy; anyone really cool would've called him a "pig." But I was happy to see him. It was lonelier out there than I'd thought it would be. When he asked what I was doing, I told him I was going home.

"Do your parents know you're out this late?"

"Oh, yeah. But they're expecting me home now. I think I might be late."

"Well, get going, then. You shouldn't be out here by yourself at night." I waved good-bye and kept walking. Though I told myself I was only going to Sylvia's to sleep in her garage, I had a vague picture in my head of kitchen light, food and talk, macaroni salad, a comradein-arms. But when I got to Sylvia's, the house was dark. I threw some stones at her bedroom window but they landed, clattering, on the side of the house instead—her mother!—so I fled.

I headed back toward the Teen Center. I didn't know where else to go. I'd had visions of camping out in the woods with a tribe of kids. Moss bed, breakfast of berries. Caves. I realized I hadn't thought it out too well. How did Bill do it? Obviously, I had the wrong friends—no long-haired, reckless boys with couches in the back of their vans. No boys at all. No one with even a driver's permit, never mind a car. All Sacred Heart girls had long ago done their homework and were now tucked safely away in bed.

When I got back to East Rock Road, I spotted the figure of a man up ahead, climbing the hill. He was tall and slim-hipped; yellow-blond hair hung to his waist. I recognized him as someone I'd seen at the Teen Center earlier. It was the same brown leather jacket, the same astonishing mane of hair. He'd been looking for someone who owed him money. He hadn't seemed too happy about it, either. He was older than the others, lean and unsmiling, cool as a movie cowboy.

"Hey!" I yelled, and went running after him. But it was as if one of us was a ghost, because he kept walking swiftly up the hill. His long yellow hair shone in the streetlight, swinging from side to side like a woman's dress. I ran faster, my feet slapping the pavement, setting off echoes, hollow and sharp, like pistol shots. My breath scraped the air. In a few easy strides, he reached the top of the hill where the drive entered the park and then, with a last shimmer of yellow, dropped out of sight.

"Hey, wait!"

I was chasing him as fast as I could when the police car appeared again, its red light flashing over me. That's all he did, no siren, just a flash, then a U-turn to my side of the road. It was as if the cop and I had found some secret code to communicate with each other.

"I thought I sent you home," he said.

"Oh, I'm going now," I told him. "I wasn't really before. I was going to my girlfriend's house. Sorry, I lied. But now I'm really going home."

"Okay, I've had enough. Get in. I can't spend the night chasing you all over Hamden, listening to your stories." He didn't sound angry and I was grateful for the way he put it—chasing me *all over* Hamden when really it was just up and down the same hill. Somebody had to put a stop to it, but I couldn't.

He told me I had a choice. Either I would tell him where I lived and he would watch me walk in the front door and see that door shut behind me, or he'd bring me to the station house, find out who my parents were, and call them down. I gave him my real address and when we got there, he waited until I'd gone inside and locked the door behind me. I slipped up the stairs as quietly as I could, woke Bill, and asked him for my letter back. My bed felt like heaven that night; everything had turned out perfectly.

I'd run away from home and returned before anyone knew I was gone. It was almost as good as being invisible. I was living in a dream. I acted without consequence, walked without a sound, left no finger-prints. But my imagination was cooking up real boys, real cops, grown men ready to take me away in fast cars. My parents couldn't pull me away from this new mystery; I wouldn't let them.

The next day when I got out of school, I slipped out of my uni-form into my jeans and returned to the Teen Center. As soon as I reached Tom's Market, I could see a big group of kids gathered out-side. As I got closer, I heard laughter, boots scraping the pavement. This time, I walked right up to them.

"Hey!" The boy named Timmy smiled. "I thought you were going to California."

"This cop picked me up," I told him, and every face turned in my direction. "He picked me up twice! The first time, I told him some story and he let me go, but the second time he was pissed. He said he was gonna give me a choice." I paused, having learned a few things about storytelling from my father.

"He said I could either tell him where I lived and he'd bring me home, or I could have sex with him and he'd let me go. Yeah, he did.

He said if I had sex with him right then, he'd open up the car door and let me go. So I said forget it, take me home."

The boys were astonished. They made me tell the story again and again. They asked me what the cop looked like, and I said he was a young, fat cop with a red face, keeping the real man, who had actually been nice to me, out of it. The boys began to tell stories about cops who had hassled them, while I sat there smoking one of Timmy's cigarettes. Their laughter and talk closed around me. Just like that, I was taken in.

Then we were all walking into the firehouse together. After the light outside, it was as dim as a cave. A stony coolness came off the concrete floors. Under the high ceiling, boys in jeans and boots studied the two pool tables; the balls spun and clacked.

"Fuckin' A," a voice said.

At the back wall, a doorway was filled with fluorescent light. I caught a glimpse of more pool tables, many more slouching, studious boys. No cathedral could have filled a true believer with as much awe.

To my right, I heard chirping, then laughter, from a couch that had been pushed up against the wall and was overflowing with girls. At first glance, they all seemed to have long, dark hair, sharp nails, and full, womanly breasts. I was impressed. They invited me to hang out with them, but it wasn't much of an invitation, since there was no more room on the couch. I had to sit on the floor at their feet.

They must've known one another forever—they kept talking about girls I'd never heard of. "That fat whore," one of them said, and the two girls named Chrissy grabbed each other's breasts, squeezed, and shrieked. That took me aback. They held the laughter for a long time until they distracted all of the boys from their pool games. I sat there awkwardly, not even able to smile. I didn't understand what was so funny.

The two Chrissys were the dark, pretty ones, commanders of the couch. Timmy's sister Lucy was more of a tomboy, stripped down and toughened up in a family of ten. She and Timmy had eight younger brothers and sisters, each one paler than the one before, so that the very youngest seemed to glow like a firefly.

All of the girls went to Hamden High, except for Joan Connolly, who was at Sacred Heart with me.

Joan was big and raw-looking, with ash-blond hair. Her eyes were a light, sharp blue, her fists as large as a man's and bright red. When certain names were mentioned, Joan would growl, "I'll kick her snotty ass," and then, clenching one fist inside the other, crack her knuckles. The girls told me that Joan had broken one girl's nose and another's ribs.

Joan had a real taste, a talent, you might say, for violence. I couldn't help but think of the girl named Georgie as her sidekick; they seemed like bodyguards for the pretty girls. Georgie was short and pigeon-toed, so when she walked, her ass waddled after her. She had a small round head, buck teeth, white skin, and black freckles, like a baseball someone had drawn a face on. Every time the Chrissys brushed their hair or snapped each other's bras or blew each other big, mocking kisses, Georgie's face turned wistful and hurt for a moment, and then she'd come up with a story about what some stupid bitch had worn to school that week, or how some other girl never shaved her armpits and how bad she smelled.

But when push came to shove, they were all good friends. That was something I'd have to come to terms with later, that the people who hate you are always friends to somebody else; their fathers love them, their sisters depend on them, they cry when their grandmothers die.

That first day the girls tried to teach me how to behave. "You smoke like a gangster, Kathy!" they said. The beautiful Chrissys showed me how I was supposed to smoke—two fingers making a V, the cigarette held between. They puckered their lips like they were going to kiss it, and smoked from the dead center of their mouths. They liked Virginia Slims and Mores. I liked Marlboros and smoked them out of the side of my mouth, sometimes letting them dangle there while I zipped up my jacket. I held the cigarette backward, the lit end cupped in my palm. I tapped the ashes onto my jeans and rubbed them in. And when I'd smoked a cigarette down to its filter, I flicked it away in a reverse snap.

The girls didn't like the way I dressed either. "Don't you ever wear a bra, Kathy?"

I didn't think they would ever just let me be. But I hadn't come to the Teen Center to find new girlfriends. I had no desire to nest with a bunch of girls on a big couch.

There were so many boys at the center—playing pool, spitting, cursing, coughing, shoving—that I felt happy as soon as I walked in the door. When I strolled to the soda machine, the air seemed to vibrate. The boys talked louder, stood taller, shoved one another harder. When I played with the zipper on my jacket, boys watched keenly. I laughed aloud and plucked grins from their faces. It was fall but I was still wearing my halter tops. I was ripe for the picking and it showed.

One boy in that lively group was a beat behind the others. He didn't know what was going on, or he didn't want to know. It seems there is always one boy like that. He turned to the others, all watching me, and asked petulantly, "Give me a smoke, man." He had to ask twice. And then, for no reason at all, it seemed, he muttered, "Motherfuckers." One day, I would know that boy—Ben—all too well, but at that electric moment, his surliness didn't even register.

"Kath! Tell him what that cop did," Timmy said, and as I was telling it yet again, other boys gathered around.

"Where did he want you to do it with him?" Timmy's friend asked when I had finished.

"Right there. In the backseat of the car," I told them, shrugging it off.

"Damn," someone said with feeling. "Fucking cop. He had balls!"

"So he just let you go?"

"Yeah, he wasn't mean or anything. He thought he'd just take a chance—see if he got lucky."

"Lucky!" the boys laughed.

They told me they were going for a beer run. They were waiting for some guy who had a car and was old enough to buy the beer.

When the older boy arrived, we piled into the backseat of his car.

This was the beginning, the first of many rides I'd take in the next six months—the only girl in a car full of boys.

There were too many of us to fit in the back, but the driver, whose name was Nicky, didn't look like he wanted anyone crowded up in front with him.

"Here, sit on my lap," one boy said, hitting his leg.

"No, she can sit on mine," another boy cried.

I sat carefully on the first boy's lap, feeling his two legs like a wobbly dock underneath me.

"Am I too heavy?" I asked him.

"Hell, no, you're light as air," he said. "I could hold ten of you." And taking a big breath, he pulled me farther back on his lap.

And then we were off! Flying down Putnam Avenue, windows cracked, cigarettes sparking and sparks sailing. We swung wildly to the right, then to the left, but I was held secure in my bundle of boys.

In the rearview mirror, I could see that Nicky's eyes were on me. Coal black and unsmiling. He was giving off a man scent just sitting there, steering.

I heard Nicky ask one of the boys in front who I was.

"What's your name again?" the boy asked, turning around in the seat. "What's her name, Timmy?"

"It's Kathy, you brain-dead moron. What's your name?"

"Fuck you," the boy said to him, and to me, "I'll remember it now."

From the start, the boys made me feel at home, with their jokes and their boasting, their tall tales of fights and cops and car crashes and someone's father chasing them around with a baseball bat. Their scattered, coarse energy warmed me, entertained me, let me in but asked no questions, made no judgment. There was something democratic about the boys, something I'd been looking for my whole life, it suddenly seemed.

It was just a matter of time, two or three days later, until Eddie Flynn walked me home one night and lingered by the front door. He backed me up against the wall next to the door and began to kiss me, bending his knees and pushing his body against mine. He was as supple as a snake. He slithered and pressed, herding me into place, and then he held me there. I'd never been kissed like that before. The way he used his body, it was like someone had tied his hands.

Eddie had a longish face, a thatch of black hair, a peppery sprinkling of freckles along his nose and cheekbones, the soft beginning of a mustache on his upper lip and that half-sweet, half-nasty manner of some mother's boy bulling his way into manhood. He was completely appealing to me. Not that it really mattered. Any bold, half-handsome boy could've done what Eddie did next.

"Come down here," he said, and jumped off the stoop. Then he pulled me behind the bushes. Here where my brothers and sisters and I had hidden from one another as children, here where Cindy and Beth and I had made little houses, knocking on the tree trunks to be let in, Eddie unsnapped my jeans and put his hand inside, his finger up in me. His hand scraped back and forth along the zipper.

He called it "finger fucking," and so that's what it was then. It was all brand new to me, anyway; speeding car, open country, crash course. "Baby, touch him, he likes you." Penis as puppy dog. "Baby, you got to let me do it. I can't stop now." Desire as runaway train.

14

Party Time

THE HOUSE FILLED UP QUICKLY WITH LONG-HAIRED, SHARP-FACED boys, and girls wearing thick black mascara and turquoise eye shadow. Like partying nomads, they arrived carrying cases of beer and bottles of scotch, vodka, and gin. Some of the girls had thought to bring plastic cups. The music blasting from the living room stereo could be heard from the lawns across the street—the J. Geils Band singing, "Take out your false teeth, mama, I wanna suck on your gums." Sebastian looked like an especially eager host, trotting from room to room on stubby legs and swinging his feathery tail so hard his rump wagged.

It was still September, but already the night had sharp, cold edges where it touched my skin. My parents had gone away for the weekend with Cindy, Beth Ann, and Stephen, and Michael was off somewhere with a friend. So Bill had decided to throw a party.

When he'd told me about it that morning, he said it as a warning, not an invitation. He was hoping I'd clear out—sleep over at Sylvia's perhaps. But instead I went straight to the firehouse and invited everyone there to the party. I hardly knew them yet, but I was going to show them that I was as cool as they were. I was excited to have something to give them.

What I didn't know was that Bill's friends and the firehouse crowd were rivals, for no other reason than the fact that they lived in different parts of Hamden—Bill's friends in Spring Glen, the firehouse kids in Whitneyville. In every other way, Spring Glen and Whitneyville boys were exactly the same: working-class kids who all went to Hamden High (except for Bill, of course, since my parents had forced him to go to Notre Dame); who all wore the same Levi's, boots, and leather jackets; who all drank the same booze (Johnnie Walker, Schlitz, Budweiser, and anything else they found in their parents' liquor cabinets), smoked pot, and occasionally took speed but preferred 'ludes. The only discernible difference in their taste was that Spring Glen boys seemed to have a preference for vans; Whitneyville boys liked their muscle cars.

In the kitchen that night, the girls were making screwdrivers while the boys were doing shots with their beer. Smoke hung from the ceiling and someone must've spilled a drink, for my shoes stuck to the floor when I walked, sucking and popping at each step. I'd never drunk alcohol before, so it didn't occur to me to start then. Instead, I planted myself on the couch in the living room to wait for *my* friends to arrive. There bottles were being passed, bongs were burbling, and J. Geils gave way to Jethro Tull. On the coffee table in front of me someone had placed a paper plate piled high with brownies. It seemed funny to me that at a party where no one had brought even a bag of chips, never mind some onion dip, someone had thought to make dessert. "Eat me," the brownies seemed to say, and I did.

When I glanced up, Michael and his friend were standing there in shorts, holding tennis rackets. They looked flushed, naked, and appalled.

"Tallyho!" a voice called out from across the living room; the crowd parted to reveal the speaker, a long-haired boy-man sprawled in my father's rocking chair, a girl with black hair on his lap.

"Where's Bill?" Michael asked stiffly. Bill's friends drew around him. "Nice socks, Mikey." Putting on British accents, they asked about his backhand.

"Where's Bill?" Michael asked again.

"Billy can't see you now."

"He's otherwise occupied."

"I think he's rolling a joint."

"Tapping a keg."

They looked up at him innocently, shrugged.

"Hey, Mikey, where can I get one of those shirts with the little alligators on them? They're keen."

"Neat-o."

"Jim Dandy." Just like that—the captain could be made a clown. It was terrible. But I felt there was a kind of justice in this. Michael couldn't be king everywhere. He was on Bill's turf now, a place where straight A's and good behavior didn't matter. In fact, they were a black mark against you.

Just then Bill walked in, surprise written all over his face. "Oh, Mike, hey, I forgot—"

"You're responsible for anything that happens here. I'm leaving," Michael said.

"Whhhoa! Can you handle it, Billy?"

"You better have it all cleaned up before Mom and Dad get home tomorrow," Michael said. "I'm not covering for you this time." And then he turned away. Bill looked like he'd been slapped. Had he expected Michael to join in? Or give him a brotherly pat on the shoulder and ask to be introduced to his friends? Bill let out a loud belch, but Michael was out the door, gone.

"Fuckin' . . ." Bill muttered, swallowing the next word in his beer.

I was reaching for another brownie when a flush-faced boy sat down heavily next to me. "You'll be flying tonight," he mumbled, and when he saw the quizzical look on my face, he let out a laugh. "Oh, shit," he said. "You didn't know? They're hash brownies." Who would've thought? His laughter made me laugh and so we sat there, the two of us, looking at each other and laughing, though I'd already forgotten what had started us off.

Then I was in the upstairs hallway with its towering doors, all closed, and some other boy was holding me against the wall, thigh to thigh, pressing, digging, teasing, torturing his own hard-on. His tongue slithered into my mouth. I took it like a climber takes a rope;

it focused me. He yanked open the nearest door and pulled me into my parents' bedroom.

In there, the air was hushed, the bed barely visible in the dark. When we had stripped off our clothes, the boy pulled me onto the bed and lay on top of me. I felt the whole weight of his boy body on mine, felt his struggle, then the thrust in. Once inside, a holy pause, before the action began anew.

It was so secretive, so intimate; he seemed to be whispering in my ear, but all he was saying was, "Uh-uh-uh-uh-uh . . ." Then the door cracked open, and ghoulish faces stared at us from the light—"He's fuckin' doin' her!" Laughter followed. The door closed, and we lay in darkness again. "Fuck them," he said, pulling me close as I tried to break away, but I could hear the despair in his voice. The moment was over, and he knew it.

I dressed and slipped down to the kitchen, where Sebastian had licked the floor as clean as he could and was now walking sideways, bumping into cabinets, feebly waving his tail. He seemed to be trying his best to tidy up after us, keep us out of trouble. Bump, wave, bump, wave; he finally made it over to me.

I emptied the beer someone had poured into his dish and refilled it with water. "Better stick near me," I told him, cupping his narrow head, but he lay down sideways on the floor in front of the cookie cabinet, one apologetic eye watching me. His tail tapped the floor, *sorry, can't do, sorry, sorry*.

The front and back doors to the house were open. There was no center to the party anymore, people were everywhere, on all the floors of the house, on the back porch, on both lawns, out in the drive-way, down the basement—inside the closets, for all I knew.

Suddenly, there was trouble out front. Word passed like electricity from room to room, and everyone rushed to the door.

Battles were erupting on several parts of the lawn, curses and grunts filled the air. I saw two figures tumbling across the grass and onto the sidewalk. The firehouse boys had arrived.

Up and down the street, lights came on. Doors opened. Men stood on their front steps, looking our way, their fists clenched, as if they'd like to toss off their responsible adult selves—just one more taste of youth!—and join in the brawl, show these punks a thing or two. Across the street, old women in nightgowns and robes watched from the other side of their screen doors.

Then, out of nowhere, a boy came charging across the lawn, roaring and swinging a log. Everyone jumped back.

I knew that log! It was the driftwood my parents had brought home from Cape Cod and put in our garden. Now this maniac was using it as a weapon, whirling around the lawn, scattering the fighters. Grinning from ear to ear.

"What the fuck?" I heard Bill mutter. "We got fuckin' Paul Bunyan here." His voice was rough and careless-sounding, but I could see the panic in his eyes.

Sides were forgotten. Every guy on the lawn crouched around the log swinger and took turns dashing toward him, but no one could get close. He had dark shadows on his jaw and his green eyes were lit. His brown leather jacket flapped open every time he swung. I recognized him from the firehouse. He laughed and, grabbing the log with one hand, sliced hard at the air, practically knocking himself over. No one was having as much fun as he was. I watched in wonder.

"Jimmy, you fucker!" Now I knew his name.

Then we heard the sirens, and dozens of kids went running . . . across lawns, into cars, over fences, through the hedges. I ran along with the rest of them; but unlike the others, I couldn't run home.

It had been my first big party, and as I headed into the woods across the street, I knew it would be my last. I didn't like the crowds or the aggressive ugliness of the music, the way the boys drove Michael from the house and got Sebastian drunk, the whole great sea of carelessness. I kept picturing Beth, not my parents, walking into that party, and I could see her face, astonished, then grave, as she bent over Sebastian and spoke tenderly just to him: "Okay, little buddy, I'm here now."

No, I hadn't liked the party. But the boy upstairs, his tongue in my mouth, his skin hot and bare, yes, I liked that. The wild, handsome man on the lawn, his reckless energy, yes, yes. No one could touch him, not just because of the log but because he had no restraint, no fear, no guilt. He wasn't even fighting because he was angry. He was having fun. I wanted to see him again.

From my hiding place in the woods, I looked out at our house, all lit up and deserted, the front door ajar. The log of driftwood lay in the middle of the lawn like a giant, half-eaten bone, and two police cars were parked at the curb. When the cops pulled away, I crossed the street and went home.

Late that night, Bill and I wobbled over brooms and mops. I was happy to be cleaning up with him, thinking we were partners at last. But he, big brother, black sheep, wasn't happy at all. He cleaned with a grim determination. As he swept broken glass from the kitchen floor, he was silent. I mopped and watched his face. My brother looked the complete opposite of Jimmy on the lawn; he was all grown-up at sixteen, already paying for his freedom and his pleasures.

"You shouldn't have been here," he finally growled. But I knew better. I had my own life now. He didn't know about the boy upstairs, didn't know that it was I who had invited the Teen Center over.

That night I was given two glimpses of my future: Jimmy, charismatic, careless Jimmy, jumping straight into the chaos on the lawn; and the ghoulish faces peering in at me through the bedroom door, laughing. But I had no hint of what the future held for me, and though I was given these two signs, I couldn't read either one of them.

No, instead I lay on my bed and composed a poem to the outlaw on the lawn with the streetlight in his eyes. By the fourth verse, my outlaw was surrounded by police, washed in a red, swooping light. They were blind to his wild, free spirit; they were going to put him in a cage. In my poem, I imagined Jimmy as someone bighearted and hungry, blissfully unaware that he was heading for trouble.

15

The Real Girlfriend

I WAS WATCHING A POOL GAME IN THE BIG FRONT ROOM OF THE firehouse, wearing my yellow halter top, when Nicky Pineda asked me if I wanted to go for a ride. One minute he was standing with a group of the older guys by the front door, the next he was coming across the room to me, saying my name. I was pleased he remembered it, and I agreed immediately. He had been our driver on the beer run and was one of the man-boys at the firehouse. Nicky, Jimmy, and Patrick Cahoon: These three made a nation.

The man-boys always arrived at the firehouse at dusk. You heard the roar of their cars outside. The firehouse doorway shrunk; they loomed, all leather and stubble.

The man-boys ruled the Center. It was as inevitable as anything else in nature. They had dropped out of school and had jobs that callused their hands, money in their pockets, tanned, muscular arms, confidence, cars, a case of beer in the trunk, a bottle of Johnnie Walker pushed under the front seat, and a divided Hamden in their heads— Whitneyville versus Spring Glen.

I didn't know if I liked Nicky Pineda or not. I liked what I knew about him so far—his full lips, olive skin, coarse hair. Sometimes the other boys called him "Nick the Spic" to annoy him. I liked the nickname, too. Everything about him seemed thick and bullish. There was nothing flirtatious about his lust; it was simply rude and strong. His T-shirt looked pressed. I was excited.

When I got in the car, Nicky drove straight to West Rock Park in West Haven. He was that sure. I watched him with pleasure—a silent boy! Driving! Smoking!

We seemed to drive up many hills, aimed each time for the slice of dark sky at the top, until finally we reached the peak of West Rock and parked at a low stone wall, a flutter of tiny lights far below us. He kept the motor running but shut the lights, turned his full, unsmiling lips toward me. "Come on over here."

When we kissed, his hand got up between us and held my breast. Then he was breathing hard and pulling my T-shirt out of my pants.

His other hand was getting busy with himself, with *it*, our reason for being here.

He unbuttoned his jeans to let it breathe and it poked straight up in his underwear, trying to get out. It was suffocating in there. He yanked his underwear down to his hips. "I've got a real boner," he said, and the word fit perfectly. I thought I'd never seen anything so ridiculous and so admirable in my life. "Let's get in the back," Nicky said urgently. It wanted what it wanted. He had trouble tucking it back in.

As soon as we were in the backseat, he unsnapped and unzipped my jeans. "Take them off," he said. Everything was happening too fast, like someone had just set out dinner and then, just as suddenly, cleared the plates and threw down dessert.

"Uh, could I have a cigarette?"

I wanted to give Nicky whatever he wanted, but taking off my pants just now? And only my pants? It didn't seem very sexy.

My capacity for desire was in its baby stages, just beginning to un-furl; instead of coaxing it, teasing it out of its nesting place and then stirring it up, Nicky was bulldozing over it, flattening my desire with his. But he had no use for my desire, and his disregard matched my own, for I had no idea what I was missing.

"A cigarette?" he said. His laugh was a snort. "You're gonna start playing shy *now*? After letting me go this far?"

With every breath, his chest rose to meet mine; heat came off his body in waves. His black eyes had turned deadly serious.

He softened enough to say my name. "Kathy," he said. "Come on, Kathy . . ." I was deeply flattered by the heat and heaviness of his wanting. He told me we couldn't stop now and then he told me why. . . . At fourteen I found it easy to believe in blue balls, in wanting something so badly that if you didn't get it, you'd be poisoned by frustration. Yes, I could believe in that.

Nicky and I had sex every night for a week, and each time he seemed unfriendlier. I couldn't get the desire and the unfriendliness to mesh in my head. It seemed a mistake had been made, and soon things would be set right.

One of those nights, he muttered the word *chinga* in my ear and my skin prickled. I didn't know what the word meant but it opened like a door anyway—and through that door I could see Nicky's mother and his sisters in a kitchen wearing aprons. The women sang to each other in Spanish, a nest of sparrows. The flowered curtains, the laundry basket, the patter of pretty feet blackened his lust. "Chinga," he said, and I felt his anger and excitement as if they were my own—the flowered curtains trembled, the mother's hands flew up, his body jerked, a shot and a soiling. Ah ha! So that's how it was.

On the seventh night, Nicky asked me to skip school in the morning. He said to take the bus as usual and he'd pick me up in the school parking lot.

That morning, I tumbled down the steps of the bus with the rest of the girls, all of us in our brown-and-white-checked skirts and knee socks, our stiff white blouses and soft, brown shoes, God's girls, dressed like Toll House cookies. Marisa and the two Lisas, Guardino and DiRosa, walked by me in the parking lot—"Hi, Kath!"—their voices friendly but embarrassed. They hesitated a second. What to say? Should they wait and walk in with me? Walk away?

Marisa and Lisa Guardino and I had been good friends since first grade at St. Rita's. As soon as we got to Sacred Heart, we gathered a group of like-minded girls, including Lisa DiRosa and Sylvia, until there were about nine of us at our cafeteria table. We ate lunch together, had sleep-overs, bicycled, played volleyball, fell in love with one another's older brothers but in a public, jokey way. We didn't seem to have any secrets except the kind we quickly shared. Everything about us was as plain as paint.

It went on that way until the end of our freshman year. Then school let out, and I started wearing halter tops and short shorts; I'd become "boy crazy," as they would've said. Since I spent much of the rest of that summer on the cross-country trip I took with my family, I didn't see any of my girlfriends until the fall.

In September, when we returned to Sacred Heart, they immediately sensed that I had changed. Marisa, a redhead with sugar-and-cinnamon skin, started blushing whenever she looked at me. Slowly, she and Lisa and the other girls gave me up that year. There was no meanness to what they did, but no choice, either. I embarrassed them, I know, confused, maybe even saddened them. I never stayed after school anymore, not for drama tryouts or the Latin Club. I swore aloud. I walked with a sexual swagger.

But they were a kind group of friends. They said nothing, let me sit with them at lunch and drift away little by little. Only Sylvia and I remained close, but she knew nothing of my nightlife, didn't even sense it, unlike the rest of them. And if she had? It wouldn't have mattered. The tie between us was stronger than that.

Meanwhile, two of the black girls in our class had begun to court me, and I them. Leslie and Linda were in my homeroom that year—Sylvia had been switched to another—so the three of us were in all the same classes. We often found ourselves sitting together in the back of the classroom. They were always joking and playing with each other, and after a while they began to include me, first by playing *to* me, a most appreciative audience. Leslie was tiny but her afro was huge, seventies-style, with copper-colored highlights. She kept her pick inside it. "That's so . . . country, Leslie," Linda would say, cooing it so you didn't know if that was a good or bad thing.

One day in Christian Womanhood class, Linda raised her hand, fluttering her fingers in the air, trying to get the nun's attention. When she was finally called on, Linda said, "I'm sorry, Sister, but as a nun how can you teach us about being women?" Shock rippled through the classroom, and several girls turned around to shoot her angry, appalled looks. But I was impressed. Within a week the three of us were playing Mod Squad in the hallway between classes. Shortly after that, Sylvia and I moved over to their cafeteria table. But meanwhile, the old gang and I couldn't just pretend our friendship hadn't existed.

So there was Lisa DiRosa waiting for me as I stood in the parking lot that morning. "Hey, Kath, aren't you going in?" It took a tomboy to cut to the chase. Marisa was blushing wildly and Lisa Guardino seemed to be watching my shoes, but DiRosa was looking me straight in the eye. A tiger in the field and on the court, a great stealer of bases and rebounds, she had short black hair and an athlete's slouch to her shoulders.

"I'm waiting for someone," I told her. "A guy I know. I'm skipping today."

"Okay, uh, well, good luck . . . I guess," she said, patting me on the back clumsily, her hand cupped like it had been molded permanently by her catcher's mitt.

Just then, Nicky's car slid into the parking lot, dented, dark, engine growling low. The door swung open. I slipped inside. Girls stared, astonished, then quickly looked away, ashamed of their naïveté. No one would tell.

We went into the woods that bordered Treadwell Street. There, in a patch of needles and sun, Nicky spread out a blanket and we got completely undressed. I liked that he had thought of the forest and the blanket. His forethought became our foreplay. There wasn't any other kind—just a kiss to get it out of the way. He pushed himself right in without any notice of our nakedness. We were completely bare in front of each other for the first time. And it was daylight. I wondered if I should be wriggling or something. The pine trees tele-scoped into a perfect circle of blue, Easter egg blue, and from some-where behind us came the sound of a work crew clearing a patch of forest. I couldn't help thinking that I should have been happier than I was right then. *You are naked in the woods, making love on a school day*, I said to myself, and though that sounded like a fine adventure, it didn't feel like one.

Overhead, a bird screamed. Nicky was putting on his pants. For a moment things went very flat, and I got scared. I had staked all my bets on this new world of mine, thinking that there I would come into my own. What if I was wrong?

Nicky wanted to leave right away. "I have to get to work," he said. He was already late. But I had nowhere to go. Home was out of the question, and I couldn't just walk into school in the middle of the morning.

"The nuns aren't even gonna notice you were gone," he told me impatiently. But of course they would. Unlike Nicky, the nuns noticed everything.

I said he could take me back to school. It was a silent ride. I spent it staring out the window, making plans.

When we got to the long drive that led through the grounds, I told Nicky to drop me off. He never asked what I was going to do, and there was obviously no point in asking his advice.

I settled in behind the statue of Jesus where the bushes hid me from the road. I'd wait here for the bus that took us home, I decided, and just try to blend in with the crowd of girls when they started to board.

Now that Nicky was gone, I began to feel a lot happier about him and me. It was amazing how quickly my natural optimism could re-assert itself. Nestled in the soft grass, I suddenly realized that Nicky and I had been going together for eight days now! By tomorrow it would be nine. Making love in the daytime suddenly felt like an an-niversary celebration. I would have to call his attention to that tonight.

When I thought about what we had just done in the woods, I became intensely aware of my skirt and my bare legs. A dark delicious humming started up along my skin. I thought of all the girls in school, rolling up their sweater sleeves and writing their equations down. I thought of Nicky lying on top of me, his thick thighs and bulletlike head, his pushing in and out while in the distance, other men hacked away at the edge of the woods. I remembered hearing the shriek of their saws, then the sharp cry of a blue jay high up. Blue on blue, I thought. I took out my notebook to write it all down.

There was the tiniest bit of unease in my mind about my ability to enjoy my "adventure" now when it was over and not at all when it was happening. It seemed a little tricky, this, a little dubious. But the vivid aftertaste was real, this pleasure, this savoring as my pen set out across the page.

The despair I'd felt in the woods was vanquished. I was writing my way out of it, without knowing that that was what I was doing. I wondered how you spelled *chinga*.

That night I said something to Nicky about being his girlfriend for more than a week now, and he looked at me with contempt.

"You're not my girlfriend," he sneered. "I've got a real girlfriend. She won't even let me kiss her."

He was driving me home from West Rock Park, and I turned and stared out the window (I couldn't bear to look at his face) but saw nothing. The fences and houses and trees had been swallowed up by a dense fog. The only image to appear out of that mist was *the real girlfriend*—lips first. They were painted bright red, set firmly together. Immediately, I assigned her all the other attributes of femininity I found most beautiful—long dark hair, high cheekbones, womanly breasts.

She was a prize, I was absolutely sure of that, but an alien creature. I couldn't imagine telling a boy *not* to kiss me, *not* to lay a hand on me. Why would I? I must have heard girls talk about not having sex so boys would respect them, but that notion held no attraction for me. All in all, it had a hollow, dusty feel to it, like a glass jar on a shelf—DO NOT TOUCH. No, not for me. The respect of a sixteen-year-old boy couldn't hold a candle to his desire.

That was the last night I spent with Nicky. I moved on.

16

The Most Beautiful Boy in the World

DOWN IN THE BASEMENT, THE STROBE LIGHT PULSED ALONG THE cement walls and floors, Led Zeppelin played on the stereo, and pool balls spun straight across the green. "Gonna make you sweat, gonna make you groove!" Timmy sang, as I took aim for the corner pocket. When a skinny boy named Pete tried to block the shot with his hand, Timmy wrestled him from the table. The old pinball machine my father had gotten from a colleague at Yale clicked and flashed and rang until Ben shoved it with his hip, sending it into Tilt mode, all of its lights shutting off. Six of the boys from the Teen Center had come home with me that day.

The basement was our turf, a Dobie Teen Center all its own. My parents had given it over to my brothers and sisters and me that year, making strong bid for our presence on the home front.

The pool table, with a big red bow around it, had appeared as the surprise gift at the end of a long treasure hunt on Christmas morning. Together we'd gone in search of it, following the clues my father had written in rhyme and hidden all over the house late the night before. During winter break, Cindy had painted wavy Day-Glo stripes down the walls and across the cement floor. With the black light on, you moved across the room as a set of glowing clothes. If you weren't careful, you'd trip over one of the beanbag chairs slumped on the floor. When our relatives first saw the room, Great-aunt Bert pronounced it "groovy," savoring the ridiculous word, and Great-aunt Emma gamely tried out the pinball machine, amusing us to no end.

I'd brought the boys in through the side door, the one that opened from the backyard directly onto the basement stairs, so that we could avoid the kitchen—and my mother. But suddenly she appeared at the top of the stairs in her flower-covered apron and her high heels. Her face was pink, her hazel eyes blazing. I turned the music down, but not off. I felt cocooned by my crowd of boys and their instantly sullen faces.

"Aren't you going to introduce me to your friends?" she asked, her voice stiff with false brightness. A hundred sullen boys couldn't protect me from that. I gave their names, the ones I knew, with a great show of nonchalance. The boys barely bothered to nod.

It was the seventies, the seventies in a small town, which meant that the sixties had just begun to influence us, and so we had more drugs to mix with our alcohol, a free-floating anger at authority, contempt for conformity, and no real tolerance for anything. God help the housewife in her apron and high heels, trying so hard.

I no longer saw my mother as young or beautiful. I saw only the old-fashioned apron, the dark support hose, the beauty parlor hair, dyed blond now; my critic, my uncomprehending mother. It must have been terrible for her, all our loving gazes receding from her that year. But I didn't want to know what she was feeling anymore.

After she went back upstairs, slamming the door behind her, the boys decided to take off. This was no Playland; this was a house with parents.

"Let's go," blond Timmy said, and when I told them I couldn't come with them, they bounded up the stairs and out the side door as eagerly as if I were the mother and they were fleeing me.

When I walked into the house a few minutes later, I found my mother cooking dinner. Her eyes were wet.

"Why didn't you bring them in the front door and introduce them to me?" she demanded. "Why do you feel you have to sneak around all the time?"

"I didn't think about it." I shrugged. "They're just some boys I know."

I couldn't explain that mothers and boys just didn't go together in my mind, family and sex, kitchens and backseats. I thought everyone knew that was so but pretended it wasn't, said "Nice-to-meet-you, nice-house-you-have-here," and "Why-thank-you-very-much" while one person was thinking, *How do I get out of here so I can fuck your daughter?* and the other was trying not to think about it too much.

"Are you ashamed of me? Do you think I'm too square?" Her voice was pitched high, imploring and protesting all at once. Behind her, the kitchen walls were plastered with inspirational posters she'd bought in the New Haven mall, quotes from Kahlil Gibran and Martin Buber printed on fields of wildflowers, on sunrises and ocean waves. Every few months, she bought a new one, as if she were trying to cheer herself up, so that over the last couple of years the kitchen had become more and more like a teenage girl's bedroom. Less a setting for the Dobie family dinner than the place where my mother strove to project her personality against motherhood, wifedom—that promised land that had become a black hole.

"No, I'm not ashamed of you," I said angrily, fighting back an enormous wave of pity. I wasn't going to feel that for her. Rage was better. Drop-dead coldness. Not pity. Not for your own mother. "It doesn't have anything to do with that."

And it didn't. There was no sense in bringing them together. I didn't want to see the boys go sullen and stupid under her gaze, didn't want her to shrivel and protest under theirs.

"They're your friends. They're in my house," she was saying.

"They're not my *friends*," I replied, dripping scorn.

"Well, then what are they?"

"Just some guys I know."

"You were the only girl!"

"So what?"

"Why weren't there any other girls with you? Why were you the only one?"

Then I thought she was insulting me, thought it was a clever way of asking why I didn't have any *girl*friends, and an even more clever way of doubting the boys' interest in me.

"The girls at the firehouse don't like to play pool," I said as airily as I could. "So they wouldn't come over."

I was feeling very sticky and strange by then. This is what could happen to the beautiful adventure if you brought it home—it could suddenly look tawdry and shameful. I had to get out of that kitchen before my dream crumbled to dirt.

I told my mother I was going to Sylvia's, though I didn't think I was. I headed swiftly up Clifford, crossed Putnam, not slowing down until I was well away from the house. As I wandered up and down the small streets that crisscrossed a hill back behind the avenue, I began to feel calmer. Men were raking leaves, kids leaping into the yellow-and-orange piles, dogs barking as I passed.

When dusk fell, and all the leaping children were called home, I headed toward the firehouse. The boys weren't there, so I went to see if they'd gone over to Pete's house, a favorite gathering place because his parents were never home. Pete's older brother answered the door. His hair was still wet; he'd just stepped out of the shower.

He went to the refrigerator for a couple of sodas and I took off my jacket and sat down on the couch to drink mine. He just stood in front of me, rolling his unopened can back and forth across his stomach thoughtfully. Because of his wet hair and the smell of soap coming off his skin and the silence that he held and held, the air was heating up, a thousand agitating molecules.

When he finally sat down, he leaned back against the arm of the couch, legs sprawled wide. He lit a joint. Squinted at me.

"Where are your boys tonight?"

"Oh, they're around."

"Aren't you cold wearing just that?" he asked, holding the smoke in and talking over it, his voice strained. He jerked his chin at my shirt, a polyester blouse that tied at my waist, leaving my belly bare. It was silvery, shimmery, printed with blue flowerpots and pink flowers; a disco blouse that never went dancing.

"No, I'm never cold," I told him. "Usually, I'm too warm. That's why I like the winter and the fall." He exhaled the smoke with a big sighing sound, then carefully pushed the glowing end into the ashtray and pinched whatever fire was left between his fingers.

"You *look* cold," he said quietly.

"What do you mean?"

Then he leaned over and with his fingers barely touching the side of my breast, brushed his thumb lightly over my nipple, the same thumb that had just put out the joint. It left a faint smudgy track on my shirt.

"Goose bumps," he said.

"Maybe that's not because I'm cold," I said, trumping his boldness with my own. If he was going to be outrageous, I'd be right there with him. It was almost a point of pride with me.

He looked shaken awake. "How old are you, Kath?"

"Fifteen," I lied, but I would have my birthday soon.

He went over to the front porch windows. I heard him murmur to himself, "Down, boy." Maybe he didn't think I was listening, maybe he didn't care whether I heard him or not.

When he came back, he stood over me, rubbing his stomach with his hand now. He let out a whistling sigh.

"I see what they're talking about." He smiled at me then and shook his head. "Trouble."

I was happy I'd made him sweat, happy to see him smile, but he told me I'd better leave, and I wasn't so happy about that.

Maybe it was a test, but if it was, I'd passed *and* failed, for the next thing I knew I was out on the street, wandering around by myself, nowhere to go but home. When I got to the house, I found I wasn't ready to go inside yet. Instead I went around to the backyard and sat on one of the swings, gently rocking myself back and forth with one leg. As I took a cigarette out of my pocket, I saw a light go on in the house. A figure appeared in the window of the living room, then disappeared on the way up the stairs. Then someone else ran by the same window, the smaller faster shape of Cindy or Beth. Now the sunporch, windowed on all three sides, was filled with light. Who was in there? Suddenly I imagined little Stephen bent over his trucks all alone, clearing his throat to make engine sounds. Grief pierced me, and I wanted to cry. I felt as if each person inside that house was secretly, terribly lonely.

What I needed right then was for some kind, sensible friend to give me a good shake and say, "Don't be silly, they're inside that house all together—you're the one out here alone. Your little brother is playing with his trucks, having fun. The loneliness you feel now is your own."

Maybe the talk started right away, started with Eddie Flynn when he emerged from the bushes that September night: *"She let me finger-fuck her!"* Maybe the boy in my parents' bedroom was a firehouse boy. All I know for sure is that Nicky talked, couldn't stop talking, in fact, and Nicky hated me. The girls did, too. I must have been driving them mad, for they heard what the boys said about me, the contempt in their voices, and then they'd see one of those boys come into the Teen Center to get me, and off I'd go with a grin and a wave—the chosen one.

They hated me for getting away with it, even though I was only "getting away with it" in my own head. But that's what must have been so infuriating. To them I was trash—it was obvious. Everyone knew it but me. As far as I was concerned, I was doing exactly what the boys were doing, which meant I was as alive, as bold, as free, as they were. What the girls would have to do, and they probably sensed this already, was pull me out of my head and into the light of day, make me see things *their* way.

"He ate her out!" I was waiting for my turn at the pool table when I heard them behind me. The boys stopped their game and looked at me to see how I would react.

"Ecchhh . . . gross!" the girls screamed, and when I turned around, the couch was writhing—girls grabbing themselves and falling into one another's laps, laughing. "That's so disgusting!"

I was taken aback. I didn't think anyone shriveled around sex but spinster aunts and little kids, certainly not beautiful girls like the two Chrissys. I thought that even if you felt that way, you tried to hide it because it was so uncool. You weren't going to see *me* talking about sex like a little girl with a frog waved in her face.

The girls succeeded only in making me feel worldly-wise, which was, of course, exactly what I wanted to be. In fact, the only time I ever felt ashamed was when I wasn't "in the know," a peculiar kind of shame that went straight back to my dream-clouded childhood. So when Patrick Cahoon had asked me to do "sixty-nine" the night before, I was mostly concerned with not knowing what that was.

Patrick was a big blond boy, built like a football player. One of the man-boys. He had a military haircut and thick lips that gleamed every time he passed his tongue over them. We were lying half naked in the backseat of his car.

"How about we do sixty-nine?" he asked.

"Okay, sure," I whispered, and then wondered why he was turning himself around and heading down there. . . . I actually started to follow him.

The day after the girls had made their scene on the couch, I got to the Teen Center early. It was right after school, the quiet part of the afternoon. None of the girls had arrived yet, and none of the man-boys, either.

The only people there were a few of the quiet, anonymous boys who hung around the fringes of the action, studying the pool tables like they were doing their homework, and the four black boys who sometimes came around, four dark faces in a sea of white.

They always appeared at the firehouse together and went straight to their table, which was the one just inside the entrance. If they weren't playing pool, they stood with their backs against the big firehouse doors watching—and more than the pool game, as I found out that day.

When I walked in, Fat Roscoe was taking a shot while Craig and the two younger black boys leaned on their sticks and waited.

"Hey, Kath," they called out, and then Craig handed one of the younger boys his pool stick and came over to me.

"Kath, we need to talk to you," he said. "It's important."

Craig was tall, whiplike, soft-spoken. He was handsome, but his handsomeness had no currency here. Fat Roscoe was fat; he was wrinkled with it, like a bulldog. He had gold teeth and a big walking stick. Roscoe made ugly cool, cooler than any white-boy prettiness. Behind his back, some of the white boys referred to him as "the coon." They were afraid of him and they adored him. He was like some kind of mascot, he so perfectly fulfilled their idea of a nigger.

"Come take a ride with us," Craig said. "So we can talk with you alone." This must have been in late November, right before I began seeing Jimmy.

Their car was parked out front. It was an old car, low-flying and high-finned, wide as a bed. Craig got behind the wheel. Roscoe opened the door for me. "Slip in the back, angel," he said, and motioned the other two boys to get in there with me. Then he sat in the front, the car bowing down like he was royalty.

As soon as we hit Hamden's main drag, Craig began.

"Kath, everybody's talking about you. You got to start being careful."

"You're getting a rep," Roscoe said in his gravelly voice.

They talked to me over their shoulders, keeping their eyes on the road. The two young boys next to me were quiet. They were about my age, maybe a year or two older, and they were listening closely, their faces deadly serious, like they were in training to be men, and I suppose they were—black men in Hamden.

"You can't trust any of them," Craig said. I turned my head toward the window, trying to hide the pleasure I felt—not only at his and Roscoe's concern, but at the very idea of being well-known. A rep. A shadow, a ripple. Something's there in a room before you enter, and still there after you're gone. I couldn't have been happier. My name would have the force, the thunder, of Roscoe's walking stick, set down with a thump every time he took a step.

He and Craig advised me to slow down and to watch out. There was nothing judgmental in their words, nothing that said I was wrong or dirty, or that having sex was. It was all about the treacherous company I was keeping. To this day, I marvel at it. Four boys in a car with me? They could've imagined a very different scenario—but all they tried to do was protect me.

Until that ride, I'd assumed that they wanted to be friends with the white boys. I thought Roscoe didn't know what they said about him. I even felt sorry for them and pictured myself as their ally. It was laughable. What did I have to offer them? A girl so foolish she didn't even know she was alone. No, it was they who allied themselves with me. They saw the danger approaching and took sides—not with the crowd, with the pretty girls or the rowdy boys, but with the weakest link in the chain. A bravery wasted on me.

I had no caution in me then, just as I had no sexual shame. And so late that afternoon, unwilling to heed their advice, I walked straight into New Haven in search of a new adventure, and soon enough I found one.

It was about four miles from my house to the New Haven Green. When I got there, I sat down on the grass and smoked a cigarette. Dusk was falling, and the old-fashioned lamps that lined the green lit up as I sat there, and under them crowds of people rushed home, dark-suited men swinging their attaché cases like boys with schoolbags, women clustered in groups, holding their coats closed at the collar and laughing with each other for no other reason, it seemed, than that it was five o'clock and they were free! Their eyes sparkled in the cold of a November evening; leaves crunched under their heels. And then a boy came across the grass toward me, the most beautiful boy in the world. He had green eyes and a fistful of blond curls on his head. His cheekbones were high; his full lips had perfect Cupid peaks. He looked like an angel, but dusty.

I had the distinct impression then of his being a wanderer. There was something worldly and carefree about him, something not Hamden. To me he seemed like a boy who rode the rails or stowed away on ships; he'd watched the prairies roll by, seen the northern lights from the deck of a fishing trawler. But perhaps he was just from New

Haven; a city boy. I don't remember what we talked about, but I know I invited him to come to my house later that night. I told him to knock quietly on the basement door and I would let him in.

It was late when he arrived, lights out and everybody in bed for the night. On the eight-track tape player, Steppenwolf sang softly about his snow-blind friend, and the most beautiful boy in the world was climbing up the beanbag chair from the floor, climbing up my legs, my belly, my breasts, his hands sliding up inside my shirt as he rose, climbing through the black light and the strobe light, looking like a water creature making his way onto land.

When he had finally worked himself up every inch of my body and lay full-length on me, he whispered, "Hey, girl," like we had just finally now and truly met, and then his mouth was on mine.

How sweet he was, how slow, how sensuous, how totally unlike Brian or Victor, Nicky or Patrick. Who had raised him that he didn't think sex was his to experience alone? That he thought there were two of us there? I had a sudden image of a spangled fat lady from the circus, holding him on her pillowy breasts.

When he left that night, he disappeared altogether, on to another town perhaps, but he would stamp himself on my brain, and so he would resurface again and again through the years, in other boys and men. Once the mind knows something exists, there's no stopping it from finding that thing again, especially when that thing is a slow, practiced, shamelessly hot and tender boy. Occasionally he appears in my dreams—he's always on a high wire, performing for a crowd. He wears a dusty bowler and will take no money for his show. He does it for the love of it; he's as light as air.

17

A Distant Coyote

THE SACRED HEART CAFETERIA HAD A FLOOR OF MARBLED GREEN linoleum—sea green with clouds of white moving across it. Dozens of windows lined the two long sides of the cafeteria, with one wall of windows looking directly into the seniors' parking lot. The room was full of light in January, and cold.

Linda, Leslie, Sylvia, and I sat together; Leslie and Sylvia across from me, Linda at my side. I was taking Spanish that year and I knew Linda's name meant *pretty*, but I thought it hardly captured her. I searched hard for the right word to describe her looks. Elegant? She wore her hair natural and cropped close to her head. She had smooth rich skin, a face that was almost flat in profile and so serene you could print it on a coin, long arms, strong legs. Finally the word *lovely* came to mind—lovely Linda—but that hardly seemed to capture her.

She was tall and sinewy, haughty as hell when she wanted to be. If she saw some of the snobbish girls from our class in the hallway, she'd crank her chin up so high you could see the outline of her windpipe and swish right by them, not even granting them a glance.

"Come on, girls," she'd call out airily to us. "We'll be late for our manicures!" Or our tennis lessons. Or the opera. Swish, swish, swish, nose in the air. But she could never keep up the act for long. Soon enough her whole body would double over and shake with laughter until tears flowed down her face. Linda could make you laugh until you cried or until *she* cried, but if the wrong people were laughing or laughing for the wrong reason, she would shut down fast. She had only to make her face go expressionless—a still black face—and the laughter would freeze midair.

There was only a handful of black girls at Sacred Heart, four or five out of five hundred, including, in our class, Linda, Leslie, and a worried-looking girl named Rita, who served on the student council. In our senior year, Rita would become class president.

At the table diagonally across from us in the cafeteria, Joan Connolly sat with a group of loud, gossipy, good-looking girls, once again playing bodyguard. It was as if she was working a double shift. Her large red hands twitched on her lap. Cuffed in the stiff white blouse, they looked as incongruous as lobsters on a leash.

From freshman year, this group of girls had elected themselves class royalty. They thought the choice was obvious, that the peasants knew they were peasants. There was Louisa with her long brown Barbie doll tresses, little Stacie, very pretty and brimming with aggression, mascaraed Rose, her dark eyes bulging slightly out of a face that was greasy with makeup, and four or five others. Like frat boys, they were always in a pack, so their presence was felt en masse, a dense and glittering force of female confidence.

They went to Florida at winter break and came back and compared their tans. They wore Notre Dame class rings on chains around their necks. They went steady. With seniors. Any fat girl, any plain or pimpled one, immediately felt their contempt.

The fact that they didn't like me was no surprise. The previous year I'd been so far beneath their radar, I might as well not have existed: I never wore makeup, it was obvious I read books, I studied Latin, didn't have a boyfriend, and I cared about doing well in school. Sophomore year I changed, and they noticed me, but they didn't much like what they saw. Recently Rose had cornered Sylvia in the bathroom and told her, "If you were smart, you'd stay away from Kathy. You're too nice to be hanging out with a girl like her."

That afternoon, as I was eating my usual lunch—Hostess cupcakes and chocolate milk—I heard little Stacie let out a yelp at something Joan had said: "You're kidding! Really? That's disgusting." And they all looked over at me. I was sure Joan was telling them about me and the boys at the Teen Center. But I didn't care. The very fact that they were gossiping canceled out anything they had to say. My mother's lessons about never saying anything bad about anyone had gone very deep.

While I'd decided to ignore the girls, I could see they'd gotten Linda's attention. Without having any idea why they were snickering—not that that mattered to her—she began to plan a response. Linda liked to play with the class queens, like a cat plays with a mouse. At first, all she did was drum her long, ringed fingers on the tabletop. Her fingers made a spiderlike sprawl—she had strong fingers, many silver rings, even on her index fingers—and they struck the table harder and harder, beating out a drumroll to . . . what?

She lowered her head to ogle the girls, and when she did, her glasses slid down to the tip of her tiny, flared nose. Improbably, they hung there. Sylvia, Leslie, and I turned to follow her gaze.

The class queens had finished discussing me and were now oiling their arms and legs. Protecting their winter vacation tans. If enough sealant was applied, perhaps they would make it until early spring, when they could hit the backyards with their aluminum reflectors.

"Ugh! I'm peeling!" one girl cried.

"Hmmmmm . . ." Linda murmured, pressing her lips together like she was seriously pondering something.

"Uh-oh," Leslie said.

"Excuse me, girls. Be back in a jiffy," Linda said in one of her peppy white-girl voices.

"Linda, don't . . ." Leslie warned, sounding alarmed but looking interested.

Linda was already sliding away in her chair. She didn't get out of the seat, just pedaled the linoleum with her large handsome feet until she had pulled up to their table.

She put her arm next to Louisa's and said, "Why, you're blacker than I am!"

"I am . . . *not*!" Louisa replied, jerking her arm away as though Linda's touch had soiled her. She had a look of revulsion on her face she didn't even try to hide. "This isn't . . . *that*! It's a tan!"

"You forgot a spot. Better rub some cream on," Linda continued helpfully while the girls buzzed. "You're getting a little ashy there."

Then she came pedaling back, waving to us as she came.

"Just having a little chat with the girls," she explained, docking at the table with a thud and reaching for her Coke at the same time. "Trading beauty tips." She smiled her close-lipped doll's smile and wagged her head back and forth, like one of those electric doggies you used to see in the back windows of people's cars.

Leslie was giggling into her little cupped hands.

"Linda, you're so droll," she said. It was a compliment they handed back and forth to each other frequently.

Then Leslie took her pick out and began to fuss with her hair. When she was done, she patted the back of her head coquettishly and announced, "I'm a lover, not a fighter."

When we left the cafeteria that afternoon, Leslie hooked an arm over my shoulder, pulling me into her.

"Hey, chum," she said and then, nestling her lips in my ear, she began to sing, "Jimmy Mac, when are you coming back . . ."

"How is that bad boy?" she asked affectionately, though she had never met Jimmy, and never would.

Later I would say that I went out with Jimmy for three months, so maybe I started seeing him in early December. But I probably cheated on the time. It might have been the end of December or early January, two and a half months that we went out or even less and I rounded it off. Three just sounded better because almost from the start I was trying to imagine telling someone the story of what happened that night in the car with Jimmy and the boys, and I didn't want the listener to take Jimmy's and my relationship lightly. So two and a half months became three. And even though I'd turned fifteen that November, in my story I was still fourteen. That's the way I would tell it, I decided, if I ever did. Because if I said I was fifteen, the listener might say what happened wasn't so bad or that I should have known better.

Whenever it was that Jimmy and I started seeing each other, I remember our first night very well. We'd had sex in his car, and as we drove out of East Rock Park I was sitting over by the door, ready for a drop in the temperature. Wasn't that how it had gone with Nicky, hot, hot, hot, then cold?

"What are you doing way over there?" Jimmy had asked, tilting his head sideways at me. "Don't you like me anymore?" *The boy asked me*. I slid across the seat and under his arm. He pulled me closer, his leather jacket crumpling softly against my back.

"Do you want to steer?" he asked.

The next day he called and we went out that night, and the night after, and the next one. . . . By mid-January, Jimmy and I were as thick as thieves.

I'd given up rubbing my legs, chattering my teeth, and stamping my feet, and now I was huddled into a tight ball on the cement steps in front of my house. But as cold as it was that winter, and it could get very cold waiting there for Jimmy, sometimes for ten or fifteen minutes at a stretch, I still wouldn't be caught dead wearing gloves or mittens, a hat or a scarf. I didn't even wear a coat, just my leather jacket, which was so short it didn't cover my hips. Socks, I had decided, were uncool, so I always wore panty hose under my jeans.

Winter break had ended and I was back in school, but the rhythm of my evenings remained the same: dinner, dishes, then out the door or back upstairs to my bedroom. I spent three or four nights a week with Jimmy, the others doing homework, chatting with Linda or Leslie or Sylvia on the phone, reading, dreaming—and thinking of Jimmy.

As I sat there shivering on the front stoop, I craned my neck toward Clifford Street. I knew that was the route Jimmy would take, because he always stopped at the Teen Center before coming to me. I could hear his engine the minute he made the turn from Putnam Avenue—a throaty, grinding noise, like the car was chewing up the street.

As soon as Jimmy pulled up, I saw that the car was full. Most of our evenings began this way, Jimmy coming for me with a carload of boys, usually the younger ones, the little brothers moving up, flunkies or friends, but none of them with cars of their own or money in their pockets or a man's need to shave—or a girl like me at their disposal.

Timmy stepped out of the front seat. "Howdy, ma'am," he said, tipping his bangs like a hat. I slid in next to Jimmy; Timmy followed.

"Hey, babe," Jimmy greeted me, kissing me on the mouth. Ben and Stevie and Neal were crowded together in the back. Hey, hey, hey all around.

"Kath, you want a beer? We got a case back here if this motherfucker gets his big feet off it."

"My feet ain't big!"

"Where we going?"

"Fuck, anywhere! Let's go!"

When they got Ben's feet off the beer, they handed me one. A can of Schlitz, wet to the touch. I popped the tab and put it on my index finger, wiggled it, watched it wink in the streetlight. Jimmy took my hand and moved the tab from my index finger to my ring finger. It was like a chorus of birds opened up in my chest, Jimmy, my love, my heart, *my man*.

"With this beer, I thee wed," Timmy said, smiling crookedly and pushing the bangs from his face. I knew Timmy had a crush on me, but he seemed to have resigned himself to the role of witness to Jimmy's and my romance. To me, Timmy was like a twin brother; he was my age, my height, school-bound, curfew-bound, always underdressed and so always cold, such a familiar combination of enthusiasm and awkwardness that I found it impossible even to imagine him pursuing a girl, or making that first move.

When I bent my head and took that first sip of Schlitz, my mind played a magician's trick, and it was Jimmy's breath I was tasting, his cold lips, and I drank it slowly in a smoky kind of swoon.

Jimmy turned the music loud, draped his arm around me, and we took off with a sense of expectation so strong you might have thought we were actually going somewhere.

The heat was blasting from the floorboards. The little pine tree hanging from the rearview mirror whirled round and round. Jimmy turned to smile at me, so close I could smell the beer and Marlboros on his breath. He hadn't shaved. His jaw was furred. From the back, a voice as deep as a drum said, "No shit." Oh, I was happy then. I'd been with all three of the man-boys who ruled the Teen Center. That didn't spell trouble to me.

Jimmy liked to drive slow. It drove the boys crazy sometimes, but it made me feel like we were king and queen of the streets, out surveying our kingdom. When he took the corner at Dixwell Avenue, he turned the wheel using only the palm of his left hand—the master of one-handed driving because he liked to keep his other arm around me. He had green eyes, charcoal lashes, and close-cropped reddish-brown hair. When I brushed my hand up the back of his neck and head, I could feel each bristle. His jaw was square—a man's jaw in profile, which was how I saw him most often, there at the steering wheel—and he had hard, thin lips, a tight James Cagney grin. His hands were rough, the fingers callused. He'd dropped out of school before I met him and worked as a car mechanic at a gas station close to the New Haven borderline.

If I were making up the story, I would have chosen sullen Nicky or rude-boy Patrick to play the part that Jimmy eventually played in my life. Call it a failure of the imagination. But Jimmy was so playful, so lighthearted, and always, until the end, affectionate toward me. I can't remember a single sharp word from him, any hint of coldness or contempt. I knew he was a troublemaker, of course, but saw no anger or despair in him, no twisted psychology. Trouble just seemed to find him, and when it did, most likely he'd be grinning at it, as if trouble was just one more guest at his party. It was his loose and easy generosity—everybody along for the ride!—that drew people to him. It made you think he was never really doing anything bad, just up to some boy's mischief.

From the backseat, Ben was yelling, "Close the fucking windows!"

"Auntie Ben!" the boys shouted back.

Ben was called Big Ben and sometimes Ben Gay. Bulky, dark-haired, and still carrying his baby fat, Ben always had something to complain about. When the window was open, he wanted it closed. When it was closed, he was suffocating.

Sixteen, but with his heels dug in hard. He was determined to be cranky.

I didn't know enough yet to realize that he was what my mother would have called a late bloomer. He didn't yet feel what the other boys were feeling about girls. That confused and angered him. I knew he didn't much like girls but I thought if I was nice to him, he would treat me the same. I know I treated him better than the boys did.

"Jimmy, it's like fucking Alaska back here!"

"You pussy," Stevie said.

"Kathy?" Ben asked.

"Kath, don't close it!" the boys yelled, but I reached over Jimmy and cranked the window up.

"Thanks, Kath," Ben grumbled. "Fuckin' assholes."

Jimmy gave me a sly smile. "The boys are acting up," he said.

"Yeah," I said happily, and we listened, proud as parents, prouder even, while they argued in the back.

Jimmy wasn't the quickest one in the car, but he was always the one having the most fun. He slid a Gladys Knight tape into the deck and started singing along. "She's leaving on a midnight train to Georgia . . ." he sang to me, changing her words so they would come out right, "I'd rather live in her world than live without her in mine . . ." until the boys began yelling for some Zeppelin. He gave them the Allman Brothers instead, and the car fell into a stillness so that there was only the music, the bass throbbing, the heat coming up at us in waves. My hand began sneaking up Jimmy's thigh and the boys exploded into another argument. "Get off my fuckin' foot!"

I ain't on your foot.

Yeah, you fuckin' are. What's this? It's my foot.

That's a fucking snow shovel. No wonder I'm steppin' on them—look at 'em! You could plow roads and shit.

Fuck you. My feet ain't big.

Kathy! Kath, look over here—are these big feet or what?

Jimmy was laughing the way a man laughs when something funny's going on, but he also has a hard-on and a hand secretly stroking it; that is, with about as happy a laugh as I'd ever heard.

"Big feet, big dick," Ben shouted in self-defense.

That's when Jimmy decided to drop them off at the Teen Center. When we pulled up to the curb, they didn't want to get out of the car.

"Ah, come on, Jimmy!"

"Why the fuck we gotta get out?"

They knew why and they weren't happy. Jimmy paid them no mind. He gave them a big cartoon grin—*what can I do, boys?*

"Party's over," he laughed. "It's past my bedtime!"

"Where you two going?"

Stevie gave Ben a shove toward the door. "You know where they're going."

And then Jimmy and I took off for East Rock Park.

Once inside the park, we left the road. The trees took us in and then stood guard over our car. They were heavy with snow and hung with so much dazzling ice that on a sunny day, it would have hurt your eyes to look at them. A deep hush came out of the woods, deeper and denser the longer you listened, and then you could hear tiny pops and cracks, ice shifting, a squirrel hunting, one bough letting go of snow deep inside the forest.

"Look, he's sitting up, he's begging," Jimmy said after he unzipped his pants. The flat belly, the stiff hairs on his thighs, the hard dick with its snake head; a triangle of warm, white flesh, almost glowing in that dark car.

He was begging to be petted, so I did. Jimmy put his head back and yowled softly, like a distant coyote.

Jimmy explained all kinds of things to me. No one else had bothered. They all thought I knew. Or didn't care whether I did or not.

He told me a man's semen built up in him so that if he went a long time without fucking, he would have so much to shoot, he would fill you up. Legs up made it easier for him to get in. Legs down, tighter and nicer. I wouldn't get pregnant if I took a hot bath when I got home.

Whenever I slipped my hand under his balls, Jimmy would say, "Aren't they heavy?" He was joking but he wasn't. He liked to think that his five o'clock shadow hurt me. "It's sharp, isn't it?" he'd ask, rubbing his jaw. "Did I scratch you all up?"

The windows steamed over and then the steam froze in a child's drawing of snowflakes. Outside this crystal curtain, there were owls in the trees, wolves in the snow, moonlight like ice, shadows like ink. Inside, we were bare-skinned, warm to the touch.

One night, he wove his fingers through my hair and gently pushed my head down, whispering fervently, "Suck it, baby, please." When I took it in my mouth, he leaned back and petted my hair, saying dreamily, "Like your Popsicle."

After he came, we always laughed, as if each time it was a complete surprise. Then we lay holding each other in the backseat. Sometimes he fell asleep gripping my hand so tightly that I was sure he needed me to save him from something, and I knew that I would.

Back then I didn't know girls could come, too; I thought what I felt was the apex of sexual sensation, the warm and shivery tingling when he touched me, the profound jolt when he pushed himself inside; shock and sense, revelation and rightness hitting all at once.

On the ride home, I sat under the curve of his arm, the fingers of his right hand falling over my right breast, all very casual, but we were slinky with pride. He steered with his left hand, a Marlboro hanging from his lips. When he glanced sideways at me and grinned, the cigarette pointed up.

"Am I your man?" Jimmy asked me, as if he had to. But that was the thing about Jimmy—he asked anyway.

He dropped me at the front door and was there again the next night. We could hardly bear to be apart. If he ran into my parents, he was as charming and clumsy as some shaggy dog, but to me he was the epitome of masculinity, and in retrospect the first wholly successful challenge to my father's dark suit and tie.

On Sundays, Jimmy and the boys and I would visit the Teen Center director, a big, fleshy woman named Donna with brown hair down to her hips. Donna was half hippie, half shit-kicker, and she lived in the only apartment complex in Hamden. It was practically across the street from the firehouse, looming seven stories above Whitney Avenue. She had a black boyfriend and they were always in bed when we arrived. They lay there naked under the sheets and we raided their refrigerator and then, Cokes in hand, pulled chairs up around their bed.

When Donna and her lover spoke to each other, their voices hummed with self-satisfaction, and I could feel their pleasure, naked under the white sheets and our gaze. She'd lean back against him and he'd reach over her to grab the menthols or lighter from her night table, pausing, it seemed, to let us see his black arm against her marshmallow skin. He was all ripples, lean and long, and she was a mountain of whipped cream.

"So what are you boys and girls up to today?"

"Boys and *girl*," Timmy said.

"Kathy and her merry men," the boyfriend said.

"Hairy men," one of the boys cracked.

"So you two are together now?" Donna asked Jimmy and me.

"Every night," Jimmy said to laughter, pulling me close.

"Better watch out for that one," the boyfriend said to me.

"Kathy's the one you got to watch out for," Donna told him. "She's a free spirit, right, Kathy? Like me."

"Better not be too free, baby," her boyfriend reminded her.

Back home, I sailed around the house singing "Midnight Train to Georgia." I told my sisters that it was Jimmy's and my song. I was madly in love. It was Jimmy, of course, but it was also the gang of boys who came with him. My tribe in the woods, the one I'd been looking for the night I ran away. My brotherhood.

Sometimes I worked on the poem I'd begun the first night I saw Jimmy, swinging a log on our front lawn. In the latest version, he was standing on a windswept cliff at midnight, still surrounded by police. *They didn't care that he loved me—and I him—or that his whole wild life was mine*, I wrote, and then those very unimaginative cops put *my man's proud body* in handcuffs and led him away.

We didn't seem to *do* much, Jimmy and I, but we did it almost every night. Once in a while Jimmy got to my house late or had to leave early. "I gotta go see my old lady," he'd say, and always with such regret, I thought he meant his mother.

I don't know how long it took me to realize that he was talking about a girl, but when I did, I wouldn't let myself feel anything about it. Then I heard the name Chrissy and knew she was one of the two Chrissys at the firehouse. I'd never seen Chrissy by herself and it was strange to think of Jimmy approaching her through a forest of shining hair, long clicking fingernails, smoke, bubble gum, and whispers. He would be an intruder there. He would have to beg. I was sure Jimmy was grateful to have found me, his true love, and equally sure he would soon break up with Chrissy. That he didn't do it right away made sense to me. At fifteen it was easier just to slide from one moment, one adventure, to the next, carried quickly, almost violently, by your deepest feelings. It would all get sorted out eventually, I thought, and the unwanted girlfriend would just disappear, along with any other inconvenient bits of reality.

On Valentine's Day, Jimmy presented me with a little white teddy bear wearing a T-shirt that said, "I Wuv You." Wasn't that the truth of the matter? His heart revealed?

By the end of February, the snow was piled high in the yards. Donna had been fired by the town of Hamden right after some of the boys at the center torched the girls' couch and pushed it down the stairs. She was replaced with a nervous-looking man named Alan.

The hostility of the firehouse girls had grown thick as brambles. When I walked in, it was so intense that if none of the guys I knew were there, I'd turn and walk out. I'd never been hated by girls before, and the ugly look on their pretty faces came as a shock. I wasn't happy about the situation, but I wasn't as worried about it as I should have been. I just stopped going to the firehouse and started spending all my time with "my boys," as I'd come to think of them—Jimmy and the shifting cast of characters that came with him.

Some nights they picked me up at home. Sometimes, in my impatience, I met them halfway to the Teen Center. I waited on the corner of Putnam and Clifford, stamping my feet against the cold. Under my boots, the lawns were crunchy with frost; my breath was a warm, moist cloud. If I was early or they were late, I'd sometimes wonder what it would be like to be stranded out here, connected to no one, belonging nowhere. But as soon as I climbed into Jimmy's car, I left the loneliness and cold behind. We made a warm, jostling world of our own, one completely cut off from the day-lit world, the world of parents and other teenagers where your behavior was closely watched and carefully controlled. Outlaws and rebels, we had each other, and nobody outside of that car mattered.

That's the way I felt then, though now I can see how it really was. The boys were still hanging out at the Teen Center, even though I wasn't. Jimmy was still best friends with Nicky and Patrick. Chrissy was Jimmy's official girlfriend. The boys who went out with us at night, and the girls who hated me, were all full-fledged members of the Teen Center gang; I was the only outsider.

The ground was eroding under my feet, but I never noticed. In fact, as my world became smaller, each aspect of it became more precious, every moment alone with Jimmy, every festival shout from the boys, every time they said "Kath" with affectionate familiarity and Jimmy held me close and whispered, "Babe."

18

Bad Cop, Bad Cop

IN MARCH, I WAS STILL BABY-SITTING FOR FAMILIES IN MY NEIGHBOR-hood—a good little girl when they all started hiring me the previous spring, who would've thought I wasn't by wintertime?

I was an excellent baby-sitter, of course, a popular one. I worked for five families and had a waiting list. It was a job I was well suited for. I knew how to change diapers, give baths, bandage cuts, I enjoyed playing with invisible friends, talking to shoes, singing lullabies. If the children wanted to stir a pot of blocks and feed me out of it and do it again and again and again—and each time I was supposed to exclaim "Yum! Yum! Pudding!"—I would.

This particular night, I was working for the Luganos, my favorite family. One boy and a baby girl. Nina was rosy-cheeked and sturdy; the boy, Johnny, was pale-faced and fragile, enchantingly serious. He found a ready nest in my heart, the place Stephen had carved out six years earlier, which has been open ever since, a place for small, unearthly boys who seem, even at five years old, to keep their own counsel. There were never any scenes when the Luganos left the house. In fact, that night Johnny waved them out the door so he and I could get back to flying planes off the living room furniture.

When someone started knocking at the Luganos' front door, I'd al-ready tucked Johnny and Nina into their beds and I was wandering through their living room, shoeless, sliding my feet across the sage-green carpet and drinking chocolate milk. Even though I liked being in other people's houses when they weren't there, after an hour of exploring the Luganos' refrigerator and kitchen cabinets, reading their grocery list and their wall calendar, and trying out each chair in the living room, an itchy kind of restlessness had come over me. There were no books in this house! I was ready to go home, but it was only nine o'clock. Two more hours to go.

The knocking started softly, with a stuttering rhythm, tap, tap-tap-tap, tap-tap, like the person at the door was signaling in a secret code.

When I'd told Jimmy earlier in the day that I couldn't see him that night, he was unhappy. "What do you have to baby-sit for?" he'd asked in a plaintive voice. "I need you to take care of *me*." I didn't think he was upset because he was desperate to see me—he just didn't like being told that he couldn't. So when he asked me where I'd be, I gave him the address, assuming that if he did stop by, we'd have a quick, quiet visit, two young lovers stealing some time. Maybe we'd huddle outside on the steps, share a cigarette, kiss.

Before I could even get to the door, the tapping changed into a harsh knocking and I flew—he'd wake the children! There was a window set high in the door and when I stood on my toes and looked out, I saw Jimmy and the boys huddled in their coats, faces pinched with cold and lifted toward the window.

"You can't come in," I mouthed through the glass. Could they even see my mouth? I shook my head but my heart was already stricken. I had never refused Jimmy anything.

But why, why did he bring all of them?

"Kathy, it's coooold!" they cried, their voices getting louder and louder. "Come on, open up!"

I unlocked and cracked the door.

"You have to go—" I started, but they pushed the door wide and piled in, Jimmy, Timmy, Ben, and Stevie, beer cans in their coat pockets but already rolling drunk. They went straight for the kitchen. Opened the refrigerator, the cabinets.

"Where do they keep the booze?" someone asked, while Jimmy snaked an arm around me and planted a cold, beery kiss.

There was nothing good to drink and nothing handy like brownies to eat, so Timmy picked up an egg, yelled, "Hey, Jimmy, catch this!" and threw it across the kitchen.

The egg splattered against the wall and dripped down.

"The kids are sleeping!" I hissed frantically, but it was as if a gong had sounded; mayhem.

"Batter up!" Stevie cried, gripping a spatula. Another egg went flying. "Strike!"

Jimmy grabbed a plate from the counter.

"Frisbee?" he asked Stevie. I tried to grab his arm.

"Fucking flying saucers!"

Timmy went reeling out of the kitchen, bounced off the hallway wall, and disappeared into the living room. I got there in time to see him lurch sideways as if the floor had tilted underneath him; a table tipped, a vase exploded.

"What the fuck?" Timmy said, looking puzzled.

He dropped to his knees and wavered over the broken glass.

"I'll clean it up, Kath, don't worry, make it nice and clean and nice," he mumbled. He dove for a piece, missed, dropped his cigarette on the carpet.

"Timmy, it's okay, I'll do it. Come on, Timmy, you gotta go now," I told him, trying to pull him to his feet.

From the kitchen, the smell of beer and burning. When I went back in there, Ben and Stevie were sliding around on the eggs like figure skaters. Then Ben's legs flew out from under him, and he landed like a rock.

A beer can lay leaking on the floor. A cigarette had been ground out on the linoleum.

"Jimmy, you gotta get out of here! Please! Please, you have to go! The parents are gonna be here any minute!" And with *parents*, not *children*, I herded them through the hallway and out the door, shutting it behind them.

I was turning back to the kitchen to clean, heart tripping with panic, when Jimmy started hammering on the door.

"Kathy!" he yelled. I froze.

"Kathy?" In the silence that followed, I could hear him listening to me listening to him.

"Kathy, let me in! Kathy, please!" Boom, boom, boom, his fist beating out a protest. Then he howled: "Katheeee!"

He'd forgotten he had a car to go to, a home, friends, days and years ahead, another night to see me. "Kathy!" he called out again. My feet were nailed to the carpet. I wanted to cry.

Then his fist plunged through the window on the door . . . glass, blood, winter wind.

"Wh-who is that?" And behind me at the top of the stairs, Johnny stood owl-eyed and shivering in his baseball pajamas.

When I jerked open the door, the boys were falling into the car, yelling, "Jimmy, let's get the hell out of here!"

Jimmy just stood there, swaying slightly and looking down at his bloody hand, his face soft with wonder.

When he looked up at me, his eyes were filled with gratitude. In his play-around, fuck-around boy's life, he'd stumbled upon something real in himself, something running deep. It was there, but by tomorrow he'd forget.

"Sorry, babe," he whispered, then turned and stumbled toward the car.

I closed the door and locked it, but an icy wind tunneled through the broken window and into the rooms of the house. It was as if the outside had come inside: Furry black tree branches looked close enough to touch with my hand, snowflakes gusted through the hallway, and the streetlight spilled onto the carpeted floor. In the window frame, jagged claws of glass were splashed with blood. Suddenly it seemed that I had always known this would happen someday, that I would bring chaos into a home, set fire to the curtains, flood the family room, hurt a child. Known it from the day Frank Lee leaned over Henry's seat with a look of great anticipation on his face and a pencil in his hand.

Upstairs, Johnny was huddled in bed. His fist clutched his pajama top like a fretful old man.

"What do they want?" he asked, his scared eyes glued to my face, still depending on me.

"They're gone now, Johnny," I told him. "They won't ever come back."

Downstairs, I taped a piece of cardboard over the window, washed the kitchen floor, dug in the carpet for pieces of glass.

Mr. and Mrs. Lugano came rushing into the house. He was first through the door, disheveled, wired, ready.

"Are you all right? What the hell happened? Are the kids . . . ?"

I tried to explain but before I could finish, their faces closed against me and they ran upstairs.

When they came down, their eyes were cold.

"We're calling the police," Mr. Lugano said. "And your parents."

I waited on the couch in the living room. Mrs. Lugano came out of the kitchen with a glass of milk.

"You will never set foot in this house again," she said as she carried the glass upstairs.

Out of nowhere, like some kind of space machine, a police car slid swiftly to the front of the house, jerked to a stop, went dark. Doors opened, slammed, a metallic crackling came from the sidewalk, and then two men in blue had their feet planted in the living room.

While the Luganos explained, the cops looked around the room, taking in the damage, their eyes always coming back to me. They had their notebooks out and were asking me for the boys' names when my father arrived.

He came in the door fast. The charge coming off of him was so strong even the cops caught it. They stood straighter, their cool cops' faces rippling into life.

My father could barely keep his attention on what they were telling him. He bent his head low, trying to concentrate on their voices. I could see his jaw clench. His lips were pressed so tightly together they'd almost disappeared. When he lifted his head, his hot blue eyes pinned me to the couch.

"Big-time," he said, coming across the room. "You've messed up big-time now." He shook his head slowly, still working his jaw and clamping down on his lips. This was personal; this was between him and me.

"What the hell were you thinking? *Were* you thinking? Do you have one thought for anyone but yourself? You had *one* responsibility here, *one* job to do, to watch over their children. That's what they hired you for, that's what they pay you for—*to protect their children.*" He paused before passing his final judgment. "You didn't even come close."

"She won't tell us the boys' names," Mr. Lugano said, and once again, all eyes were on me.

"You won't do *what*?" my father said.

"This isn't a game," one of the cops told me. "You've gotten yourself into some serious trouble here."

"So, you're going to protect the guys who did this," my father said, as if the cop hadn't even spoken. "You put two kids at risk, you didn't protect them, you didn't protect this house, but you're going to protect the guys who wrecked it. I bet you think you're being honorable. Tell me, is that what you think?" He was shouting now, his face shoved close to mine. "Huh, dummkopf? Is that what you think?"

"Do you know how Johnny feels now?" Mr. Lugano said. "Do you know what you've done to him?" This was worse than anger. These people hated me, hated me so much it made them hate my parents, too. Even years later, when the Luganos saw my mother and father at a party, they turned away, refusing to speak.

"Do you think we'll ever leave him alone again with any babysitter?" I knew they wouldn't—they were good parents, they loved those children to death.

"He's up there shaking, afraid to go to sleep," Mrs. Lugano cried out angrily. "Afraid they're going to come back."

"Just give us the names of the boys, and then we can talk with them," one of the cops said to me, and I knew he was saying: *Give us the names, for your sake, for ours*. With the boys' names, they could leave this family drama behind and get down to business, round up the boys, be their cop selves pitted against something surly out there in the street.

But I couldn't. Say the name Jimmy out loud and watch it being written into a cop's notebook? No, I couldn't. There wasn't even any choice about it. Every teenager knew you didn't rat on your friends, and every Dobie knew you never, ever gave in to pressure—standing alone against the crowd was the very definition of moral courage for my parents, especially my father.

The second cop had said nothing the whole time, just stood there watching. They seemed like bit players, the cops, dressed for a more major part.

"You *owe* them the names," my father said. "Have you given one thought, one tiny thought inside that thick skull of yours, to what could have happened here? They could've set this house on fire! They could've hurt those kids! This is *your* responsibility, *your* fault, your mess to clean up now. Crying? *You're* crying?"

Mr. Lugano started shouting then. "What the hell about my little boy crying in his bed upstairs?"

"This isn't about you," my father told me. "Nobody here cares about you anymore."

"We trusted you!"

But still I couldn't give their names.

The silent cop stepped forward then. "I might have a solution," he said.

First, he went into the kitchen with the Luganos to work it out with them. My father said nothing while they were out of the room, just stood there glaring at me, while the other cop shifted back and forth on his creaky shoes.

When the three of them returned, the cop explained the deal to me, one that the Luganos had agreed to reluctantly. He told me that if I convinced the boys to pay for the damage, then they would let the matter drop. No charges, no arrests, no more questioning.

"You tell the boys that either they come here this Saturday, meet with the Luganos, and make good for the damage, or you'll give us their names and they'll be arrested and charged. Okay?" His voice was stern, but there was no anger in his eyes. I held on to his gaze almost desperately.

I would have to make the boys believe I really would turn them in, he explained. "Even if you won't—"

"She will," my father interrupted.

"That's the only way this will work. Those boys wrecked this house. They owe the Luganos. You know that's only fair." He was appealing to my sense of justice, the only person in the room who seemed to believe that I might have one.

"The boys pay up and that will be that. No more questions. It's a good deal for them. Okay? You got it?" I nodded. "So you'll get them over here on Saturday?"

When I agreed, he told my father, "You can take her home now."

My father charged down the empty street, still not talking to me. He couldn't even bear to look at me. I watched our shoes. His were moving fast, mine made a pathetic ticktacking sound on the concrete as I tried to keep up. Occasionally I lost my footing and skittered over the icy sidewalk. I thought we might walk this way forever, my father's anger burning next to me like a furnace, the two of us rushing past snow-filled yards and low box hedges, our footfalls and our breath the only sounds.

He was a mast of moral fury, the worst kind, towering over me. I had no defense against him. If I trusted anyone on morality, it was my father.

My mother and father fought over what to do about me. My father wanted to straight-out forbid me to go to the Teen Center. He didn't know that I hardly went there anymore. My mother didn't think that was a smart idea. She was afraid of driving me away altogether.

My father ignored her. No more Teen Center, he told me. And worse—no more Jimmy.

"That's it. It's over. You meet with those guys tomorrow night and tell them to get themselves over to the Luganos' next Saturday, and then you can consider yourself permanently grounded."

I didn't know then that they'd argued over me. Didn't know what they had been saying about me since that night. But at fifteen, I told myself I didn't care what my parents thought. I certainly acted like I didn't—and wasn't that halfway there?

My father stopped speaking to me after that. For several days, maybe even a week, my dinners would be passed in a kind of exile: "Would you tell your sister to pass the peas."

I met with the boys and gave them the message. They couldn't believe I'd set them up.

"You fucked us over," they said, before turning their backs on me to discuss their next move. It was as though I had ceased to exist.

On Saturday, they went to the Luganos'. They went grudgingly, but with money in their pockets. The Luganos must have talked to the other families I baby-sat for, because I never had another call. I couldn't be trusted with children anymore.

The day my father began speaking to me again, I immediately wished he hadn't.

"Jimmy has an arrest record a mile long!" he roared. How had he found that out? I knew Jimmy was on probation when I first met him, though I'd never asked why. All of the boys got into trouble for the same things: drinking and driving, brawling in public, and then taking a swing at the cops when they arrived. They lived on probation like souls in limbo, neither good enough nor bad enough for a final judgment. To me, Jimmy's "probation" was just part of the package—his leather jacket, the James Cagney lips breaking into a Gladys Knight song, that rough calloused hand gripping mine tightly as he slept. Tough, tender, hapless; in charge, in trouble; big man and little boy all wrapped into one. But my father knowing about the probation was a completely different thing. I felt like he'd reached into my secret nighttime world, yanked open the door to Jimmy's car, where we lay naked, and shone a flashlight in.

   I waited until my parents were in bed that night and then snuck out the back door to meet Jimmy—the first of our secret rendezvous. Back then, I thought I was a clever little escape artist. Years later, my parents told me they used to hear me going out. Short of locking me in my room, however, they didn't know what to do.

I wasn't going to give Jimmy up. But holding on to him wasn't anything like those stories of star-crossed lovers in the books and movies I knew. I saw him only three or four times in the next two weeks, and each time we used our old meeting place, on the corner of Putnam and Clifford. He came without the boys those nights, so I figured they were still angry about the Luganos. And Jimmy himself had changed. There was nothing obvious; he wasn't hostile or mean. He just stopped reaching from the driver's seat to open the door for me, and no longer greeted me with the big, dancing grin I loved so much—simple omissions that had me scrambling to get back what I had lost.

Everyone was angry at me—my father, my mother, the neighborhood families I knew through baby-sitting, Ben, Timmy, Stevie, the girls at the Teen Center. Even Jimmy, it seemed. Except for my three Sacred Heart girlfriends—Sylvia, Linda, and Leslie—all the people in my life had turned against me. There were no eyes that brightened with love or pleasure when they saw me. The light had gone out and I couldn't figure out how to turn it on again.

That winter the weather was bitterly cold; the skies were steel gray. I imagine that I acted as if I were extraordinarily cheerful.

The Bottom of the Sea

THAT NIGHT BEGAN AS ALL OUR NIGHTS HAD ONCE BEGUN—JIMMY came for me with a carload of boys.

It was the middle of March, snow high and crusted over in the yards, Christmas lights long gone. The sidewalk, patched with ice, gleamed dully beneath the streetlamps. I hurried down Clifford, my hands, red and stinging, jammed into the pockets of my fake leather jacket, my chin buried in its fake fur collar. No one else was out. Between the tapping and skittering of my boots, I heard the soft thump of snow falling off the trees. Steam rose from my mouth. My eyeballs felt dry, my lips peeling; I bit at the little flags of flesh, then fumbled in my pocket for Chap Stick. I had the look of a thousand other suburban white kids, slatternly and a bit desperate.

When I got to Putnam Avenue, I leaned against a tree. Stamped my feet and waited. Twenty minutes? Thirty?

When Jimmy's car finally pulled up, it stopped several yards from me and then just idled, smoke pouring from the exhaust pipe, windows blank. I felt as if my whole body had paused to watch, to listen. Why was Jimmy doing that? Didn't he see me?

I walked over to the car and when I bent to look inside, I saw the boys had come. Then the passenger door swung open and flooded me in a wave of heat and smoke. Neal slipped out—"Hey, Kath"—and I slipped in. There behind the wheel was Jimmy. The smile was back on his face, his eyes were reddish, dancing. "Hey, babe," he said.

Ben was in the backseat with a man who occasionally appeared at the Teen Center, the one with the long blond hair I'd chased up the East Rock hill that night in September. His name was Scott, and he'd never come out with us before. He was a lot older than we were, in his thirties. Since the boys always owed him money, I assumed he was selling them drugs—he didn't have any job that I knew of.

Scott didn't know I'd tried to catch up to him as he climbed the hill the night I ran away. Only six months before, and it already seemed like years. He wore the same brown leather jacket he'd worn that night. His blond hair still hung to his waist. He had a hard face, a lean, mobile body. I was surprised he was out with us, tucked in the backseat like that. I didn't think cruising the streets with boys who still hid beer in their coat pockets would be very interesting to him. It was a compliment, I thought, his coming along with us.

In the backseat of the car there was a case of beer and a bottle of gin. Another couple of six-packs were stashed on the floorwell under Neal's feet.

Hey, hey, hey all around. Jimmy jerked the music loud, draped his arm over me, pulling me close, and we took off.

The road stretched ahead, then disappeared around a curve. Jimmy chased it down, sent it spinning under his wheels, only to see it unroll ahead of him again.

"It's cold as a motherfucker," Ben said from the back.

Neal asked me for a cigarette. His lips were the color of cherry candy.

"Whoa, your hands are like icicles," he said.

"They don't feel cold," I told him, trying to curl my fingers. "They feel like they're on fire."

Neal was always the smartest and quietest of the boys, middle class, college-bound. Unlike the others, he never got drunk, and he was always trying to get me to wear his gloves.

"I'll warm your hands up," Jimmy volunteered. He took my hands and pulled them inside his thighs, closing his legs around them. Then he spoke in my ear, "It's warm there."

The little pine tree hanging on the rearview mirror swung from side to side, smothering us softly with its scent. I felt like I had a reprieve. They weren't angry about the cops—not for tonight? Not ever? On Dixwell Avenue, Jimmy took a right and Ben grumbled, "Why you going this way?" It was just like old times, I thought, and I laughed aloud from a relief so pure, it felt like happiness.

We were across the street from the Dunkin' Donuts when Jimmy turned to reply to Ben and we veered off the road and crashed into something, throwing us back against our seats.

"Shit!" Jimmy yelled and got out of the car to see what we had hit. In the headlights, we watched him bend down. When he stood up again, he was grinning.

"A snowbank!" he shouted.

"A goddamn snowbank!" he laughed as he got back inside. He gunned the car backward while cars behind us honked angrily.

He screeched forward and we took off, the boys giving the other drivers the finger. If someone had started chasing us then, we might have been saved. But no one did. The boys laughed. "Fucking snowbank." "Sneaky motherfucker." "*Big* motherfucker." But the snowbank had jarred something loose. There was a heavy restlessness in the air.

"Don't open that beer, man. We get stopped, I'm fucked." The boys wanted to drink, but Jimmy wouldn't let them. He was on probation again.

They began to get irritable. "Man, shit, what did we get all this beer for?"

"Fucking pull over somewhere!"

Usually this was about the time Jimmy would choose to drop them off at the firehouse with some of the beer, but tonight he just kept driving.

"Jimmy, let's go somewhere we can smoke this joint," Scott said, and suddenly there was silence, like a dip into darkness. My neck prickled, but it was only Ben and Scott crouched back there.

"Maybe later," Jimmy said. "I want to cruise around some."

He asked me to light him a cigarette, and after I'd slipped it in his mouth, he pulled me closer to him. As I leaned against his chest, smelling his leather jacket, I felt like I'd been taken into a safe hiding place, and I could stay here and never, ever have to go home.

We cruised down Dixwell Avenue, by the strip mall with its barren parking lot, then under the railroad tracks, passing nothing but an office complex closed down for the night, a boxy building in a big square lot. Then some scraggly brush, buried in snow, and another darkened strip of stores. Traffic lights blinked on deserted corners. Grimy mountains of snow stuck to anything that stood still—lampposts, mailboxes.

The boys got quiet looking out. Their boredom began to weigh on me.

Greg Allman was singing about being tied to the whipping post; the bass held the song down and then turned slow and deliberate.

"Let's get the fuck out of here," Jimmy said, and he made a wide U-turn using all four lanes of Dixwell Avenue, letting the back of the car shiver a little. "Let's go up to East Rock."

We cut through the reservoir on that cement bridge, took the dark hill, up, up. . . .

How hard I'd chased Scott that night! Running, yelling, spurred on by that rope of yellow hair that swung from side to side. He'd vanished, right at the crest of the hill, at the entrance to East Rock. I guess you could say that tonight was the night I'd finally caught up with him.

We rolled into the park, our headlights revealing the black bodies of trees, their roots swamped in snow. The road had just begun to climb steeply when Jimmy veered to the left, plunged straight into the woods. The car churned, cleaved snow.

Jimmy cut the headlights. The snow glowed; shadows slipped wetly from trees. Scott lit a joint and when it was passed to Jimmy, he told me to open my mouth and he put his lips to mine and breathed the smoke in. I took off my jacket and a little hum went through the car.

"Kath, hand me one of those beers up front, they're colder," Scott said.

"Me, too," Ben mumbled and then repeated himself. "I want one, too, Kathy." I leaned over the backseat, propped myself there, and watched. Jimmy slid his hand up the back of my shirt.

I don't remember what we talked about: a concert they'd been to, pot deals they got burnt on, a fight, a cop, a father? I do know that they would have done most of the talking. I wasn't one for words back then, not in a car full of boys. And my recent brush with their anger, with so much anger inside and outside of my family, had made me cautious. The fear I had of losing Jimmy and the boys had gnawed a hole inside. I felt emptied of thoughts and feelings; a creature in waiting. So I sat there smoking, drinking, handing out beers, and taking the boys in through my skin, their harsh voices, their laughter, their thick-knuckled hands and tight jeans, the essence of them—that whole hard-ass, shaggy-dog, boys-to-men thing.

I drank my beer, pressed leg to leg against Jimmy. When I held the flame under his cigarette, he wrapped his hand around my wrist. They began to pass the bottle.

Neal leaned back against my right shoulder. His arm rested on the side of my breast. It seemed to have landed there by mistake; the car was that crowded. But then he noticed. I could feel him noticing. He didn't move.

Every time I took a breath, my breast swelled against his arm. The quiet between us was like an urgent, whispered conversation. My chest rose and fell. Neal turned his head stiffly to say something to Ben or Scott, keeping his body where it was. When he turned back around, he looked down at his hands. I held my breath for a few seconds, but that only made it come harder and faster. It was so obvious now, it was like my breast was petting him. Jimmy left the car to piss and that broke the spell. There was no reason to be crowded up against each other anymore. Once, by mistake, yes, that was the trick. Again and planned? No longer so enticing.

When Jimmy came back, he put his mouth to my ear. "I want you." He kissed me, filling my mouth with his tongue. It cleared the air, dissipated the heat, put me back on track.

"What did Chrissy do to you, Jimmy? Decide to fucking brand you?" Scott said roughly from the backseat.

Was it only then that I noticed the bruises on his neck? It was dark in the car and the collar of his jacket had hidden them but his jacket was open now and I could see them, big purplish red welts covering both sides of his neck. They were fearsome. She'd marked him with her teeth. That desire! That confidence! claiming him for all to see and he, yes, he letting her.

Unbidden, the image of Jimmy laughing as Chrissy dug her teeth in came to mind. Did her long hair fall across his face and did he lift it up, winding it around his fist? Did he almost burst with wanting to have her because he couldn't? He wore the bruises openly, I could see now—he wore them with pride.

"Ring around the collar," Ben smirked. They were laughing and that is the moment I began to change, not quick quick quick, like sweet Cinderella at the stroke of midnight, but slowly. Something was dissolving inside of me; the air itself seemed to shift, a dingy light coming up from the floorboards.

Jimmy put his arm around my neck. "You're mine, right, babe?" And pulling me close, he took my hand and put it on his crotch. "Feel that?" He wanted me now, he whispered again, and I was still thinking this was just a profession of desire, not a plan, still stumbling through the thicket of dark hair and long sharp teeth, when he said, "The boys can leave."

Leave? Go where?

"They'll wait outside if I tell them to." He turned to the backseat. "You guys can wait outside, right?"

"Outside? What the fuck . . . nah, man!"

"Fuck, I ain't freezing my balls off out there."

"Come on, don't be a bunch of pussies."

"It's cold out there, man."

But they grabbed their jackets anyway, grumbling and cursing, and opened the doors. A question stirred the air, a ripple of wonder and doubt, of expectation, of something very close to awe.

"Wait a minute, babe," Jimmy said and got out with them. I heard him yell, "Ben, close the fucking door! She'll freeze her ass off." And then I sat alone in the car, listening to the rise and fall of their voices outside, a stranger to myself, a "she" who could freeze her ass off.

Jimmy opened the door grinning rakishly, held out his hand. "Come on, babe, they said it was okay. Let's go in the back." It was a done deal.

"Come on," he cajoled. "They can't wait out there all night." I felt awkward getting out of the car in front of them and then crawling into the backseat with Jimmy.

"Jimmy, give us the bottle!"

"And my smokes!"

"And don't take all night, man."

They didn't say anything to me, though they were all watching. Their eyes had changed. They were regarding me with a cold, lively interest. There wasn't anything friendly about it.

Sex went fast with Jimmy, and everything felt wrong. My shirt stayed on and being half bare didn't feel seductive, it felt babyish and obscene, more like I'd forgotten to put my pants on. My body was cold and dumb. Heavy luggage being moved about. My feet looked white as fish.

Outside, I could hear them stamping their boots on the snow, spitting, talking, laughing. The windows had steamed and then frosted over, curtaining us in ice.

When Jimmy was done, he was full of gratitude—"Oh, babe, that was good," he said, nuzzling my neck—but it wasn't the same. There was something false in his manner, something slick and keening.

I pulled on my pants, thinking of the boys freezing outside.

"Wait a minute, babe," Jimmy said, and leaning close, wrapping his arms around my shoulders so I could feel the soft cotton of his T-shirt, the hardness of his chest, he asked, "why don't you let the boys have a taste?"

Does it matter what was said next?

He pressed his case with his usual charm and some schoolboy

logic, only he wasn't Jimmy anymore and I wasn't Kathy, wasn't Jimmy's girl, wasn't any girl I recognized. But there she was in his eyes: a girl who would fuck four boys.

"Come on, babe, do it for me," he said. "I want them to see how good you are." His smile then was the smile of a man who knows how charming his smile can be. "It's no big deal. You do it with me." The boys were hollering to come in out of the cold.

"Jimmy, hurry up, fucker!" And then someone said "Fuck *her*," and I heard them laugh.

"They're freezing their balls off out there, babe. What do you say?"

"But . . . I don't want to."

"Why not? You like them, don't you? They like you. They're out there freezing their asses off for us. Come on, Kathy."

"Hey, Jimmy, here comes Chrissy!" With her name came a flash of the day-lit world, all that was public and acknowledged, and another flash, not a thought at all, though I write it down here as one: They had decided to put me in my place, to, in a sense, finish me off. From now on, this is where I would always belong, in a car parked in the woods, late, late at night, here and nowhere else, like a dirty secret.

After that everything seemed to come at me through a haze, like I was hearing the echo and not the original sound.

"Hey, fuck it, we're coming in!" Jimmy opened the door, yelled, "One second!" and as he closed it, the boys were coming toward us.

"What do you say, babe?" he asked. "Okay? For me."

They stood at the car doors, darkening the frost on the windows.

"Babe, you got to. I told them you would."

He'd told them? I guess certain elements tumbled into place then, Scott's presence, the ill-tempered restlessness, Jimmy's rush, the slick sweetness afterward—they must've thought it out beforehand, discussed it with one another. But all I really remember is a great rushing and clashing in my brain. The dream, worn and frazzled already, held together only by my desire to have it so, disintegrated and I woke, as my parents and teachers always warned I would.

Another girl might have . . . But what does that matter? I wasn't another girl. "I"—that mysterious concoction of desires and history, relationships and inclinations, hope, fear, pleasure—was nothing but a raggedy coat wrapped around the thing they wanted.

Fists banged on the car roof.

"Okay, babe?"

I know I whispered it, but I said it. "Okay."

Scott must've gone first. He was so much older than the other two and not at all nervous. I guess Ben and Neal crowded into the front seat, though maybe they took turns waiting outside, I'm not sure. But I know Jimmy was there because I remember what he did. When Scott got on top of me and pushed himself in, and I started crying, Jimmy reached over the seat, took my hand, and said (for the first time), "Kathy, I love you." He kept hold of my hand.

When he was done, Scott decided I should suck him. He pushed me down on him, but I gagged and threw up. He leapt out of the car, cursing, "Stupid bitch," while somebody in the front seat laughed. "Hey, hey!" Jimmy said. "Go easy, man."

When Neal got into the back, he looked angry. I kept my face turned into the seat.

Ben was soft and had to use his fingers to push himself inside. He was so heavy, he was pressing the air out of me.

"I can't breathe," I told Jimmy.

But Ben kept going, his breath huffing in my hair. Panic swept through me and I started screaming.

"I can't breathe! I can't breathe!" And then he stopped.

More beers were cracked open. I dressed. Bent down into the backseat, into the darkness near the floor, I pulled my panty hose up over each foot, then up over my legs, thinking how ugly they were, the color, a pale pasty hue called "nude," the white crotch at the top, so modest and sanitary, poked through with little breathing holes. Above me, the boys talked loudly, laughed, passed the bottle.

Jimmy put the car in drive. No one suggested I move up front. Neal slid into the backseat with Ben and me. On the drive home, I hugged the door, staring silently out the window, seeing nothing until the gray house came into view, its porch lights on.

As I got out of the car, one of the boys said, "Kath, don't tell anybody and we won't." I headed up the driveway toward the back door and the kitchen light, tripped, and fell over a snowbank.

(In the years to come, that would be the image I would fix on, not anything that came before, but that stumble and then my face in the snow. Each time I conjured up that moment, I made myself taste the rough dirty ice, feel again the cold moisture seeping through my jeans. It was as if I wanted to punish that girl, push her face into the snow for what she had done.)

I fell once more just trying to get into the house and up to bed. My mother had been washing the kitchen floor, so she'd moved all the chairs over by the back door. I walked into that blinding kitchen light, my panty hose sticking to my skin—they were strangling me! I had to get them off!—and my foot hooked onto a chair leg so that I went crashing to the floor. As soon as I landed, I burst into tears.

"Honey! Are you all right? Did you hurt yourself?" My mother hurried over to me and all I could think was *Uh-oh, she's gonna know I'm drunk*. No one but a baby would cry at this fall. I had to invent something fast.

"Jimmy and I broke up," I told her, climbing to my feet.

"Oh, I'm sorry, honey," she crooned, helping me up from the floor. Not a word was said about the fact that I wasn't supposed to be seeing Jimmy; that hadn't been her idea anyway. There were just the two of us alone in the kitchen, and the only thing that mattered to her was that her daughter was crying, her stubborn, difficult daughter. "What happened, honey?"

I backed away from her so she couldn't smell my breath.

"He was mad about something and we had a fight."

"Well, maybe you two could work it out, talk about it when he's cooled down some." Gently, she brushed the hair back from my face. I kept my mouth closed, my head down, and breathed through my nose. I knew she was grateful for this mother-daughter moment, for—finally!—this child's confidence. She would have liked it to continue, for me to need her, be close to her again, but suddenly a great wave of sleep was arching over me. I could feel its cool darkness all the way down to my bones.

"I'm really tired," I told her. "I think I need to go to bed."

"Okay, honey, go get some sleep. Things will seem better in the morning," she said. "And, Kathy, even if you two can't work it out, someone else will come along that you'll care about just as much, maybe even more. I know it doesn't seem that way now but it will happen." Her face was very close to mine.

"All right?" She was nodding, hooking me with her bright eyes. "Okay?"

The rope was thrown. I had to at least look like I was reaching for it, though my spirit was sinking down into that hole in the bottom of the sea; hooks and lures couldn't catch it.

"All right, Mom."

20

Commander and Foot Soldier

THE SKIES WERE LEADEN THAT SUNDAY, THE SNOW SOOTY, BUT ST. RITA'S Church was lit up as bright as a banquet hall. Father Sheridan took his place at the altar, giant Father Sheridan in purple Lenten vestments, raising his large white hands. Everyone stood, and then everyone knelt, bones crackling and popping, and then, in one voice, everyone prayed: "In the name of the Father, the Son, the Holy Ghost . . ."

My family took up a whole pew. Beth Ann knelt on one side of me, my mother knelt on the other, her face lifted expectantly toward the altar, refreshed and hopeful. The light streaming down from the ceiling had flattened the stained-glass windows that lined the church, turning the saints into opaque blocks of blue and red. They seemed to be trapped inside the glass, looking out at us with their dark, tragic eyes.

Father Sheridan's blond hair was shorn close to his head, and he wore thick black-framed glasses like the kind they issue to grunts in the Army. He was a young priest, more drawn to the hope of Jesus' resurrection than his great suffering.

"This is the blood of Christ," he intoned, as he lifted the gold chalice high. He always spoke as if he'd never said Mass before, as if he was infusing each word with its own essence. This made the older people twitchy and my parents swoon. Father Sheridan was good friends with my mother and father, good enough, and worldly and compassionate enough, to have told my mother she could start using birth control. After six children and two miscarriages, the doctors were worried about her surviving another pregnancy, and Father Sheridan said it was more important that she be around to be a mother to the children she had than to give birth to any more.

At the Kiss of Peace, I turned as I was supposed to and shook the hand of the man behind me, avoiding his eyes. I'd always felt more in tune with the old people in the parish, who preferred to take the Mass in a solitary fashion, not forced to touch their neighbors or be sociable, but never more so than now. "Peace be with you," I heard the man say. "And with you, too," I replied as we shook hands, relieved to have gotten that over with.

When Father Sheridan took his place behind the lectern, he paused before starting the homily, his gaze moving over the faces of his congregation. Then he began talking gently, softly, meaningfully, about the Virgin Mary, and a black curtain fell across my brain.

As soon as we returned home from church, I pulled on my jeans and boots and went out the door, heading up Clifford toward the Teen Center.

For two days after the night in the car, I'd stayed huddled in bed, telling my mother I couldn't go out, couldn't go to school, because I was sick. And I was, of course, lying there hour after hour in dumb misery, stripped of thought, feeling, motivation. Why get up and dress? Why wash? Why eat? I felt as if I were on a high bridge suspended in fog, unable to see the land I'd left behind or the one I was heading into. I didn't know what had happened that night, only that it was big and awful. I hadn't seen it coming, had no idea what to do next.

But on Sunday, the third day, I had risen from my bed, as if my Catholic upbringing demanded that of me. As I dressed for Mass that morning, I felt as if I'd been erased from existence, like someone pummeled and then left on the ground—to survive, or not. I suddenly decided that I had to go back to the Teen Center and walk in there *with my head held high*, as I put it to myself, because I needed to show them that I was still alive, that I existed on the other side of that night in the car. And, just like that, with "head held high," I had a plan of action. Instead of hiding away in my bed, I would face the Teen Center crowd—and that night in the car—head-on.

Mountains of frozen, dirty snow filled every yard I passed. Winter still had Hamden in its teeth. When I reached Putnam Avenue, my father's words began to circle in my head: *Time to face the music, kiddo.*

My father's belief that you should never run and hide or shift the blame or take the easy way out was rooted deep in my bones. He'd made it clear in the stories about his own life that the finest form of bravery was to stand alone against the crowd, and that he expected his children to be forthright and brave, too, to do the right thing even when it wasn't easy. Of course, the challenges he would have imagined us facing were those of a child—owning up to undone homework, or defending an unpopular opinion in the classroom. My own situation was one he could never have dreamed of.

If my father had known what happened, what would he have done? Gone to the cops? The boys' parents? Or hunted the four of them down? And what would he have wanted me to do? All I know for sure is that he never would have wanted me to act alone. But as I walked toward the Teen Center that afternoon, I thought my father's morality was a perfect fit for my circumstance, and I heard his words as marching orders. *Time to face the music.* Only one and a half more blocks to go; I could do it. I had to.

When I stepped inside the firehouse, all hell broke loose. "Look who's fucking here!"

"That douche bag coming in like . . ."

"Gang bang!" Their astonishment and delight couldn't have been keener. A group of girls who were sitting on the floor, knees tucked up against their chests, began to open and close their legs. Some of them held up four fingers. Boys crowded in from the poolroom in back.

My vision refracted, and as bizarre as the scene already was, it became more so with faces split in two, revolving around and around one another, a circle of mouths, twin tongues wagging, half a leer, a startled eye. And below the kaleidoscope of faces, down on the concrete floor, the crowd of girls kept spreading their legs and clapping them shut like singing clams in some hyperactive cartoon.

Alan, the new director, came racing into the front room and ordered me into his office. Once we were inside, he slammed the door shut behind us and told me I had to go home.

"They've spent the last two days talking about beating you up," he said. He would drive me home, but I had to go *now*.

"I don't know why you had to come back here," he said irritably. He told me to follow him out, and to stay close behind. We cut through a throng of kids. The girls were off the floor now, their faces rubbery with rage.

"Fucking sleazebag!"

Boys grabbed their crotches when I went by. "What about me, Kathy? Gag on this."

They followed us out and amassed by the entrance. *(So long, rebels, so long, outlaws.)* Alan's car was in the driveway. He ran around to the driver's side, yanked open the door, and hopped in, leaving me standing on the sidewalk, waiting for him to unlock the door on my side. Instead he turned the ignition over several times, trying to start the engine in the bitter cold. The girls began to scream, "Fuck her up!" and all I could think about was how much I wanted to be in that car. But then a snowball hit my back. Suddenly all the Westerns I'd watched with Sylvia, all the boys' adventure books I'd read, merged with my father's tales of heroism. I turned to face the mob.

Whap! A snowball hit my chest and sprayed up into my face. "Fuckwad!" they yelled, a brand-new word to me. Snowballs flew by my head, a stick hurtled through the air, whirling like a boomerang, a crumpled soda can bounced off the car, and then, finally, the door opened, and I ducked inside.

Alan dropped me off at my house with advice I no longer needed—not to return.

I went through the kitchen—"Hi, honey!"—and straight upstairs. Halfway to the attic, a thought stopped me dead in my tracks: *Life will never be the same.* The life I'd thought of as my creation from that day when I had stepped onto my parents' lawn wearing a candy-striped halter top—that life was mine no longer. Before I could bear even to think about what had happened that night, they'd named it. Before the shock had even lifted, they'd begun to spread the word of a gang bang and the disgusting girl who had let it happen. As narrators of my story, the kids at the Teen Center weren't compassionate or insightful or even very imaginative, but the tale they told was remarkably convincing; it had the ring of hard truth, for what kind of girl would let four boys do what those boys had done to me?

To be honest, I don't remember much of that March. I must have moved through it like a sleepwalker. I was shaken awake in April—not by a kiss, but an errand run. Usually my mother sent Beth Ann, but she wasn't home that day and there was a prescription that needed to be picked up at the pharmacy.

I stepped out of the house cautiously. In less than one month, without my having noticed, the world had been transformed. Winter was gone, not one gritty trace of it left behind. The trees were suddenly sprinkled with tight green buds. Across the street, big black birds filled the old people's lawns. They moved across the grass with their heads bent down, eyes intent on the ground, more herd of cows than any winged thing. It was time for short-sleeve shirts and nylon windbreakers. Spring again.

I set off down Treadwell on my errand, avoiding the route I would usually take, because I didn't want to go past the firehouse. But immediately the sidewalk began dragging at my feet. Was I really going to let fear control me now? Less than a month had passed since the night in the car, but I told myself that they'd thrown me out, they'd had the final say, what more could they want? I turned around and made myself head up Clifford toward Putnam Avenue.

When I reached Putnam, I was a block and a half from the firehouse, two blocks from the Country Club Pharmacy. I kept up a steady chant: *Go on, get going, you can't run all your life.* I was commander and foot soldier, ordering myself along, grim in all that birdsong.

At Tom's Market, I saw a group of kids gathered outside the Teen Center. I could cross over to the other side of the street, but they'd still see me. They would have to yell. Everyone would hear.

As I drew closer, I didn't recognize any of them, but then again I was blind with panic. My ears were roaring. Three houses, two, one— *What can they do to you? What's the worst thing? Don't be a chickenshit*—they were coming down the firehouse drive, blocking the sidewalk in front of me.

Then a group of boys walled me in, but I could only concentrate on the face right in front of mine. It was large and beet red with pleasure and loathing. I stared at it as if mesmerized. Everything else was a blur.

He wet his lips. I could smell the inside of his mouth. He laughed, leaning close.

"Remember me?"

I shook my head.

"Yes, you do," he said loudly. "I fucked you."

This beet-red boy?

"But I don't even know who you are," I protested.

He thrust his face into mine. "Then how the fuck do I know you?" I forced myself to move, pushing past him and through the crowd. As I headed toward the corner, I heard their machine gun laughter at my back.

I never walked by the firehouse again. Not that it made much of a difference. A few days later, when I was heading down Whitney Avenue on my way to buy groceries for my mother, a car screeched to a halt in front of me, and a group of girls jumped out, yelling obscenities and then surrounding me. They wanted to beat me up, but, as I was beginning to learn, it isn't all that easy to throw the first punch. They needed some sort of trigger—my yelling back, or trying to run— but I froze and my fear saved me, that and the fact that the driver of the car started honking for them to get back inside. They were block-ing traffic.

My name had a life of its own now, just as I had wanted, just as Roscoe and Craig had warned me it would. Boys said whatever they wanted about me. Suddenly everyone had had sex with me. My de-nials sounded pathetic, so after a while, I stopped. I'd become the route by which timid boys lost their virginity without losing their timidity. It was too valuable a route for them ever to surrender.

My house seemed much too bright and loud that spring. Windows crashed open, people banged up and down stairs, shouting, Sebastian barked sharply, chopping the air into bits. At the dinner table every-one ate and talked at breakneck speed. My mother's face, as normal as could be—those hazel eyes and full lips, the small furrow running along the tip of her nose—now seemed to belong to a stranger.

I hadn't told anyone, not even Sylvia. Not about the night in the car, not about my reputation, not about what was happening now on the streets. Of course I hadn't. Wouldn't, couldn't, never, ever.

My secret was the reverse of most secrets, which, if you tell, you tell only to your closest friends. That girl in the backseat was hidden from my friends and family but well-known, unforgettable even, to an ever-growing number of people. Without her, I was an imposter. But I wanted to be that imposter, and was willing to do whatever it took to keep her alive. So I knew I'd have to be careful not to go any-where outside of school with either Linda or Leslie. That way I'd avoid having them see a carload of girls shrieking names at me or guys sprouting from the sidewalk insisting that they, too, had had sex with me. That way I wouldn't lose them as friends, for I was sure that was what would happen if Linda and Leslie knew. I wasn't as nervous about Sylvia. Her mother kept her on a tight leash, so we spent most of our time inside her house or mine. She floated in her own dream-world anyway. She could easily miss what was going on. Or not un-derstand it even if she saw it.

I began riding my bike on errands, a blue bike I hadn't been on since I was twelve. I went fast, telling myself that if I could run over that leaf up there on the road, right over the center of it with my front tire, I could win a fight with half a dozen girls. Gliding silently downhill, I scanned the street, every nerve in my body alive and sharp. I could hear a footstep in a thunderstorm. I could brake on a dime. I had eyes in the back of my head. My fingers itched at the brake levers, not touching them but ready to draw. So I tried to imagine myself: gunslinger at high noon.

But no matter how fast I bicycled or what stories I told myself about cowboys and gunslingers, all it took was one blast of a car horn and imagination fled. I was Kathy Dobie, that slut, pedaling fast and looking stupid on a girl's blue bicycle.

21

Sister, Sister

I WAS READING JIM CARROLL'S MEMOIR, *THE BASKETBALL DIARIES*, MY schoolbooks stacked around me on the kitchen table like fortress walls. Musician, poet, high school basketball star and onetime junkie, Carroll told the story of his early teenage years in the deadpan voice of a city boy who flinched at nothing. From the opening line—"Today was my first Biddy League game and . . ."—I felt like Carroll had taken me into his confidence.

I'd read my first memoirs that spring when Leslie gave me Nicky Cruz's *Run Baby Run* and Piri Thomas's *Down These Mean Streets*. Like Carroll, Cruz and Thomas had grown up in New York City, and as young boys all three of them had known the life of the streets—the cops, the gangs, the sad old alcoholic men and sexy neighborhood girls, the local junkies and preachers—as well as any homeless person did. Carroll seemed to get by on wit and bravado alone. Whether boosting clothes from a department store or diving from high cliffs into the dirty Harlem River, he displayed a great disregard for rules— and an equally great desire to plunge right into whatever action he could find. I loved him for that. And for all the mistakes he made, the way his life just seemed to spin out of his control. Carroll became a junkie before he turned fifteen, while he was on a search for something entirely different, something he called "purity." No one I knew would speak as honestly about his or her life as Carroll did. And so I read *The Basketball Diaries* with the kind of ravenous hunger I'd once thought was reserved for food.

As I sat there lost in my book, I was surrounded by my mother's relentlessly upbeat posters, hung one above the other all the way to the ceiling and bearing messages like "This Is the First Day of the Rest of Your Life." Jim Carroll would find that sentiment as depressing as I did, I was sure. But the bond between Carroll and myself was to be short-lived, for when I arrived at one of the diary entries from the summer of '64, there was a description of a sexual encounter that instantly jarred me out of my easy alliance with him. Enter Winkie and Blinkie, blond twins identical down to their leather-trimmed underwear. Carroll had sex with one sister, his friend with the other, and it didn't matter which was which, for they were both exactly the same—two big-breasted, dim-witted, enthusiastic girls who would have sex with any boy who asked. Here, in a book that anyone could read, thirteen-year-old Winkie was described as "a Bronx poodle walking slut." And this by the same writer who wrote of "the stars breathing down" and just wanting to be "pure." I loved this writer, but he felt the same way about girls-who-fuck as the boys of Hamden did. That's how all men felt, I concluded. Even the poets. It was as if my case had been presented to a higher court, and I'd been convicted. I'd never find a better place than Hamden.

Summer was approaching. School, which had unexpectedly become my safe haven, would end. Though Joan and her Sacred Heart friends were bubbling over with malice toward me, excited by the turn my life had taken that night in East Rock Park, they were held in check by Linda's presence at my side. They were afraid of her, so all they would dare were gleeful, hostile glances in my direction, and gossip among themselves, loud enough for me to hear but not so loud as to attract Linda's attention. No screaming, no threats; no being taken by surprise. I could live with that. Never knowing what would happen or when, which face at the mall or on a crowded street corner might suddenly light up in recognition—that was the hard part. The faces always looked the same, disgusted and alive; *douche bag* and *fuckwad* were their favorite words.

Thinking about the summer, I realized that once our vacation started, there would be no safe place for me outside the house. For three long months, no one jollying me along or petting my head and calling me "munchkin" or "Scooby Dooby Doo" or any of the dozens of tender, ridiculous nicknames Leslie and Linda had for me. I had no defense against that future, against thought or dreaded memory, not even the book in front of me. Especially not the book in front of me. I put *The Basketball Diaries* facedown on the kitchen table and headed upstairs to disappear into sleep.

I couldn't think about that night, but I felt as if it was always thinking about me, a stalker without respect for civility, for daylight, or privacy. I might be eating a bowl of Cheerios or taking notes during class or climbing the attic stairs, when suddenly it would leap out at me, not in a whole, coherent memory, but in a stream of filth: shock, shame, guilt. I would try to duck and flee, but a black swarm would explode, swoop, cackle in my head—Scott's furious face when I threw up on him; my naked legs; the girls' mouths dropped open, appalled; Chrissy's neat, shiny ponytail, and Big Ben, soft as a worm, using his hand to grimly tuck himself inside . . .

The afternoon of Winkie and Blinkie I dreamed of little men in yellow cowboy hats and twirling mustaches chasing me down. I kept trying to fly away from them—I knew I could fly, I'd done it in other dreams—but I could only rise a foot or two from the sidewalk, and as my feet furiously pedaled the air, I kept descending, inch by awful inch. I could feel their hands pulling at my shirt. I sobbed in fear and frustration—why couldn't I make this dream come out right?

In May, Michael graduated from Notre Dame High School, Cindy from St. Rita's. I was at the end of my sophomore year. At Sacred Heart we gathered in the back garden to offer prayers to Mary the Queen of Heaven on the month of her Ascension. Instead of studying for my final exams, I took long afternoon naps and then read unassigned books late into the night. For the first time in my life, I received barely passing grades in all my courses. My religion exam was marked with a large D and a note from Sister Mary Margaret in the margin that said *If you need to talk, I'm here.*

And then suddenly it was summer. I planned to spend all three months of it in my room.

That's where I was the day my mother drove Cindy into New Haven for her back brace. Earlier that spring our family doctor had discovered a curvature in Cindy's spine. The only cure was a brace she would have to wear for the rest of her teenage years. The fittings had been done with measuring tape and plaster, so Cindy had no idea what the brace would actually look like. None of us did. *Though by now, Cindy knows,* I thought as I lay there on the bed waiting. And I found myself staring at the door, willing her to walk through it.

Then the doorknob turned and there she was, fluid, tomboy Cindy with her narrow face and rakish widow's peak, strapped into a bulky contraption and walking into the room like a zombie. A rod with a cup attached had been placed under her chin, forcing it up. In order to look at me she had to turn her whole torso sideways, and as soon as she did, she burst into tears. Instantly our mother came up from behind and put her arms around Cindy, desperate to offer comfort. Just as fast, Cindy's tears dried up, her eyes snapping open so wide that I could see the angry red veins at the edges: She was fourteen and caught twice; embraced when she most wanted to fly free.

"It's what's inside a person that counts, Cindy," our mother was saying. Marriage and motherhood must have made her simple, I decided.

After one or two more unsuccessful attempts to find something consoling to say, our mother left the room, and Cindy slid her pants down to show me what had been done to her. She had to wear an elastic waistband now, because of the thick armor of plaster encasing her hips. When she opened her shirt, there was a metal bar that went from the plaster girdle up to her chin and stood stiffly between her breasts. Two more bars went up her back, their ends poking from her shirt collar and through her thin blond hair as if she were a parcel ready to be hooked and carted through the air.

"All the kids in school are going to be looking at me—that girl in the brace!" she cried. "How can I go anywhere in this ugly piece of . . . this stupid, horrible, this dumb, disgusting . . . ?" She couldn't find an adjective scathing enough. But she was looking at me. As she sat straight-backed on the edge of my bed, her hands at her side to balance her, she was asking a real question—how could she be seen in that brace?—and she was expecting me to provide an answer. She assumed I could, that I was wise enough, that I cared enough—I was her sister Kathy, after all, fellow adventurer and ally since she and I were three and four years old. I'd forgotten that person, but she hadn't.

"Let's go outside and walk around the block and see what happens," I suggested. "It might not be that bad. But the longer you wait, the harder it's gonna be."

Cindy protested at first, but soon we were heading down the driveway, Cindy staring straight in front of her with her head held unnaturally high. Halfway around the block we ran into a friend of hers, an excitable girl named Grace. Cindy froze as Grace ran toward us, ready for her shock or pity.

"Hey! What are you doing? Where are you two going?" Grace asked. And then she noticed the brace. "What's that?"

Cindy gritted her teeth. "I've got a curve in my spine," she explained bitterly. "I have to wear this until it straightens out."

"What a bummer," Grace said, cocking her head in sympathy. But then her face brightened, "Jennifer's having a pool party! Are you going? She wanted to borrow one of my bathing suits—as if it would fit her!" Then she started talking about how tall and skinny and flat-chested Jennifer was, and which neighborhood boys would be at her party.

When Grace's mother called her inside, she took off, shouting over her shoulder, "See you later! Don't forget the party!" Three thuds up the stairs, one bound across the porch, and she was gone.

"She didn't even care," Cindy said into the silence, sounding stunned.

"She hardly noticed."

We walked on, past the house where Patrick Cahoon lived, Patrick the Teen Center King who'd taught me the meaning of "69," past

Timmy and Lucy's house, too, where any one of the Teen Center gang could have been visiting. But the fear that had become my constant companion had somehow receded. I'd thrown my lot in with Cindy that afternoon. This was an emergency. At that moment, her life seemed more real than my own.

When Cindy and I returned to the house, we poured ourselves two glasses of Kool-Aid, and went to the living room to discuss her situation. As we sank to the floor, folding our legs Indian-style, Cindy, who wasn't yet used to the brace, toppled over backward.

Shock blanched her face and she looked at me accusingly. Then she burst out laughing. After I pulled her upright I squatted there on my heels, doubled over. Tears ran down our cheeks, our laughter so helplessly out of control that Cindy had to get to her knees or it would have knocked her over again.

Once, when we were younger, Cindy had made me laugh so hard that I'd almost died, but then she'd saved my life. We'd gone snorkeling in a pond on Cape Cod, where our family was camping. We were far from shore, paddling around facedown in the water with our flippers, masks, and tubes. When she turned her face to me, she looked so strange—somber and goggle-eyed, lips distended like a monkey's—that without thinking I laughed. The breathing tube popped out of my mouth, and my next breath in was all water. Gasping and coughing, my mouth working the air like a beached fish, I was unable to draw a clean breath. I began to panic.

"Turn over," Cindy commanded. She put her arm around my chest and began swimming me in. We'd both taken lifesaving courses at summer camp. We knew the drill. When we reached the shallows, I leaned over while she thumped my back, knocking the water out of me. As soon as I could breathe, I tried to tell her why I had laughed in the first place, but she wasn't amused.

"You could've drowned out there," she said severely.

The truth of this was suddenly real. I could have died; she had saved my life. We thought that's what being sisters meant. We went over the event again and again, exhilarated by the close call and by our achievement, hers as well as mine—I didn't struggle, did I? I felt like a model drowning person.

We were enormously proud of our relationship. Who knew what else we would be called upon to do, what battles we would fight to the death, what people we would save if only given the chance? And hadn't we promised each other that if either of us became a "vegetable" the other would sneak into the hospital and pull the plug?

So there we sat on the living room floor, trying to plot the future. Cindy was allowed to take the brace off for one hour a day. One hour of freedom. How to use it? Or as Cindy said, "What can we do with one lousy fucking hour?" The brace was already teaching her how to swear. We were as close as we'd been for the last year. And now I had a chance, through her, to have some kind of summer, after all.

We would bicycle to New Haven. That was my idea. I, too, wanted to be free—free of Hamden. I convinced Cindy to wait until ten o'clock at night, steering us to an hour when the streets would be empty. That evening we took our bicycles out of the garage and set them up in the driveway, ready for takeoff. At exactly ten, Cindy unstrapped the brace, cracking it open as if she was breaking the back of a chicken, and spreading it flat. Then she set the brace on the floor next to the bed, where it stood upright, all hanging leather straps and buckles, thick white pads and gleaming metal.

Cindy slipped into her shorts, a gauzy Indian shirt, and buffalo sandals, and then we ran down the stairs. Our watches were fixed to our wrists.

"Good-bye, girls!" our father called, his face suffused with pride. Much later, when we were all adults, gathered together for a Thanksgiving dinner, he said to my mother, "Our children are friends. At least we did that right."

"One hour now, Kathy!" Our mother made it clear that I was in charge. If anything went wrong, I would be responsible. Before I could even ask myself the question that had begun to plague me—why didn't she and my father ever see any vulnerability in *me*?—we flew out of the house.

Cindy and I hopped on our waiting bikes, pushed off with our feet, and rolled down the driveway onto the street, not a car in sight. Our tires hissed on the pavement, and the wide black river of Tread-well flowed before us. We passed by our neighbors' houses so swiftly that they seemed to be blowing away, then took the turn onto Whit-ney in a big, sweeping curve, our bodies leaning to the right, letting the slope power us around the corner. Cindy sped past, taking the lead. She stood up on the pedals, her short hair waving like a flag, turning now to grin at me.

Past the fruit and vegetable market, faster and faster. All I wanted was to get away from here, away from the pizza place, the Country Club Pharmacy, the beauty parlor, the movie theater, the Texaco gas station.

And then, the beginning of freedom. We left the town center be-hind, and Whitney Avenue swooped down and curved to the left. We were entering a tunnel lined with windy trees. Tall wild grasses and Queen Anne's lace had sprung up between the narrow sidewalk and the avenue; they swayed toward the street like river weeds. I could hear the sound of the waterfall to my left, coming down hard, a sheet of noisy glass, a man-made waterfall pouring over a concrete wall, overflow from the reservoir.

"You Are Entering NEW HAVEN." We shot by the white sign and Cindy checked her watch. She whooped. "Six minutes!" The city had closed for the night but wrought-iron lamps shone on empty side-walks and apartment doorways. A soft, skyward-pointing beam of light traced a Gothic church spire. Back alleys, spidery fire escapes, even empty lots were illuminated by hidden spotlights, and suddenly the whole scene appeared to me as if it were a stage waiting for some-one—Dylan Thomas? Eugene O'Neill? Marlon Brando?—to step out and say something grand and transforming.

Cindy and I rode on, reaching the green in the center of New Haven in twenty minutes. We bought two Cokes at the McDonald's, then sat down on the grass. We had the green to ourselves; our Cokes, which we were forbidden to drink at home; and another thirteen minutes. We discussed clothes—was there a way to look sexy in a

brace, or at least hide the rod at her neck?—and tried to find a solution to two of her more immediate problems: the difficulty of sleeping in the brace, and the way the plaster girdle made her sweat and
then itch. We decided baby powder was worth a try, but as far as
sleeping went, I could only come up with the lame reassurance that,
though she had to sleep flat on her back without a pillow, the metal
rods digging into her back and the chin cup holding her head rigidly
in place, she'd probably get used to it.

On the way back, we left ourselves some extra time and rode
slowly, taking the downhill stretches without pedaling, gliding side by
side. As we hit the curve in the road that takes you from New Haven
into Hamden, I heard the waterfall again but couldn't see it. At that
moment, the night seemed to be making a promise to me.

I'd sailed up and down this street, around this curve, in cars
packed with cursing, laughing boys, happier than I'd ever been in my
life. I rode it now on my bicycle, not happy exactly, but aware of
something unalterable in the world, its richness and its beauty. No
matter what happened, and regardless of whether I was happy or not,
the world would go right on being beautiful. It would always be
there, waiting.

22

The Bridge Back

I HAD TO SEE JIMMY AGAIN. FIVE MONTHS HAD PASSED SINCE THE NIGHT in the car. It had taken that long for the numbness to wear off, and when it did, what emerged from the fog was the image of Jimmy. The apparition was so vivid, it was almost a physical presence.

There had been four boys with me in the car in East Rock Park. What happened that night tied me to them in an awful intimacy that had only deepened as each month went by and I hid the truth from all the people closest to me. I couldn't have explained why I needed to see Jimmy's face, the face that had hovered over the front seat watching the whole time, but it's obvious to me now that I was looking for some acknowledgment of what I'd gone through and was hoping to find it in his eyes. Jimmy would have to see that night as something terrible that had been done to *me*—a girl he knew well, whose hand he had clutched while he slept. I needed someone to see it that way. It would inject some sense, some tenderness, back into my universe.

They say people return to the scene of the accident to try to absorb what happened there. Jimmy's face was my accident scene.

One Friday night in August, I went to stay at Sylvia's house for the weekend. The gas station where Jimmy worked was only a few blocks away. I told Sylvia I wanted to see him the next morning and asked her to go with me. Unlike my return to the Teen Center, I was going to take this trip with a friend at my side.

Sylvia knew that I'd had a boyfriend, that after our freshman year at Sacred Heart I'd found a life that was separate from hers. But she'd never seen Jimmy, and had caught only glimpses of that life from the clothes I wore, the pack of Marlboros in my pocket, and the way I sometimes arrived at her house not in my parents' car but on foot or dropped off by a stranger I'd hitched a ride from, coming up the front walk surefooted and happy, almost swaggering. Since I hadn't spent much time with her that year, she assumed my other life was more enthralling than the one she and I shared. She didn't know it had ended.

We woke that Saturday to a bright, steamy morning. The light outside the window was the yellow of pollen and bees. As soon as we dressed, we headed out her back door and down the two cement tracks of her driveway. Sylvia was singing, "In the summertime, when the weather is hot, you can swish right up . . ." She was so rarely let out of the house, it was like we were setting off on an adventure.

Sylvia's street, Park Road, was lined on one side with trim white houses that had small front yards, and backyards crisscrossed with laundry lines attached to porches by pulleys. No one ever sat out on their front steps, and all the little sunporches were curtained. I thought old people must live in all the houses; it was that careful a neighborhood.

My street, by comparison, was filled with kids on bicycles, hop-scotch squares drawn in pink chalk on the sidewalk, and older broth-ers noisily mowing the lawns. My family's power lingered in my mind—I still thought they lived in the center of things.

Even the name of Sylvia's street, *Park*, seemed dull. I thought it showed a lack of imagination. Unlike Treadwell. These days, when I looked at our street sign, I thought it was solemnly nodding to me. "Tread well," it said, offering encouragement and warning, both at once.

We walked along under big shade trees across the street from a city-run nursery, where rows upon rows of red, yellow, pink, and white roses bloomed and baked in the sun. Between the insects and the hot, glancing light, I had the general impression of an unpleasant busyness over there. After four short blocks, Park Road curved gently to the left and ended abruptly, rudely almost, after all those billowy trees, and there we were at State Street. The gas station was right on the corner.

There was a man at the pumps, a rag stuck in his back pocket. I asked him if Jimmy was working that day.

"Jimmy, there's a coupla young ladies here to see you!" he shouted.

Jimmy came out of the garage. His face looked thicker than I'd remembered, and his jaw, scraped clean, was pale. No wolfish shadow there. I'd never seen him this early in the day, so soon after he'd shaved. I had no plan in place, no words rehearsed.

"Uh, Kathy," he said, looking surprised and then, I couldn't deny it, uncomfortable.

He glanced behind him, as if his work was waiting for him in the garage and waiting precariously, a car barely balanced on a lift, perhaps.

Jimmy, it's me! I wanted to cry out.

"This is my friend Sylvia," I said instead. Sylvia looked as if she had just taken a bath. Her cut-off jeans were perfectly trimmed, each thread the same length, making a fluffy fringe of white on her olive thighs. Her shirt was pressed. She never sweated. It suddenly seemed important for Jimmy to know that I had a girlfriend, and a girlfriend who was this clean and cute, so obviously girlish, so obviously good.

Before I could say anything further, a carload of girls screeched into the station like an unfunny cartoon. The two Chrissys, Joan Connolly, and Georgie. It seemed unbelievable, this bad luck, as if they'd been waiting five months for their cue.

"What the fuck are you doing here?"

"You fucking slut—you show up here!"

They were tripping over one another in their indignation. They couldn't believe I'd popped up again, here of all places, on their turf, and more important, on their time. From their point of view, my life had stopped that night in the car, never to go forward. They could move on—graduate from high school, make new friends, fall in love, get married—but my life story had already been written.

"You don't fucking take a hint, do you?"

"Fuck her up and she'll take a hint," Georgie said, looking like an enraged dwarf next to beautiful, long-haired, red-lipped, white-toothed Chrissy—she who was so obviously the right girl for Jimmy.

"What's going on here?" I heard the man ask.

"Yeah, I'll fucking break her nose," Joan said, ignoring him and rubbing her clenched fist like a lucky stone. Violence became her. Her blue eyes were electric. Those big, rawboned hands made admirable fists. The girls made a circle, closing us inside.

"Who do you think you are, douche bag, coming around here?"

Chrissy stepped in close, her face a breath away from mine. "This is *our* turf—" Joan cracked her knuckles while Chrissy shouted, "Don't you know what you are? You're nothing but a dirtbag. Dirt-bags don't belong here."

"Jimmy, I think you should take these two girls home," the man said.

"You're gonna drive that douche bag home?" the girls wailed.

"Break it up now," he told them. "Time for you all to leave. Jimmy, you two girls, get in the car." And while he stood watch, we made our escape.

"You better not come around anymore," Jimmy said to me as we drove off. "They come over to the station a lot." He might as well have been the mousy director of the Teen Center driving me home that March afternoon, put out by all the trouble I was causing him.

"Well, it was nice to meet you," Sylvia said as he pulled up in front of her house. She thought Jimmy had saved us.

"Uh, nice to meet you, too," Jimmy replied.

"Be cool," he said to me. Be cool?

I almost said *okay*. The word jolted me.

Do it for me, Kathy. I told them you would.

Okay.

I plunged from the car.

"Bye, Kath," he added, my name on his lips like a knife. But it meant nothing to him; he hadn't even intended to wield it.

Once inside Sylvia's house, I didn't offer any explanation and she didn't ask. To Sylvia, what had just happened made perfect movie sense: We'd been surrounded by a violent mob and told to get out of town by sundown.

"I believe they was in a hanging mood," she said gaily, rubbing her neck. She zipped around the kitchen, from stove to refrigerator to cabinet, getting things ready for the family dinner that night, while I sat at the kitchen table watching her.

I'd taken off my earrings, delicate silver loops with three blue stones strung on each wire. As Sylvia sang and chatted, sliced and chopped, I twirled the earrings around on the tabletop with my finger, then stuffed them in my pocket. I wouldn't wear them anymore. They were very pretty. They reminded me of girls I knew, slim girls with willowy hair who burned incense in their rooms and smelled faintly of patchouli.

I no longer remember what we did the rest of the day. But around ten or eleven that night, after we'd eaten and Mr. DeAngelis had gone up to bed, we heard a car horn blasting outside. Sylvia and I had been watching TV, with Mrs. DeAngelis and Albie asleep on the couch behind us.

"Hey, fuckin'—" Boys' voices. A carload of them, parked across the street. "Come on out! We know you're in there!"

Mrs. DeAngelis woke with a start. "What's that yelling? Who's out there?"

"Come on out!"

"What are those boys yelling? They yelling for you?" she said, looking at me. She went straight to the window and drew the curtains. Now they were leaning on the horn and all yelling at once, but nothing was coming through clearly except my name.

Mrs. DeAngelis jerked open the front door and yelled, "You get out of here now or I'll call the police! You hear me? Get out of here!"

She didn't look like some lady who was going to call the cops. She looked like someone who would grab the thing nearest to her—a pot, a leg of lamb, a meat cleaver—and take care of the problem herself. Her black eyebrows had shot straight up to the roots of her hair like dangerous birds ready to swoop down. She had God, the sleeping houses, the leafy trees, and every white lacy curtain in every kitchen window on the block on her side. That's why the boys fled, I think—someone else had grabbed the moral high ground.

When she came back in, slamming the door shut, Albie was pacing the floor like an animal whose cage had been rattled. His eyes were wide and he was breathing hard. It had a kind of ha-ha-ha sound—was he going to start giggling?

"You get out, too," Mrs. D. told me. "I want you out of this house now."

"Ma! It's not her fault!" Sylvia protested, but her mother had gotten hold of the movie script and it wasn't a Western anymore.

"I'm not having any trouble here. We never had anything like this here. This is a quiet neighborhood! There's old people sleeping right next door! I'm not having it. She goes. Now."

"But, Ma, how's she gonna get home?"

"She can call her father. She can call him and tell him we've got a store to run in the morning, we work hard around here, and I'm not having carloads of boys coming around here howling for her all hours of the night, we don't live like that—"

"Ma, she doesn't live like that, either," Sylvia said, laughing nervously.

But Mrs. DeAngelis had always had her doubts about me. "She's years ahead of you," she had warned Sylvia. "And you're too much of a follower." Now she'd been proven right.

"Albie! Go up to bed! And you, too, Sylvia." She turned to me. "Call your father and then you can go wait for him outside."

"Ma! Outside!"

But Mrs. DeAngelis was past arguing.

My father answered the phone right away, so I knew he was up late.

"Mrs. DeAngelis doesn't want me to stay overnight" was all I said.

I walked out the back door and crouched down on my heels, hiding in the shadows against the side of the house, in case the boys returned. I lit a cigarette, pulling on it hard. It flared for a moment and then settled into a steady burn. It seemed alive to me, quiet and alert, as loyal as a dog.

I listened for cars—dangerous cars and my father's car. My ears were like eyes as I followed the road past the shuttered greenhouses of the city nursery, around the curve and uphill toward the entrance to East Rock Park.

Above me, a window screen scratched open.

"Psssst . . ."

I stood up. Sylvia, hanging out of her bedroom window. "Kath, I'll call you tomorrow," and she was gone, the screen sliding back into place with a snap.

I settled down on my heels again, and pictured my father sitting in his armchair in the living room, going over the papers he often brought home from Yale, Muzak playing softly, a drink on the lamp table next to him, ice cubes melted into slivers, the rest of the house sleeping. I thought of him on the road now, gliding smoothly toward me.

And then there he was, pulling into the driveway. He leaned over to open the door for me.

"Mrs. DeAngelis changed her mind, huh?" he asked as I climbed inside.

"Yeah, she's got to get up early tomorrow," I said. He didn't seem to require any further elaboration.

The patter of voices on the talk radio station eased us into a comfortable silence. At the entrance to East Rock Park, the road veered downhill and he drove as if he were cutting that road himself, through the dark trees, past the plush lawns of the big white houses, straight across the reservoir. How powerful and swift the big station wagon seemed in his hands!

Sitting there watching the streets fly by, I felt newly calm, the way a child feels after a long cry. Exhausted, yes, but also opened up, no defense against the truth and no desire for that defense, either. It had dawned on me that there was only one way those boys could have found me at Sylvia's house: Jimmy had told them. In fact, Jimmy must have brought them there. He was in that car. I wasn't going to pretend that wasn't so.

The second betrayal drove home the first. Somehow Jimmy had managed to deny any connection to me—and to the night in East Rock Park. The burden was mine alone to carry.

As my father drove me home, I sensed how much strength I would need to hold on to my own vision, my own truth, and I became even more protective of my memory of that night, more distrustful of other people's interpretation. Everyone must be kept away. It was like keeping a crime scene intact until the big boys, the experts, got there to examine it.

Only in this case I would be the expert—who else could say what that night meant to me? And so I would store the experience away, keep it guarded for years.

23

Metamorphosis

"THE EXPENSE OF SPIRIT IN A WASTE OF SHAME . . ." MRS. COLASANTO sat at her desk reading one of Shakespeare's sonnets aloud while we followed along in our textbooks. Junior English with Mrs. C. was the only class in which Linda, Leslie, and I chose to sit up front, though at the moment Linda was resting her head on her open book. Shakespeare always affected Linda this way. From the first "how oft" or "thine outward thus," Linda's eyelids would droop, and her body would slump in her chair. But the line had jolted me. The classroom walls seemed to melt away at those words, as did the parking lot, visible through the windows, the statue of Jesus, the green and well-groomed grounds. Nothing existed but the voice of this long-dead writer shooting straight across the centuries, speaking directly to me. I refused to believe Shakespeare was talking about sex, though Mrs. Colasanto said that was so. He seemed to be describing my life exactly and warning me against it, but not unkindly, for he was warning himself, too.

Mrs. Colasanto was short and plump with a small, pug-nosed face, nut-brown hair, and slightly protruding eyes that were dark and lively and moist. She reminded me of a fairy tale frog—a noble prince resided within. She was my favorite teacher. She thought we were perfectly capable of being moved by Shakespeare and Chaucer and Emily Dickinson. The only lay teacher I had at Sacred Heart, she was married and the mother of college-age daughters. I envied those girls and liked to imagine them studying for careers in math or science, as engineers perhaps, or lab technicians, anything that didn't require a passion for reading and writing. For that, their mother would have to come to us.

One day that fall, I paper-clipped a poem I'd written to the last page of my regular homework, and handed both poem and homework to Mrs. Colasanto at the end of class. The poem's opening lines were an obvious imitation of Shakespeare: "Darkness unrelieved holds no curse / But in the shadow of the sun some hearts are born . . ." Unfortunately every time I'd read those lines back to myself, the Beatles broke into song in my head—*Here comes the sun, dah-dah-dah-dah*—and I had to continually wrest myself away from that rhythm to make my poem sing a different tune. It had taken me almost a month to write five verses. But when I'd finished, I was sure I'd created an astonishing piece of work to show Mrs. Colasanto.

The next day I took my place in class, too nervous even to look at her; I told myself she probably hadn't had time to read my poem, which now seemed unmistakably awful—how could I have showed it to her? As she moved up and down the aisles, returning yesterday's assignment to each student, I pretended to be reading my textbook. When at last she drew near my desk, all I saw of her was the pleated skirt that covered her knees and her square-heeled brown shoes.

"Kathy, your poem is wonderful," she said. Her voice was warm and serious. I fixed on that seriousness, and the matter-of-fact way in which she'd spoken. Perhaps she meant it. I'd begun to think that the only image I would ever project would be the slut, and that anything good inside me, anything valuable, was going to remain hidden. "If you have anything else you'd like to show me, I'd love to see it," she continued, handing me my poem and my homework. She made no mention of the assigned essay at all. Maybe she'd decided that I was above such banal requirements. If I could write poetry, then homework was mere child's play. It was very easy for me to swing from self-loathing to self-glorification in those days, slug to genius and back again.

Not long after that, Mrs. C. stopped me as I was leaving class. "You must keep writing," she said. She wanted me to write more—today and tomorrow and the next; she meant for me to make myself into a writer.

Every day after I got home from school, I would put on a pot of coffee and slip into my jeans and a black sweatshirt—which seemed to me a serious, writerly sort of outfit. I'd set out my pens and note-books, push up my sleeves, and get to work. On the stories and poems that I began to hand to Mrs. C. regularly, as if she had given me an as-signment, she wrote comments like, *Beautiful description!* and *The per-fect metaphor!* I lived for those compliments, became greedy for them, noting the presence of every exclamation point—and also mourning their absence. If she wrote *Beautiful!* I felt blazingly happy. *Nice* made me scour the writing for what was wrong. And a blank margin meant that my writing was so bad it had embarrassed her into silence. But I had a reader—and what a reader! Mrs. Colasanto loved language, as I did, and for the first time I had the feeling of being unique and valu-able to an adult. When I gave her a short story or a poem that she liked, I felt I had served her something delicious to eat.

I wrote to please Mrs. Colasanto, and I wrote to fill the hours. There was nothing else for me to do, no place for me to go at night or on weekends, not even Sylvia's. After the night when the boys had showed up at her house, Mrs. DeAngelis wouldn't allow her to see me. And since Sylvia had switched to Hamden High that year, our only contact now was over the phone. But one afternoon that fall, when her mother had refused once again to drive her to my house, Sylvia took a stand: "Fine," she said, "I'll *walk* there," and marched out the front door. Her parents, always so protective that they had never allowed her to walk the mile and a half between our homes, followed her in the car, driving slowly alongside, her mother yelling to her fa-ther, "Grab her!" and her gentle, mild-mannered father absolutely re-fusing. "It's not right, Norma," he told her, shaking his head gravely. Her mother relented—halfway.

From then on, Sylvia was allowed to come to my house, but I was still banned from the DeAngelises'. So except for school, I was almost always home.

Most evenings, I worked at the kitchen table while my father worked in the living room. He had his papers and coffee and I had mine. We both worked late. The house would go quiet and dark on the upstairs floors, with everyone else tucked away for the night, except Bill, who was always out. When I wasn't writing, I was reading—poems, novels, plays—memorizing lines that moved me or were playful or simply contained a catchy rhyme.

I felt I had company, secret company, wise to the ways of the world and not at all shocked by my situation. If someone were to recognize me at the back-to-school sale at Sears, I wasn't alone. I had T. S. Eliot with me, whispering in my ear: *In the room the women come and go / Talking of Michelangelo.* He enjoyed a place like Sears, I was sure; it was grist for his mill. And as I waited in the long line at the cash register, surrounded by a sea of overflowing shopping carts and hoping not to see anyone I knew, it was Robert Louis Stevenson who observed: *The world is so full of a number of things / I'm sure we should all be as happy as kings.*

All my early stories were cheats. I simply wrote down the bad dreams I was having at night as if they were the inventions of my conscious mind. Our class was reading Kafka that fall, and if a grown man could wake up as a cockroach, why couldn't a girl discover a doorway cut into her bedroom wall? And when she stepped through that door, why couldn't she find herself in a gloomy mansion, moonlight streaming through one window, illuminating piles of white sheets huddled against the walls, each sheet covering the body of a dead woman?

After she read that story, Mrs. Colasanto sent me to the school counselor. Until then I hadn't even known that we had one. Though she was obviously trying to help, it was the only time that Mrs. C. disappointed me. I had thought she of all people would understand that there was no subject, no thought or feeling, forbidden to a writer.

When I told the school counselor, a young nun, that the story of the murdered women was just a dream I'd had one night, she said, "Oh, that's all right, then, we thought you made it up," and I was free to leave. After that, I stopped giving my creepier stories to Mrs. Colasanto, but I began to conjure up an audience for them nonetheless. The readers I imagined had hearts and minds that were large and tolerant, of course, and unafraid of anything dark or strange; in fact, they had a passion for it. My audience was simply the distilled spirit of every writer I'd ever read—Dickinson, Poe, Thomas Hardy, and Victor Hugo; Sylvia Plath, Carson McCullers, and Graham Greene; Madeleine L'Engle and Lorraine Hansberry; Robert Louis Stevenson, Bernard Malamud, and Mario Puzo; Xaviera Hollander, Saul Bellow, Eugene O'Neill, Jim Carroll—and Lewis Carroll, too.

With my notebook and my pen, I could amuse myself for hours, even as my long-held fear that the world was passing me by became real—the world of dates and dances, rock concerts and Friday nights at the beach or the local pizza parlor, surrounded by a group of friends. In fact, this was the world that Cindy had now entered. Every time she sailed out the door in one of her gauzy Indian blouses and silver jewelry, I bent deeper into "my work." I sensed another world, invisible but immense, one to which I was hooking my fate through the act of writing.

That fall I set about remaking myself. It's a process I've watched many teenagers go through in the years since I became a journalist—one that is both reactionary and immensely creative, and never fails to fill me with admiration. There was the seventeen-year-old black girl from Newark, New Jersey, who, in the middle of a tumultuous adolescence filled with too many boys, too much heartbreak, a pregnancy, and an abortion, decided to become a Muslim. She found peace, and some breathing room, by veiling herself and praying to Allah five times a day.

There were the squatter kids, more drifters than runaways, who gave themselves names like Pain Dog and Peasant Rose, Chronus and Dirtbag Mike, pierced their tongues with bolts, and wore dirt-encrusted clothes like suits of armor. They turned abandoned buildings on the Lower East Side into the homes they'd never had.

And there were the white girls in California, who were so envious of the black and Mexican kids who made up the majority in their schools that they decided to become skinheads, donning Doc Martens and shaving their heads, trying to make their white skin into a tribal flag, a symbol of belonging.

My own self-transformation wasn't as colorful as many I've witnessed, but it, too, had to have a physical manifestation. So that fall I asked Sylvia to cut my hair. She used pinking shears and chopped it off at my chin. Then we renamed ourselves—Maxwell for her (inspired by the coffee can in my mother's kitchen), and Winchester for me. Winchester sounded intriguing, but it was also the name of a gun.

I started digging through my mother's classical records, and her collection of Gershwin recordings, listening to them in the privacy of my bedroom. Rock belonged to the Teen Center, to the boys in the car, the two Chrissys, the strangers cornering me on the street. I was determined to carve a new space for myself, one without a trace of teenage culture. But Chopin was too dry, Beethoven too big and certain; only Rachmaninoff, Tchaikovsky, and Gershwin's *Rhapsody in Blue* were romantic enough for my fifteen-year-old heart.

Once I even borrowed a recording of the opera *La Traviata* from the school library, but as soon as the soprano's voice came soaring out of the tiny speakers of my bedroom turntable, setting all the dirty coffee cups on my desk a-tremble—I'd never heard anything like it in suburbia—I jumped up in alarm and turned it off. What would Bill and Cindy and their friends think? Bill's friends already made jokes about me as the grim and bookish sister. In trying to escape one label, I'd never considered that I'd be stuck with another.

Sometimes I despaired that everything worthwhile had been taken, leaving me only the scraps. From the opening bars of the Rolling Stones' "Paint It Black," my skin prickled. Why should this be *their* song? *Fuck it, I don't care.* And so I learned to let go of songs, clothes, streets, whole seasons. Good-bye, spring and summer; that was *their* time, warm days when *they* would be outside. I only liked nighttime now, late at night when Hamden was so quiet it seemed as if everyone had died, and I liked the rain and I liked the cold because *they* didn't.

The next project was my half of the bedroom. One Friday evening when Cindy was out, I took the bells I'd been collecting for years, the exotically costumed dolls, the big chunky candles, put them into cardboard boxes, and shoved the boxes into the crawl space that ran behind our bedrooms. I said good-bye to my jewelry, all of it too delicate for the person I was becoming. Bye to the music boxes, the incense and perfumes, the children's books that still sat on my shelves. Good-bye to the angel bookends.

I even dismantled my private chapel—the plaster saints and dried rose petals and shells I'd arranged in the bottom drawer of my dresser. There was no God, I'd decided (though I still talked to Him incessantly). Since I'd already announced my atheism to my parents and stopped taking Communion at Sunday Mass, disposing of my chapel felt like I was finally making a clean sweep of the last remnants of my old life.

I had just finished putting a conch shell, a beeswax candle, and St. Teresa in a box when my mother knocked on the bedroom door. She came in carrying a load of clean laundry. "What did you do with everything?" she asked, stunned by the sudden emptiness. When I told her I had packed up all my belongings, she said, "Don't those things mean anything to you?" Her voice was angry, but she was peering into my face like she might see right through it and into my mind—what was going on in there?

"They just don't fit me anymore," I told her.

"Some of those things were presents from people who care about you."

"Well, that doesn't mean I have to hold on to them forever."

"So you're just going to throw them away?"

"No, I *put* them away. They're right there in the crawl space."

Her eyes were glued on mine, and after a long moment of silence, a silence that I found acutely uncomfortable, she said, "I don't even know who you are anymore."

I couldn't tell my mother that I was no longer a girl who would collect angel bells and china hearts and that I didn't want to live a lie—or more of a lie than I was already living. So I simply shut her out, ignoring both the despair and anger I heard in her voice. The trouble with having a family was that we were all tangled up with one another. It was like living in a crowded room—every time I moved I knocked something over.

My clothes were now as stripped down as my bedroom—black sweatshirts and threadbare T-shirts that said I had more important things on my mind than appearances; straight-legged jeans and scruffy, low-heeled boots. With the boots on my feet, I felt strong and swift and determined. I didn't want people to see me as a girl—too risky. I suppose I wanted them to see only a brain or a soul. I began to think of my hidden self as winged, and one day I would fly out of Hamden for good.

24

The Christmas Gift

ON CHRISTMAS DAY, I WOKE TO THE SOUND OF A BELL RINGING AND my parents' voices on the floor below as they moved from bedroom to bedroom waking us. At the window, the darkness had just lightened into a blue-gray and the horizon was a ribbon of pale white. The clock said seven A.M. Now the sound of the ringing bell was heard on the stairs, the door was swinging open, and my parents, Beth Ann, and Stephen, all of them in their pajamas, were piling into the room, calling, "Merry Christmas!" Every year it was the same, our Christmas ritual. My parents' faces were doughy and pale from lack of sleep; their breath smelled of coffee when I kissed them.

Downstairs, the fire was lit, the stockings my grandmother had knitted for each of us when we were born stuffed to overflowing, packages heaped in gleaming mountains around the tree. We always opened our presents in our pajamas, though this Christmas Bill was wearing his jeans and a T-shirt and he was sprawled on the couch, yawning vigorously. Had he just come home? I didn't know. Michael sat in one of the armchairs, grinning and rubbing his hands. "Let the games begin!" he proclaimed. He was completely unabashed in his appetite, his confidence, his enjoyment of us all. When he'd returned from his first semester at college a few days earlier, we saw that he'd grown his hair long, but it was so curly that instead of falling down his back it rose in a halo around his head, a bushy orange afro. He had even grown a beard.

I sat down on the floor with Beth Ann, Cindy, and Stephen; there we bobbed back and forth like shuttles on a loom. It would take the entire morning and half the afternoon to get to all the presents. We opened them one at a time, taking turns while everyone else watched.

When we were little, we made all our gifts. One Christmas, Beth Ann made my father sandpaper by gluing salt and sugar onto sheets of brown construction paper. Sometimes there were joke presents, like the year that someone—was it Bill or Michael?—gave a gift-wrapped turnip to Stephen. The first joke this year was in Michael's stocking, a rolled-up poster of a gorilla with the caption "When I Want Your Opinion I'll Beat It Out Of You," which was something Michael always used to say. "That's perfect, just perfect," Bill called out from the couch, laughing along with the rest of us. It was like Michael had never left for college, Bill had never run away, I'd never tripped out into the world in my halter top and hip-hugger jeans. We'd always teased and celebrated Michael's self-confidence; it was part of us, like a family pet.

"Well, I think this package has your name on it, kiddo," my father said, placing a large, square-shaped box wrapped in green and gold on the floor in front of me. From the look on my parents' faces I knew this was the big present, something special. Every year there was one for each of us. When Cindy and I were six and seven it was two black kittens wearing red bows and hidden away in the laundry basket in the basement; when I was nine it was a blue bicycle.

I was nervous opening my present while everyone watched. What if it were something awful? Something girlish that would've been right for me a year ago but no longer. Or worse, what if it was something practical and grim? Family surprises were treacherous; if my parents had misread me it would cut to the bone. I knew I spent all my time at home now, reading and writing and arguing politics with my father, but I couldn't bear it if they gave me the complete works of some radical nun.

When I tore the paper across the front of the box, I could hardly believe my eyes—was this a joke? Was it only a typewriter *box* with something else tucked inside? I looked up at my mother and father. "A typewriter?" I said carefully.

They were beaming and nodding. A typewriter! The first one in our house. A writer's present, and just in case I didn't understand that they understood, my mother said, "That's for all that writing you're doing now."

I leapt up to thank both of them, happy to be carried toward my parents on a genuine wave of enthusiasm, for I was rarely affectionate with them anymore—in fact, whenever they reached to touch me, without thinking, I cringed. The two of them felt like large furry bears when I hugged them; my father's flannel robe was warm from the fire. I knew they were relieved.

As everyone continued opening presents around me, I sat on the floor in front of the typewriter, rolled a piece of paper into the carriage, and began to hit the keys.

Silver spider legs high-stepped onto the page, leaving wet black footprints behind. Tiny, precise; I'd never seen a prettier *a*. I felt like I was playing the piano, clack clack clack clack clack, a bell dinged, I hit the carriage, and zing!

For a long time my mother kept smiling at me, trying to catch my eye. I was completely happy with the present but unable to meet her expectant gaze. Random letters gave way to words, *georgia, lipstick, alley, shadow,* which gave way to sentences, then rhymes, *merry merry christmas bells. merry merry christmas hell.*

"What are you typing there, honey?"

"Now I know my ABCs," Bill recited in a simpleton's voice. "Tell me what you think of me."

"Nothing, just playing around," I told her, ignoring him and typing, *a tisket, a tasket, a green and yellow casket.* I was thrilled with the present, and deeply, stubbornly unhappy with my life.

That wasn't the only big present from my parents that year—they also gave Cindy and me tickets to a Sunday matinee of *Grease* on Broadway. And on this, our very first trip to New York, we'd be going alone. Two train tickets to Grand Central were inside the package, money for cab fare, the theater tickets, and a handmade certificate announcing that we were having dinner at Sardi's, already paid for. At the end of the evening, my parents would pick us up outside the restaurant.

With a typewriter and train tickets to New York, my parents had given me the wings I would need to fly away from them—did they know?

Late that night, I sat on Michael's bed looking out the window at the empty intersection of Clifford and Treadwell. Ever since he had left for college in August, that window had become my eye on the world, this room my refuge, and my jail. Bill kept vampire hours, coming in just before dawn, so I always had the room to myself. When I wrote up here, I leaned my notebook on the windowsill so that I could watch the streets below. By keeping the world that I'd lost in view, I felt a little less cut off.

I watched the flashing traffic light swinging on its wires, dreaming of New York City, only two hours distant and yet impossibly far. That is where I would move as soon as I graduated from high school. Where else would you go if you were leaving a small town to become a writer? But there was only one acceptable route away from my family—college. Since my freshman year at Sacred Heart, everyone—my parents, my relatives, my friends and teachers—assumed I'd be going, and because of them, I did, too. I'd decided to apply to New York University, knowing nothing about it except the most important thing, right there in the name.

Though I'd not yet actually been to the city, I'd always felt its presence. It was there in my books and my music, in the old movies I watched with Sylvia, on the silky labels inside Grandma Callahan's furs, on TV every Thanksgiving when we went to Great-aunt Bert's house to eat jelly doughnuts and watch the Macy's parade. Sometimes New York appeared to me only in black and white, the city as seen from a distance at night, a dark island shooting up immense towers of pearly light. Other times, I imagined the city as a great jumble of people, characters, really, from those books and movies, burly cops and wisecracking newsboys, jazzmen and businessmen, dockworkers who coulda been contenders, desperate gang kids turning to Jesus, beautiful women in sequined dresses smoking, drinking, never thinking about tomorrow, a junkman singing right before dawn. Everyone was hungry—for money, for love, for fame or purpose; survival wasn't a given. I knew I'd fit right in.

I fantasized about my future in New York City with the same fervor a prisoner serving a life sentence might bring to his thoughts of heaven. But my sentence was not interminable. As I sat there on Michael's bed that night, my eyes glued to the flashing traffic light, I told myself, *Less than two years and you'll be free.*

25

Seaward on the Waves

THAT NIGHT IN THE CAR HAD THE UNFORESEEN EFFECT OF OPENING UP a Pandora's box of ugly feeling in me—emotions I never wanted to feel and couldn't remember ever feeling before: jealousy, bitterness, rage, self-pity, self-disgust, despair.

I fought with everyone that spring, driving a wedge between me and my family that would last more than a decade. I pushed my mother into fits of exasperation, made Cindy cry.

"You care too much about what other people think of you. I don't care," I told her one evening, in what might have been the most astonishing lie of my life. "Most people aren't worth thinking about." All Cindy was doing at that moment was choosing a shirt to wear, as I lay in bed with a book watching her. Whenever she went out now, she put clothes on under the brace, ducked into the alley that ran behind our garage, slipped out of the brace, and left it there until she came back home. She was like a fairy tale princess who escaped her father's castle each night after he'd fallen asleep and danced until dawn, only to sneak back into bed before the king awoke.

She stood in her white bra, her dungaree shorts, a beaded strand of leather around her neck, examining two blouses, both white, both pretty and faintly crumpled, so no matter which one she wore, she would look wonderful, and also like she didn't care how she looked. She had a large crowd of friends, boys and girls in equal numbers.

She told me I was a snob. "That's not exactly an insult," I replied evenly.

"I hate you!" she shouted, her eyes brimming with tears. "Sometimes I wish you weren't my sister."

"Well, just pretend I'm not." I cracked open my book.

We were supposed to be above such ugliness in my family. Was I a sinner? No, a sinner confesses and then she's free: "Go forth and sin no more." But I had no way of banishing these feelings, my anger at my parents, my envy of Cindy, my wariness around Bill and his friends. I couldn't rid myself of the sense that mine was the black heart buried and boiling inside my loving family.

My mother and father would have had to work hard to reach me during this time. It would have taken a sustained effort, and a willingness to rise above rebuffs and failures and keep coming back for more. But they had five other children, as well as aging parents, aunts, and uncles to take care of. My grandmother had suffered a massive heart attack earlier that year and undergone a quadruple bypass. My mother was worried about her, and as I found out years later, secretly fighting a depression of her own. My father had been promoted to director of operations at Yale, reporting only to the provost and the Yale board, and was facing enormous pressure himself. He loved working with people, and now he was working with budgets.

And I? I was playing the part of a tough girl. I wanted my parents to see through that act; they swallowed it hook, line, and sinker.

I could have turned to religion or drugs or some cult where you shave your head, marry a stranger, and play tambourines all day, but instead I discovered Ayn Rand—Rand and her superheroes, Rand and all her contempt for flawed humanity. As soon as I began reading her, I was completely in her thrall. I began to fashion myself after an Ayn Rand hero, and after reading *The Virtue of Selfishness*, my third Rand book, I passed it on to Sylvia with a note: *Sylvia, I know it's hard at first but if you stick with it, it will become clearer and clearer. If you have any questions, I'm always here.* Now the disciple had a disciple.

An Ayn Rand hero invariably has high cheekbones and a contemptuous mouth. His eyes are cold and clear. And except in Rand's first book, *We the Living*, the hero is always a man. He might be an architect, a composer, a sculptor, an entrepreneur, but whatever he is, he loves his work, loves it so much that the world will try to destroy him for it. He is pure, he never compromises, never says what people need him to say.

According to Rand, the vast majority of people smile too much. They try too hard to get along. They flatter and simper and cringe. One time Sylvia reduced the entire Ayn Rand philosophy to the pithy phrase "The masses are asses." And, of course, she and I weren't. We began to ration our smiles, curb our enthusiasm, disdain emotion, softness, shoppers in the mall. I learned another walk—neither male nor female—a swift, long-legged stride. Gone was the girl who sashayed down the street swinging her hips and licking her lips. But not because I was ashamed, no, not that—I was an Ayn Rand hero.

My pariah status suddenly acquired nobility. I wasn't sitting home alone every night because I was scared of people; I simply didn't need them. I wasn't bewildered by the world, unsure of how to enter it again; there was nothing and no one worth my time in Hamden. And, so, the girl they called a *douche bag* began to tell herself she was actually superior to most of the human race.

My mother could hardly stand to be around me. One day as she was driving me home from school, I announced that I didn't need anything from her. I'd missed the school bus and had to call her for a ride home. She and I were crammed together in the Pinto, our bucket seats close to the floor.

"I don't do things because I *need* to. I do them because I want to," I proclaimed, this distinction being very important to me at that time in my life.

"Well, what about other people? What about their needs?" she asked.

"That's not my responsibility. If I do something for someone else, it's because I want to, not because I'm being selfless."

"Well, you're my responsibility. I'm not picking you up from school just because it gives me pleasure. I still have to get dinner fixed and—"

"Well, you shouldn't have come, then."

"Kathy, sometimes you have to make sacrifices for other people!"

"Well, you shouldn't."

"So, I should've left you here at school? Let you find your own way home?"

"Yeah, if you didn't want to pick me up."

"Agh!" my mother yelled, gripping the steering wheel.

We argued all the way home. But when we arrived, my mother suddenly calmed down. Or so it seemed to me then. Now I think she was fighting back.

"You know what?" she said casually. "If you and I weren't related to each other, if we just met on the street, I don't think we'd even like each other."

I stomped up the stairs and into my room, slamming the door behind me. *My own mother!* I kept exclaiming to myself, trying to work up an outrage or pump out some tears. But neither came. I was stunned, but I knew I'd driven her to it. Besides, I thought she was right. It surprised me that my mother had shown herself to be just as capable of the hard truth as I thought I was. It was as if a wish had been fulfilled, a painful wish, one of those they tell you to be careful of. And now that the truth had been revealed, the guilt removed, our ties could be cut. I was free to leave her, and my whole family, behind.

But within the hour, my mother came upstairs to take it all back. She sat next to me on the bed, asking for a hug to show that, underneath it all, we really did love each other. In her embrace I felt my insides kick and struggle.

It was only my father who accepted my challenge to duel. Everyone else wanted me to be nicer, more agreeable, or at least apologize at the end. But my father and I were like two men fighting, fighting hard, no punches pulled, no tears, either. He never even winced, never seemed to take our arguments personally. How I enjoyed fighting with him.

One night I used my smoking as a bait. If I was old enough to drive, I was old enough to smoke, I announced. It was a Saturday night when Cindy and Bill had taken off with their friends, a spring night with the scent of lilacs drifting in through the open kitchen window.

"You *do* know smoking causes cancer," he said to me, as we faced off from opposite ends of the kitchen table.

"There's no proof of that," I replied rashly, and he looked at me like I'd landed from Mars. Sometimes I argued with my father about serious things, like the death penalty or the meaning of patriotism, sometimes about ridiculous things, like this argument right now. It hardly mattered to me what we fought about. I had only one guiding principle: Whatever my father said, I took the opposite view. I was angry; I needed his company. Engaging his attention was surprisingly easy.

"What do you mean, there's no proof?" he said, almost shouting in frustration. "That's all there is."

"I'm talking scientific proof, studies and things."

"What do you think *I'm* talking about?" I took a swig of my coffee, he took one of his. Our cups hit the table with a clank-clank. His blue eyes were flaring. I stared right back at him. It seemed unbelievable that I'd ever been afraid of him.

I thought my father enjoyed our sparring matches—a worthy opponent at last!—but when I asked him recently what I was like during that last year and a half at home, he answered steadily, without any hesitation at all, "Aggressive. Defensive. And offensive."

That spring, when Sylvia and I decided to make a movie that would display our Ayn Randian selves to the world, we couldn't come up with a narrative for a heroine whose main attributes were disdain and pride. She would be deeply passionate, of course, while also being unmoved by most human beings, for they hardly deserved her attention. But what would a woman like that *do*? We decided our protagonist was dying and we would show her last day on earth, filled with extravagant, romantic gestures.

I was to play the heroine and Sylvia would do the filming, since she was taking a television broadcasting course at Hamden High and she knew how. She borrowed the 16-millimeter camera from her class. The camera had no sound, so the script was easy. Just think: wild, aching, doomed.

We decided the heroine would go to the ocean and . . . what? Swim naked? Walk restlessly? No! Scratch the ocean. She would down a glass of champagne in one thirsty swallow and then hurl it against a wall. "Could you catch the falling glass in slow motion?" I asked Sylvia.

And she would ride a horse, very fast, tearing her hair on branches of low-hanging trees. I didn't know how to ride a horse, but how hard could it be?

In the yellow pages, Sylvia and I found a stable in the nearby town of Milford where we could take out horses by the hour. As soon as we arrived, the three men who worked there took a lively interest in us: our camera, our movie script, my long skirt and lack of horsemanship.

"You've never been on a horse before? I think I better give you lessons," the youngest of them said to me, smiling broadly. His yellow-blond hair was pulled back into a ponytail; he had pointy satyr's ears, devilishly pretty and pale white.

"I'm sure I can figure it out," I said, "if you'll just show me the horse." The men laughed.

"You planning on riding sidesaddle in that skirt?"

I didn't know what he was talking about.

"If she ain't riding sidesaddle, I'll give her lessons."

"Who do we pay?" I asked, not even glancing over at Sylvia but sure that her face was as disapproving as mine.

"You can pay me," the ponytailed man said. "And John will saddle you a horse, but I'd hate to see you thrown to the ground—that's not supposed to be in the movie, is it?"

"Where's John?" I asked.

They pointed out a man by the fenced-in area where they kept the horses.

"You sure you don't want some help getting up on that horse?" Ponytail was smiling at me in a friendly and interested way; his blue eyes were so clear I could see feathery gold flecks in his irises. But I knew I couldn't respond. If I opened myself to Hamden again, to any part of its day-to-day, prosaic life, I was sure I would be swallowed up for good.

I lifted my chin in the air and turned swiftly away, grabbing the back of my skirt as I turned because it was a wraparound and there was a bit of wind that day—wind I would ride on my horse, I thought, like Eliot's mermaids "riding seaward on the waves."

Heads held high, Sylvia and I went striding off. We heard hooting and hollering behind us. Was that applause?

Out of the corner of her mouth, Sylvia hissed, "You're holding your skirt *open*."

I blushed straight to the roots of my hair, got up on that horse, and rode it not through low-hanging branches and whipping leaves but a tangle of embarrassment.

The horse and I never got into any kind of rhythm. We rolled along like two weary workmen—I could feel his huge chest and inside it, his slab of a heart. He seemed to be laboring. Whenever he tried to break into a trot, I bounced up and down in the saddle, smacking it with my rear end—but who was spanking whom? It wasn't at all like I'd imagined it would be.

A year and three months left, all of it stuck inside this stiff and cheerless Ayn Rand persona. I couldn't figure out how I was going to last that long.

26

As Happy As Kings

THE SUMMER AFTER MY JUNIOR YEAR, I FINALLY MANAGED TO REENTER the world—as a union-dues-paying pot washer wearing a blue work shirt with a bulldog on the breast pocket, thick work pants, and heavy, rubber-soled shoes. In June, I began to work in the Yale kitchens. It was my first job, not counting a two-week stint providing service with a smile at McDonald's.

My official title was "general service assistant" and I was part of a small crew that swept and mopped the floors, washed the heavy kettles, made sure the chefs had everything they needed, and kept the storerooms stocked, unloading fifty-pound bags of potatoes and onions and rice from delivery trucks. New Haven seemed miles and miles away from Hamden, and the hard work released me from my head. Five days a week I had somewhere to go, a job to do. And I had company. I'd become a citizen of the democracy that I'd been hearing my father describe at our dinner table for years.

There were black, brown, and white faces, male and female, young, middle-aged, gray-haired. We worked in the din of pots and pans clattering on stoves, water running, meat frying, voices hollering, "Hand me that towel there, love!" and "Where the hell is that boy with those potatoes?" Clouds of steam rolled off the stoves, and behind those clouds the cooks labored. In their white chef's jackets and pillowy hats, they looked like sturdy angels.

Whenever I picture that summer, I see myself striding happily down a long concrete basement corridor, pushing a metal trolley filled with cans of tomatoes that jiggle and rattle against one another. Every time I turn the light on in one of the basement storerooms, there's a sudden scurrying motion on the floor. These are the first cockroaches I've ever seen—leggy, three-inch-long creatures with a lacquered reddish shine to their shells. But I'm not afraid of the water bugs, or the long, empty corridors that wind and turn, or even the windowless storerooms, though I'm claustrophobic. I'm completely at home here.

Riding the freight elevator up from the basement, I feel a jerk as it lands, opening on to a high-ceilinged, white-tiled kitchen with a shiny island of stoves as big as a banquet table. On weekdays, Geraldine runs the kitchen. A short, wide, chocolate-brown woman buttoned into her chef's whites, she has forearms as bulky as a dockworker's, the skin darkened in patches from burns. "Honey, open those cans for me," Geraldine says. Here everyone is called *love, honey, sweetheart*, and even—especially if the woman being addressed is older and married—*baby cakes*. This is exactly the kind of easygoing atmosphere that suits me right now in my life, for if I open my mouth to try to say something serious, all I can do is spout Ayn Rand, make declarations. I've built a self to present to the world, but it is all a construct, hollow and artificial. In the bustling kitchen, with a job to do and a place on the team, I can just *be*.

My uniform suits me, too. It's a badge of membership. There is hard work to be done and it has to be done right, so if I have to wear a hair net or a blue and white paper hat when I work the serving line, I just wear it. A paper hat is a laughably small price to pay for belonging. The people I work with like me, and I like them. Life is suddenly very simple.

Every dining hall has a first, second, and third chef. Besides Geraldine, our first chef, we have Freddy, who is very round and very white, his hands like soft dinner rolls, and grouchy Julius, a big-bellied gray-haired man with a crumpled face who lumbers around the kitchen like a bear, leaving dirty pots and pans, egg splatters, puddles of pancake batter, and charred towels in his wake. Julius is close to retirement, slowing down, and sometimes a whiff of panic comes off him as he throws pots onto the stove and jerks smoking pans out of the oven. Ilsa, our desk clerk, who checks the students in at each meal, is a grandmother, a Polish woman whose blond hair is piled on her head in swirls like a pastry. I always take my fifteen-minute breaks with her, the two of us smoking and drinking coffee out of juice glasses with such camaraderie you would have thought we were two confirmed drinkers meeting in a bar. We also have a couple of Yale work-study students who come in at mealtimes to help me on the serving line and at the dishwasher: wisecracking Jason, a cute, curly-haired Jewish boy from Manhattan; and Ruben Gonzalez, a slight-boned, big-afroed, sweet, cynical, strong-willed Brooklyn boy, both of them reaffirming my belief that New York City is the place for me.

As I wash the kettles in the deep steel sinks, Julius and Freddy argue behind me. "Move your big black ass," Freddy calls out airily. When Julius calls Freddy a fat white cracker, Freddy challenges him to a duel. "Choose your weapon!" he cries, and I turn to see Freddy raising a spatula, his legs set apart like a fencer's. The insults, the shouts, even the water running into the sink seem joyful. A burden has been lifted, and whenever the chefs send me downstairs for eggs or onions or potatoes, I feel light on my feet, quick and strong.

At the end of that summer, the head of our GSA crew asked me out. Carl must have been in his mid- to late twenties. His full name was Lawrence Carlson, but only management called him Lawrence. He was a man of few words, quietly dependable, and handsome. Though Carl and I worked side by side, and I worked just as hard as he did, he treated me with a gentleness that was close to courtly. When the two of us worked alone together in the storerooms, he talked even less than usual, and in the silence that grew as we dragged boxes across the floor, cut them open, and filled the shelves, the air became moist and charged. His skin appeared to shimmer.

After I finished my last day of work, Carl and I left together. It was a warm breezy night, I remember it well. We were sitting in Carl's Pontiac with the windows rolled down, outside a red and yellow neon-lit bar in the black part of New Haven. He'd gone in and bought us two beers and we drank them in the car, listening to the music spilling out of the open doors. The tar on the street shone like water, and the leaves on the trees were a silvery green. As we sat there nursing our beers, Carl told me the manager of our dining hall had called him into the office early on in the summer and had warned him away from me. "He told me you're Mr. Dobie's daughter and you're off-limits." Carl looked pained as he said this, as if what the manager had really meant was that he, Carl, wasn't good enough for the daughter of the boss. Wasn't good enough because he was a black, working-class man. And perhaps that is what the manager meant.

"He did that on his own!" I told him, surprised. "My father never would've told him to say that!" I don't remember anything else that we talked about, just the look of humiliation on Carl's face and my view of the summer shifting to include Carl's restraint, his frustration, the threat of losing his job hanging over his head, the way he, a grown man, had been talked to like a bad little boy, and how admirable he seemed to me now. After we finished our beer, Carl drove me home, parking on the Clifford Street side of the house where the tall hedges hid us from view.

"Well, good night, thanks for the beer," I said, hesitating, for I knew I'd never see him again. School was starting in another week and I was being moved to another dining hall where I'd work only on weekends. How does one say good-bye? And for no other reason than that you're young, and life is taking you somewhere new? Carl didn't bother with words. He leaned over, his face suddenly large, the skin glowing and . . . His lips moved over mine with the utmost attention and tenderness, sending my breath into a hard run. I held the side of his face; it was larger than my hand.

Who thought of this? I wanted to cry. *Who could live without it?* With the air buzzing and my body as charged as a racehorse at the gate, I said good night to Carl again. I just *couldn't* have sex with him, or any man.

At fourteen, my body had still been a child's. I didn't feel much sexually but I didn't care, because I didn't know what I was missing. At fifteen, I ached to be free of my body and go flying down some lonesome (but poetically moonlit) highway. At sixteen, well after I'd learned sexual shame, my body woke up. The timing seemed designed by someone with a not-very-funny sense of humor.

That fall, the beginning of my last year in high school, the sun felt almost holy, swinging in the sky like Father Sheridan's censer, showering light down on emerald lawns and yellow trees. The air was sharpening; it gave a glint to everything as it honed itself into the cold knife tip that would one day drive in winter.

Senior year, and at the very moment when the class queens had reached the apex of their lives, they began to lose their stranglehold, so that everything felt slightly disarranged. Nine months later, this world would dissolve. The days seemed to pick up pace as if time itself was tunneling toward that change. No one seemed to be what they once were. Even the shy, awkward girls, the ones who had faded into their uniforms like freshly shaved recruits in boot camp, suddenly had a brightness in their faces, an almost feverish look.

Sylvia and I had sent in our applications to NYU. She was nervous about being rejected because it was the only college we'd tried to get into, but I was so certain of my future in New York City that the application process seemed almost a formality. Of course they'd let us in.

I was beginning to feel happy, and less cautious. So when I went into the senior lounge one afternoon to get my chocolate milk, having abandoned my usual practice of checking to see who was there before entering, I found myself surrounded by the class queens.

"The Teen Center? Is that on Putnam Avenue?" Louisa asked Joan loudly. They so rarely got a chance at me alone, they had to jump at it when they did. I put my money in the vending machine. I didn't even think about responding. What was I supposed to say to them—that I wasn't the grotesque cartoon they'd reduced me to?

"That's right, at Putnam and Whitney."

"Oh, I heard some story about that place." They started laughing, and the shrill sound drove a timid freshman out of the lounge before she even got to the vending machine. They *owned* the senior lounge; they'd come into their inheritance. The rest of us were looking ahead. The future was ours—it always belongs to those who are unhappy in the present.

Just then Linda came gliding into the room. When she saw the cluster of girls, she tossed her head, making a show of it, like she was flipping back her hair, though her close-cropped afro didn't even stir. Leslie was right behind her, wearing a faded blue, silver-studded dungaree jacket over her uniform. While Leslie stopped to talk to the girls, Linda went straight to the soda machine. She made a great pretense of studying her choices. "Eanie, meanie, minie, mo," she said, enunciating each word. Her silver bracelets slid down her arm as she dropped the coins into the machine slot.

"Ohhhh, Leslie, you're so cute!" Louisa cried.

"She's like a little puppy dog."

"Can I feel it?"

They were petting Leslie's afro.

"It's like a bush, it's all springy."

"It's soft!"

"What happens when you wash it? Does it stay up like this?"

"Isn't she adorable?"

Leslie was soaking it up, cocking her head and batting her long lashes at them. A lover, not a fighter; she just couldn't help herself.

Linda looked sideways at me and then slid behind Louisa, cobralike. She reached for Louisa with her right arm in slow motion . . . and then she brought her hand down on Louisa's head and began petting her.

"Ohhhh," Linda cooed. Louisa jumped. I could see her skin flinch, eyes flash furiously. But whatever word was on the tip of her tongue, she bit it down.

"I just wanted to feel it," Linda said sweetly, but her eyes were dead cold. "It's like a . . . a . . . pancake! It's so smooth and flat."

The girls shot looks of pure hatred at Linda. Leslie was giggling. "A pancake!"

Linda put her arm around Leslie's shoulders, squeezing her close, and said haughtily, "Come on, buddy-o'-mine, let's go." Then: "Ta ta, girls! See you around the quad!" She turned once to see that I was following, gave her beauty queen wave, fingers closed, hand shifting, back and forth like a metronome. "See you later, alligators!"

Leslie was doubled over in laughter, but there was a breathlessness to the sound, a note of shame.

When we got close to our table, Leslie ducked out from under Linda's arm, whirled around on one foot, came to a stop, one hand raised, and sang, "Stop! In the name of love . . ." She did Diana Ross *and* the Supremes. Gladys Knight *and* the Pips.

"You're gonna make me pee in my pants!" Linda hollered, clutching her stomach.

The bell for class was ringing.

Leslie turned to me. "Okay, Dorothy, ready?" Sometimes she called me Dorothy, sometimes Chief.

"Ready when you are," I said, meaning exactly that, for I had no idea what she was going to do next.

She put her arm out for me to grab, sounded the first note, and we went skipping out of the cafeteria, singing, "We're off to see the wizard!"

Linda caught up to us in the crowded hallway, her skip a giant's version of ours. She floated right by us, all swinging arms and legs and lifted chin, completely straight-faced. Girls scattered and giggled helplessly. Was there anyone luckier in friendship?

27

After All

THE BOYS OF HAMDEN HAD ONE LAST MESSAGE FOR ME.

The summer was coming to a close and my new life was about to begin. In one week I would be leaving for New York. Today was my last day as a Yale food service employee. To celebrate, Sylvia and I were taking ourselves out to dinner at Sam's Pizzeria.

When I finished up work at four, I shed my GSA uniform and put on the black sundress and the ankle-laced, wedge-heeled shoes I'd long ago moved to the back of my closet but never quite forgotten. Three summers had passed since I had dressed up and played the part of a beautiful girl. Only now did I feel free to do so again, for I was on my way out of town—and I was in New Haven, not Hamden, after all. I had a few hours to kill before meeting Sylvia, so I decided to stroll down to the green, where I could listen to one of the city-sponsored jazz concerts that were put on almost every Friday evening in the summer.

Stan Kenton and his band were playing, and the New Haven green was filled with picnicking couples and families. Sitting down on one of the benches at the edge of the green, I watched as fathers struggled to open bottles of wine and wandering children were coaxed back to their blankets with bribes of fruit and cookies. Here and there, a solitary Yale student sat on the grass reading. The sound of jazz trumpets swirled over us, like a canopy. The beep of a car horn seemed tinny and festive. A breeze pulled at my hair and sent an occasional napkin or paper plate flying.

I saw them coming from far away. My heart started hammering, even as I doubted my eyes.

Don't be stupid. It can't be, I told myself. This was the city, it belonged to strangers, hundreds and thousands of them, *they* wouldn't be here. Besides, the boys were on the opposite side of the green. They couldn't possibly have spotted me from that far away.

There were eight of them, and they seemed to be heading straight toward me, stepping around picnic blankets, dodging the small children in their path, never looking down. I kept thinking: Any minute now they're going to veer right or left, find the person they're looking for, call out a name, and turn into somebody's harmless friends, sons, or carousing brothers.

Their steamroller progress began to attract attention. People who had glanced up from their blankets only because those feet were so close to their sandwiches now became riveted; *What was going on?* Unbelievable and yet inevitable. While my body objected and my thoughts froze, two and a half years dropped away. And then the boys were assembled in front of me. Leering. Their leader had a wide-nosed, fleshy face that I recognized but couldn't place.

(And wouldn't until fifteen years later, when out of the blue it came to me and suddenly, I knew his name: Paul DiRusso. He was one of my brother Michael's friends, someone who went on family picnics with us when we were kids and once had almost drowned me in a lake, holding me down between his legs in a game that went on too long; a Notre Dame boy.)

"Are you Mike Dobie's sister?" he asked, the grin never leaving his face. Michael? Notre Dame? They'd known about me in a private Catholic high school in West Haven? I shook my head rapidly. "No."

That made him laugh out loud. "So you're not Bill Dobie's sister either?"

"I don't know who you're talking about," I said, and the thought of

Peter's betrayal, three denials, the cock crowing, flitted through my head.

They were all laughing now, except for the ringleader, whose sweaty face suddenly shone with hatred.

"Come on! We know who you are." He dug into the pocket of his jeans. The jeans were tight, so it took him a while to extract what he was looking for—a fistful of change. As he held it out to me, his palm opening slowly, I froze. I had no idea what was going to happen next.

"There are only eight of us," he said. "This should be enough."

I got up and walked away fast.

"Fucking dirtbag!"

"Go back to Howe Street where you belong, you cunt!" they shouted. Howe Street: That was where the prostitutes trolled in New Haven.

And then the coins came flying at me, some of them hitting my bare back. On the green, people stared and, I thought, clutched their children to them.

The boys didn't know me, of course, but I knew them, knew they were still virgins, and because I had gone (again and again) to the place they hadn't yet been, they hated me, even as they envied the boys I'd had sex with. I knew, too, that it gave them as much pleasure to hurt a girl, to poke her and see her twitch, as it would to make love to her. Either way, they would feel more like men when they were done.

I got to Chapel Street, took a right. But where could I go? There was no safe place.

Just keep walking, I told myself, and suddenly I pictured myself walking straight through time—out of that day, into the next, through five more, until I got to New York City. It still feels like I arrived here on foot.

I only lasted one semester at NYU, dropping out after I was put on academic probation. I hadn't considered how difficult it would be for me to live in a dorm with a couple of hundred boys and girls my age. The past wasn't to be banished so easily. But failing at NYU didn't really matter—the city, not college, had been my dreamed-of destination.

From where I sit writing this, on the fourth floor of a house I rent in Brooklyn, I can see tarred rooftops, wooden water towers, flocks of birds, a small silver plane crossing a huge expanse of milk-striped blue.

This row house used to be a boardinghouse for sailors passing through (the docks are only seven blocks from here), and it still is, in a way. Not that the three people I live with are transients, but they are currently without spouses or children, healthy bank accounts, or predictable futures. In the morning, I can hear the adjunct professor of philosophy singing in the shower.

In the more than twenty years I've been in New York, I've never lived alone, never wanted to. But I've never lived with a boyfriend, either. I need more freedom, and solitude, than I could manage if I lived as part of a couple. I once saw a photograph of Diego Rivera's and Frida Kahlo's home in Mexico City: two houses built side by side, connected by a second-story walkway that went from her bedroom to his. This seemed the perfect living arrangement to me then, and my boyfriend and I now have our own version—with the Brooklyn Bridge as the walkway between us.

Loose domesticity suits me. As long as I have a place I can retreat to, a hideaway—this top floor, my attic room—I enjoy being surrounded by other people. While I work, I like hearing the sounds of whistling or laughter coming from the floors below or the clunk-clunk-clunk of Tim's sneakers in the dryer; like knowing that Ed is reading Kant at the kitchen table downstairs or Chris is fixing his bike in the living room. Sometimes Chris, a New Orleans boy, stops at a phone booth on his way home from work and asks if I want some Popeye's chicken, biscuits, rice and beans; sometimes I cook dinner for all of us. Their girlfriends spend the night, leaving their French shampoos and herbal facial scrubs on the shelf in the shower; Ed's friends from his university days in Germany use this house as their New York City hostel; Tim holds a Fourth of July barbecue, attended entirely by musicians, and late in the evening guitars, accordions, and horns are pulled out and a chaotic babel of sound gradually finds its way into a tune they all recognize. I know each of my housemates and both of my cats, Fate and Will, by their footfall, much as I once knew my brothers and sisters by theirs. Chris's feet make a snapping sound as he comes upstairs in his hard-soled office shoes at the end of a workday. He flies down them on weekends, though. Tim's footstep is the most solid, and I can imagine him as the small Indiana farmboy he once was, whose first words were the proud declaration "I carry." And when Will comes thumping down the stairs, you'd think he was a grown man, not a fourteen-pound cat. In short, I live much as I did growing up—amid the sensual, comforting ruckus of a large family.

From my attic perch, I can see my neighbor Daphne sitting on her stoop across the street waiting to greet the bus drivers, the garbagemen, the UPS, FedEx, and postal workers, all old friends. Daphne's a large, baby-faced woman who suffers from diabetes and various heart ailments. She was born in Trinidad but raised in that redbrick house, and she took care of her mother and father there until they passed away. She's always dreamed of visiting Venice, where she'll meet the love of her life—an opera singer with a robust appetite. Whenever a bus driver honks on this block, I know Daphne's on the stoop.

Every neighborhood needs their Greek chorus, and ours is sitting on orange milk crates outside the El Beriyah deli right across the street: three older black men from the projects one block away. There's kind, no-nonsense Cyril with his spotted dog, slender Cooper, the retired cop, and Bear, who has only one tooth. When I need a break from writing I join them on the milk crates and trade stories, especially with Cooper; I have a few of my own to tell now.

When I was a teenager, I thought I'd write fiction and poetry, but real-life stories turned out to be a better fit. I start each one hungry for contact, and filled with trepidation. Will they trust me—the Navajo gangmembers or the skinhead girls, the death-row prisoner, the mother whose daughter was murdered? Will we connect? Will I be taken in? The stakes feel very high. Most of the people I write about would be considered outsiders, and what I listen for in every interview are the stories they tell themselves about their own lives. What narrative has this person fashioned to help him or her survive?

Once, when I was interviewing runaway teens at a local shelter, I came across a girl whose face was like a shuttered house. Even her voice was a monotone. She was sixteen but big-breasted and big-boned. Between that and her sullen face, she could easily be mistaken for someone in her mid-twenties, an unpleasant someone, and my hunch was that it had been a long time since anyone had treated her as a young person—if ever.

She gave only two answers to most of my questions: "yeah" and "uh-uh." The interview wasn't going well, or so it seemed. Then she asked if I wanted to hear something she wrote, and pulled a crumpled sheet of notepaper from her jeans pocket, something she'd obviously been carrying for a long time. The title of her poem was "To Someone Who Was Always There." She read: *When I was hungry you fed me / You held me when I cried / You gave me your coat when I was freezing in the cold . . .* When she had finished, I asked who it was written for. "Nobody," she said.

What could I possibly do to honor that moment? Bear witness by writing about it.

Last year I met a Harlem street minister named Reverend Betty Neal, a seventy-five-year-old woman with a poodle haircut and Bette Davis eyes. Reverend Betty used to minister to the prostitutes in Times Square, anointing them with holy water on the sidewalk in front of a porn theater while their pimps, who were sure the girls would make more money after receiving the reverend's blessing, stood by and watched. When she told me this, Reverend Betty hollered with laughter. She had a great sense of fun and a natural-born affinity for the street; she loved hookers, pimps, homeless people, EMS workers, firemen, and especially cops. Her storefront office was decorated with toy police cars. When cops were in a jam—and there's no trouble quite like a-cop-in-trouble—they came to Reverend Betty for advice and counseling.

When the police commissioner retired, Reverend Betty brought him a singing fish, Billy the Big Mouth Bass, as a going-away gift. "Billy" was mounted on a plaque, with a motion detector hidden inside. All morning as the reverend and I waited outside the commissioner's office, I watched the fish turn its head, open its mouth, and start singing, "Just call me angel of the morning" to every big, burly, dark-suited detective who walked in the door. And every time the song started up again, the seventy-five-year-old reverend, as skinny as a fence post, danced across the oriental carpet with her head thrown back and her fists pumping the air. The detectives, those with a good sense of humor, anyway, sang along with the fish. The commissioner didn't seem to enjoy it that much when we were finally let into the office and the reverend made her presentation, but the rest of us had a good time. I took the Brooklyn Bridge home that day, laughing all the way across, so that anyone passing me would have thought I was mad. I kept repeating to myself, *Someone* pays *me to do this?* So I have found a way to enter in, after all.

There is a quote that hangs on my computer—I no longer know where I got it, or who it's from, but it reads: "No interesting project can be embarked on without fear. I shall be scared to death half the time." The wisdom and encouragement I draw from that quote seems to me to come straight out of what happened to me during my teenage years.

As I blindly circled the New Haven green that day, I told myself to keep walking—walking out of that town, into the future. What I didn't know then, but surely know now, is that my future had already begun. I'd stepped straight into it one night in March, an ice-cold night when I was fifteen.

Acknowledgments

I always knew I would write this story someday, but without the prodding and encouragement from Sandy Close and Richard Rodriguez of Pacific News Service that someday may have been many years from now. Thanks to both of them and Mark Schurmann for their wise friendship throughout my writing life.

I must thank *Harper's Magazine* for publishing the article that was the genesis for this book; to Colin Harrison for taking me into *Harper's*, Lewis Lapham for his gallant support, and my editor, the tough-minded and loyal Ellen Rosenbush, most of all. A special thanks to my former editors at *The Village Voice*, Ellen Willis, Amy Virshup, and Jon Larsen, for opening the door to writing for me, and then letting me run loose. They knew how to support a writer's obsessions but never her flaws. And to *Vibe* magazine for their continued support.

To my fellow writers, all of them, but specifically in this case to Donna Gaines and Ruben Martinez—thanks for many late-night conversations about the pitfalls and joys of the writing life; i.e., the tricks of the trade. And my thanks to James McGoon, Lee Gershuny, Sylvia DeAngelis, Peter Burnett, Joe Rodriguez, and Barbara O'Dair, who have helped me feel less alone and made me a braver person. Lt. Joseph Heffernan and Mauricio Mule have each in their own way helped me to remember the past more precisely, and more joyfully.

To my sister Beth Ann Dobie and my friend Marisa

Steffers, my undying gratitude and deep respect for their close, thoughtful reading of the manuscript.

My love and thanks go out to my aunt, Barbara Dobie, and my father and mother, for digging through many old photographs and supporting a project that I can only imagine must be the cause of some pain.

To my siblings, Michael, Bill, Cindy, Beth, and Stephen—you are my first tribe, and writing about our early years was a great joy. Their children, my nieces and nephew, Cara, Tracy, Jamie, Corissa, Alana, Nicholas, and Julia have renewed my sense of family. As three-year-old Alana once put it, proudly, "These are my people." They are. And so are my "street godchildren," especially Amalh Mendelsohn.

I can hardly offer enough praise to the three women who made this book happen. My agent, Kris Dahl, who stuck by me through thick and thin, who knew when "I wasn't waving / I was drowning," to quote Stevie Smith, and dove in to save me. And she made it all look easy. Simply put, this book would not have seen the light of day if it weren't for her. Susan Kamil has made me feel truly lucky; she possesses editorial brilliance and plain old human caring in equal measure. Thank you for taking this book under your wing, and making me a better writer. And to my co-pilot on this journey, Beth Rashbaum, the deepest respect and love. It's a rare editor who can honor and protect the writer's voice while also remaining a reader who requires clarity and honesty from that writer. Beth's acuity and sensitivity and hard work have made this a far better book than it would've been if I'd been left to my own devices. And never was the editing process more memorable or fun. This time around, I was hardly the only girl in the car.

And a great big kiss and hug to the three people who have lived with this book more thoroughly (and patiently and lovingly) than anyone else—my sister Cindy, my dearest friend Chris Waters and, of course, James Hamilton.